Andrew McCoy was  outh Africa and educated at
the University of St___ ___ ____ _____ business he embark__ _____
Since then he has _____ _____
adviser, an industr_____ _____
fessional polo playe_____ _____ ___
racing yachtsman ____ _____ _____
McCoy is a bachelo_____

ANDREW McCOY

African Revenge

PANTHER
Granada Publishing

Panther Books
Granada Publishing Ltd
8 Grafton Street, London W1X 3LA

Published by Panther Books 1985

First published in Great Britain by
Secker & Warburg Ltd 1980

ISBN 0-586-06171-1

Printed and bound in Great Britain by
Collins, Glasgow

Set in Times

*For Nick Austin and John Blackwell, because they know
that, without freedom of expression, civilization reverts to
the bigots and the apparatchiks*

The wheel spun, the ball clattered. Lance kept his eyes on the green baize in front of him. If he won his winnings would be added to the small stack of chips by his right hand. If he lost . . . he would not lose. The ball fell. Lance did not listen to the croupier, did not hear the low tense voices elsewhere in the room, did not smell the smoke and sweat and perfume drifting around him. No new chips appeared at his right hand. He had lost. New bets were being called. There were thirty or forty rand of chips before him. He pushed them all on to the rectangle numbered 11. The wheel spun, the ball clattered. Lance kept his eyes down. Perhaps, if he did not look, his luck would change. The ball fell. No chips appeared at his right hand. He had lost again.

Lance raised his head slowly, caught the eye of the croupier, looked him full in the face. The croupier shook his head almost imperceptibly, looked away quickly from Lance's silent pleading, continued with his work. The croupier felt vaguely sorry for Lance but he had his orders: no more credit for Lance Weber. Everyone had the same orders.

Lance sat for a long moment, rubbing the back of his neck. Around him play continued. Nobody looked directly at him but he knew they were aware of him, uncomfortable in the presence of a loser. That made him uneasy. He knew nobody would ask him to leave but he had not been a public figure long enough to revel securely, arrogantly, in the ability of a celebrity to impose on others. He pushed his chair back and rose.

He stood in the middle of the room, looking around, savouring it. He wondered if he would ever return here, would ever be able to return. A passing steward, his fawn face sympathetic above his clinic-white jacket, gestured with his tray towards Lance. The drinks were free. Lance almost took a drink. Then he shook his head, smiling with an effort. 'No thanks, Johnny. I'm in training.' The coloured servant passed on. Lance headed for the door. He had to get someplace where he could think. His mind refused to function in here.

Near the door a man stepped unobtrusively in front of Lance. 'Mr Colin wants a word with you.'

Lance considered trying to brush past him. But he had a companion, cut from the same pattern; they were not as big as Lance but heavily built under their dinner jackets and had viciously determined eyes and set faces. 'All right.'

'You know the way.'

Lance walked down the passage, followed by the two men. The door to the office was open. One of the men closed it behind them.

Mr Colin looked Chinese. He probably was Chinese. But somehow, Lance knew, he must have obtained papers classifying him as White because he operated a restaurant – the front for his illegal gambling operations – in a White area and was married to a brittle blonde with ice-blue eyes, a shrewish voice and a bosom that could equally serve as a cushion for the Pekinese always in her lap. Lance had never found out Mr Colin's other name, if indeed he had one. Everyone, including his diamond-dripping wife, called him Mr Colin; everybody called her Missus without qualifier. Mr Colin was old – his skin was smooth but it was in his eyes – and she was approaching thirty. He sat behind the desk, she beside it in an easy chair, the Peke dozing in her lap. It was three o'clock in the morning.

'Mr Colin. Missus.' Lance nodded. Neither returned his greeting.

Mr Colin stared at Lance for a few seconds. 'You owe me three thousand rand.'

6

Lance suppressed the urge to shuffle his feet and watch himself doing it.

'And you have no way of repaying it.'

There was another long silence. Nobody seemed to breathe. Lance looked at his feet. 'I could win it back.'

'You could try. With my money. But you won't and I won't lend you any more.'

After more than a minute one of the men pushed Lance in the back, none too gently. 'Answer Mr Colin when he talks to you.'

Lance cast a resentful glance over his shoulder. The shove had not been hard enough to warrant any greater reaction and he did owe Mr Colin an awful amount of money. He shrugged.

'Show him what happens to people who don't pay,' Mr Colin said without inflection. He always spoke like that.

Before Lance could even assess the implications of this threat, not to mention protest, the two men had pulled him out of the door by his arms and were hurrying him down the passage, away from the restaurant and the gaming-room. Lance kept his footing with difficulty as they shoved him down the stairs, through a storeroom and out into the service alley behind the building. In the alley Lance found his balance and swung his fist at the man nearest to him. The man ducked so that Lance's fist bounced glancingly off the side of his head, caught Lance's arm and pulled him off balance. His fist slammed into Lance's stomach while the other man rabbit-punched Lance in the kidneys. Lance gasped as he was swung up against the car and his face forced down on the dewed roof by the hold one of the men had on his hair. He kicked out behind him and hit nothing. His arm was twisted higher behind his back.

'You can come easy or we can take you. That hurts. Which'll it be?

'I'll come,' Lance ground out against the roof of the car. The hold on his hair went. He heard one of the men

7

opening the door. The other man pulled him away from the car, then shoved him contemptuously towards it. 'Get in the front. Remember, I'll be sitting behind you.'

Lance sat slumped against the door of the big sedan. He had never in his life been so humiliated. Or so frightened, he admitted to himself. It was almost like the thrill of gambling. Except that the stakes were something more than money he didn't have. He should stop feeling sorry for himself and start thinking of evading these frightening men. He surreptitiously rested his hand on the door handle. The man behind him leant over to cuff him heavily over the ear. Then Lance heard the click of the lock on the sill of the window being pushed home. He would have to make his move when they stopped.

They drove up Kloof Nek and turned left at the roundabout to the parking area servicing the Table Mountain cable car, deserted at this time of night except for another darkened car. Two men were standing beside it, featureless in the dark, grim silhouettes with glowing cigarettes against the cloud-fringed bulk of the mountain.

Lance tensed. The man in the back climbed out and opened the door, standing to the rear of it so Lance could not slam it into him. The driver pushed Lance out of the car and slid across the seat after him.

'Over there.' Tha man who had sat in the back seemed to be the spokesman. Lance walked reluctantly towards the men leaning against the other car. There was nowhere to run: behind him the two toughs who had already subdued him, to his left a low stone wall protecting a sheer drop of several hundred feet, in front of him two more men – with another drop beyond them, to his right the rockface where the parking area had been cut from the mountain.

'He's passed out. He knows what's coming,' one of the men with cigarettes greeted them. He dropped the butt on the ground and immediately lit another cigarette. He held the lighter to Lance's face. 'Hey, I know you. You're the

Springbok centre, Lance Weber. I saw you score a try on telly yesterday.'

Lance wished fervently he had never heard of the game of rugby. Always, after a good game, especially if he had scored, he felt the urge to keep the excitement alive a little longer by gambling. And he would never have found out that he liked gambling if certain rich rugger fans had not introduced him to it.

'Just another high-roller who can't pay,' the more talkative of the men who had brought Lance said. 'Let's get on with it.'

'Pity,' said the man with the cigarette. 'We'll do the other one first.'

The flung open the rear door of the car and dragged something out. A fragment of cloud cleared the moon and Lance could see that what they were dragging was a man. From the way he banged around – they were dragging him by his feet – without putting out a hand to save himself, Lance supposed he was unconscious. Only unconscious men and drunks are that limp. As they pulled him around to the front of the car, one of the men said, 'He's pissed himself. They always do. It's disgusting.'

The car lights were put on and it occurred to Lance that they must be very sure of themselves to commit murder coolly between the four of them when surely two would be sufficient and also reduce the chances of someone talking. He had never seen anybody killed before, or even seen a dead person. He shivered.

Lance breathed deeply. When their attention was on killing the other man, he would break past the two behind him and make a run for the road, the only exit from the parking lot. If he was lucky, there might be some more cloud and they wouldn't be able to see him to shoot at. Once at the roundabout he could run into the brush beyond it and their cars would be useless. He was pretty sure none of them would be able to catch him on foot. He played at centre because, despite his weight, he was an excellent sprinter, often using his mass and momentum to barge forward to the touchline despite the restraining efforts of several lesser men, delighting the crowds.

One man went to the boot of the car and returned with two bricks while the other bent over the unconscious man and stripped away the wet-stained pyjama trousers. Lance could see now that the victim was a man in his forties with thinning hair and a paunch. The pyjamas were luridly striped in orange and lilac.

The man with the bricks kneeled on the ground beside the unconscious man. 'Ready.'

Lance settled his breathing. His blood was oxygen-rich now and any more would lead to hyperventilation, dizziness and a resulting impairment of his judgement. Where had his judgement been when he got himself into this shit?

The other man flipped away his cigarette. He bent over and, between forefinger and thumb, gingerly pulled the unconscious man's limp penis upright. 'We keep forgetting the rubber gloves. Watch my fingers.'

Lance made his break, turning in his first stride, intending to run between the two men behind him, counting on surprise. Instead of stepping apart, they stepped closer to each other. Lance swerved slightly so as to hit only one of them. He was going to steamroller the man, striking him on the chest with a lowered left shoulder. The man went down with a satisfying thud and Lance stumbled only slightly over him. In his next step, gathering momentum, he felt the boot strike the side of his foot, his heels click together. He was flying through the air, bringing his arm up too slowly to break the fall against the side of the car, hitting the ground hard enough to drive the remaining wind from him.

Lance was still rolling when the man who had tripped him pulled him up by forcing his arm behind his back. The man was laughing! 'Very nicely done, very.' He gave Lance's arm an additional twist and Lance gasped. 'Don't try it again, eh?' Another twist. Lance thought his arm would come out of the socket.

The man Lance had run over rose groaning and stood bent over, gasping for breath, the air rasping in his throat, his hands pressing ineffectually at his chest. Lance's rising, accelerating shoulder had caught him under the short ribs, striking his heart a great blow. They stood in silent tableau until the hurt man could breathe easily enough to straighten, though his breathing was still far from regular.

The pain from the arm being twisted further forced Lance forward towards the man he had hurt. The man swung his arm and his fist exploded in Lance's stomach. Lance had had the presence of mind to stiffen his stomach muscles. Seeing the blow had little effect, the man kicked Lance repeatedly in the shins. Lance thought his arm would come out of its socket for sure this time as he twisted and turned to avoid the painful kicks on his shins. The other one said, 'That's enough for now.'

'That's – only – an – instalment,' the man gasped as he kicked Lance one last time.

'Can we carry on now?' one of the men kneeling beside the unconscious man asked, amusement in his voice.

'Just let me get this one in position to get a really good look.'

Lance spat out some blood from where he had cut his lip when he crashed against the car. The man holding his arm must have thought it a sign of defiance for he kneed Lance in the back before turning him around and marching him slowly, excruciatingly into the rectangle of the car's lights. Lance was still trying to catch his breath from the blow in the kidneys but there was no escaping the vision in front of him.

One man again picked up the limp penis with evident distaste and said, 'Watch my fingers.'

'Yeah, you told me.' The other man had a brick in each hand, holding the bricks on either side of the flabby testicles shrivelling pathetically.

11

This only happened on farms, not to people. It was worse than being killed. The remains of his dinner tasted foul in Lance's mouth.

The bricks made a sound like a sock of wet sand dropping on the ground when they came together, then a sharp click as some edge touched around the ruin in between. The unconscious man screamed and arched his back. There was a sulphurous smell from his released bowels and a stain grew under him; it looked like blood in the distorting light of the headlamps but Lance knew it was excrement. Vomit dribbled from the side of the man's mouth.

Lance hurled what little was in his stomach in a curve in front of him. His arm was released as his tormentor stepped back to avoid being splashed. Through the glaze over his eyes he heard a laugh.

'Does it hurt?'asked the man who had wished for rubber gloves. Lance could dimly make out that he was wiping his hands with fastidious care on a handkerchief, finger by finger.

'Not if you keep your thumbs well clear,' said the man with the bricks. Nobody laughed. It was obviously an old joke. 'You'd better knock him out before we do him. I don't much fancy him struggling.'

Lance tried to move towards the freedom of the road but his feet only shuffled.

'Naw, Mr Colin only sent him to watch the demonstration. He'll get his if he doesn't pay up.'

Lance fainted from relief.

He hurt everywhere. Yet he remembered it as a good clean game, an early-season friendly between Stellenbosch University and the South Western Districts visiting team, played at Coetzenburg before a good crowd. The stompings and the fouls wouldn't come until later in the season when teams started getting desperate for points to keep their positions in the ratings. And why the hell should SWD want to 'mark' him, the only other reason for this bashed feeling? Only one SWD player stood a chance of being selected for the Springboks in the coming All Black tour and he played a different position; Lance was certainly not in competition for a place as a scrum-half.

He moved his limbs one by one. All present and active. He sighed in relief. He rolled his head and raised it slightly. Legs would break and heal and so would arms, but a spinal injury could invalid a rugger-player for life. Lance didn't like wheelchairs. His pillow was as hard as a rock and grittily damp.

'On your feet and in the car!'

Lance remembered. He rolled frantically to avoid choking on vomit but there was nothing in his stomach. The retching wracked him into a tight foetal ball on the tarmacadam. A shoe crashed into his side and he staggered up and towards the car. His hand ran blindly along the sculpted side, searching for the handle.

'In the back, you!' The contemptuous implication – that he was no longer a danger to men who would have their backs to him – seared Lance. He found the handle and opened the door. He slumped into the car. The door was slammed and Lance wound the window down for fresh air. His own smell was sickening him.

There was no sign of the other car or the three people who had come in it.

Halfway down Kloof Nek the driver, the one Lance had winded, spoke. 'So, Rugger-Player, nancy-boys don't run too well with the ball. With no balls, hee hee!' Lance made no reply and the man continued, 'Yeah, and how would you go in the shower with the other guys with your balls all squashed?'

'How old are you, Weber?' the other man asked.

'Twenty-one,' Lance mumbled.

'You could drink a bottle of wine every day for the rest of your life and chances are it will do you no harm. Driving a car is twice as likely to end your life prematurely as a bottle of wine a day, riding a motor cycle a hundred and fifty times as likely. Do you understand what I'm talking about?'

'Probability.' Lance was sullen, wondering where this was leading.

'Relative probability. There are only two absolute certainties. The first is that we all have to die, the second that those who owe Mr Colin money they can't pay will get knackered.'

The car had stopped in the alleyway where they had started from less than an hour before. Without being told, Lance climbed out and walked up the stairs to Mr Colin's office. There was no point in resistance now; he had to find out what the real threat was. He waited until the door was opened for him and walked through numbly, ignoring the anonymous shove in the back.

Mr Colin and Missus regarded him steadily for a long time. Lance looked at his shoes; they were splashed with vomit, as was the rest of his clothing. He gagged on the smell and stared at the carpet a little way in front of him. At last Mr Colin spoke.

'He's seen?'

'Yes.'

Mr Colin turned his agate eyes back to Lance, his head motionless. 'You have one month to pay.'

Lance knew he could not, but hope springs eternal. He nodded.

'But you won't pay.'

Lance nodded automatically, then shook his head half-heartedly.

'You saw what happens to people who don't pay.'

Lance nodded again.

'But I'm willing to make an exception for you.'

It took a moment to sink in. Then Lance looked up at Mr Colin and tried to smile.

'When the All Black rugby players from New Zealand come here – ' Mr Colin waited, his eyes boring into Lance.

'You will have until after they leave. When they have left, I may decide the debt is no longer due. Do you understand?'

Lance nodded again, trying to keep his fear from passing across his face.

'We will be staking large amounts of money on the outcome of the matches between the Springboks and the All Blacks,' Missus said coldly, mistaking the fear on Lance's face for bewilderment, not trying to hide her exasperation. 'Are you stupid or something?'

'I . . . uh . . . I –'

'Did you really think we'd let you gamble here, losing more money than several times your total scholarship, if we didn't want something in return?'

Lance cringed under the scathing voice. He was actually glad when Mr Colin spelt it out for him.

'You'll get instructions on how to play,' Mr Colin said. 'Sometimes we'll tell you to play as you usually do. Other times we'll tell you to be less effective, slowing down a little, fumbling the ball, stumbling over your own feet if necessary. Is it clear now?'

Lance nodded again, not trusting his voice. It was all only too clear. Even if he wanted to do what they demanded, he could not. Dr Danie Craven, doyen of the selectors and an instructor of Lance's at Stellenbosch University, had already told him in confidence that he would not be selected to play against the All Blacks this year. He was not doing too well at his academic courses and the selectors, conscious that academic failure would void his scholarship and lose him to them, wanted him to concentrate on his studies; they were not unaware of his youth, of the fifteen years or more of first-class rugger before him, and several were of the opinion that there was little sense in risking him against the heavy and experienced New Zealanders just yet. As a consolation Dr Craven had promised him a certain place in the Springbok side to tour France later in the year. Lance had not objected. His objection would have changed nothing; besides, he had faith in the selectors and was content to let his rugby career progress at the rate thought suitable by these very experienced men. It would be madness to tell Mr Colin. He would be immediately taken back up the mountain and . . .

But the news that such an obvious choice would be left out of the side would be in the newspapers in a week or ten days when the 'trials invitation list' would be published. Then – Lance kept nodding like a marionette. A week was better than nothing.

Missus stroked the Pekinese with one hand. The other hand she held out, palm up. She closed her fingers into the palm, folded her thumb across them and squeezed. Lance watched mesmerized as her knuckles whitened. The Peke growled in its sleep, affected by the tension in the room.

'Or else,' Missus said with relish.

CROCODILE

Lance sat on the steps of Ewart's house halfway up the hill at Clifton, carefully keeping his mind blank by staring at the waves rolling on to the beach far below. His brother was the only one he could ask for help. It was no use asking his parents: they lived on a small pension in a council house in the grim suburb of Maitland, his father's main concern keeping alive the two struggling rose bushes in the front garden, the only greenery on the street, against the pervading poisonous air. Asking them for help they could not give would only distress them pointlessly. Ewart was different. Ten years older than Lance, Ewart had always been strong, resourceful and self-sufficient. At fourteen he had run away from home to go to sea. Later he had served a stint in the French Foreign Legion. He came home infrequently, every several years, and never wrote, but every month an envelope with a blank sheet of paper folded around assorted banknotes arrived and was used for Lance's education. Well trained by the French, Ewart had become a mercenary. When Lance went to university, the envelopes were sent directly to him. A year ago Ewart had appeared without warning from the Congo and rented the house at Clifton, living there with a succession of girls.

At exactly seven o'clock Lance walked up the last few steps and knocked on the door. He was frozen to the marrow but glad of the bleary sun; it often rained right through a Cape winter and a soaking, while washing the smell from him, would only have added pneumonia to his other problems. A blonde girl he hadn't seen before opened the door. Her hair was tousled and her peignoir transparent. She rubbed her eyes.

19

'What do you want?'

'I'm Lance Weber. I'd like to see my brother. If he's not up yet I can wait.'

She turned to open the door wider and her breasts swayed. Lance felt an erection pressing in his trousers. He breathed deeply, caught a whiff of himself, remembered the humiliations of the night. Immediately the erection slumped. He walked behind her to the kitchen at the back of the house, looking at the play of her buttocks against the cloth without much interest, his mind elsewhere. In the year that he had been back in South Africa, Ewart had visited Lance twice at Stellenbosch and had turned up at the parties after a rugger match a few times, never embarrassing Lance by fawning over him like their father did, never staying long, always somehow distant. Did he have any right to ask Ewart for help?

Ewart sat at the kitchen table, eating a breakfast which, from the look of the girl, he had cooked himself. He was dressed, as always, in superbly pressed short-sleeved shirt and lightweight slacks with highly shined shoes double-welted around the thick soles. He was obviously impervious to the cold and gave the impression of a man whom discomfort, dirt or superfluous creases in clothing approached on pain of instant death.

'You look terrible at this time of day,' Ewart said to the girl. 'Go back to bed.'

She showed him a middle finger and pressed closer to Lance than she needed to pass. 'You jocks all smell,' she said to Lance as she disappeared down the passage.

'The bathroom's through there. Wash your face and hands and I'll make you something to eat.'

Lance stood uncertainly for a moment, shifting his weight from foot to foot, then went into the bathroom. When he returned to the kitchen, Ewart was grilling bacon and frying eggs with an easy economy of movement. 'None of these girls can make even a cup of tea without leaving the kitchen looking like a guerilla war had been fought in it. Sit down.'

Lance sat down. 'Ewart, I'm in trouble. Very bad trouble.'

'I can see that. And smell it.' Ewart put the plate down in front of Lance. 'Eat first. You can tell me afterwards.'

The bacon was crisp, the eggs had firm whites and runny yolks, the quartered tomatoes gleamed brightly red. Lance gagged on the first two bites. Then his appetite took over and he finished the rest of the food in short order. Browned bread popped from the toaster just as he finished the bacon and eggs and Ewart put a mug of coffee at his right hand. When Lance had eaten two slices of toast and was warming his hands around the mug, Ewart said, 'Now tell me.'

Lance didn't know where to begin. He opened his mouth and closed it again.

'Start at the beginning,' Ewart said, lighting a cigarillo.

'Some people I know took me to gamble with them. Later I went back on my own. I . . .'

'You're in gambling debt?'

'Yes.' Before his cool, competent brother, Lance felt like a lout. Bit by bit the story came out. At the end, Lance said, 'They're threatening to . . .'

'To crush your balls between two bricks as well?' Ewart seemed amused.

'Yes. But there's more. I made a mistake, an additional one. I'll tell you about it.'

The two toughs had pushed Lance down the stairs to the back door – Missus had said, 'Take him out the back way, he'll smell the customers out if you take him through the front.'

Lance's damaged pride had given his common sense no opportunity to protest. Without planning it consciously, when they had come to the back door and one of the men was leaning forward to open it, he had pushed the man

21

violently into the door, rejoicing in the crack his head made against the fireproof metal. He had swung around in the same movement and kicked the other one in the groin and then in the face when the man had bent over to clutch his testicles with both hands. At the same time he had brought his clenched hands down on the back of the man's neck, knocking him out like an ox going down at the slaughterhouse. When he had turned around the man he had pushed into the door (the driver, the one who had kicked his shins), was rising fuzzily and pulling what looked like a sockful of sand from his pocket. Lance had kicked him heavily on the shin, then stood back and help up both hands, palm out.

'You'd better not hit me with that, Mister. Remember, I'm the goose that's going to lay the golden eggs.'

Ewart laughed heartily, choking on the words. 'And he let you go?'

Lance was offended at his brother's merriment. 'Yes.'

'Uh, you're not as stupid as I thought.'

'It only means that they're going to come after me all that much more enthusiastically when they find out I'm not going to be selected – in addition to not telling Mr Colin the truth.'

Ewart shook his head. 'They're scum, easily dealt with. The problem is that there will be more behind them, always more.' He smiled grimly and did not see Lance shiver. 'And you think it'll be a good idea to get the money from me to pay them?'

Lance looked into his mug. 'Well, yes.'

'For a guy who's going to get a university degree this year, you're a bit naive, Lance. The hold they have on you is not the three thousand rand. They'd never have let you get that much in debt even if they thought they could frighten you into finding the money somehow. Even if you pay it back now, they'll still have a blackmail hold on you.'

'Huh?'

22

'What would happen if the South African Rugby Board found out you gambled regularly and lost more money than you could afford?'

'Oh shit!' Lance put his face in his hands. 'Even if I won, just the fact that I gambled . . . I'd be finished in first-class rugby.'

'You'd also be finished as a university student. With your academic record your scholarship wouldn't last one day after you got thrown out of first-class rugby.'

Lance looked up, trying to see if Ewart was enjoying this. But Ewart's face was sombre. There was a long silence. Ewart rose to put on more coffee, automatically taking the plates from the table to the sink.

'If I paid them, at least they wouldn't . . . there'd be no business with the bricks.'

Ewart sat down again. 'No, perhaps not. But, since they now have a personal grudge against you – not that I wouldn't have done the same, except I wouldn't have left the scum alive – you'd better disappear until their disappointment over your non-selection blows over. Say a couple of months or so.'

'You will give me the money then!' Lance was enormously relieved.

'No, I won't give you the money. You will earn it and quite a bit besides. When do the varsity holidays start?'

'Next week. But I can't go anywhere, I'm in training for the French tour.'

'If you stay here, they'll come for you and I won't be here to deal with them.'

'Oh.' Lance was glad Ewart hadn't said 'to protect you'. He already knew sufficiently well what a helpless halfwit felt like.

'Any exams? Can someone take notes for you?'

'No. Yes.'

'Then you'll go on holiday with me for a week. Later we'll think up some story to account for a two-month absence. When we return you'll have the money to pay them and the business about not being selected against the All Blacks will have died down a little. I'll also make it clear to them that I'll take it personally amiss if anything should happen to you.'

Lance shivered again. His brother spoke calmly but his very confidence in contemplating threatening underworld toughs was frightening. He inspired absolute awe. Lance wouldn't want to do anything his brother could 'take personally amiss' in that chilling tone of voice and had no doubt that even Mr Colin would feel the same way.

'How can I thank you, Ewart?'

'By thinking before you act, by not making an idiot of yourself again.' Ewart rose, taking the mugs to the sink, the subject closed. 'Go on, shower while I clean up. We'll pick up clothes for you in Stellenbosch on the way to Paarl.'

Lance Weber was a big man on campus at Stellenbosch, a star rugger player in a place that had produced more Springboks than any other institution or group or club. It had been like that from the day he arrived from school, already with a certain place in the Junior Springboks, and so had not made as much impact on him as a change in circumstances would have. His lack of assertion was taken as the most becoming modesty. His status had been assured on his first day at his residential house, Simons-berg: each *jokkel* – athlete – was assigned to room with a *swot* and Lance, the star *jokkel*, was roomed with the star *swot*. The idea was that *jokkels*, who were often dim and always had to spend a great deal of time in training, needed all the help they could get with their studies if they weren't to be thrown out of the university for failing grades and so lost to the team. In return the *swot* would share in the girls and general popularity that always grativated to a *jokkel*.

Lance's *swot* was sitting at his desk, staring over the thick text on it through the window. He had been a happy choice. He was short, slim and pale, his black hair falling lank and greasy despite daily washes in lemon shampoos. He was a Jew whose family had long been assimilated into the Afrikaner farming community, his father farming many thousands of acres of maize in the Orange Free State. His social confidence and sensitivity had been a boon to Lance, a poor boy suddenly transplanted into an affluent environment. On his first morning at Simonsberg, Lance had, as always at home, made his bed neatly. His room-mate had watched until he had finished, then pulled the cover from the bed. 'Your servants at home must have an easy life.'

'We don't have any.'

'Well, we have them here. They make the beds and take the laundry away and sweep and so on. You don't do anything.'

'I don't mind making my bed.'

'Sure. But consider, if you make your own bed, some poor Coloured is going to be out of a job.'

'Oh'

'However poor you might think you are, there's always someone poorer. Okay?'

'I'll remember.' Lance had pulled the rest of the bedclothes off. He had soon learned to avoid embarrassing solecisms by letting his roommate make the going in any situation in which he felt unsure.

'Whose is that blue E-type?' Lance's roommate asked now.

'My brother's.'

'The Baluba Butcher himself?'

Lance gave him a sharp look. 'I thought you told me not to believe everything I read in the papers.'

'Sorry. You're in a mess.'

Lance changed. 'They had me surrounded.' One of the social graces he had learnt from his roommate was to pass off lightly subjects you didn't want to discuss. 'My brother's taking me for a week's holiday. Will you take notes for me in class?'

'Don't I always. What about training?'

'Tell them I'll be back next week.' Lance felt himself blushing. He couldn't remember when he had last told a lie. He closed his small suitcase. Ewart had told him to pack his passport, dripdry shirts and slacks, under-clothing, and chukka boots.

'Where are you going?'

'My brother didn't say.' Lance had wanted to ask on the drive down here but Ewart had seemed occupied with the Bach emanating from the stereo tape player in the car. Lance was also wondering what he would have to do to earn the enormous sum of three thousand rand – and some besides, Ewart had said – in the seven weeks until term started again after the vacation.

'A strong silent man, eh?'

Lance left with a wave of his hand. In the parking lot he put his case next to Ewart's in the back of the car and climbed in. The music was still playing, Ewart still silent.

Lance looked around him as if for the first time as they drove through Stellenbosch. He realized he loved this quaint old-fashioned university town with its straight white buildings, its dripping oaks, its slow sleepy air of unconcerned self-sufficiency. Without the education – however superficial – his skill in rugby was instrumental in obtaining for him he would instantly be back in a nothing job, poverty and living in a dull and dirty place like Maitland instead of clean white tree-rich surroundings like Stellenbosch. He had taken too much for granted too soon. He had been incredibly stupid.

'It's peaceful, isn't it,' Ewart said, turning the music down.

A flush of gratitude gulfed in Lance. 'I don't want to lose it.'

'You won't.' Ewart punched the button to eject the tape in mid-note. 'I was thinking while you were inside. What we are going to do is dangerous. Instead of coming with me, I might be able to arrange for you to stay with friends

of mine in Durban while your gambling partners overcome their disappointment.'

'No,' Lance said, 'I'll come with you and earn my way.
Maybe I made a mistake with this gambling but I'm not a
charity case.'

'Have it your own way.' Ewart pushed the tape home
and the tinkling sounds of the harpsichord filled the car
again.

Lance admired the way Ewart sent the car hurtling
along the narrow old road between Stellenbosch and
Paarl, his hands resting easily on the controls, his move-
ments totally unhurried. Lance, a natural athlete and a
good driver, knew that to get anywhere near the speed his
brother was making his own hands and feet would have
been moving frantically from control to control and the
car would be slewing all over the place. Yet Ewart did it so
smoothly that it seemed easy and relaxed, every twist and
turn and irregularity anticipated as if Ewart had planned
them himself.

They drove through Paarl and, beyond the town, turned
off on a graded gravel road. They drove around the
imposing Cape Dutch farmhouse with its thatched roof
and curved shutters to a large cottage behind it. There
were several acres of garden and, beyond that, vineyards
stretching in all directions as far as the eye could see. It
was obviously a rich man's farm, the workshops and
storehouses and labour accommodation out of sight of the
living area. A man came from the cottage as they levered
themselves from the low car. He walked with a slight limp.
One could have put Lance, Ewart and this man in a row
and there would be exactly two inches at each step, Lance
tallest, his brother in the middle, the limping man shortest
at six feet. What the other two lacked in height they made
up in muscular bulk. The effect was that they all made the
same impression of mass. There the similarity ended.
Lance wore his hair touching on his ears and curling at the
neck. Ewart wore his sandy hair short, every hair trimmed

27

into place and framing his square face. The stranger too had short hair but it was dark brown and his face was long and narrow, his nose hooked.

'Jacques, this is my brother Lance. He's coming with us. Lance, this is Jacques Roux, my partner.'

Lance shook hands with Jacques Roux. 'How d'you do.' He had never met him before but the man was famous – his roommate would have said notorious. The black-sheep son of an established Afrikaner family which had been a power in the land since they landed with the French Huguenots in 1688, he had been a brilliant Law student at Stellenbosch but had refused to enter the profession on graduation. Instead he had become a diamond smuggler, been caught and served a gaol sentence. After that he had become a fundamentalist preacher and Old Testament scholar. Finding verbal blood and thunder unsatisfactory, he had joined the security division of one of the Belgian mining consortia in the Congo and had shortly afterwards emerged as a colonel in the secessionist Katangese army (backed by his late employers who in fact still paid his wages) and aide-de-camp to Moise Tsombe. It was in this capacity that he had hired Ewart's services. When Tsombe had been installed in office, he had retired to the family farm, now run by his elder brother, a Member of Parliament, and sold his life story to be serialized in the country's biggest-circulation newspaper.

'Put your car in the garage round the back and your bags in the station wagon,' Jacques said. 'Briony's just made coffee and immediately after that we'll leave for the airport.'

Briony Roux was of medium height and handsome rather than pretty, her strong bone structure accentuated by the bob of her blonde hair. She had a notable bosom but was otherwise boyishly slim with almost no hips to speak of. When she was told Lance would be going with them she said, 'Does he have any experience of this kind of thing?'

'No,' Ewart said equitably, 'but neither do you and Jacques is bringing you.'

Lance who still didn't know where they were going or what they were going to do, resented her immediately. She had the attitude of one who wished she were the tallest person in the world so she could look down on everybody else. He was dammed if he would expose his ignorance to her.

Four hours and nearly 1800 miles later, Lance had still had no opportunity of asking Ewart in private. At Salisbury airport they were met by a slim Coloured named Pietie whose ancestors had served the Roux family through nine generations. He had driven the Landrover overland from Cape Town to meet them here. Lance was impressed by the idea of having a servant do a tedious three-day drive for you while you took the plane. Pietie had his front teeth missing, extracted, in the manner of the Cape Coloureds, to make his kissing sexier. He smiled continuously, nervously. Briony pushed him every time she gave him an order and called him 'Hotnot'. Lance knew that, strictly speaking, Pietie was not a Hottentot, that the word was applied as an insult, but Pietie didn't seem to mind so Lance said nothing. The Hottentots had been the original inhabitants of the Cape coast, and had been indiscriminately exterminated by the black tribes migrating southwards into South Africa and the white traders spreading northwards. Pietie was the result of miscegenation between the Dutch settlers and their Malay slaves.

The Landrover was a thing of beauty, custom-built. On the outside it was the standard long-wheelbase stationwagon with the little windows let into the curvature of the roof over the doors; there were the usual trans-Africa accoutrements of bull bars front and back with water bags and multitudinous fog, driving and long-range lamps affixed to the front and twin-Cibié spots to the rear, the spare wheel on the bonnet, the heavy-duty aluminium roof rack, telescopic swivelling spots beside each front door, at the rear a permanent ladder to the roof and two more spare wheels on either side of the door, a fifteen-foot whip aerial for the two-way shortwave radio. Inside it had been totally refurnished to luxury car standards: walnut trim to the fully instrumented dashboard, walnut cappings on the doors, electric winding windows, five leather-trimmed Recaro bucket seats, reverse-cycle air conditioning, a complicated stereo radio and tape player with many speakers strategically placed, thick sound-proofing to enable the music to be heard, plush carpets.

They immediately set off on the two-lane blacktop north-westwards, Ewart driving, Jacques in the front passenger seat, Lance and Briony behind, with an empty seat between them, Pietie in the back with the cases. Pietie had caught Lance's surprised look when he had climbed into the luggage compartment and said *Die Hotnot sit agter* – The Hotnot sits behind. Pietie had confirmed the pecking order of the expedition: he called Jacques *Grootbaas*, Ewart *Baas*, Briony *Mies* and Lance *die kleinbaas* – Big Boss, Boss, Madam, the little boss. There was no talk in the car except when Briony distributed food and drink from a styrofoam cooler, Mozart, Beethoven, Brahms and Bach emanating continuously from the speakers. Lance wondered if Ewart and Jacques, old comrades in arms, knew one another so well that they had nothing to say to each other.

An hour out of Salisbury they stopped at a house in a small town and Ewart went into the house for ten minutes. When he returned, he gave Lance an envelope. 'That's a letter to your coach from a doctor. You've slipped a disc and will be on your back for at least seven weeks. Later he'll discover the diagnosis was mistaken and it was nothing more than a pulled muscle. That way they'll not suspect your fitness. Write a note to your coach on the back of the doctor's certificate and address the envelope.'

As they drove away from the post office, Ewart said,

'Remember the name of this town, Sinoia. It's where you pulled the muscle in your back and the hick doctor kept you in bed for a slipped disc.'

'I'm not stupid,' Lance snapped. His resentment soon evaporated. This whole business did after all stem from his own foolishness. And he certainly knew no doctors who would give him a fake certificate; more, he could not even conceive of asking a doctor for such a thing. Not that he thought Ewart had asked for it; Lance was reasonably sure Ewart had simply told the doctor what was required and waited for it to be handed to him.

An hour later, while Jacques was changing the tape in the stereo player, Lance asked, 'Where do you know that doctor in Sinoia from, Ewart?'

Ewart looked away from the road into the back of the Landrover, surprised at the question. He had to think for a long moment before he answered. 'Aden, 1956.'

'He owed you,' Jacques said, a statement rather than a question.

'Some Arabs had him. I took him back.'

Jacques pushed the tape home and music filled the car, cutting short Lance's questions about what the doctor owed Ewart for, what Ewart had meant by 'Some Arabs had him. I took him back.' What kind of debt would bind a man for ten years? How did Ewart know where to find the doctor so fortuitously? Lance wondered if Briony felt as excluded by the wordless understanding between Ewart and Jacques as he did. He glanced at her and caught her staring at him. She did not lower her gaze. Lance closed his eyes and went to sleep.

An hour later they stopped again. Almost immediately they heard the drone of an aeroplane though they could not see it. Lance was glancing around the treetops when the plane shot over the topmost branches and, without circling, immediately dropped to the ground then came rolling straight at them. Lance was already ducking when the plane turned in a large circle in front of the Landrover,

31

the shadow of the wingtip sweeping across the bonnet, and stopped facing the way it had come.

'Bloody show-off,' Briony murmured.

Jacques and Pietie were running towards the plane. A deeply tanned man with curly black hair swung the door open and jumped down. He reached into the plane and loaded whatever he fetched – the overhead wing was casting an obscuring shadow – into Jacques' and Pietie's arms. While they were still running back to the Land-rover, the man jumped back into the plane and set it rolling to take off with the wheels rustling the treetops. Lance held his breath. Behind the plane the grass straightened and before the sound of the engine had faded, there was no evidence that it had ever been there. Except the firearms Jacques and Pietie were carrying back to the Landrover. They put the arms in the luggage compartment, Pietie jumped in, Jacques climbed in the front, and they drove off.

Lance looked back. There was just a road without any markers, beside the road just grass and straggly flat-topped trees. How the hell had Ewart known where to stop? He would ask him later. Behind him Pietie was putting the rifles up on a gun rack Lance had not noticed before. What would they need rifles for? Perhaps they were going hunting. He would like that, he had never hunted before. And it was quite conceivable that the Rhodesians wouldn't like mercenaries as well-known as Jacques and Ewart to bring firearms into their country, even for hunting. Lance drifted off to sleep again.

He was fully rested when he woke again. 'Where are we?'

'Between Karoi and Makuti,' Briony said. Lance was none the wiser; he had never heard of either. They were slowing down and Jacques was turning one of the focusing spots to the side of the road, illuminating the trees flanking the road one by one. Ewart recognized one of the flat-topped trees dotting the savannah here and there and pulled the Landrover off the road under it. Lance looked at his watch. It was nearly ten o'clock in the evening though here, nearly two thousand miles nearer the equator than Cape Town, there was still a glow of faint light in the northern sky. It was eerie, Ewart recognizing one tree out of so many of the same breed, but Lance was willing to trust his instinct that they had arrived at another predestined point in their journey.

After five or ten minutes, filled with Bach and the shushing of the cicadas, a lantern appeared out of the long grass and with it the elongated shadow of a man. Ewart started the engine again and followed the lantern for a few hundred yards through the grass. Near another tree their headlights picked up a truck. Underneath the tree was a folding table and over it, from the lowest branch, hung a Coleman lamp. Beside the table stood a black man.

Ewart drove the Landrover in a circle around the tableau to park it next to the truck. By the time Lance realized Ewart was inspecting the surroundings for some reason it was too late for him to do the same. A thrill of danger passed through him and suddenly he was glad he was with Ewart and Jacques. He wondered why, if they suspected danger, they had not armed themselves from the arsenal behind him.

Ewart switched everything off and opened his door. 'You can all come,' he said.

They walked in tight formation behind Ewart. Once Lance bumped into Pietie in the dark and found him shivering with fear. There was also a sour smell of fear on the Cape Coloured servant.

The man beside the table was as black as midnight, taller than Lance, broader than Ewart. His faced gleamed impassively in the light of the Coleman. He waited until Ewart was only three paces from him, then snapped impressively to attention.

'Sergeant Sambo,' Ewart said mildly.

'Major Weber.' He had a deep, soothing voice.

33

Lance thought the big black man was going to salute but instead Ewart stepped forward and embraced him. Briony sniffed her disapproval audibly, then gasped as Jacques dug his elbow into her side.

'You've come,' Ewart said.

'I have.'

Lance had seen the black man before though he had never met him. There had been a picture on the front pages of newspapers throughout the world. In it his brother Ewart and Sergeant Sambo stood looking down on a scene of indescribable carnage. Anti-Tsombe rebels had raped and killed twenty-six nuns. Ewart and his men had arrived too late to save the nuns but with time in hand to kill more than three hundred of the rebels. The papers had made much of the obvious fact that not a single prisoner had been taken. He had again been photographed with Ewart when other nuns had been saved from a similar fate – again no prisoners had been taken.

'This is Colonel Jacques Roux.' Ewart indicated those behind him. Jacques stepped forward to shake the black man's hand. This time Briony was silent.

'We met when His Excellency decorated you,' Jacques said.

'I remember with pleasure.'

'His wife,' Ewart continued. 'My brother Lance. Mr Roux's servant Pietie.'

Sambo nodded at each in turn. 'You asked for twenty men I trust. With me my brothers, all those who survive.' Sambo turned to the four men standing in the shadows behind him. They were carbon copies of him but where he was sombre they smiled. 'You remember them.'

'One does not forget brave men,' Ewart said. He stepped forward and greeted each of the four brothers by name. Each in turn bowed his head.

'And fourteen men of my tribe, all the men who survive. I am ashamed to say I could not find another man whom I could trust.' Sambo indicated the shadows behind his brothers and for the first time Lance saw the row of men sitting on their haunches in the darkness.

'N'kosi,' they chorused as Ewart raised a hand to them.

'Nineteen will do as well as twenty,' Ewart said to Sambo. 'They can all drive a truck?'

'They can.'

Jacques fetched a map from the Landrover and spread it on the table. Sambo joined Ewart and Jacques while his brothers and the men stayed where they were. Lance stood with Briony near the table while Pietie cowered behind them. The map was the standard Michelin of Central and Southern Africa to the scale of one inch to every sixty-three miles. The southern edge of the map threatened to pull off the section on the table: Jacques picked the map up, folded it and put it back on the table.

'Cameroun. Central African Republic, Sudan, Ethiopia.' Jacques tapped his finger along the top of the map to orientate them. 'Here – ' his finger tapped the map to the south ' – the Congo Brazzaville and the Congo Kinshasa. Between them, until it runs into the River Congo and that becomes the border, the river Oubangui. At its northern end the Oubangui is the border between the Congo Kinshasa and the Central African Republic but of that less than a hundred miles will concern us.

'The rivers of this part of Africa, as everyone knows, teem with crocodiles. With the decline in game, the crocodiles have taken to eating domestic animals and, increasingly of late, the villagers.

'The governments of both the Congos agree on at least one thing: it is undesirable to have the people eaten by crocodiles.'

Jacques paused for the brief laughter from Ewart and Sambo before continuing.

'Perhaps it would be more accurate to say that I have persuaded them, in person and through intermediaries, to agree on this at least.

'The upshot has been that they have given me and Mr

35

Weber a licence to kill all the crocodiles in the Oubangui from Mougoumba in the north to where the Oubagui joins the River Congo three hundred miles south. This is in the nature of a test. If we are successful we shall get a licence to eradicate every crocodile in both Congos.

'To get the agreement of the Congo Kinshasa we have had to undertake first to eradicate the crocodiles in the Oubangui from Mougoumba north towards Zongo, a matter of about a hundred miles. Here the Oubangui forms the border between the Congo Kinshasa and the Central African Republic whose co-operation could not be obtained. They will not, however, obstruct us. In summary, we will eradicate the crocodiles in the River Oubangui for four hundred miles, starting at the juncture of the Oubangui and the River Congo, northwards till Zongo, attending to the northernmost hundred miles first.

'The Oubangui is a wide river, fertile in crocodiles. Estimates vary between sixty and a hundred crocodiles per mile of the Oubangui. Some even think the higher number conservative. But let us work on the lower number, sixty crocodiles per running miles. That means twenty-four thousand crocodiles in the four hundred miles to which our present licence extends.

'I have arranged for a guaranteed price of forty American dollars per skin delivered to either Bangui or Kinshasa.'

Jacques gave all his listeners time to do the arithmetic before supplying the answer. 'That is near enough to one million American dollars as to make no difference.'

Sergeant Sambo whistled politely.

Lance did not whistle but it occurred to him that the ability of his brother and Jacques Roux to achieve so much with such ease while he had gambled his manhood for so little must surely be a sign of their superiority.

'The licences, the bribes to the Central African politicians for not interfering,' Jacques continued, 'cost Mr Weber and me about forty thousand American dollars.

36

There were additional expenses. All of this we will forego. Out of the total income of the expedition, we will pay you one-fifth for the services of you and your men. The rest will be divided equally between Mr Weber and me. Are you satisfied?'

'Your terms are generous indeed. How you distribute your share is not my business.'

'But we want you to know,' Ewart said, 'in case of eventualities.'

'Ah.'

'In case of eventualities,' Jacques said formally, 'my share to my wife, Mr Weber's share to his brother.'

'I understand.'

'All right. Those are the general arrangements. From here on Mr Weber, having more recent and more extensive experience of active service than I, will be in total command while I shall deal with any further political or commercial questions that may arise.' Jacques nodded to Ewart.

'May I ask a few questions?' Sambo asked politely.

'Certainly,' Ewart replied.

Sambo folded the map open and held it on the table with one huge hand while he pointed with the other. 'We are here, just inside the Rhodesian border. To get here, near Mougoumba, where we start work, we will have to travel many days through the territory of hostile tribes. White men are not welcome and white women fair game.'

'How dare you!' Briony strode forward and would have said more but Jacques gripped her arm, his knuckles whitening, until she cried out in pain.

'Quiet, Briony,' Jacques said softly. To Sambo he said, 'She is my responsibility. She has been many places with me. I apologize for her and thank you for your concern.'

'No apology is necessary.'

Briony was flushed and would have spoken but Jacques led her firmly away from the table. 'Stand here and be quiet,' he said between clenched teeth when they reached Lance. He returned to the table.

Sambo stood with bowed head while the unseemly scene played itself out. When Jacques was back at the table he looked up. 'There will be further expenses of matériel for operations on the scale we propose.'

'The Lord will provide,' Jacques said and laughed.

'No doubt aided by a little force of arms,' Sambo replied with a chuckle.

'I'll explain about that tomorrow,' Ewart said.

'We shall wait.'

'Do your men have food and bedding?'

'Yes, thank you.'

'Till tomorrow then, two hours after first light.'

They spent the night in *rondawels* at the rest camp at Makuti. Lance lay awake for a long time, revising his earlier opinion that the riches of the crocodile hunt would come easily. Otherwise men like Ewart and Jacques would not speak of 'eventualities' and bequeath their share of spoils. Why this should be necessary Lance did not know and was not sure he would be enlightened if he asked Ewart: the question would embarrass his brother.

In the morning they breakfasted on sausages and bacon and eggs and toast with fresh butter and honey. Pietie, wearing a white jacket, was lording it over the rest camp's Matabele servants. Briony looked strained. Lance wondered if Jacques had reprimanded her for what was, Lance had sensed the previous evening, inexcusable and perhaps dangerous behaviour. Briony and Pietie remained behind at the rest camp. Lance was glad Ewart saw fit to take him along to the planning council.

Lance was flabbergasted at the grand robbery Ewart proposed at the planning session, not only by its scale but by the sensitive nature of the material to be stolen. When they arrived, the men sat in their half-circle, Sambo's brothers standing smiling before them, as if they had not moved since the previous evening. Sambo stood over the table in the shade of the tree, studying the map Jacques had left the night before. He straightened and folded his arms as they approached. After the greetings Ewart said something fast to him in French in which Lance caught his own name.

'What was that about me?'

Sambo smiled broadly. 'Perhaps you'd like to take a walk with me, Mr Lance.'

Ewart was already walking away with Jacques, saying, 'Let's get to know the men.'

Sambo took Lance's arm and Lance perforce had to walk with him. Sambo had the grip of a vice. Lance flexed his muscles and shook his arm free.

Sambo smiled. 'Your brother tells me you are an athlete of renown. *Le rugby*. It makes you strong.'

'I try. Did my brother also tell you why I'm here?' It was impossible to be angry with this man.

'He did mention in passing that youthful exuberance had led you into indiscretion. He doesn't seem to think it fatal.'

Lance laughed with the big man. 'No not fatal. But the next best thing. They're threatening to crush my testicles between two bricks.' Here, walking in the sunshine with a strong and competent and friendly man, it seemed unlikely and far away.

'Ah. Painful. But more than just painful. You can be sure your brother won't allow it.'

Lance didn't know what to say in the face of such certitude. They came to a stream and Sambo sat down on the bank. Lance sat down beside him.

'There might be some danger in what we are about to do,' Sambo said.

'I guessed that. Though yesterday, when Jacques first explained it, it seemed a great deal of money for quite little effort.'

39

Sambo chuckled. 'Nothing is for free, Mr Lance.'

'You can call me Lance if you like.'

'Thank you. But it would offend Mrs Roux and perhaps Mr Roux. Your brother worries about you exactly because you are an athlete with quick reflexes.'

'Oh'

'Quick reflexes are only an asset in our business if they are controlled. Mr Weber and Mr Roux are immensely experienced men. I was with your brother throughout the Congo troubles and had ample time to observe and admire him. He moves slowly and surely, always first securing his back.'

This did not square with what Lance had seen of his brother. Ewart was one of the quickest-thinking and -acting men he had ever met. 'What do you mean?'

'I express myself badly. You see your brother is a very alert man. That is true. But did you ever observe his driving?'

'Yes. He sets very high and consistent average times. I couldn't match such averages.'

'Exactly. Because you, though a superior athlete, do not have his experience in harnessing your reflexes. What I meant when I said your brother moves slowly is this: he plans exhaustively for all risks, then moves decisively in the direction in which he can best control the risks. To an outsider that seems like reflex action, to him it is the professional trick of survival.'

'You make it sound as if we could be killed just hunting crocodiles.'

'That is true. We could be killed before we even get there.'

'My brother could tell me all this himself.'

'From him it would be patronizing. He has made me responsible for you.'

'I see,' Lance refrained from saying he didn't need a nursemaid; that would be pointless ill manners.

'In my turn I shall take the opportunity of assigning one

40

of my brothers to you as a bearer. It will be a big opportunity for him to learn much from you.'

'A bearer?

'He will carry your rifle and, in return for what you choose to tell him of the wider world, point out the unfamiliar pitfalls of the jungle to you until you learn to recognize them yourself.'

Sambo's personal authority was so great that, before he could stop himself, Lance was telling the black man of the *jokkels* and the *swots* at Stellenbosch.

'Exactly so,' Sambo said when Lance had finished, 'except that here more is at stake than meeting a few girls or getting academic credits.' He rose without explaining the cryptic remark. 'We must return. There is work to be done.'

'There is one more thing,' Sambo said as they neared the camp. 'I hope you won't take offence.'

'Say on.'

'Once, after a battle, your brother told me he was from a city. It was difficult for me, who grew up in the jungle, to understand but he said that Africa is strange and a law unto herself who will not allow a man to survive until first he learns humility before her. Once said, it was obvious that that is exactly what the manhood training of the African tribes is aimed at. Do you understand what I'm saying?'

'I think so. Watch, listen and learn. Do not move too quickly.'

Lance was consumed with amazement at the man walking beside him – Sambo must surely be truly exceptional if Ewart should so confide in him. And no doubt it was a compliment to be put in his care.

All the men were sitting in a circle around Ewart and Jacques, listening intently to Ewart speaking in a low voice in their native language, occasionally breaking into French rather than searching for an unfamiliar phrase. Once they laughed delightedly.

Sambo called one of his brothers away from the circle. 'This is my brother who will be your bearer. Call him Jimmy. His native name was not made for white men to get their tongues round. Even your brother can't say it.' Sambo spoke a few words in their own language to his brother. The brother immediately stepped behind Lance's right shoulder, smiling all the while.

Sambo sat down in the circle around Ewart and Jacques, and Lance followed suit, Jimmy taking his place behind his right shoulder. The talk was meaningless to Lance but he laughed when the men laughed. It was just like joining a new rugger team, you had to earn your place by observing the group mores (a phase from Psychology I – how far away Stellenbosch now seemed).

Ewart finished an anecdote, waited politely for the men to stop laughing, then rose without another word. Lance had never seem him like this before, or known him to tell a story. He had always seemed at ease, almost offensively self-contained everywhere else, yet here somehow, with these men, he seemed to have grown a new dimension. Jacques, by contrast, seemed a little less at ease with the common men than he had the day before with his peers or with Sambo.

Jacques and Sambo followed Ewart to the table. Halfway Ewart turned. 'You come too, Lance.' When Lance turned to walk around the table he found Jimmy behind him. He hoped it would be all right.

'You're a lucky bugger,' Jacques Roux said to him. 'Not everyone has a prince of royal blood as a bearer.'

'Huh?'

'Jimmy here. He can trace his lineage through fifteen generations of Supreme Chiefs.'

Jimmy cast his eyes down. Sambo said easily, 'Alas now dead and their tribe murdered by our enemies except for the few here. A man cannot be a chief of eighteen men, at best he can be a sergeant.'

'And younger brothers corporals,' Jimmy said.

'I don't know that I would take such adversity with fortitude,' Jacques said.

Sambo nodded. 'Unto every day sufficient its own evil.'

Jacques smiled. 'And an eye for an eye when you can.'

'You two scholars can swop biblical texts some other time,' Ewart said. He put his finger on the map. 'We're here. Over here a dam is being built. Kariba. They have dynamite and trucks. We will need a great deal of dynamite and as many trucks as we can get. We will take them from Kariba after dark tonight.'

'Lake Kariba is really very beautiful,' Sambo said to Lance. 'It's a pity you can't see in the dark.'

Lance shifted on the front seat of the truck, peering anxiously into the night. Sambo on one side of him and Ewart on the other, both bulky men, left him very little space. He was frightened but did not want to admit it against their calm. If he spoke his voice would betray him.

'You came to see?' Ewart asked.

'Where else would one need so many men who can drive trucks?'

Ewart held the arm with his stainless steel Rolex out of the window to read the dial by moonlight. 'It's time.'

Sambo started the engine and put the lights on. He drove slowly down the gravel road. When they came to the roadblock he stopped and sounded the horn. A middle-aged black man with a blanket wrapped around him and a heavy staff in his hand came from the hut next to the barrier.

'Men of the Matabele for the compound,' Ewart called to him. 'Raise the barrier, Watchman.'

The barrier was raised and they drove on. About half a mile further on they came to the compound of the workmen where all was darkness and drove past towards the huge concrete and earth bulwarks silhouetted by the moon. Sambo took them to the right and soon they were among orderly rows of heavy dumping trucks. They drove past these and around the back of the compound of workmen. Here, behind the commissary, were the stores and two neat rows of flatbed lorries. Sambo stopped the truck. The men piled from the back and, chattering excitedly, each ran to a truck. Ewart made no attempt to silence them. They were like children promised new toys. They opened the bonnets and stood waiting beside the trucks as Ewart had repeatedly told them to do during the afternoon. He and Sambo went from truck to truck and re-arranged the wiring under the bonnet.

Lance found Jimmy behind his right shoulder and went to the truck at the end of the line with him. When Ewart had finished rewiring the engine of their truck, Lance and Jimmy climbed in and Jimmy turned the starter. The engine caught immediately and all the other engines were turned over to make the night hideous with sound. Surely somebody would come now, Lance thought. He was sweating in the cool night.

Jimmy laughed delightedly. 'They're all Mercedes Unimogs. Very good for rough terrain, high off the ground. Only the very best for us!' He switched the lights on as Ewart drove past them in the truck they had come in, turning to follow its muddied red tail lights. With roaring engines and clashing gears the other trucks swung in behind them. Lance thought the noise would wake the dead but the hundreds of men sleeping around them had begun their labours at dawn and seemed to sleep soundly enough.

The lead truck stopped near a high barbed-wire fence, angled outwards at the top against intruders. Set in the fence was a gate wide enough for two trucks to pass side by side with ample space to spare. To one side, outside the gate, was a large shack. Lance incredulously heard Ewart add to the racket of the engines by blowing the hooter of his truck continuously. The other drivers joined in exuberantly.

A white man wearing only a pair of shorts stumbled

44

from the shack, rubbing his eyes with one hand and waving a torch with the other. Obediently the hooting stopped. He kept waving the torch and one by one the engines switched off. When there was only silence, he stepped aggressively towards the lead truck.

'You realize this is overtime?' he said to Ewart. 'You people have no concept of time.'

Ewart climbed down and gently pushed the torch shining in his face aside. 'I can't drive a truck full of dynamite through the dark if you ruin my night vision.'

'Where's your authority?'

Ewart reached inside the cab of the truck and cocked the rifle in the same smooth movement with which he produced it. 'Here.'

The torch lingered on the rifle, hanging casually in Ewart's hand. The arming click had been unmistakable. 'You realize it is a criminal offence to hold up a government inspector of explosives, don't you? And stealing explosives by the truckload contravenes at least half a dozen laws?'

'Turn around.'

'Besides being, most probably, high treason?'

'Turn around.'

The man in the shorts turned around. Ewart hit him under the ear with the side of his hand and, using the same hand, caught the torch before it had fallen more than six inches.

Lance drew a deep breath, more in admiration for such superb reflexes than for the audacity of the act. Ewart went into the shack and returned almost immediately with a bunch of keys. Meanwhile Sambo had come running up and was tying the explosives inspector to the gatepost. Ewart opened the padlock with the first key he tried. He and Sambo flung the gates wide and the trucks drove through into the explosives compound. At widely spaced intervals on cleared ground stood seven conical huts built of stones that appeared in the headlights to be ashblocks

45

but which Lance knew, because Ewart had said so at the briefing earlier in the day, were fireproof asbestos blocks. Their own truck and thirteen of the stolen trucks split up, two to each hut. Ewart ran around opening the huts with his keys. The men fell to loading the cases of dynamite. They sang as they worked, throwing the cases fearsomely from hand to hand.

Ewart stood to one side, watching for a moment. Somebody, Lance knew not who, had put on lights in the compound. He wondered if it was the beginning of the end for them.

'Lance, Jimmy, come with me,' Ewart said and started towards the gate at a lope without looking to see if they were obeying. Lance trotted beside his brother, knowing Jimmy would be behind his right shoulder. The black man had been there all day and already Lance had become used to it, a strangely reassuring feeling.

'You remember what I told you?' Ewart asked.

'Yes.' Earlier in the day Ewart had taken Lance aside and told him twice, making him repeat his instructions each time. 'All those trucks we have were refuelled at the end of work today but you want Jimmy and me to get two full tankers of diesel for the journey.'

'If you meet any opposition, let Jimmy and the other one handle it.'

'Yes, you told me.'

'Don't forget it.'

'All right, all right!' Lance remembered what Sambo had said about humility, about watching, listening and learning, not moving too fast. This was not his kind of business but it had seemed ridiculously easy till now. 'Sorry.'

Outside the gate the remaining six trucks had been turned to face away from the explosives compound, their engines left running. Lance jumped into the nearest one and the driver immediately drove off in what seemed to Lance to be the wrong direction. 'Hey,' he shouted at

46

Jimmy on the running board beside him, 'we're going in the wrong direction.'

'No sir. We're going right,' Jimmy shouted back.

The three minutes it took to cover the mile from the explosives compound to the fuel depot were the longest in Lance's life. He was flattered that Ewart had assigned this responsibility to him – although with a warning to heed Jimmy's counsel under any and all circumstances – and he was worried about failing.

At last the fuel depot loomed cylindrically before them. The driver slewed the truck in a tight circle. There was nobody guarding the fuel as far as Lance could see. He looked nervously at his watch. Three of the eight minutes Ewart had allocated him had gone. Jimmy had to jump aside nimbly to avoid the door striking him as Lance swung it open.

Lance ran around the first tanker he came to, looking for the fuel gauge under the curvature of the belly. He could see nothing in the shadows the overhang of the tanker caused. He came on their driver, inspecting the gauge by the light of a match.

'Put that out!'

'Diesel doesn't burn like petrol, N'kosi,' the driver said calmly in bad English and lit another match. 'This one is full.' Without waiting for further instructions he swung the door open and climbed up into the cab. 'Key in here too.'

'Over here, Mr Lance,' Jimmy called. He was already in the cab of another tanker, turning the engine.

Lance felt foolish. He ran around the front of the tanker and climbed up beside Jimmy. He felt like crying. As a leader of men he was a signal failure. Even the modicum of leadership Ewart had expected of him, guided by Jimmy, he had not been able to exert.

Jimmy hummed under his breath but stopped when Lance spoke.

'I'm sorry.'

'You've succeeded. You're bringing two full tankers, as

47

requested, and ahead of schedule.' Jimmy drew the tanker up outside the gate to the explosives compound. The other tanker pulled in neatly beside them.

Sitting still, waiting, was getting on Lance's nerves. He craned his head out of the window to look into the explosives compound. The last lorry was just being loaded, the others pulling up one by one beside them. He saw Sambo and one of his brothers come out of the inspector's shack, gingerly carrying a large aluminium trunk between them.

A closed truck pulled in beside him, cutting off his view of Sambo. Ewart was behind the wheel.

'What's that?' Lance asked.

'A refrigerator truck full of frozen meat and green veg,' Ewart said. 'We only needed two trucks for the tools and spare parts, so I took this for the spare driver. Did you have any trouble?'

'No. The fuel depot wasn't guarded.'

'Good work.'

'Thanks to Jimmy and the other man.' Lance had an idea Ewart had known the fuel depot would not be guarded.

'Learn his name as soon as you can. You're in charge of the fuel tankers. That man and Jimmy will be your drivers.'

'I don't –

'Just be careful and think before you act.'

Lance had been about to say he didn't think he should be put in command over Jimmy and the other man. He drew a deep breath to repeat the assertion.

'It'll be an honour to serve under your brother,' Jimmy said over his shoulder.

'Good,' Ewart said, climbing down. He strode off.

'You're a sarcastic bastard,' Lance told Jimmy without heat.

Jimmy managed to look surprised without losing his perpetual smile.

Lance climbed down and walked to the front of the

truck. Instantly Jimmy appeared beside him. Sambo, the other brother, and Ewart were lashing the aluminium trunk carefully on one of the trucks with spare parts. 'Fuses and detonator,' Jimmy said. 'Very dangerous.'

'I'd have thought, with all this dynamite, we wouldn't worry too much about one small box of detonators.'

Jimmy shook his head. 'No, Mr Lance. Dynamite is inert. You can shoot it with a rifle or burn it and nothing happens. But those detonators, they're – ' he searched for a word. 'They're volatile.'

Ewart and Sambo were going from truck to truck, inspecting the fastenings of the nets holding the boxed dynamite on the trucks.

Lance was sweating at their calm, their apparently leisurely pace. He glanced at Jimmy in the headlights but Jimmy was apparently unconcerned, staring into the distance over Lance's shoulder.

'They're stirring.'

Lance followed Jimmy's outstretched arm. Lights were coming on in buildings half a mile away. Involuntarily he looked at his watch and was amazed to find they had only been inside the contractors' camp for twenty-six minutes. It felt like hours. His shirt was drenched with sweat and clammy against his back.

'Ewart!' Lance called. 'They're stirring at the camp.'

Ewart finished pulling at the cords of the last truck, then looked in the direction of Lance's arm. 'Not before time,' he said loudly enough for Lance to hear. 'All right,' he raised his voice, 'everyone to his truck and follow Sergeant Sambo.'

Yet the men still moved with what seemed to Lance suicidal slowness, walking to their trucks rather than running. Lance, sitting in the passenger seat of his tanker, could see one set of car or truck lights coming on in the distance, then another and another. Somebody was coming to investigate the commotion they had caused for the last half hour.

It seemed an hour before it was their turn to pull out into the line, even though they were near the front. First was Sergeant Sambo, driving one of the trucks loaded with spares and tools, then the other similarly loaded truck, then an empty truck, then the two tankers, behind them the trucks loaded with dynamite. It had taken Lance a while after Ewart had expounded this arrangement at the briefing to work out the reasons but in the end it was obvious: they had far to go; there were only three (now reduced to two) trucks of spares which they would certainly need on their journey and there were also only two tankers with diesel without which they could not progress at all; but there were many trucks loaded with dynamite – so that they could afford to lose a few at the tail-end. Jimmy let the other tanker go before them. Lance saw Ewart look up from something he was doing on the truck they had come in to wave the refrigerated truck in behind the second tanker.

'What's he doing?'

'Giving us a screen.'

'No, with the dynamite.'

'He's arming it.'

'Why?'

'I don't know. Perhaps he's going to blow up something.'

'Jesus!'

Jimmy laughed easily. 'Don't worry. Your brother doesn't make mistakes.'

Lance changed the subject. 'Why do we need a screen?'

'Diesel oil will just smother an open flame thrown in it but if you shoot a bullet into a tankful of it there will be an explosion.'

'I want to go home to my mother!' Lance would wonder for a long time afterwards if this remark was the genesis of the same casual courage his brother and Jacques Roux had or simply a nervous release.

'Don't tell my brothers, but me too,' Jimmy said,

sending the truck up the incline of the dam wall, little more than a dirt track at a slight angle in the horizontal plane climbing steeply up a wall of packed earth. 'But Mr Weber could hardly give his own brother one of the less dangerous commands. It would not be seemly.'

'He brought me here to keep an eye on me, to see I didn't get into more trouble.' To his surprise Lance found the thought, once spoken, funny. He laughed with Jimmy.

They had passed the middle of the wall. To the left and to the right stood concrete pillars, sprouting metal rods. Far below the moon glinted on water. Lance looked in the mirror beside him. Behind them there was a snake of lights and beyond the snake more lights gaining on the snake. A light at the tail of the snake stopped, wiggled dementedly as Ewart backed and filled, then glared out across the water as he positioned the truck across the narrow road, blocking Lance's view of the vehicles giving chase.

Lance counted aloud as he had seen people do in films. After a while he stopped, feeling ridiculous. He had reached thirty. Nobody in the movies had ever had to count that far.

'Two-minute fuse at least,' Jimmy said. 'To give him time to run clear.'

'Oh. Who's picking him up?'

'I don't know.'

'We can't leave him behind!'

'He will have made his arrangements,' Jimmy said, looking straight ahead though the driving, following the lights of the tanker in front, did not take much concentration.

Lance cursed his own impetuosity. Was he doomed forever to be making a fool of himself? It seemed likely, for just then they passed the Landrover, Jacques sitting behind the wheel with his head well back against the restraint, obviously listening to some favourite piece of music. Briony was beside him. As soon as the trucks had passed they would fetch Ewart.

As they started the long descent into what had been Northern Rhodesia and was now Zambia, they heard faintly the boom that lit up their mirrors. The sound of rushing water soon drowned the explosion.

They had stolen the trucks and dynamite they wanted, complete with tools and spares and diesel for the trucks, and driven away. And now they were safe from pursuit. It had happened so smoothly and without any drama that it compared most unfavourably to what Lance had seen in films. He was reminded of what Sambo had said about his brother's planning for the minimization of risks. It was almost, but not quite, disappointing that no one had fired on them or even challenged them, excepting only the government inspector of explosives whose resistance had been more comic than effective. Escaping, they were not even driving very fast on the beautifully graded gravel road they now found themselves on, no more than thirty miles an hour.

After five minutes at this pace the Landrover came past them, feeling its way cautiously in the dust the trucks threw up. A little later, after the Landrover had reached the front of the cavalcade, they speeded up to fifty miles an hour. Presently they passed a large number of idle roadmaking machines and came on to a hard-surfaced road. Their speed increased again, to sixty miles an hour. Lance knew, because Ewart had stressed it at the briefing, that this was the crucial stage of the operation, this seemingly innocuous stretch of good road to Lusaka. They had to cover the 114 miles to Lusaka and pass through Lusaka before the contractors at the Kariba Dam could persuade the Zambian army or police to set up road blocks. Lusaka, Ewart had said, was the obvious place – because nobody would believe white men would steal trucks and dynamite in Rhodesia only to branch off at the only possible junction which led back to Botswana and the Caprivi Strip of South West Africa – and Lusaka was, anyway, the only place with adequate communications and sufficient men for a big operation short of Kitwe 223 miles further. Sambo had been worried about this, saying, 'Many of the white administrators stayed on after independence, especially in the police and army.'

Ewart had nodded thoughtfully. 'That's true. But after the Unilateral Declaration of Independence of the Rhodesians the relations became a bit strained. We're counting on that.'

Sambo had seemed satisfied. Lance had heard or read somewhere that the Kariba Dam was a joint venture between the two countries and was sure that that would make them co-operate more closely, on matters affecting the dam at least, but had said nothing. Before today he could not even have pointed out the position of the Kariba Dam on a map, nor did he know exactly where the Zambezi, on which the dam was built, was to be found.

A little more than two hours after they had left Kariba they drove without incident through Lusaka, a pleasant country town that reminded Lance of Stellenbosch with its white buildings.

After Lusaka it became pretty boring, staring at the lights of the truck in front, catching the occasional glimpse of a tree in the sidespill of the lights. Lance had long since ceased to find the signs funny; they were the same in Rhodesia:

DANGER ELEPHANTS CROSSING

DANGER LOOSE RHINO

When Lance woke the dawn was just breaking. 'Where are we?'

'Three hours from Lusaka,' Jimmy said.

'Oh.' He felt guilty at having dropped off. He tried to

picture in his mind the map he had seen several times during the previous day but it was a confused jumble. 'How far are we from the border?'

'That way – ' Jimmy gestured to his right ' – fifteen or twenty miles. Up ahead along this road at least another two and a half hours.'

Lance studied the red glow in the sky. 'Soon they will be able to send planes after us.'

Jimmy nodded.

The line of trucks was slowing down and turning right. Lance caught a glimpse of a sign: NDOLA. 'I'm sorry I called you a sarcastic kaffir last night.'

'You didn't say kaffir.'

'I apologize for what was in my mind.'

'It's all right. I think all white men smell funny.'

Lance sniffed his armpits. 'You should smell me before a big rugger game.'

'No, not sweat. All men sweat. It's the perfumed soap white men use that make them smell funny to blacks.'

'You speak damned good English for a black man, even a prince.' It was true, Jimmy's English had the fruity intonations of some of the upper-class English students at Stellenbosch.

'I was at school in England for a while,' Jimmy said. 'I didn't like it as much as the mission school back home . . . in the Congo.' There was a brief pause. 'I liked school best in Belgium when I later went there.'

'And then you fought with my brother in the Congo?'

'Yes. That was a bad time, right after my family and my whole tribe . . .' Jimmy let the sentence trail away.

'I'm sorry.'

'Don't apologize. The man driving the other tanker, you can call him Ben. He's a good man.'

The helicopter clattered its way over them. They were approaching Ndola. 'Shit!' Lance said.

'Ai, ai ai-ieeh!' Jimmy keened.

Ewart had said, 'Taking the trucks and dynamite will be

easy. But remember, the job isn't over until we cross the border into the Congo.'

At the front of the convoy the helicopter took up station above the Landrover. A man was shouting into a bullhorn to make himself heard above the roar of the trucks and the clatter of the helicopter. 'Stop immediately. This is a police message. Stop immediately. If you do not stop we shall deal harshly with you.'

'Can't we go any faster?' Lance shouted as the message was repeated.

'Not on this road,' Jimmy said, watching the helicopter over the tail of the tanker in front of them.

'What about the Ndola police?'

'They'll be waiting.'

'Where?'

Jimmy shrugged. Lance hopped up and down in his seat in frustration as the convoy progressed at the same even pace, the helicopter hanging over its head like an evil omen. The Landrover and the trucks would be easy targets from the helicopter. As if to satisfy Lance's every thought, the loudhailer ceased its addition to the cacophony and was replaced by a rifle barrel peeking coyly from the glass bubble of the helicopter.

'Hey, Jimmy, they're going to shoot us!' The rifle barrel did indeed seem to be aimed straight at their truck.

Jimmy gave Lance a look as if to say: what did you expect? Lance missed it; he was staring mesmerized at the barrel of the rifle. Shots rang out. The cavalcade continued inexorably forward. Lance ducked under the dashboard, then came out again, shamefaced, when the shooting stopped and the loudhailer started again, informing them that the next shots would be into the trucks, not over them.

'Look,' Jimmy said conversationally, pointing.

Lance reluctantly tore his eyes from the helicopter to look where Jimmy was pointing. They were rushing into the square of a small colonial town. Lance first saw a man with an unbuttoned uniform jacket; the man was rubbing his eyes with his knuckles. Others were carrying sandbags and barriers or rolling forty-four-gallon drums.

'The Ndola police are building a roadblock for us,' Jimmy said. Men were diving for cover and then they were through the square and racing down a wide avenue for the open country. Behind them they heard sirens starting and a few scattered shots. It had all happened so quickly that Lance had not even been able to duck under the dashboard again before it was over. He looked in the mirror beside him but there was nothing to see except the line of trucks.

'Watch out!' Lance heard Jimmy call but it was too late; Lance was thrown violently back in his seat and only his excellent reflexes saved him from hitting the dashboard on the rebound. The wide avenue had suddenly become a narrow dirt road but the convoy had not slowed. Almost immediately Lance became used to the jolting motion.

'How far is the border?'

'Five, six miles,' Jimmy said as the helicopter came over them again.

'There they are again!'

The helicopter turned wide in front of the convoy, then came skimming over it so low Lance thought it would surely crash into them and ducked, his arms over his head.

Jimmy laughed. 'They're trying to slow us up.' The convoy had not slowed one whit.

'You're enjoying this!'

Jimmy cast Lance a quick glance. Lance looked away: he was enjoying it too. 'They're also spotting us for planes with heavy machine-guns,' Lance said. As a boy he had built plastic models of fighter planes.

They heard the shots before the helicopter came into sight over the tanker in front of them. Ben took his tanker to the left, Jimmy his to the right. Lance hit his head on the roof as the wheels struck the ridge of the ground the graders had left at the side of the road, then held on for dear life while Jimmy fought the huge truck back on to the road.

No sooner were they in the middle of the narrow road again than an open Landrover bouncing in the rough veld beside the road overtook them from behind. Men were bracing themselves in the back, pointing rifles at the convoy. This time Lance was sure he could see down a barrel.

'Jimmy! This side!'

'Down, Mr Lance, down!'

A shot rang out and the whole cab rang with a painful high ting! Then the Landrover hit an anthill and slowly turned on its side, men flying in all directions.

They passed Jacques' Landrover, parked beside the road, Briony at the wheel. Jacques was standing beside it, a rifle to his shoulder. Ewart had a rifle hanging in his hand and was looking back to where they had come from. Lance glanced in the mirror but saw nothing. Some pieces of a barrier pole striped like a barber's were still falling to the ground when they passed through the Zambian customs area. Lance caught fleeting sight of a sign: OPEN AT 8 A.M.

'We can't wait,' he said and laughed nervously.

On the Congolese side there was no barrier and no sign of any customs officials. The trucks drew up in two neat lines as they arrived. Lance jumped down and stood beside the tanker looking back. The Landrover was just coming through the broken barrier. As it passed the Congolese customs hut, another Landrover full of armed men came to a sliding halt at the broken barrier. The men jumped down and aimed their rifles at the convoy but an officer shouted at them and struck the rifles down. The helicopter hovered forlornly above the border, not daring to cross. All round Lance their drivers were shouting epithets and making rude finger signs at their frustrated pursuers.

The cool dawn breeze plastered Lance's wringing wet

shirt uncomfortably to his back. The Landrover came by beside the road and slowly the convoy got under way again. A mile further they stopped to refuel the Landrover and all the trucks from the tankers. Then they set off for Lubumbashi where, in the early afternoon, they camped on an open piece of ground within sight of the town.

Ewart immediately came to Lance. 'You've done well.'

'Thanks.'

'What we did back there was easy. The most difficult part is still to come. Have a look at this when you get a chance.' Ewart gave Lance a map. 'Another thing, Lance. You're in charge of refuelling. Thirty-four minutes for refuelling is too long. I want you to work out something to refuel all the transport in ten minutes if we ever have to do it under pressure. Just have Jimmy commandeer as many men as you need to do it properly.'

Lance, who had not known the refuelling had been timed, nodded. 'Okay.' He was bursting with pride at being given some real responsibility and it was only later, when Ewart was busy elsewhere, that the question occurred to him. He asked Jimmy, 'What does my brother mean, "under pressure"?'

'If we're attacked.'

'Christ, I thought we were safe now.' Lance took the map from his pocket. 'My brother told me what we did back there was easy, the difficult part is still to come, and gave me the map.' He folded the map as he had seen Jacques do. After several tries he still couldn't get Lubumbashi and Bangui on the same section. He refolded the map again. 'Still, what's the big deal – I mean we're only going to travel from here to – ' he pointed, turned the map over and pointed again ' – to here.'

'Just add up the distance, Mr Lance.'

Lance started adding up the red mileage figures but soon stopped. He had a total of nearly a thousand and he

58

could see figures of 500 and 300 and 200 looming in the sections ahead. 'Something over two thousand miles.'

'Look at the roads.'

To Lance a road had always been a road. He looked up the key. He looked back at the map. He consulted the key again. Then, unbelieving, he traced the road from where the map indicated the tarred road stopped. 'What's an improved road?'

'One that's been scraped and perhaps graded.'

'And a partially improved road?'

'A dirt road with places for cars to pass each other.'

The other components of the key were self-explanatory: 'Recognized or marked tracks' and 'Dirt-roads, suitable for cross-country vehicles.' They were going to travel over more than two thousand miles of roads the mapmakers had obviously thought substandard or difficult. 'Okay, so it isn't going to be easy.'

'Some of those roads marked there, Mr Lance, exist only during the few months of the year when it is the dry season. For the rest of the year they're streams. You'll see. But that wasn't what your brother meant. Most of the two thousand miles is hostile territory.'

'Huh?'

'The people are going to resent us travelling across their land.'

'So they don't like us.'

'They usually show their resentment by armed attack.' Jimmy was amused.

'Come on, Jimmy! You're having me on.'

'I assure you, Mr Lance, I'm in earnest. Would your brother joke about such things?'

'No, but I thought he was talking about the crocodiles.'

Jimmy raised his hand to make a small dismissive movement. 'Crocodiles don't have guns.'

Lance read some of the names of the provinces inscribed on the map. 'Kazai, Mongo, Shaba, Kivu, Bangala.'

'All have tribes hostile to strangers and especially to white men,' Jimmy said. 'All warlike and dangerous.'

Lance pondered this for a while. If a man like Jimmy, who had been through the Congo troubles with Ewart, called someone dangerous that someone was bound to be at least lethal.

'Anyway, you left out the most immediate danger, the Baluba,' Jimmy said.

Lance found the Baluba tribes on the map, then scanned the low hills furtively. 'The Baluba?'

'Sure. Very warrior-like. Very fierce. Good men to have on your side though their excesses can be a bit sickening. Bad enemies.'

Lance just didn't believe in the threat. He looked at the map again. There were still hundred miles of tarred roads, several large towns before they reached the green rain forests where, even Lance was willing to believe, anything could happen.

'You're bullshitting me, Jimmy. That's like being unkind to strangers.'

Jimmy stubbornly shook his head. 'They're unkind to strangers as a matter of course. Their cultural heritage, you might say. Some of them will even eat you.'

'Cannibals?'

'Yes. Not common but not unknown. But that's not what we have to worry about. There are rebel groups for about two or three hundred miles all round Lubumbashi who're going to want all this lovely dynamite we're carrying, and our high-quality trucks, for purposes of their own.'

'What are they rebelling against?'

'Government. Any government. They want independence. The Katangese want Shaba Province, the others all want their own areas. Some are professional rebels; they just fight any authority because they like fighting.'

'Jesus, you paint a horrifying picture. On the map the Congo looks just like any other country, except it's bigger.'

'Being bigger, it is less easy to govern. All the tribes used to be independent until the Belgians came. With the Belgians gone the Congo is one huge country artificially conglomerated of disparate and hostile tribes.'

'*Pygmées?*' Lance read from the map. 'Pigmies!'

'Right where we're going to end up. White men, and for that matter strange black men, get shot with poisoned arrows several times a year.'

'You'll never get a job as Santa Claus, Jimmy. Instead people will hire you to frighten children.' Lance still only half-believed Jimmy. It was simply too much to credit. Jimmy shrugged.

It wasn't until three days later that Jimmy was proved right between Kamina and Kaniama. They had stopped a day and a half in Lubumbashi while Jacques visited government officials with his letters of introduction and the inevitable gifts and Ewart bought equipment and supplies to put on the so-far empty truck.

Ewart had approved of Lance and Jimmy's plan for speeding up the refuelling: two lines of trucks, each line in the shape of a V, one V inside the other. That way the overlapping trucks, the dynamite trucks on the inside, should provide cover for the men working the tankers and for the tankers themselves.

Lance still didn't believe in any possible attack but entered enthusiastically into the game of practising for it. First he selected his men. Then he had the trucks drive in line through the open space outside Lubumbashi where they were camping, forming up in the nestling V on the sound of the whistle Briony had found for him in the Landrover. The fuel tankers would drive down the lines and Lance would time their dry runs. At the end of the day the whole operation, getting the trucks formed and refuelling them (this time for real), took fourteen minutes, of which the actual refuelling took twelve minutes. Ewart expressed his satisfaction. 'That'll reduce with practice. Send all the men except your drivers back to their other tasks. Then take the tankers for refuelling.' Lance felt like a general, marshalling his forces. Later, when he signed with a flourish for the diesel to refill the tankers, credit arranged by Jacques, he felt like a capitalist; this was nothing like signing a chit at roulette – it was somehow a better, clearer, cleaner feeling. He had also asked Ewart to include cleaning materials for the tanker-men in his shopping list and Ewart had bought a small bale of waste cotton and a huge drum of stuff you could rub on your hands to make the diesel disappear and which then washed away in water without the need for soap.

Among the equipment Ewart had bought were two small diesel generators and floodlights to attach to them. These were set up in two banks after the evening meal and the trucks driven one by one between them, unloaded and tightly repacked under Ewart's watchful eye. Simultaneously each truck had its oil changed and was greased. Every tyre was inspected minutely for cuts or the slightest wear and replaced if necessary; hard work, as Lance found out when he volunteered to help. When they were moving the heavy spare rear axle units, complete with springs and shock absorbers, a contest of strength developed and Lance found to his surprise that several of the men were stronger than he.

It was nearly midnight when they finished. The men went to wash off in a pool in the nearby stream and Lance went with them. They splashed about in the water, laughing exuberantly. Lance wondered what good these men would be in an attack; they were strong but unused to even moderately complicated machines and totally childlike. True, his brother had greeted them by name like old comrades-in-arms but Lance clearly remembered reading in a news magazine that a modern army marched on its brains rather than its stomachs or feet, which was why, the writer concluded, the few white mercenaries had been so devastatingly successful against such overwhelming odds.

In the morning a large closed truck arrived and the

white driver, wearing a side-arm and accompanied by a fierce-looking black man armed with a short-barrelled shotgun (Lance was later to learn, from Jimmy, that it is called a *riot gun*), asked for Jacques. Lance was still trying to work out the name of the company that owned the truck, painted quite small just in front of the door, when Jacques came, accompanied by Ewart. He had got as far as deciphering that it was a mineral company of the Belgians – *de Belgique*. The crates inside the closed truck were unloaded. Jacques stood patiently by while Ewart had each crate levered open with a crowbar and inspected the contents. Only when Ewart expressed himself satisfied did Jacques sign the paper on the driver's clipboard. The men gathered around excitedly to inspect the arms and ammunition in the crates.

'Jesus,' Lance said to Jacques, who was standing next to him, 'you can't go around arming private armies in foreign countries.'

Jacques laughed, a sound Lance found chilling. 'It's not a private army. As of now they're on the payroll of the mining company as security guards.'

'Did you have to give the mining company a cut of the crocodile skins?' Briony asked from the other side of Jacques.

'No. They want to prospect in the River Congo itself for diamonds and other valuables and to do that, they must first be rid of the crocodiles. Even the arms are free, in return for my promise that I would tell both governments of their co-operation. For people as rich as they are these arms are peanuts and even our riches from the crocodiles would be a drop in the ocean.'

'I suppose so,' Briony said judiciously.

Lance restrained himself from whistling. He couldn't conceive of people for whom a million dollars would be a negligible sum of money. He looked around at Jimmy, who was smiling as usual but shrugged his shoulders to show he knew how Lance felt.

63

'This company used to make thousands of millions out of copper and chrome in the old days,' Jimmy said softly. 'Even now they probably make hundreds of millions of dollars. They financed the mercenaries and the whole war out of petty cash.'

This time Lance did whistle. 'Thousands of millions, eh?' It was amazing the things Jimmy knew, even if he were a prince.

'That was what the war was about.'

'Yeah. Most wars are about natural resources or trade,' Lance said. He had learnt that at school but not understood it till now. 'Aren't we going to get into trouble carrying all this stuff about?'

Jacques had overheard him. 'It's going to keep us out of trouble. Don't worry. Nobody's even going to ask us about it.'

Sambo brought Jacques one of the firearms. 'All good ay-one stuff in beautiful condition, Mr Roux.'

'Thanks, Sambo.' Jacques inspected the weapon, trying the moving parts, and then turned to Lance. 'Do you know what this is?'

'A submachine gun.'

'Near enough. It's a fully automatic medium-calibre machine pistol.' He handed it to Lance. 'It's what you win wars with in Africa. You don't have to be a trained marksman, you just spray the approximate area of your target with bullets and you're bound to hit something.'

Lance held the thing uncomfortably. It felt cold in his hands, yet seemed to fit naturally.

'The beauty of it is,' Jacques continued, 'that it is almost indestructible. It can be field-stripped and cleaned by a regular moron after ten minutes of instruction. And it's versatile. You can switch it to single shot, fit a longer barrel in seconds and turn it into a fair long-range weapon. You want to try it?'

'Here?' Lance looked at Lubumbashi not two hundred yards away.

'In Africa, only a fool investigates gunshots not specifically aimed at him.'

Jacques was obviously referring to a different Africa than the one Lance had hitherto known. 'Yes, I wouldn't mind,' Lance said.

Jacques called for a clip of ammunition, inserted it into the weapon and cocked it. 'That's the safety catch. Click it over.'

Lance clicked the safety catch. It made a most satisfying though small precision sound. He looked around for something to shoot at.

'Try hitting those drums,' Jacques said. 'From the hip, you don't put it to your shoulder.'

Lance's first burst went over the drums and he immediately released the trigger. What the devil, the thing was pointed straight at the drums not more than twenty-five feet away. He felt Jimmy's hand on his wrist, pressing it down, and squeezed the trigger again. This time he hit the drums.

'A natural,' Jacques said drily. 'You've already worked out that the torque of the bullets will lift the barrel and to fire short bursts not to overheat the barrel. Try it again.'

This time Lance aimed low and the bullets climbed across the ground and into the drums. He wondered what the hell 'torque' was.

'Good, good,' Jacques said and wandered away, leaving Lance to wonder what to do with the firearm in his hands.

'Thanks, Jimmy. What's this "torque" business?'

'Put the burp gun on safety, Mr Lance.'

'Oh,' Lance was flustered. 'Shall I take this thing out as well?' He tapped the clip of bullets.

'No. Just the safety. Torque is just the spin of the bullet. You see, the barrel is rifled, grooved in spirals you might say, and the turning of the bullet in these grooves causes a sideways and upward force.'

'I see.'

'Here, I'll clean it for you.'

'Thanks but you'd better show me how to do it for myself.'

Calling it a burp gun was apt, it did go *burrp* when you pulled the trigger. 'It's not quite as easy as Jacques . . . Mr Roux makes out.'

'You'll need very little practice It's as he says, Mr Lance, you're a natural.'

Lance blushed and Jimmy tactfully cast his eyes down.

The arms and ammunition were distributed. For each machine pistol there were also a longer barrel and a stock to turn it into a rifle as well as a clip with self-tapping screws to fix it inside the trucks. Ewart inspected the fittings after they were screwed on and had two changed because in a sudden stop the men could be thrown against the weapons. Lance noted and filed away for future reference his brother's attention to minute detail.

After lunch Ewart declared a holiday, telling Sambo the men could go into Lubumbashi until ten o'clock that night. Soon all the men had gone, chattering happily, except only Sambo and Jimmy.

Ewart came over to Lance. 'Do you want to inspect the brothels of Lubumbashi?'

Lance was acutely embarrassed. 'No, I don't think so. Thanks.' He had never been inside a brothel in his life.

'You won't see another white woman for a long time.'

'I'll last out, thanks.'

'Okay. That's probably wise. It's not worth the diseases you might pick up.'

'You're not going?'

'No. But I'm willing to take you if you want to change your mind.'

'No. But what about Jimmy?'

'You can go, Jimmy,' Ewart said. 'I'll look after Mr Lance.'

Jimmy looked at Sambo, who nodded, but decided against it. 'Thank you Mr Weber, but not this time.'

'Suit yourself. You go, Sambo. Enjoy yourself.' With a

66

wave of his hand Sambo went off after the men. 'Join us, Jimmy. I have bottle of good bourbon.'

The three of them sat around the folding table under a tree, drinking the smoothest liquor Lance had ever tasted. He was not a heavy drinker and drank slowly, only a third as much as the other two each consumed. It didn't seem to diminish their faculties and they made no attempt at pressuring him into a competitive drinking bout. Jacques and Briony had gone off in the Landrover and when they returned in the late afternoon the bottle was nearly empty. They had been silent for a long time when Briony's sniff of disapproval at discovering a black man sitting down with white men disturbed the quiet. Jimmy immediately stood up to take his place behind Lance's shoulder. Lance was irritated with Briony for her tactlessness. They weren't in South Africa now; besides, Jimmy was a prince.

Jacques came from the Landrover with a rifle in his hand. 'Your brother's a natural with a burp gun,' Jacques said to Ewart. 'I want to see how good he is with a long barrel.'

'Jimmy held my hand down the second time,' Lance said.

'I saw. Do you want to come, Ewart?'

'No. I'll stay and watch our stuff and give Briony a drink.'

'Okay, Jimmy, fetch an FN with a stock and a barrel and a couple of clips.'

They walked out of the camp for about a hundred yards, Jacques carrying the rifle and a pair of binoculars, Jimmy carrying the burp gun with stock and long barrel fitted.

'What's an FN?' Lance asked.

'FN is Fabrique Nationale. It's the Belgian factory that made our arms,' Jacques said. 'That rifle is a Mannlicher custom-made for me in Austria.'

They came to a flat grassy spot and Jacques stopped. 'See that hill? How far is the small white spot about halfway up?'

It took Lance a while to find the spot, even with the directions. It was a very small spot.

'About a mile.'

'If you don't know, say so. Don't guess.'

'Yes, Jacques.'

'It's about a thousand feet. What do you think, Jimmy?'

'Nine fifty, thousand,' Jimmy said.

'Can you hit it?'

'Maybe.'

'Let's see.'

Jimmy took his time to set the sights and to aim. When he squeezed the trigger Jacques had the binoculars to his eyes. Lance could just see the white puff as the bullet hit. 'Again,' Jacques said. 'Two more shots.'

There were two more white puffs.

'Dead centre,' Jacques said. 'The rifle's sighted in. You try it, Lance.'

Lance was well into his second clip when Jacques said, 'You got the right-hand edge this time. Okay, we've demonstrated how difficult it is. Jimmy is a top marksman and you've caught up with him in remarkably little time.'

Lance didn't know whether it was a compliment. His shoulder hurt. He kept quiet.

'Now try this.' Jacques handed him the Mannlicher. 'This thing on top here is a zooming telescope, built especially to my order. Don't worry about the elevation – that's the distance; it will allow for that. This knob at the side here is for the windage – the wind blowing the bullet aside. Don't worry about that either as there is no wind today. This button here switches on the batteries to operate it. This button you press with your left thumb to zoom it one way or the other. It's preset for something the size of a dinner plate at a hundred feet. If you zoom it forward it automatically elevates for distance. Look through it.'

He handed Lance the rifle. Lance took up his stance, rifle to his shoulder. He felt Jimmy gently pressing his right elbow closer to his body. 'I see a small circle with a cross in it in the middle of the big circle.'

'Right. Now you just zoom in until the little circle is

68

filled by some part of your target no larger than a dinnerplate and shoot. You'll hit it right in the middle. You got it?'

'Sure. It sounds foolproof.'

'Right. Try it on that tree over to your right first.'

Lance hit the tree first time, the force of the bullet shaking the trunk visibly.

'Now, on that white spot there's an empty beer can. See if you can hit it.'

Lance lowered the rifle. 'A beer can on that postage stamp?'

'That spot's two feet across.'

Lance stared unbelievingly. Then he raised the rifle to his shoulder and sure enough, as he zoomed the telescope in he found the bright red can. When it was inside the inner circle and the crosshairs defined it he squeezed the trigger carefully. To his surprise the can jumped into the air. The second it landed he hit it again, followed it and hit it in the air. And again. And again. Then the clip was empty.

Jacques lowered the binoculars and stared unbelievingly at Lance. 'God, you're like something from the movies.'

'It was easy with your scope. I'd rather be able to shoot like Jimmy.'

'It's not easy. Machinery doesn't turn you into a good shot unless you already have a basic aptitude. And one day you will shoot like Jimmy and even better, even with an open sight. But you might not have the time to learn, so meanwhile the scope is your salvation.'

Lance saw Jimmy looking hungrily at the rifle in his hands. 'Jacques, can Jimmy try it please?'

'It's your rifle. You let whoever you want use it.'

'You mean – You can't –

'Indeed I can. The man who can use it best should have the equipment. Come on, Lance, reload the rifle.'

Lance had been holding the rifle out to Jacques. He reloaded the clip carefully from the box of shells Jacques held while Jacques and Jimmy watched. Then he handed the rifle to Jimmy. Jimmy too made the can dance and laughed gleefully about it.

'Every man dreams of a rifle like this, Mr Lance,' he said when he handed it back.

Lance disintegrated the can with the next clip and all too soon it was over and they were walking back to the camp. Jacques gave Lance the case, cleaning materials and ammunition for the rifle. There was also a box of the very small round Mallory hearing-aid batteries that powered the scope and a small leather case of precision-made tools for disassembling the rifle into its minutest parts. Lance and Jimmy spent a happy hour under the light of a Coleman lamp cleaning the two rifles.

At ten o'clock sharp Sambo came into the camp, singing cheerfully. He reeked of beer but seemed sober enough, rock steady on his feet. The three brothers who had gone into town were with him, less steady. One immediately fell asleep beside the fire; Sambo and the other two sat beside the fire humming sad ditties.

At quarter to eleven Lance yawned, stood and said, 'I'm for bed.'

Ewart made a negative sound. 'Uh-uh.'

Lance sat down quickly. 'Why not?'

Jacques answered him, 'Your men aren't here.'

'Oh.' Lance was absolutely baffled. 'What can I do about it?'

'Fetch them. You're responsible for seeing that they're ready to move out at dawn tomorrow,' Ewart said.

'Me, fetch fourteen big drunken men?'

Ewart laughed. 'Just the ones on the refuelling team. Sambo and I'll get the rest.'

'You're not frightened, are you, boy?' Jacques asked.

'No. Just realistic.'

'That's good. Overconfidence is a fast way to get hurt. Fight only if you have to and then fight dirty.'

Lance resented being patronized. 'Are you coming?'

'Wouldn't miss it for all the world. You never know when we might next see some little excitement.'

Lance watched Jimmy give his brothers large mugs of black coffee and throw a bucket of cold water on the head of the sleeping one, who groaned loudly, rolled over and went back to sleep. Sambo rolled the sleeping one well clear of the fire and then they walked into Lubumbashi.

On the edge of their camping site stood a green Peugeot 404 with two white men in it. It had been there since morning. Everybody had ignored it and Lance had been too busy to ask questions. Now he asked, 'Who are they?'

'Cops,' Jacques said. 'Let's find out whose cops.' They walked over to the car and Jacques rested his arm on the windowsill. 'Good evening.'

'Good evening,' one of the men replied in a thick Afrikaans accent. There was a heavy silence.

'What do you want?' Jacques asked.

'We want the trucks and dynamite you stole.'

Jacques laughed delightedly. 'You guys have cost us a lot in extra bribes to the local officials.' He stepped away from the car.

'We'll catch up with you,' the voice called after them.

Out of earshot of the car they stopped. 'Shall we do something about them?' Jacques asked.

'No,' Ewart said. 'They have no official standing here. We'll only attract more attention to ourselves if they don't return.'

Lance shivered at the casual way Jacques had suggested murder.

Jacques was in a talkative mood. 'Before the Belgians pulled out, there were nine brothels in Lubumbashi,' he said to Lance. 'Now there are only four parlours where the oldest profession in the world still trades. The whores know that, as soon as a white government is replaced by a black one, law and order breaks down and they're at the mercy of all kinds of toughs. That's why they're pulling out.'

Lance nodded in the dark.

'When the whores pull out as soon as a black government takes over, how far behind can the technicians be? Think of what that means for the minerals extraction industries; you can't run sophisticated machinery with unskilled labour.' Jacques sounded infinitely sad. 'Africa is turning slowly black, from the equator outwards, going to the dogs at the same rate.'

'I thought Africa would last forever.' Ewart too sounded sad.

'So did I, till recently,' Jacques said.

Lance was surprised to find he knew what they meant. He was amazed to find they loved Africa. He should start looking for what had attracted their love before it was too late. He had never before thought it possible to find sentiment in his brother or Jacques.

They walked without speaking until they reached the first port of call. Behind them Sambo and his brothers hummed a melody of such infinite sorrow that restless shivers ran up and down Lance's back. But he didn't want it to stop.

To Lance it looked just like any other seedy bar. Cigarette butts almost covered the multiple burns on the floor and half the mirrors behind the scarred blackwood bar were broken. At the back were stairs covered in worn carpet; the stairs looked dangerously rickety. Not that Lance would have wanted to ascend the stairs with any of the women in the place. Black or white, and all shades in between, they were sleazy and some were obviously diseased. He was glad he had refused Ewart's invitation of a tour of inspection. Then another woman entered the room, changing Lance's mind. She came sweeping from a beaded doorway, a slender Eurasian in a dress slit to the hip and clinging everywhere else. Her skin was a smooth cream, her hair raven. She was tall and took long strides, her slim legs flashing in the dress. She came to a stop in front of them.

72

'The former splendour is no more,' she said to Jacques, 'but old friends can still find a clean glass and a sealed bottle.'

'Rosie, Rosie,' Jacques said sadly. 'You're going? You too?'

'Alas, yes.' She looked at a black girl with an open sore on her cheek who was passing them on the arm of a man, on their way to the stairs. 'It is no longer possible to keep prices up in order to protect standards. I've sold and by the end of the month I shall be gone. Hong Kong perhaps. Or Singapore. Who knows?' She turned to Ewart. 'Major Weber. Always a pleasure to see you.'

'And you, Rosie. I'm afraid we can't stay. We've just come to fetch our men.'

'Your men? You no longer command forces here!' The man who had interrupted their conversation stood halfway up the stairs, a sleazy halfdressed mulatto on each arm. He wore khaki pants and a singlet in which his stomach bulged alarmingly over his belt but Lance noted that his boots were meticulously laced.

Ewart sighed. 'Teddy Bruun. I should have known I'd find you presiding over the decline and fall.'

'Mr Bruun to you, Butcher Weber.' The untidy man pushed the mulattos aside and strode over to join them, muscles rippling under the fat on his stomach. There was no fat on the heavy muscles of his arms. 'You command no men here and if you had any sense you wouldn't show your face here either.'

'Crawl back in your hole, Teddy,' Ewart said distinctly.

'My name is Theodore!' Bruun screamed. He noticed Lance. 'Hallo, what's this? A younger, taller, handsomer version of the Butcher, or have I been drinking too much? What's your name, boy?'

His finger poked painfully at Lance's chest. Lance stepped away from the finger, but it followed him. Flustered, he said what came into his mind: 'You smell.'

Bruun laughed. 'And sassier too.' The finger poked harder.

Lance intended only to take the man's hand and push it away. He misjudged and got only the pointed finger in his hand. As he pushed the finger broke and Bruun screamed. Yet he was alert enough to hit Lance stunningly in the face with his other hand. Lance remembered what Jacques had said. He didn't want to fight this man but if he had to, it was going to be dirty. His foot lashed out and caught Bruun in the shins. Surprisingly, Bruun only laughed. He stepped back, carefully folded the broken finger into his hand, then stepped forward to take Lance by the shirt. His damaged hand, now a fist, slammed into Lance's stomach repeatedly. Lance was pushed back against the bar. He brought up his knee but Bruun turned and took the blow on the thigh. Lance butted him in the face with his head but Bruun laughed at this even though his nose started bleeding.

'That's enough!' Ewart couldn't have spoken sooner. Lance knew he would pass out after only a few more blows.

Bruun stopped striking Lance. 'What?'

'That's enough. He doesn't have your experience and you provoked him.'

Lance used the respite to stomp his foot on Bruun's instep. Bruun slugged him casually in the stomach. The man had the arms of a gorilla and, after Lance had butted him in the face, had stepped back out of reach of Lance's arms though still holding him by the shirt. 'I'll decide when enough is enough. He still has some fight left in him.'

Lance's hands, scrabbling on the bar behind him, found a bottle. The bottle extended his reach. He hit Bruun in the side of the head with it. Bruun let his shirt go and stepped back a pace to look at Lance.

'See? He's still game.' He started forward, towards Lance, feinted and, as Lance blocked with the bottle, took the weapon from him. 'But you're right. He's useless.' Bruun hit the bottle on the edge of the bar and turned the broken end on Ewart. Lance slid down against the bar.

Ewart stood quite still, his arms at his sides, as Bruun advanced on him. When Bruun was in range, the bottle already moving for Ewart's face, Lance saw his brother weave ever so slightly, the wickedly jagged bottle passing within millimetres of his ear, take Bruun's arm to pull him off balance, and kick him in the groin. Bruun dropped the bottle and grasped his groin with both hands. Ewart stepped back, swung his leg lazily and kicked Bruun in the face. Bruun went down silently, shaking the floor with his weight but Ewart had already turned around to search out his men.

Lance rose shakily. It had all seemed so easy for Ewart but he knew from his own painful experience how quickly Bruun moved, how easily Bruun had avoided his own attempts at attack, how defenceless he had been against Bruun. Jimmy was helping him up. 'Fat lot of help you were.'

'It would not be seemly to interfere between white men,' Jimmy said. 'You did very well by yourself.'

'Aw, shut up, Jimmy. He beat the shit out of me.' Lance kicked Bruun in the back as heavily as he could, hoping to burst a kidney.

'No more of that,' Ewart said softly. 'You're spoiling your reputation.'

'It hurt me more than it did him.' It had: the leg muscles strenuously used jerked his painful stomach excruciatingly.

'What's Bruun still doing here?' Jacques asked Rosie, who throughout the fight had been standing by uninterestedly.

'I don't know. But he has money. He's been buying the bordellos.' She pointed to a roughly painted sign over the bar.

'M O F W H,' Jacques read.

'My own fucking whorehouse,' Rosie said without a trace of humour. 'He said he'd been thrown out of so many that one day he was going to own one and do exactly as he pleased.'

'It's shameful, a Sandhurst man owning whorehouses,' Jacques laughed.

'All the same, you'd better go. He has armed men.'

'We'll be gone at dawn, before he even wakes up,' Jacques said. He kissed Rosie's hand.

Sambo came down the stairs, bringing one of the men. Sambo was holding his arm turned up behind his back; with his free hand the man was trying to do up his flies. Lance chuckled at the comic spectacle but it hurt his stomach and he stopped. He followed the party out. Sambo counted the men and reported to Ewart, when he came out after saying goodbye to Rosie, that there was one missing.

'Ben isn't here, sir. He's in the Laverne, they say.'

The men were a sorry-looking lot, half of them being held up by the other half, most with clothing in disarray, all drunk. Lance had seen one of Sambo's brothers strike a man heavily through the face to wake him and divorce him from the bottle in his hand. Lance didn't think they'd be leaving for another twenty-four hours at least: the men would need that much time to recover from their hangovers.

'You and Jimmy fetch Ben,' Ewart told Lance.

Lance nodded and started off. 'That's gratitude for you,' he muttered. Ben alone had lifted one side of a heavy axle while Lance had needed help to lift the other side in the contest of strength that had accompanied the unloading and repacking of the trucks. Lance didn't much look forward to the possibility of another beating.

They found Ben at the Laverne, another sleazy bar. Jimmy had led Lance unerringly to it. Ben was sitting at a table, drinking beer from a bottle and staring with red-eyed belligerence around him. Nobody in the place dared look directly at him. He had been in a fight already, if the swelling bump on his forehead and a discoloured and lumpy lip were anything to go by. Lance was fast learning to read the signs.

Lance stopped before Ben's table and looked at Jimmy behind him. When Jimmy said nothing, Lance said, 'Time to go, Ben.'

Ben raised red eyes to him. Lance shivered. Ben's half of that axle had weighed more than Lance.

'We've an early start tomorrow.'

'Not going,' Ben said flatly. He drank from his bottle.

Jimmy said something fast in their own language. Lance caught nothing of it but it caused Ben to look curiously at him. Lance just stood his ground, not knowing what to do. Then Ben rose and flung the bottle into a corner. Nobody seemed to take any notice. Ben walked out in front of them.

Once outside, Lance sighed. 'What did you tell him to make him change his mind?'

'I told him you beat on Mr Bruun,' Jimmy said.

'But – ' Then Lance got it and couldn't help laughing, no matter how painful the glee. 'Yeah, I did beat *on* him a bit. Jimmy, what's there between Bruun and my brother? And what makes Bruun so special?'

'Mr Bruun once held a command. Because he hates black men and is brutal to them he was inefficient. His command was taken away and given to your brother. My brothers and our tribesmen served in that command. Mr Bruun once beat Ben and, as you've seen for yourself, Ben is very strong.'

'What makes Bruun special?'

'He's a feared man. News travels. Bad juju, bad luck to cross him.'

'Jimmy, don't talk native, just give it to me straight, eh?'

'It's a native thing, Mr Lance, or at least African. There's something about a man that the people sense,

77

either good or bad. Then things happen and a myth builds.'

'What things?'

'Mr Bruun's enemies have a habit of turning up dead, messily dead. Once or twice is a coincidence, after that an aura builds around a man.'

'Something like the feeling you have about politicians? Some do everything right, others do everything wrong.'

'Exactly, Mr Lance.'

There was something wrong with Jimmy's argument. 'But both kinds of politicians get elected. And I shouldn't imagine the enemies of my brother and Mr Roux sleep all that easily at night.'

'Even so,' Jimmy said. It was agreement, not justification. 'There are survivors, men who don't go under. Survivors can be good or bad. Each has this aura but you must decide for yourself which survivor is bad or good.'

Lance had learned on the rugger fields and in university classrooms that some men have natural power and confidence while others do not. Now Jimmy was adding a new dimension for him. 'Ah, but that's the trick, deciding between good and bad.' He stumbled and would have fallen had Jimmy not caught Lance's arm and hoisted it around his neck.

'You chose right tonight, Mr Lance. Is it bad?'

'It hurts.'

'Hold on, it isn't far now.'

It wasn't far but it felt like a mile and the last few paces to his tent Lance was being carried by Jimmy. Sambo was standing by with a tin in his hands. Jimmy put Lance on his camp bed and unbuttoned his shirt, then stood back to make space for Sambo, whose big hands were surprisingly gentle as he explored Lance's stomach.

'Doesn't feel like anything ruptured. Just bruised muscle,' Sambo said to Ewart, who had appeared without Lance noticing his entrance. Ewart nodded and Sambo took the lid off the tin, dug out a handful of the contents and slapped it on to Lance's stomach. The cold slimy shock made Lance gasp. Sambo began rubbing his stomach and Lance gritted his teeth not to cry out from the excruciating pain. Soon, however, warmth spread from Sambo's hands and Lance felt pleasantly drowsy.

'What're you doing, you bloody black witchdoctor?' It was Briony, bringing the first aid kit from the Landrover.

'Rubbing in axle-grease,' Sambo said without stopping.

'Well, stop it at once and stand aside so I can get at him.'

Sambo continued rubbing. Before he slept, Lance heard Ewart saying, 'Oh, it works and Lance is going off to sleep. We don't want to wake him, do . . .'

The attack happened two days later and more than four hundred miles further. Lance's bruised muscles had now subsided to the level of pain after a rugger game in which he had taken several hard tackles square in the midriff but in fact he was more concerned with what the steadily worsening roads could be doing to his kidneys. He was getting bored with the savanna, the ever-spreading grassland with each shrub and straggly tree a welcome break in the monotony. He had thought the sub-equatorial region would be greener and could, in fact, find on the map fingers of green spreading down from the solid green of the equator; but these fingers ran parallel to the road they were taking and as yet they had not passed through any of the small pockets of green either. They were still several days' hard travel away from any really solid green, Jimmy said. For the first time Lance realized what an immense place was the country at whose very southernmost tip he had been born. Jimmy often pointed out animals but you had to be very quick to see them and few of them were the larger, more spectacular beasts. Of people they saw little sign, only when they passed through towns. The immense sameness seemed not to bother Ewart or Jacques. They did not hurry the convoy and took a quarter hour every morning to make sure that their campsite was spotless, all the detritus of more than twenty people picked up, burned and buried.

Lance talked to Jimmy and confirmed what he already knew: Jimmy was not only bigger and stronger than he but very intelligent and more experienced as well. He was surprised to find that Jimmy was a year younger, twenty to his twenty-one. Jimmy's competence was too unobtrusive to bother Lance and Lance was quite pleased with himself when it came to him that, having been put in command over Jimmy by virtue of a white skin and kinship to Ewart, he could probably learn valuable skills from Jimmy if he didn't presume on his position too much – after the gambling debacle it was exhilarating to find such common sense in himself.

Jimmy was saying, about his tribal initiation into manhood, 'just like the Boy Scouts. You learn to rub sticks to make fire and other useful tricks for survival in the wild. It's a – ' when he brought the tanker to a lurching halt three inches from the tanker in front. 'Out, Mr Lance, out!' He leant across Lance to fling the door open and pushed Lance bodily out of the cab.

'What is – ' Lance fell heavily on the road.

'Roll down the bank!' he heard Jimmy call and rolled, not in response to the instruction, but to avoid Jimmy jumping on him. He rolled over the edge of the road and crashed, winded, on the gravel drainage pad beside and below the road.

Jimmy jumped down lightly beside him. He had found time to snatch up Lance's rifle, his own machine pistol, the long barrel and stock for it, and ammunition. All of it except Lance's rifle spilled from his hands on to the gravel as he landed. Jimmy gave Lance the rifle and picked up the other items, inspecting each carefully.

'They were shooting at us,' Jimmy said.

Lance could see all their men against the inclined banking of the road. He had heard nothing and now all was silent. Lance inspected his grazed elbows and knees through the rents in his shirt and trousers.

Ewart came running past in a crouch and conferred with Sambo at the rear of the line for a moment. When he came back, he stopped where Lance and Jimmy were sitting. 'You're the only casualty so far. I hope you aren't going to prove accident-prone.'

'I was slow and Jimmy pushed me out.'

'All right. Next time try to get out under your own steam.'

'What's happening?'

'There's a hill on the other side of the road. Don't look.' Ewart pressed Lance down by the shoulder. 'They shot at us from there.'

'Who?'

Ewart shrugged. 'Baluba, Katangese, perhaps even Kiokos or Luenas – somebody who wants our dynamite and automatic arms.'

Lance knew from his study of the map that the Baluba and Katangese were Congolese tribes. 'What are Kiokos and Luenas?'

'Angolans from across the border. Angola is only a couple of hundred miles that way.' Ewart pointed through the road and trucks and hills. 'News spreads very fast in these parts.' Ewart walked away in a crouch. His clothes showed not a single superfluous crease and were unstained.

'What now?' Lance asked Jimmy. 'Thanks for pushing me out.'

'We wait.'

'Huh?'

'We wait till dark and then we leave.'

'Aren't we going to attack those people?'

'That's for your brother to decide, Mr Lance. But I don't think he will. You see, they hold an impregnable position. We'd lose many men storming that hill. And for what? We have no interests in killing them, only to get away from them.'

81

'But they shot at us.'

'True, but do you want to die to punish them?'

Lance laughed nervously. 'Not if you put it like that. Won't they realize that we will slip away as soon as it is dark and try to come round the back?' Lance pointed at the tall grass waving twenty feet from them, the edge of a hard artificial line where the roadmakers had stopped gouging.

Jimmy picked up two large pieces of stone. 'Look, each piece not quite the size of a man's fist. Now, watch the grass.' Jimmy threw the rock in his right hand in a curve over the grass. It fell too far for Lance to see it land. Immediately the grass in front of them stirred in a strange pattern. Jimmy threw the second rock and suddenly the grass waved dementedly. 'They won't come through the grass.'

Lance nodded. 'What about along the road from the front or the rear?'

'Only if they have armoured vehicles, Mr Lance. Otherwise they'd be exposed and we'd cut them down easily.'

'And if they had armoured vehicles, they wouldn't need to hide in the hills,' Lance said. 'Is soldiering like this?'

Jimmy nodded. 'Mostly waiting. Brief infrequent spurts of action. The thing is not to get bored. You must be alert when action is required.' He pointed.

Jacques and Briony were playing with dice and counters on what looked like an open briefcase. 'What's that?'

'They're playing backgammon, Mr Lance. It's a gambling game.'

'Don't tell me any more. That's how I got into trouble. Christ, that bloody Ben is sleeping!'

'Why not? Nobody's shooting at him right now. But look at that poor half-breed.' Pietie was sitting near Jacques, his hands over his head, his body hunched up as small as possible. He was shaking with fear.

'I suppose you're right.' Lance settled himself against

the gravel, determined to be as nonchalant as anybody present. He felt ashamed for Pietie.

'You could check your rifle before you go to sleep, Mr Lance,' Jimmy said with a straight face. 'And if you stand it upright like that, it could fall over and cause a nasty accident to you or somebody else. Always lay it flat.'

'You're a pose-wrecker, Jimmy.' Lance did as he was told. 'Any other lessons for today, Maestro?'

'If they drove us from this position, where would you hide?'

Lance looked around. 'Not in the grass. Probably behind that tree or the rocky outcrop over there. Where would you hide, Jimmy?'

Jimmy shook his head. 'They're both nice and solid and bullet-proof, Mr Lance, but they're isolated. You can't move away from them without making yourself a target. You see that dip in the ground beyond Mr Jacques? That's where I would hide, moving along it as necessary.'

'Okay. But they won't attack us from the front. They'd be outlined against the sun and we'd have a clear view of them under the trucks.'

Jimmy nodded and his mouth was open but Lance never found out what he was about to say; just then the first truck tyre exploded almost simultaneously with the sound of a distant rifle shot. In quick succession several more tyres were hit and exploded. Jimmy was fitting the long barrel and shoulder stock to his FN.

Jacques came running up to Lance. 'Can I have the rifle please.'

Lance didn't want to give the rifle back to Jacques. 'You want to shoot at something, let me do it for you,' he said without thinking about it, an automatic reflex.

Both Jacques and Jimmy looked at him strangely. Jacques shrugged. 'If that's what you want. Is the rifle loaded, cocked, safety catch off?'

Lance turned the safety catch but said nothing.

'Okay. Don't look over the edge while I explain. You

climb up to the road behind a truck tyre, crawling on your belly until you can see the top of the hill under the trucks but not right up to the tyre because some light might fall on you then.' Jacques held one hand out at arm's length to let the shadow fall on his chest. 'Stay in the shadows, understand? Only as far forward as to see the top of the hill and no more.'

'Yes.'

'You'll see a tree right at the crest. At the right-hand side at the bottom is a rock. In the angle between the tree trunk and rock is your target. You have time for one shot only. Hit or miss, and don't wait to see, immediately roll back down here after you've fired. You'll have about one second to aim and fire, so be quick about it. Do you want me to repeat any of that?'

'No thanks Jacques, I got it.'

Lance checked his rifle once more, than paced six exact paces which he calculated would bring him up behind the double rear wheels of the tanker, and peered cautiously over the edge of the gravel bank. He was behind the wheels, Jacques' hand was on his shoulder. 'Remember, one shot and back here. Do your searching through the scope, the rifle to your shoulder and ready to fire.'

Lance felt the tap on his back and then Jimmy boosted him up the embankment. He crawled forward ignoring the pain in his grazed elbows and knees until he could just see the top of the hill and the tree on it past the wheel with its fat tyre. He brought the rifle to his shoulder, moved a little right and zoomed in on the tree trunk, moving the sight down all the time. There was no target in the angle between the tree trunk and the rock. Lance was about to search elsewhere when he caught a glimpse of light flashing on metal and, immediately afterwards, a man's head square-on in his sights. The man was aiming a rifle with a telescopic sight straight at him, face squashed to a mean pinched look against the stock. The man was black and grinning. Almost of its own volition Lance's finger squeezed the trigger. It could have been a cramp. A red spraying mist flecked with specks of grey and fawn – instinctively he knew they were brains and bones – filled the scope. At the same moment the tyre in front of him exploded from the dead man's shot. Lance felt a stunning blow on his chin and chest and then he was flying through the air in slow motion, quite at peace with the world, his arms spread out, floating, floating past Jacques and Jimmy and others frozen in mid-air as they reached for him. Far off he heard rifle shots.

Lance came to giggling, thinking of how he had 'beat on' Bruun. From the neck down he had no feeling. He looked incuriously at Sambo leaning over him, feeling his ribs. Next to him lay what was obviously a large piece of burst tyre. Nearby stood Jacques and Ewart and Lance heard his brother say in a low voice, 'Next time I send you to do a job, you do it yourself, eh.'

'It's his rifle and he wouldn't lend it to me,' Jacques said. 'Man, is he ever a natural. That sniper was fast and damn cool, not distracted by the covering fire at all, but Lance was faster.'

Lance remembered. He had killed a man. Vomit gagged in his throat and Sambo turned him over to let it run out. The blood and the brains and the bone . . . It could have been his blood and brains and bone. His chest was aflame.

'Nothing broken as far as I can feel,' Sambo said.

'Let me feel,' Lance heard Briony say. Her hands moved over him, making him gasp with pain. 'No, nothing definitely broken. If he isn't okay in a few days he should have X-rays for cracked ribs. This vomiting might be something, some organ bruised.'

Jacques laughed. 'No, it will go away as soon as he gets used to having killed a man. The first time is always the hardest.'

Ewart nodded. 'I wish it hadn't been necessary. Can he hear me?'

'Yes,' Lance groaned. 'What hit me?'

'That piece of tyre next to your hand. You're lucky it glanced off you at an angle, it would have gone through you if it had hit straight on. Good work just now.' He leant over to squeeze Lance's shoulder.

Lance couldn't remember his brother touching him before and it was a pity to spoil the occasion by vomiting again but the 'good work' had been killing a man. Lance rolled over by himself this time. In one part of his mind he was glad he wasn't going to die. He even wondered if having your balls squashed between two bricks could possibly be more painful than the thudding of his heart against his ribs. Belatedly he caught fright at the way there had been, when he came to, no feeling from the neck down. He had heard of such things happening to rugby players . . . he passed out again, a vision of a wheelchair in his mind.

Jimmy was hanging upside down over him.

'Fear is a fine emetic, Jimmy,' Lance smiled at knowing such a fine word.

'Even so,' Jimmy smiled and Lance was disappointed that Jimmy too knew the word. 'Drink this, Mr Lance.'

It was coffee with bourbon in it. Lance gagged once but got it all down. Nearby a fire was burning and men were walking around upright, fetching mugs of coffee. Lance fancied that they looked admiringly at him. He brought up the coffee and bourbon. Jimmy patiently made more and held his head while he drank it, saying, 'It's for the pain when we tie up your ribs. Would you prefer morphine? That'll make you drowsy.'

'No, this is fine. What's happening?'

'My brother and some men are on the hill, making sure they're gone. Everybody else must stay this side of the trucks for the time being. Can you sit up?'

The bandaging was a painful process. Briony wrapped the tape around Lance's chest and pulled it tight while he groaned. But once the tape was on he felt better and could stand up and walk around, Jimmy at his elbow to catch him in case he stumbled. Reassured that he was functioning properly with nothing broken or impaired, Lance sat down against the gravel bank and stared at his rifle lying nearby. The scratches on the highly polished stock were a shame. He made no move to pick up the rifle and after a while Jimmy picked it up and cleaned it.

Sambo came back at the head of the men who had searched the hill. He was carrying a stick to which was tied a piece of red cloth.

Ewart took the cloth from the stick. It was a square, folded diagonally to make a triangle and tied at each corner.

'It was planted on top of the hill,' Sambo said. He sounded very subdued, more sombre than usual.

'Know what this is?' Ewart asked Jacques.

'No, but I can guess. Bruun.'

'Yes. This is his symbol.'

'He couldn't have got here before us.'

'True. But he spread the word to all who wanted to know. We have dynamite and trucks and we're travelling north from Lubumbashi.'

'Shit!'

'What else did you find up there, Sambo?' Ewart asked.

'Nothing to tell who they are. They took the one Mr Lance killed with them. They had come on foot and left the same way. Only Mr Bruun's sign on a stick. It is a warning to us that he will not forgive the beating you gave him.' Sambo gave Ewart a handful of spent shells.

Ewart gave Jacques half the shells and they inspected them. Jacques shrugged. 'Russian, Czech. Doesn't really tell us much.'

'Except to confirm that they aren't Brunn's own men. They would probably be using Belgian ammunition. Can you see the commos hiring Bruun?'

'No. Is he going to persecute us all the way?'

'What do you think?'

At Kananga the next evening, one of the nun-nurses at the mission felt and prodded Lance and pronounced him no more than severely bruised, recommending a week in bed. The next morning at dawn they turned north for Kisangani, 900 miles away. Lance had angrily refused Ewart's suggestion that he stay with the nuns at the mission for a few weeks until Ewart thought it safe to arrange transportation back to South Africa for him: 'I've come this far and intend seeing it through.' Ewart had not insisted. 'Have it your own way. Just be warned – the roads are going to get worse.' Lance hadn't quite believed him. Ever since Kolwezi the roads had been bad, earth roads hardly more than tracks with improved roads having the high ridge between the wheel tracks scraped away. 'Partially improved roads' were on the map but, to Lance, they seemed only semantically different from dirt roads and tracks. An hour out of Kananga they had done thirty miles and Lance's bruises were taking a beating. Lance was quiet. Every time he opened his mouth he thought of the man he had killed and wanted to vomit. So he kept his mouth resolutely shut. That didn't keep him from thinking about it but it did keep his food in. They rode in silence until the late afternoon.

'The man you killed wanted to take something from us by violence,' Jimmy said.

'Stuff we stole anyway,' Lance said.

'Even so. We did not kill for it.'

'But we would've done if it had been necessary.'

'I don't believe so. However that may be, we have the dynamite now and the arms were freely given. Those people would have taken it and then killed us out of hand.'

'They would have killed us?'

'Yes. Even if we had given them the dynamite and arms.'

'Why?'

'You come from South Africa, Mr Lance. You should know all about racialism.'

'All right, I don't. You tell me.'

'We're not from their tribe. Or of their political persuasion. Each in itself sufficient reason to kill us out of hand, even if there were no dynamite or arms to be taken.'

Lance digested this for a while. It was quite likely Jimmy was telling the literal truth. Not so long ago, he knew, Zulus in South Africa had killed Pondos on sight and in the previous century the Zulus had almost annihilated the Matabele – who were not warrior-like – not for their land but simply to make war against someone.

'You know, Jimmy, that man was grinning while he had me in his sights. If he had enjoyed the sensation . . . whatever it was that made him grin . . . if he had done that for a fraction of a second less, he might have squeezed the trigger first. As it was he nearly got me anyway.'

'Killing is a job that sometimes has to be done. But to enjoy it, surely you need something wrong up here.' Jimmy tapped the side of his head. 'And, I saw it in the war, the minute a man starts enjoying it, he's finished. It's only a matter of time before he waits too long for another second of pleasure and is killed in that second. You are lucky to have seen it yourself the day before yesterday.'

'Let it be a lesson to me?' Lance was aghast at the thought that he might ever enjoy killing for its own sake. Or any other reason.

'Yes. Forgive the presumption, Mr Lance.'

'Let's drop this master and servant shit, eh, Jimmy. It fools nobody except Mrs Roux.'

'It is worth fooling her because otherwise she'd make life unbearable.'

Lance didn't want to pursue the argument. He had other things on his mind. 'You know, when Jacques explained the target to me, I . . . I never thought it would be a man.'

'I noted his choice of words.'

'You mean he did it on purpose?'

'No. The most dangerous of enemies, like Mr Jacques, can be strangely gentle on occasion. Your brother and Mr Jacques are no more brutal than they have to be.'

'Unlike Bruun.'

'Aha! There, Mr Lance, is your handle on the good and the bad: the good use no more than essential force, the bad use all the force at their command because they enjoy it for itself.'

Every 300-mile day consumed at least twelve grinding hours of hard labour and more often fifteen hours. On the evening of the second day they camped in the rain-forest. It had a sound of its own, Lance thought as soon as his ears had become accustomed to the absence of the roaring of heavy trucks, a sort of singing broken now and again by the sharp cry of a small animal. Once Lance thought he heard the trumpeting of an elephant but Ewart said sadly there had been no elephants here for more than sixty years; what Lance had heard was the death-cry of a buck no higher than his knee caught by a predator. They sat around the folding table, waiting for their meal to be served, silently counting the aching muscles of the day's journey. Lance moved his leg so that Briony's thigh no longer rested against it and studied his knuckles, painfully skinned on a recalcitrant wheelnut while changing a flat tyre. Immediately Briony shifted her leg to resume the pressure. Lance gave her a sharp look but she was studying the whisky in the glass with an innocent expression. Bitch!

'Tomorrow night we'll be in Stanleyville,' Jacques said.

Lance automatically took his map out of his pocket.

'Kisangani to you, Junior,' Briony said.

Lance put his map away. Kisangani was the next big town on the map, about two hundred and fifty miles away by Lance's reckoning. He moved his leg again but couldn't escape the pressure of Briony's thigh.

'Fond memories?' Jacques asked Ewart.

'No,' Ewart said shortly. 'Tell them to get a move on with the food, will you Lance. There's work to be done afterwards.'

They ate their meal in silence, a sudden tension over the table. The voices of the blacks had become hushed too. Lance looked around into the dark woods around them, suddenly lurking with menace just beyond the circle of light thrown by their generators. 'Keep your eyes on your plate, Lance,' Ewart told him.

When his coffee was served, Ewart added a shot of brandy and lit a cigarillo. He pointed with the cigarillo. 'If that's a monkey in that tree, about two-thirds of the way up, I'm his brother.'

Jacques didn't turn to look but Briony's chair crashed to the ground as she jumped up. Lance turned his head fearfully but could see nothing except darkness. The hair at the nape of his neck rose electrically.

'He's not shooting, just watching,' Ewart said to Briony, his amusement clear.

'Shut up, you goddam cardboard man!' Briony stormed off into the tent erected for her and Jacques. Lance wished he could follow her. Being watched by an unseen, and for him personally unseeable, enemy was an unnerving experience.

As always Jacques was ahead of him. 'All kinds of watchers out there,' he said. He picked up a torch from the ground beside him and shone it around the perimeter of the camp. Here and there the light picked up reflection from the eyes of night creatures in yellows and cool greens. 'All waiting to see if we're food.'

Lance shivered. He wished he had his rifle beside him. He looked over his shoulder to reassure himself that Jimmy was, as ever, behind him.

'Have you marked him, Sambo?' Ewart called.

Sambo waved his mug from where he sat beside the fire thirty feet away. 'Do you want him alive, sir?'

'Yes. We'd better find out who he's scouting for.'

Lance peered into the darkness beyond the light. Still he could see nothing.

'Ewart *felt* him first, then searched until he saw him,' Jacques said to Lance. Ewart was wandering casually to one of the floodlights. 'It's a most useful sixth sense, developed by hunters and guerilla fighters.'

'I'll never trust this bloody forest again,' Lance said.

'You'll live longer that way,' Jacques turned around in his chair. 'Watch now.'

Sambo called something in his own language from where he sat beside the fire. Two of his brothers who had moved unobtrusively to the edge of the light suddenly melted away into the darkness. Lance heard the snapping of branches under a heavy body in a hurry and fixed the direction of the man spying on them a moment before Ewart turned on the floodlight to illuminate the man scrambling desperately down the tree. He was black and dressed only in tattered shorts. He fell into the arms of the two men waiting for him at the bottom of the tree. They each took an arm and marched the watcher easily into the camp, ignoring his struggling. They threw him on the ground before Ewart, where he remained lying with his arms over his head, moaning continuously.

'Pick him up.' They picked him up but the man continued moaning. 'What do you think, Sambo?'

'Kivu, sir.' Sambo said something to the captive in a native dialect. The man looked sullen, stopped his moaning and shook his head. 'He's more frightened of someone else than of us,' Sambo said.

'Change his mind.' Ewart resumed his seat at the table. Briony came from the tent and sat down, a high flush on her cheeks. Immediately her thigh was warm against Lance's.

Sambo rose majestically and walked to the prisoner, who twisted around with all the sinewy strength of a lean man but was held firmly by the big man on either side of him. Sambo stopped three paces away. He took a huge clasp knife from his pocket and held it before the prisoner's eyes as he slowly unfolded the largest blade. Pietie, pouring brandy for Briony, was so rapt in this performance that he poured the brandy into her lap. She sent the thin Coloured flying with a forearm blow to the head. Jacques caught the brandy bottle in the air.

'Stupid Hotnot!' Briony said between clenched teeth. 'I should give you to that big black.'

Pietie chattered on the ground. Jacques said, 'Go to bed, Pietie. We won't need you again tonight.' He turned to Briony. 'I don't really think – '

' – this is the place for a woman,' Briony interrupted him in a sanctimonious voice. 'I'm here now and I'm staying!'

Jacques shrugged.

Sambo turned the blade slowly, throwing beams of light into the eyes of the erstwhile watcher. The man cringed backwards even in the hold of the two strong men. Then Sambo took from his shirt pocket a yellow fire-starter. He cut it diagonally across to make two tapering sharp pointed wedges. One wedge he put in his pocket. He folded the knife and put that in a pocket as well. He fetched a burning stick from the fire while the prisoner watched with rolling eyes, deadly silent and pale. When Sambo was standing absolutely squarely in front of the prisoner, he lit the tapered fire-lighter with the burning branch. It flared up brightly and Sambo dropped it on the ground to burn out. All eyes went to it and stayed there for a minute. Lance was unaware that Briony's thigh was pressing harder and harder against him.

The wedge of fire-lighter on the ground burned out. Sambo took the other wedge from his pocket and held it up for the prisoner to see. He nodded at his brothers. They swung the man around and forced his arms up against his back until he was bent double. Sambo kicked his ankles apart and ripped his shorts down, quickly

93

inserting the sharp end of the fire-lighter wedge into the man's anus. The man stared at this from his upside down head between his legs and started moaning. Sambo waved the flaming branch in the man's face and raised it to the fire-lighter. The man started babbling. Sambo had him repeat everything he said, then pulled the fire-lighter from him and threw it into the fire where it flared into a bright high blaze. The captive fell to the ground and took to moaning again.

Lance became aware of Briony's quickened breathing beside him, of her thigh pressed hotly against his, of the brightness of her eyes. He moved slightly, fearfully away from her. The female spider eats the male after they have mated.

'He's scouting for the bandits between here and Kisangani,' Sambo said. 'Shall we kill him now?' He obviously didn't find the information of consuming interest.

'Bandits?' Lance asked.

'Free-lancers,' Ewart said. 'Ex-soldiers, free prisoners, soldiers that haven't received their pay.' Lance was as much in the dark as before the reply.

'They throw up unauthorized roadblocks and confiscate the goods of people passing through,' Jacques said. 'Just like old-time highway robbers. They won't touch us. We're armed and prepared to use our arms.'

'Let him go,' Ewart told Sambo. 'He'll warn them off.'

Briony looked disappointed.

Just before dawn Lance was wakened by the sound of the Landrover leaving the camp. A few minutes later, just as he was dozing off again, his tent shook and Briony fell through the flap. She'd fallen across Jimmy, who slept each night outside the entrance to Lance's tent. Lance started laughing.

'You stupid fucking kaffir, can't you look where you're going!' Briony raged from the floor. She struck away

Jimmy's hand as he tried to help her. 'Don't touch me you black bastard!'

Lance laughed louder. Jimmy had done it on purpose, letting Briony fall over him in the dark; once, when Ewart had come to the tent at about this time to discuss refuelling, Jimmy had been up and challenging him while he was still ten paces away.

Jimmy went out. Lance, still laughing, helped Briony up and picked up her towel and toilet kit. 'You really shouldn't speak to Jimmy like that, you know. He's a prince.'

Briony seemed to know he was needling her. 'He's a kaffir,' she said without heat, 'and he probably did it on purpose.'

Lance stopped laughing. He hadn't suspected her of a sense of humour.

'Jacques and Ewart went off in the Landrover to look at the road ahead. I want you to come down to the stream while I have my bath.'

Lance was flustered. 'If they're gone, I'd better stay in the camp.'

'Sambo will look after the camp. Jacques said to take you, I can hardly have a black watching me bathe, can I?' She smiled winningly. 'I'll wait outside while you dress.'

Halfway to the river, Briony turned on Jimmy who, as always, was following Lance. 'Where do you think you're going?'

'I have my orders,' Jimmy said.

'And I'm giving you new orders,' Briony snapped. 'You stay here and let nobody pass, understand? Mr Lance has his rifle and that's all the protection I need.'

Jimmy nodded and, as soon as Briony turned her back, smiled broadly at Lance, winking grotesquely at the same time.

Lance looked furtively around the trees and creepers beside the path. If there was any danger hidden here he would not see it until too late but Jacques wouldn't let

95

Briony out of the camp if there was any threat. Nevertheless he cocked the rifle Jacques had given him. If anything happened he would just have to slip the safety off . . .

There was a small pool in the stream which, in only a few months during the rainy season, would become an uncontrollable torrent sweeping giant trees before it. The damage from the last rainy season was still visible as fallen and rotting trunks overgrown with new greenery. To Lance it was strange that almost nothing grew sideways except the parasitic plants which fed off the others; every plant which was not a parasite had to fight its way upwards towards the sun which would soon be peeking shyly through the dense foliage.

Lance sat on the trunk of a fallen tree, his back to the pool. He heard Briony splash into the water and tried to blank from his mind the warmth of her thigh pressing urgently against his the night before. He pictured in his mind the rainfall charts for this area which were printed on the top of his map. In this month of June even in a 'dry' year four to eight inches of rain would fall over all the area between here and their destination. Temperatures would range from 70° Fahrenheit on a 'cool' day to well over ninety. Jimmy had told him it wasn't the heat that was so debilitating but the humidity. Why had Jimmy winked?

He swung around violently, startled by the hands over his eyes. A nipple hardened by the cold water caught him in the eye. Both his eyes starting tearing.

'Ooh, let's see where the flying tittie hit the man in the face.' She opened his eyelids and looked at his eyes. 'It'll go away in a moment.'

The pain had already gone. She saw his eyes on her body and stepped back a pace, arching her back. 'Collar and cuff matches,' she said, touching her blonde hair and the self-coloured curls in the thrusting triangle at the base of her flat belly. 'Here, let me have another look.'

She bent over him again, one hand on his head to steady it as she looked into his eyes, the other resting high up on his thigh. 'Nice and hard.'

Lance wiggled uncomfortably, lustfully. 'Now look here, Briony.'

She was slim all over except for her breasts, which stuck out at right-angles to her body.

They fell backwards over the log, Briony on top, her lips on his, her hand on his manhood. He found a breast in one of his hands and involuntarily, in his surprise, squeezed it; the nipple grew harder still. She had the zip on his trousers open and was nimbly extracting him from the folds of his underpants. She swung her legs apart over him. She arched her back expectantly and her hand curved over her bottom and between them to caress the sac of his testicles.

Even as Lance tried to squirm away, lust and fear and duty and Calvinism whirling in his mind like a St Catherine's wheel, the moss felt and smelt good under him. He had an image of two bricks crashing together, crushing his testicles between them, Jacques' hands on the bricks, Jacques' face smiling calmly above. Lance threw the breast from his hand and rolled violently to dislodge Briony from his body.

'Are you crazy?' Lance caught his erection in his trouser-zip. 'You stupid bitch, Jacques will kill us both!'

She laughed and rolled on all fours, raising her bottom so that he looked straight into the pink wetness between her legs. 'You think I'm a bitch. Well then, fuck me into the river like a bitch, doggie style. Ram that thing home, Rover!'

His erection looked ridiculous sticking through his underpants and his trousers. She was walking backward towards him, still on all fours. Lance retreated. Through a red haze Lance saw the lips splayed by her fingers, the face of Jacques Roux superimposed, Jacques, a man feared by all who had met him and many who had not, moreover a man who had given him a prized possession. Yet he found her coarseness strangely exciting but noticed clinically that his erection was subsiding.

'Jesus, you're a pale shadow of a man,' she said bitterly and, rising, pushed him over backwards into the water.

The water was a cool shock. He rolled away and, as he rose in the knee-deep water, managed to get the flies of his trousers and underpants to cooperate. He sighed as he zipped his trousers up and almost ran from the water to where he had dropped his rifle beside the log.

He didn't have long to sit nursing his damaged dignity in his wet clothes. Briony stalked past him and he hurried to catch up.

Lance didn't want to seem ungracious; he didn't want her to cause further trouble. So he tried conversation. 'Why did you call Ewart a cardboard man?'

'Because he is. He and Jacques both. They have this strong silent man thing.'

'They don't seem reticent to me. Or inarticulate.'

'It's the way they deliberately show no emotion. Ewart's proud of you but he'd rather die than show it.'

'Oh.'

'And it's beneath Jacques' dignity to take part in fun and games like we just had.'

'All right! I don't want to know.'

'You asked.'

'Well I'm sorry I did.'

They came up to Jimmy. 'You waited for nothing, kaffir,' she said to him.

Just outside the camp they met Jacques, who was carrying an FN under his arm. 'I told you not to leave the camp,' he said to Briony.

'I had to have a bath. I had Lance and Jimmy, both armed, for protection.' She walked past him.

Jacques gave Lance a searching look which Lance wouldn't meet, then turned back to the camp.

Lance ran his hand over his hair. It was still wet. So were his clothes.

'Today we'd better stay close to Mr Weber,' Jimmy said softly behind him.

Lance knew what he meant: *in case Jacques causes trouble*. He turned and walked towards the camp and breakfast. He was ravenous. The hell with Briony and Jacques and Jimmy. He was going to eat first then worry about it. Already he felt as if he needed another bath but this time with soap, it was so hot and humid. Yet the sun had been up for less than half an hour.

The convoy came to a halt. It was nearly ten o'clock in the morning.

'Bandits,' Jimmy said.

Lance climbed out on the running board to see past the other tanker in front of them. The Landrover had drawn up at a barricade but nobody had got out. Blacks were removing the drums and planks and sandbags of the barricade reluctantly.

When the obstruction was cleared, the convoy drove by.

Lance peered out of the window at the bandits standing sullenly beside the road, staring greedily at the expensive trucks loaded with spares, fuel and dynamite. They were just black men. If he met them in the street he wouldn't find anything sinister about them. They were armed with revolvers and automatics, a few rifles. One black man was peering over the sights of a machine pistol at Lance, finger on the trigger. Lance ducked frantically, banging his head on the dashboard. The bandit laughed and Jimmy said, 'He has no ammunition for it. See, there's no clip.' Lance looked, feeling sheepish. It was obvious that the bandits resented this well-armed convoy intensely.

'They must have pretty slim pickings in this God-forsaken place,' Lance said.

'Anything is better than nothing to them,' Jimmy replied. Lance was reminded of what his roommate had said: No matter how poor you think you are, there's always someone poorer. 'They're pitiful, these *bandits des grands chemins*.'

'What's that?'

'Highwaymen.'

'Oh. There's nothing grand about them or this "highway" either.' Lance grabbed for a handhold as Jimmy accelerated on the rough track.

'It's the only road there is. It's going to be worse when it rains later this afternoon.'

Lance looked up at the sky through the branches overhanging the road. It was a clear cloudless blue. 'How do you know?'

'Black man's magic,' Jimmy laughed.

When the rain came, about four in the afternoon, Lance said, 'Christ! I've read about curtains of rain and sheets of rain but I've always thought it was just an expression. That stuff looks solid.'

'It won't last long.' Jimmy pulled the knob to engage four-wheel drive. 'But in the rainy season it's like that all the time and this road becomes a river.'

The rain was over in ten minutes but the road was left drenched and dangerous for the next fifty miles. Trucks kept getting stuck in the mud or sliding into the gullies beside the road and having to be winched out by the other trucks, the Landrover and pure brute manpower. Even the ancillary task of cutting branches to put under wheels to provide traction was physically exhausting. It took them five hours to do the fifty miles. Lance was covered from head to foot in sulphurous-smelling mud.

'The smell comes from the dead leaves,' Jimmy told him. 'You can wash it off when you go swimming with Mrs Roux.'

'Shut up, Jimmy, just shut up.' There was nothing of Jimmy to be seen except his teeth, grinning evilly through the mud, and the whites of his eyes. Lance had to laugh at the spectacle.

100

Two hours later Lance held his tattered and dirty map out to Jimmy. 'We're here?'

Jimmy glanced at the map. 'About.'

'Then we have a thousand miles to go. If we have any more rain –'

'Once a day. If it isn't too bad we can do two hundred miles a day.'

'Five days.'

'It's pretty hard going. Your brother will declare a day of rest before we get there. Call it six and add a day for unforeseen circumstances. Seven.'

It took eight days. One day they rested, one was spent servicing the trucks and another stripping the refrigerated food truck of all its mechanical parts – even the generator driving the refrigeration unit – when it broke down. They crossed the River Congo at Kisangani, a town Jacques persisted in calling by its old name of Stanleyville. Lance was impressed by the width of the slow-flowing river but Jimmy told him nearer the sea a man could spend half a day rowing across it.

Of Briony he saw little, only at their snatched meals. Ewart had found that Lance had an unerring eye for the geometrics of the forces involved in extracting large heavily loaded trucks from deep mud or impossible gullies and had put him in charge of keeping the convoy moving. It was backbreaking, dirty work and every evening Lance would wash with the men in the nearest stream, eat his food quickly and fall exhausted into bed. Jacques came occasionally to stand watching a truck being pulled out and made some useful suggestions; he did not mention the bathing incident and Lance had little time to think about it: when he wasn't pulling some truck out of thigh-deep mud, he was seeing to the refuelling or eating or sleeping or washing. Though he had always preferred being warm to being cold, in this humid equatorial heat – they had crossed the equator sixty miles short of Kisangani – he was starting to feel nostalgic about the sinus-searing cold of the bitter Cape winters. His shirt clung wetly to his back from before dawn till he went to bed at night and his sweaty underpants chafed him raw. Yet Ewart looked as cool and immaculate and comfortable as ever, insisting everybody take foul tasting salt tablets twice daily.

They came on the Oubangui at sunset, without warning. The convoy had turned off the 'improved road' on to a narrow track and Lance assumed that for some reason Ewart wanted to strike camp earlier than usual. Lance ducked as a branch brushed the windscreen and slashed at his face through the open window. When he looked up he was first surprised at all the open space before him, a refreshing sight after days of staring at nothing but thick green foliage. And a clear blue sky above. Then he saw the water, stretching for more than a mile to the far bank and to his left and to his right for miles. He felt a sudden premonition, an irrational fear of the dark, ponderously creeping blackness before him. This river had been here since time immemorial and would still be here long after his dust had crumbled into nothingness and been washed away. For a long moment the convoy sat silently, the engines going off one by one until there was no sound but the gentle swish of the river as it flowed around an almost submerged tree-trunk. The very gentleness of the sound made by so massive a force of nature was somehow sinister. Lance was first shocked and then glad when the first hooter went and then the others.

They struck camp in a natural clearing in the forest, a hundred yards from the river, after first cutting down the scrub and creepers. They had not seen a living soul since passing through the village of Lisala two days ago, though the map indicated that, somewhere near them, there would be an airstrip. When Lance mentioned the absence of people, Ewart shook his head.

'There are people here all right. Pigmies on that side of

102

the river and Bangala tribesmen this side. But if they don't want to be seen you won't see them.'

'What about the airstrip?'

'That was when the Belgians were here,' Jacques said. 'The blacks will have no use for it so it will be overgrown. Chances are you'd walk right through it and not notice it as an airstrip, thinking it another overgrown clearing in the jungle.'

The brandy after the evening meal was making Lance sleepy. He said his goodnights and went to bed. It was, he felt, a great achievement for them just to have reached here. The others weren't celebrating because tomorrow the crocodile hunt would start – or perhaps they took travelling thousands of miles through armed attacks by rebels and bandits and over unspeakable roads in their daily stride. He hoped he would not let his brother down in the actual crocodile shoot.

Lance overslept. His body was catching up for the last few days. He heard Jimmy whistling outside his tent and smiled. He had always nudged Jimmy through the canvas with his foot for his shaving water. Apparently Jimmy thought he nudged too hard. Yesterday Jimmy had rolled a log against the tent and invited several of the black men to hear Lance howl when, after nudging the bulge gently and getting no shaving water, he kicked it. Now Lance first tested to see that it gave, that it wasn't another log, then kicked lustily at the bulge Jimmy's back made in the canvas. 'Watch out, you bloody maniac,' he heard Briony's voice. What the hell was she doing, sitting against his tent? Pietie brought him hot water for shaving. 'Where's Jimmy? Why wasn't I woken?' Lance asked him. Pietie shrugged, and slunk out. Lance had a theory that the coloured man's fear grew with the distance they had travelled from Cape Town. Here on the far side of the equator, Pietie was petrified and almost speechless. He was always looking furtively over his shoulder and Briony kept threatening to give him to Sambo and his brothers to eat.

Dressed, he took his rifle and went outside. He looked down at Briony; her attention was on something else. He followed her gaze. Ben, the tanker driver, was sitting on his haunches at a fire twenty feet away, a heavy cast-iron frying pan in his hands. Beside him on the ground stood a row of open one-pound fruit canning jars, their lids off. There was also an open box from which Ben was taking something, putting it in the frying-pan and putting the frying-pan on the fire. His hand reached into the box again to –

The box was clearly labelled DANGER DYNAMITE.

Lance dived for the frying-pan, kicking Ben aside. He hurled the pan and its contents away from the fire and stomped on the fire with one boot while with the other he kicked the box of dynamite away. He found his hands shaking Ben, who was surprised and terrified, rolling his eyes.

'You stupid bastard, what'll my brother say if you blow us all up?' He shook Ben until the black man's teeth rattled. 'Answer me!'

Lance became aware of the laughter around him. He slowly stopped shaking Ben. His feet were hot. He was still standing in the fire. He thrust Ben from him and jumped out of the fire. Everybody in their party was standing around. He glared at them. Slowly, slowly the laughter stopped.

Lance looked around for somebody to strike. He had never felt like this before.

'That was a very fine display of instant action and excellent co-ordination,' Jacques said. 'But it did look as if you were dancing around in the fire. Forgive us.'

Lance wondered if this was another of the elaborate practical jokes the people in the camp played on each other, like the log against the tent.

Ben was rebuilding the fire, carefully avoiding Lance; Ben hadn't forgotten that Lance had 'beat on' Theodore

Bruun and nobody had enlightened him about his mis-understanding – in his mind it was clear that Bruun had beat him and Lance had beat Bruun and therefore Lance could beat him.

'All right,' Lance said, his fury abating as he grasped the picture of himself, one foot stomping out the fire, the other simultaneously trying to kick the box of dynamite away, while his hands were shaking Ben. It probably had been comic. 'What's going on here?'

'Ben's melting the dynamite down to nitroglycerine,' Ewart said. 'We're waiting for the first batch so I can demonstrate how dangerous it is. I want everybody to understand the nitro must be handled with the greatest care.'

'Oh. What about that bloody fire with dynamite in it while I'm sleeping peacefully in the tent not ten paces away?' The adrenalin of fear and action was still coursing in Lance's blood.

Ewart shrugged. 'There's no danger.'

'Modern dynamite only explodes with the help of a detonator. It's very stable stuff,' Jacques said. 'Here, look.' He picked up one of the sticks of dynamite that had rolled from the box when Lance kicked it over in his attempts to shift it from the fire. He bent over the fire and held the dynamite in the small flame Ben was fanning.

Lance took an involuntary step back.

'The dynamite itself is not dangerous at all,' Jacques said. 'The danger is only when it gets hot and starts sweating nitro.' He pulled the stick of dynamite from the fire with two fingers. At the end that had been in the flames globules of colourless jelly had oozed through the outer skin. 'Nitro is volatile. The slightest bump sets it off.' He cautiously and slowly brushed two of the drops of jelly on to his middle finger. 'This much is enough to blow your hand off, perhaps most of your arm up to the elbow as well.'

'Be careful, Jacques,' Briony said from where she still sat against Lance's tent.

Jacques smiled mirthlessly. 'I was blowing out tree stumps while you were still in your cradle. Now watch.'

The assembly held its breath, every eye on the two fat globules glistening evilly on Jacques' finger. He shook his hand, the two drops flew off and hit and ground. There was a loud crack and two holes appeared in the earth. Everybody took a step backwards except Jacques and Ewart. Behind him Lance heard Briony draw a sharp breath.

'Aah!' said the black men as one voice, all smiling whitely. Lance was sure they considered it a powerful new toy, much as they did their firearms.

Jimmy brought Lance his rifle from where he had dropped it. They stood watching Ben preparing another frying-pan full of dynamite to hold over the fire. The black men were keeping a respectful distance. After a while Ewart produced a tablespoon from his pocket and stood tapping it in the palm of his hand. He motioned Ben away from the fire and took the frying-pan off. From the sweating dynamite he scraped the nitroglycerine until the spoon was full. He walked with it to a nearby tree and everybody followed.

'They drilled a hole in the tree before you came,' Briony said beside Lance.

Ewart held the spoon in front of him. 'See how little it is?'

'Yes, N'kosi,' the black men chorused.

'Now see what it can do, why you must be very careful not to drop it or bump it.' Ewart poured the nitroglycerine into the hole drilled into the tree at a downward angle. It flowed reluctantly and took a long time. Then he shooed them all back.

When he was satisfied they were far enough from the tree, Ewart held the spoon up between forefinger and thumb. 'You've seen how little of the jelly is in the tree. You all know how little a spoon weighs. Now I'm going to show you what a little bump can set off a big bang.'

He threw the spoon overarm against the tree. For a moment time hung and Lance feared nothing would happen. Then the tree blossomed in shreds around its trunk, the explosion lost in the sound of tearing fibres. Slowly, slowly the huge tree toppled away from them. Lance went forward with the black men to inspect the stump still standing in the ground, rising three feet to end in a frayed edge as if some god had angrily torn it in two. The stump was nearly four feet across where the spoonful of jelly had sundered it.

The black men wandered silently back to the camp. Lance inspected the stock of his rifle for scratches. It had been badly scratched when he had dropped it the time he had killed the man who had ambushed them so long – could it truly have been only a week ago? There were no new scratches.

'Jesus, I've never seen anything like that,' he said to Ewart. 'But what do we need such dangerous stuff for?'

'To kill crocodiles.'

'Huh?' Lance looked at his rifle.

'Good God, Lance, you didn't think we were going to shoot twenty-five thousand crocodiles one by one with rifles, did you?' Ewart sounded genuinely amazed.

Lance nodded.

Ewart smiled. He shook his head. 'The bwana big white hunter who shoots crocodiles one by one with the aid of a rifle, an eagle eye and an endless supply of bullets is strictly a character out of romantic fiction. I didn't know you fancied yourself as a sort of Ernest Hemingway or Robert Ruark character. I didn't even know you read much.'

'I don't. But I've read them. How do we get the crocodiles then?' Lance asked, looking around to make sure nobody was near enough to overhear his ignorance. There was only Jimmy behind his right shoulder, looking extremely thoughtful and very interested. 'You didn't know either, Jimmy?'

'No, Mr Lance.'

'Then why the hell didn't you ask?'

'Black men do not enquire into the business of white men. It is not polite.'

'Bullshit! You were saying, Ewart?'

'The way you hunt crocodiles is dictated by the habits and habitat of the crocodiles themselves. Isn't that obvious to you?'

'No. Maybe. I would have thought the resources at your disposal, weapons – '

'Ask yourself this: Last night you were at the river. Did you see a crocodile?'

'No.'

'There was one right in front of us, taking air,' Jimmy said.

'I thought that was a log,' Lance said.

'You were lucky to see one,' Ewart said. 'I've spent half a lifetime up and down Africa and I've seen perhaps thirty crocodiles of the estimated million or more.' They came to the camp and Ewart stopped a little away from the others, all standing near the fire watching Ben at his work. 'And that includes perhaps ten I've seen full-length, basking in the sun on a river bank, waiting for the intrepid hunter to shoot them. Remember, a crocodile is a reptile – it generates no internal body heat and therefore moves extremely sluggishly until the sun has warmed it. Of the other twenty or so I saw the tips of their noses and their eye-bulges floating in a river just like that log you saw yesterday. Again, don't forget a crocodile has no lips and must come above the water to eat or it'll drown in the water it swallows with the food.

'The crocodile is a reptile left over from prehistoric times. Its brain, relative to body size, is extremely small. Nobody knows much about their behaviour. But crocodiles do seem to sense the presence of alien beings and slip into the water to lie in wait for them or from pure fear.'

'You seem to know a lot about it.'

'As much as is necessary for the job at hand,' Ewart said. 'Now, what can you tell me?'

'Crocodiles live in water. It's not easy to see them out of it because they go back into it when you come. Once in the water they're hard to spot. Conclusion: Shooting them one by one with rifles, it'll take us years to clear even the hundred-mile stretch we're starting on first, of all the crocs in it.'

'Right. So, the nitroglycerine. We're going to blow up the river and the crocodiles with it.'

'Why not just use the safer dynamite for the same purpose?' Lance looked over his shoulder to see Jimmy nodding agreement.

'Good question. The dynamite is simply not concentrated enough for what we want to do. And one other thing, we want to do approximately ten miles of the river at one time. There's no way we can set off the many batches of dynamite required all at the same time. Nitro goes off from any kind of shock, as you just saw, so we need only explode one batch and that sets off the rest.'

'I see. Who thought this up?'

'I did.'

'It's clever but it sounds bloody dangerous.'

'Ths rewards are commensurate with the danger. Ten miles a day, the first hundred miles in ten days. That should come to a quarter of a million dollars.'

It was the longest conversation he'd ever had with his brother and Lance was content when a companionable silence settled over them as they stood watching Ben at his work. Ben now had a rhythm with two frying-pans on two fires a little distance apart so that there would be no danger of bashing the pans together and setting off an explosion. When the dynamite inside the pan had sweated enough, Ben would take the pan from the fire and put it in a nest of the cotton waste the tankermen used to clean their hands on after refuelling. He would take each stick of dynamite and scrape it gently against the rim of a fruit canning jar to let the nitro run down the inside of the jar which, with his other hand, he held at an angle. When a jar was full to the brim, he would take three rubber rings and fit them inside the metal and glass combination lid and screw the lid on tightly so that a little of the jelly squeezed out. He would wipe the excess jelly with a piece of cotton waste which would immediately be taken away by another black man to be carefully placed in a hole some distance from the camp. Every time Ben closed a new jar the cotton was taken away. Each jar was taken away and carefully placed on the river bank as soon as it was filled. It was a painstaking, slow business. Once a drop of sweat fell from Ben's forehead into the pan. A few drops of nitro jelly had gathered in the bottom of the pan and there was an explosion which had everybody diving for the ground. The pan was dented but Ben was unharmed and apparently unconcerned. Ewart spoke to him earnestly in his own language and then Sambo repeated everything Ewart had said before they allowed him to continue. Lance drew Ewart aside.

'Look, Ewart, that bloody Ben is too stupid to be scared. He's going to kill us all.'

'That's exactly why I chose him. He has steady hands. Could you do it?'

Lance saw his own shaking hands crashing the pan into a bottle with half a pound of nitroglycerine in it, minute pieces of his own flesh and bone flying over the camp. 'No. But you could. Or Sambo.'

'No. We're needed elsewhere. It's going to take more than just steady hands to mine the river with that stuff.'

Lance was about to turn away when Ewart laid a hand on his arm.

'Don't be offended. You're right to tell me if you have something on your mind. You've been very helpful on the

110

trip up here and you're developing into something of a leader of men. Your advice is always welcome.'

'Thanks.'

'Don't thank me. You get only what you've earned. We'd better get back. If they're not watched those blacks could get very careless.'

'Even after the demonstration this morning?'

'Especially after the demonstration. They might try to have a little demonstration of their own and misjudge the quantity and blow us all to kingdom come. Or they might just get careless with nitro-soaked cotton waste and the next time you wipe your hands on it *bang,* no arms.'

By late afternoon there were forty jars of nitroglycerine standing in a row along the river bank with one of Sambo's brothers standing guard. Ben was told to stop. Everybody watched while Ewart, Jacques and Sambo tied a piece of string around each jar just under the lid where there was a slight indentation in the glass. The tension was tangible throughout the hour this operation took. When they finished, Lance was breathing shortly and shallowly, his muscles tired, his whole body limp.

'Right,' Ewart said, 'let's see how it works.' There was no sweat on his forehead or in the armpits of his shirt, and his clothing was uncreased.

By contrast, Sergeant Sambo was drenched in sweat as if he had been in a steam room. 'That kaffir's got more sense than you,' Briony said to Jacques, who had the faintest sheen on his forehead.

'If I allow myself to admit I'm frightened, my hands shake,' Jacques said with dignity and walked past her, calling an addendum from twenty paces: 'In which case you'd better hope my insurance is paid up.'

Two flat-bottomed glass fibre skiffs were brought to the water's edge. They had been taken at Kariba and Lance had fancied they were just the right length for pulling in a dead crocodile and bringing it ashore. They were driven by small aircooled motors mounted on their rear decks,

111

turning large airscrews inside protective wire cages. When one was put in the river Lance could see it drew little water, that its passage would not disturb the surface much. Ewart checked both skiffs with his customary care, then had them refuelled and started up. He took each in turn out on the water to make sure it handled predictably, paying particular care to the wake. On each skiff he practised with the throttles until he could make them move from rest with almost imperceptible acceleration and leave no wake at all. Then he had one skiff carried back to the camp, leaving the other in the water.

'Sambo and I will do this one,' he said. 'Jacques, please make sure everybody stays well back from the river. A couple of tons of water falling on you will kill you just as surely as a truck overturning.'

They watched from a distance as Lance and Sambo carried the jars to the skiff and placed them in the sectioned corrugated boxes the jars had come in. When all the jars were on board, Ewart took the controls, and, ever so slowly, like a held breath, the skiff moved away from the shore. Ewart took it upriver at a leisurely pace. When the skiff and the men on it were small against the horizon of the river, he stopped in near the bank. Jimmy had fetched Lance's rifle without being asked to do so. He handed it to Lance and indicated the scope. Jacques already had his binoculars to his eyes. Lance made sure the safety catch was on and there was no bullet in the breech, then peered through the eyepiece and zoomed in. The propeller was turning lazily, just holding the skiff's head into the slow current, every now and again seeming to falter and stop, an arresting optical illusion. Ewart held the string attached to a half-pound fruit canning jar of nitroglycerine and lowered it cautiously into the water, paying out string a handsbreadth at a time until the string became slack. He tightened the string and wiggled it to make sure the jar was firmly settled on the bottom, held well by the silt. If it fell over it would explode and the nitro still on the skiff would also go up, set off by the concussion. Ewart dropped the string in the water and took the controls from Sambo. Now the skiff seemed not to move at all. Lance heard somebody expelling held breath like a long violent sigh. It was himself. He took several deep breaths and when he looked again the skiff had hardly moved. Only the turning of the propeller indicated movement.

Ewart put four jars across the river in a row, then moved downstream, towards the camp, at the same funereal pace for nearly two hundred yards before he laid the next line of four jars. In all he laid ten lines, a process which took two hours. At the end Lance was drained of emotion.

Ewart brought the skiff gently to the edge of the water and he and Sambo carried it up to where the rest waited. This time Sambo's clothes were black with sweat. Ewart was as cool as ever though Lance noticed that the lines from his nose to the corners of his mouth were more pronounced than usual, a lightening of the skin under his tan emphasizing them.

Jacques let out his breath slowly.

'What are we waiting for now?' Lance asked him.

'Oilskins for Ewart.' He seemed to feel a compulsion to talk. 'That jelly detonates at nearly five thousand degrees celsius and produces ten cubic feet of gas per pound at a pressure of two hundred thousand pounds per square inch. We have twenty pounds of jelly in that mile of river. When it goes off, thousands of tons of water are going to be instantly compressed. Every living thing in the water will die when the compression bursts all the blood vessels in their bodies: instant haemorrhage of the brain.'

Ewart shrugged into the oilskins one of the men brought him. He pulled on the watertight boots and laced them. He pulled the hood over his head and pulled the cords tight. He climbed into the safety harness Sambo held for him and buckled it tight. Then he walked towards

113

the river. Halfway between the spectators and the river he selected a tree and slung the rope attached to the safety harness around it, fastening the clip of the loose end back on to the harness and pulling it tight through the friction clip. Somewhere along the way he had picked up a small log. He now stood tightly against the tree, swung his arm beside it and let the log fly at the river. The log struck the water and for a long second nothing seemed to happen – an illusion, as the log had not even started to sink when there was a ripple across the whole width of the great somnolent river, running upstream against the tide. The ripple moved very quickly indeed, covering nearly two hundred yards in the micro-second before there was a dull, deep, voluminous explosion and the whole river rose in the air like a huge flat fountain. Lance stumbled back with the rest of them. He could no longer see Ewart's bright yellow clothing through the solid water. The force of the water struck him down. He choked for air as he fell and in midair swallowed a good deal of water. He was drowning. Still he tried to rise above the water but the pressure was too much. Then it was over and he was coughing out water, turning over in the mud to avoid choking on the water coming back out.

Lance saw the wave of water coming at him down the incline only out of the corner of his eye and too late to get his head down. A large log carried by the force of the water struck him a glancing blow on the shoulder and he cartwheeled with it. When the water had gone, he was left standing on hands and knees in the mud, facing down towards the river. There was a backwash but it was only three feet high and Lance laughed as its muddy murk washed over him, swallowing more of the foul-tasting stuff.

'I don't think it's bloody funny,' Briony said beside him. She was plastered with mud and her nipples stuck like angry thumbs through her thin shirt. 'Ewart could have told us to stand further back.'

'I didn't know quite how big the explosion would be,' Ewart said reasonably as he came up to them. He had thrown back the hood and was unzipping the top of the waterproof suit. Underneath it his shirt looked as if he had just fetched it from some exclusive laundry. Even the hood had not ruffled his short hair and he had already wiped the water from his face. He was smiling. 'Now we know.'

Briony snorted and turned her back on him. Her clothes went swish-squish as she waded away towards the camp.

'All right,' Ewart said. 'We can't just stand around here congratulating ourselves. There's work to be done.'

Ewart took one group of men to the far bank while Jacques took another group along the side they were on. Both groups were to fetch back any dead crocodiles that had been left on land by the exploding water. If they were left overnight the scavengers would find them and tear the skins, making them worthless. Lance was told to make sure there wasn't a drop of nitroglycerine anywhere in or near their campsite and to find a suitable spot outside the camp for further jelly production.

Lance and Jimmy, with the help of Ben, beat the earth around the fires and where the fires themselves had been with spades. There were several small explosions where drops of nitro had fallen on the soil. Lance wondered that nobody had had his foot blown off but he supposed the drops were too small because they couldn't be seen by the naked eye. This finished, they cleared an area in the forest more than half a mile from the camp where several fires could be lit to sweat the nitro from the dynamite. Lance wanted to carry the dynamite there but Jimmy stopped him.

'If we leave it here overnight, by dawn it will be gone, Mr Lance.'

'There's nobody here to steal it, Jimmy.'

'They're here. We just haven't seen them.'

Lance looked around at the trees around them. A man

115

could hide there . . . or there . . . He didn't like being watched by alien men of unknown intentions.

'I see them,' Ben said. He hardly ever spoke unless spoken to.

'Where?'

'Before the big bang. They go back.'

Jimmy had an interchange with Ben in their own language. 'Local tribesmen,' he said to Lance when it was over. 'Men of the Bangala. Violent and proud people.'

'Will they attack us?'

'They're not stupid. They've seen the other armed men in the camp and know they will come after them if they kill us.'

Lance still wished he had his rifle and lengthened his stride to get back to the camp with all speed. Only pride restrained him from breaking into a run even though logic told him Ewart would have warned him to carry a firearm if there was any chance of danger and, if perchance Ewart had forgotten or assumed he would know, Jimmy would have said something. Anyway, his rifle was full of mud from the deluge. He would clean it immediately he got back to camp.

It was quite dark by the time the last crocodile found dead on land had been dragged to the water and ferried into the camp by the skiffs. There were nearly sixty fully grown dead reptiles. Jacques and Ewart were smiling jubilantly. They had counted on sixty crocodiles per running mile of river.

'No more than a quarter would have fallen on land,' Jacques said. 'I think we can fairly count on more than two hundred fully grown crocs per running mile.'

'If this mile is typical of the rest of the river,' Lance said.

'Sure. But there's no earthly reason it shouldn't be.'

'It's going to take longer than ten days to clear the stretch to Bangui,' Ewart said warningly. 'We're constrained by how fast we can skin the crocodiles. And once all our trucks are loaded we have no men left to guard a stockpile of skins.'

'What are you getting at, Ewart?' Jacques asked thoughtfully.

'What you're thinking already. We have no contract with the Central African Republic. Once they see what a rich haul we're taking, they may interfere.'

'I'll keep it in mind. Meanwhile I think we should move as quickly as possible.'

As they walked back to the camp, Lance said, 'I thought Jacques had bribed the politicians of the Central African Republic not to interfere.'

'I did,' Jacques replied. 'But an African sees a bribe as a gift. No responsibility towards the giver devolves on the beneficiary. When it becomes obvious that the patron can give more, the African demands it as another right. But it's not more bribes Ewart's worried about – that's my part of the operation, not his. You see, the greater wealth we'll be taking from the river may well induce someone to try taking it from us by force as the smaller riches we'd originally expected would not. And our safety is more definitely Ewart's business.'

Sambo had laid on pumped water from the river and latrines had been dug behind the jury-rigged showers. Lance went to shower.

They dined on a baby hippopotamus blown up in the blast. Lance felt sorry for the animal – not because it was small, it stood over three feet high, but because it had had no chance to grow up. But the alternative, a huge fat catfish, simply looked too revolting. The baby hippo tasted fine.

'It's a pity about the others animals, the hippo and the fish, that we blow up with the crocs,' Ewart said.

'They don't add much to the diet of the people,' Jacques said. 'But the crocodiles cause a great deal of hardship. Actually, if the government could persuade the people to use the river more, it could add considerably to their protein intake. But I don't think it will happen.'

Jimmy brought Lance a section of a six-foot eel the blacks were grilling over the fire. Lance, eating out of politeness, found it tasty but Briony said, 'If that eel and that revolting catfish is the protein you're talking about, I'm not surprised the kafiirs stick to maize and cow and buck. This hippo's okay but the kaffirs wouldn't have any way of trapping and killing the grown ones, would they?'

'That's true. A grown hippo is a most dangerous animal, much more dangerous than an elephant or rhino for instance.'

'I once saw a hippo bite a man in half,' Ewart said.

Lance pushed his plate away but Briony served herself the last of the baby hippo's liver. 'Well, I'm biting this hippo in half.'

Lance decided to change the subject. He held his glass up for Pietie to pour more of the champagne Jacques had produced to toast the success of their venture. 'What happens now?'

'Tomorrow we wait here for the dead crocodiles to drift down. We take them out of the water and skin them,' Ewart said. 'Meanwhile we blow up ten miles of river upstream and repeat the process. The day after tomorrow in the evening, we move camp ten miles upstream, and so on.'

'The dead crocs come downriver to where we are?'

'Yes. They bloat and float. We have to get them out of the water before the crocs or eels or fish downstream start eating them and ruining the skins.'

'Crocs eat other dead crocs?'

'Sure. And the live little ones too. They breed out literally thousands of eggs and the big ones eat the little ones by the mouthful. Crocodiles who escape being eaten by their elders live to a ripe old age, some say hundreds of years. So they keep the population down by eating their own young. They also eat anything that's dead. They don't have jaws suitable for chewing and so prefer carrion to fresh meat. They drag their catch under an overhang and leave it to rot. Once it's rotten, they tear off large chunks and swallow them whole. Then they don't eat for weeks while they digest what they've swallowed.'

'Are you ever expansive tonight,' Briony said. 'Pietie, open another bottle of champagne.'

'Yes,' Lance said, baffled, 'but if the crocs drift downstream when they're dead, why are we moving camp upstream? Why don't we start at the top and move downstream and save ourselves a lot of travel?'

'When you're laying nitroglycerine by the box, you don't want anything to bump even one jar of the stuff, not a croc, not a hippo, not a piece of wood, not a fish, not a stone, not even an eddy of water. When one jar goes up all the rest go up too. You saw this afternoon. It would be ironic if some dead croc came drifting downstream and nudged a jar of nitro you'd just laid and blew you to kingdom come.'

'Necrorevenge,' Jacques said.

Ewart laughed. 'Yes, that's a good word for it. Pass the champagne. Necrorevenge.'

Lance pushed the flap aside and breathed deeply of the humid air. He'd had a restless night, disturbed by dreams – or the same dream over and over again: Lance hiding behind a fat black tyre filled with nitroglycerine, shooting past it at a black man with Jacques' face, disintegrating Jacques' head on the black body a moment before the bullet from the dead man exploded the tyreload of nitro in his face; in the dream he saw his own body fly apart as a fine red mist swirling up and then sinking slowly, slowly to the ground. Necrorevenge.

'Who're they, Jimmy?'

Jimmy looked along his pointing arm at the black men sitting on their haunches just outside the perimeter of the camp. 'Don't point, Mr Lance. They might think you're putting a spell on them.'

Lance jerked his arm down.

'They're the tribesmen who were watching us yesterday. They've probably come looking for work.'

'I thought they lived off the land.'

'A common misconception. Most of them probably worked on the white plantations until independence. Then the white plantation owners went back where they came from. These people don't have the skills to run modern plantations.'

'They don't look dangerous to me. You said yesterday . . .'

'Even so. They're fierce fighters. They do not mind dying because they believe their time will not come until their ancestors want them – need them – in the hereafter. They venerate their ancestors. Most blacks do, as you no doubt know. It is also against their . . . one of their taboos is staring at people, Mr Lance.'

Lance noticed they had their eyes cast down. He dropped his own. 'They still don't look dangerous.'

'Hunger only makes them fight more fiercely.'

'Some of them have pretty straight noses for black men.'

'An Arab influence, Mr Lance. There are Arabs not too many miles that way.' Jimmy pointed northwards.

Lance had always associated Arabs with deserts, large expanses of sand. He looked at the lush greenery all round their camp. 'Is that right, Jimmy? I thought most blacks were against interbreeding even outside their own tribes. That's what I learnt at school, anyway.'

'You learnt right, Mr Lance. But Arab slavers have raided these people for centuries and raped their women. They still do.'

'Come on, Jimmy! Even I am not that gullible.'

Jimmy shook his head and allowed his smile to slip from his face. 'No, I'm serious. Ask your brother or Mr Roux. They too know about these things.'

Lance nodded. (Over dinner that evening he would ask

and be assured that the slave trade, though greatly reduced, was still carried on.) His attention was taken by Ewart and Sambo walking up to the line of squatting men. Jacques also appeared and came to stand with Lance. Ewart and Sambo stood looking at the trees and chatting inconsequentially about crocodile-skinning for a moment.

The row of black men sat silently, looking at the ground. Lance noticed that some wore wicked-looking chopping knives fully eighteen inches long at their side. 'Why don't they say something?'

'An African waits for his superior to greet him first,' Jacques said. 'Ewart's being polite. It would be aggressive to greet them too soon. Discourteous too.'

'Shit!'

'When in Rome. They don't have your conception of time.'

Finally Ewart said, not too loudly, 'Men of the Bangala, we greet you.'

There was a murmur. Sambo tried them in several dialects until he found one man with whom he had a common language. A long conversation ensued.

'Let's have breakfast,' Jacques said. 'That'll go on for a while.'

They were having their third cup of coffee served by Pietie when Ewart sat down at the table.

'Well?' Jacques asked him.

Ewart shrugged. 'Slowly, slowly catchee monkee. Sambo is bargaining with them. They say they're warriors, not animal skinners. That's one count on which they want more money. They say blowing up the river is sacrilegious and may bring the wrath of the ancestors down on them. For that they want danger pay. They say we're too near their natural enemies, the pigmies just across the river. That's another bonus.'

Jacques and Ewart burst out laughing and, after a moment, Lance joined. Chafing at the delay could only bring frustration. Briony came out of the tent in a wrapper to see what the laughter was about but went back inside without asking for an explanation.

'I should think they'd start work mid-morning,' Ewart said when he stopped laughing. 'Lance, I'll clear the dead crocs from the river with the men we've got. Meanwhile I want you to take charge of the dynamite sweating. For God's sake be careful. Select the men you need to make it and watch them every minute. If you have to take a pee, do it facing them. We need enough for ten miles, ten pounds in twenty jars to the mile.'

Lance didn't much like the idea of being anywhere near a hundred pounds of nitro but there was nothing he could say. Ewart probably thought he was giving him the safest job.

By lunchtime, Lance was sure he had sweated ten pounds from pure funk. He had to be extremely vigilant or the six men making the jelly would start chatting and laughing and get careless with the volatile stuff. But the hundred pounds had been made without incident and carried, a single jar at a time, to a flat grassy area near the river. Jacques on one skiff and Ewart on the other were just bringing in the last of the crocodiles. The total haul was two hundred and forty-four. Lance found it difficult to believe there had been that many crocodiles in a single mile of river, no matter how wide. The crocodiles were spread in five long rows with space to walk between them, grim grey scaly animals ranging from six to sixteen feet, every mouth gaping open to show the rows of pointed yellow teeth. A few birds, apparently now perceiving their hosts were dead, sat on the open jaws searching teeth already picked clean for another morsel of food.

Sambo was just bringing the Bangala to the crocodiles. 'What did you settle for, Sambo?' Lance asked.

Sambo winked. 'An American dollar per day per man. Once a week every man gets a pound of salt. We also have to give them three meals of maize every day and meat from a buck or a goat or a cow once a week. Finally, if we kill any pigmies, they must be allowed to take the heads as trophies.'

'Fucking savages,' Jimmy said behind Lance. He rarely swore.

'Will they travel north with us?' Ewart asked.

'Yes sir. They won't cross the river, though.'

'That won't be necessary. Your men can fetch the crocodiles from that side. We'll do all the skinning this side.'

'They'll also go south with us when we return. Not quite to the end of the Oubangui but for a hundred miles or so.'

'All right. At that stage we'll hire new men. Do you think they'll work well?'

'Yes sir.'

'All right. Put them to work. And warn your people, Sambo, that unless they want to do the filthy work of skinning crocodiles themselves, to leave these people alone. They're not to stare at them and not to play any of their jokes on them.'

'Yes sir.'

'And make it quite clear to the Bangala that they can't bring their women anywhere near the camp.'

'I already have, sir. Since the plantations closed they've been in a bad way. They're keen for work.'

'Tell them any man who stays until they all return home will get a bonus of ten American dollars.'

Sambo told them and then showed them how to skin a crocodile. Lance was surprised at how easy it was – when done by an expert. Sambo borrowed one of the machetes. Eight men turned a one-ton crocodile on its back. Sambo chopped the knife into the inside of each of the four legs. Then he used the point to cut around the two short sides and one long side of the softer belly skin. He peeled the belly skin back and loosened the skin around his incision with the point of the machete. He put his fingers into the incision near one ankle of the beast and stepped on the claw, tilting the whole stiffened body of the dead crocodile. With one jerk he sundered the bone and with the machete cut through the sinew and flesh around the bone. He repeated this at each claw. The crocodile rolled flat on its back again, bloody fleshy stumps sticking grotesquely into the air, claws hanging by empty skin. Sambo stuck the point of the machete into the crocodile's body at the junction of head and body and moved it to sever the backbone. He chopped one way with the point and then the other way to cut the muscle and sinew. He had four men roll the butchered crocodile on its side and stand on the flap of belly skin. He motioned to the Bangala who approached tentatively, to take the stumps of the crocodile's legs. When they had a firm grip, two men to a stump, he told them to pull. They heaved this way and that and just as Lance thought whatever it was they were doing would fail, the trunk of the crocodile and its tail slipped out of the skin. It made a comic plopping sound.

The carcass was chucked on the ground to one side and the skin spread out on the grass where the head and claws made it look like a real crocodile creeping up on some prey.

They watched for a time while the skinners tried emulating Sambo. They strugged and mangled a few crocodiles.

'It doesn't matter if they ruin a few skins,' Jacques said. 'As long as they learn to do it properly.'

'They will,' Sambo assured him. 'It's the only work for hundreds of miles around.'

As they walked back to the camp to wash up, Lance asked Sambo, 'Where'd you learn to skin crocodiles?'

'I didn't, Mr Lance. Mr Roux told me to make sure the belly skin was not damaged. He also told me if we could get complete skins with head and tail and claws still attached, the price will be ten dollars more per crocodile. I just worked it out from there. Most animals have loose skins. I thought, if you skin a lion one way, why not try the same on a crocodile.'

'Are we going to salt those skins?' Lance couldn't remember seeing among their stores the huge amounts of salt they would need to treat the skins of thousands of crocodiles.

'No,' said Jacques. 'No harm will come to the skins in the short while before we deliver them to the buyers.'

After lunch Lance stood a safe distance from the water and watched Ewart and Jacques mine the river with the jelly prepared that morning. When they came ashore, Jacques was white as a sheet and sweating profusely. He looked at his watch and said to Ewart, 'We could do twice ten miles every day.'

'My nerve wouldn't last, 'Ewart said shortly. He was not sweating but Lance had never heard him being abrupt before.

Jacques didn't press the point. Lance, standing next to him as Ewart donned his oilskins nearer the river, asked, 'What's the rush, Jacques?'

Jacques mopped his face. 'Same thing we talked about yesterday. Down the middle of the river there runs the border with the Central African Republic. Technically we're killing their crocodiles without permission. Once their politicians find out exactly how many crocodiles we're taking from the river the bribes we already paid aren't going to be enough. They're going to want much more – perhaps all.'

'How will they hear? We haven't seen a soul.'

'They'll hear. News travels fast in the bush. Tom-tom news.'

'Native drums?'

'Yes.'

Ewart threw his log. Ten miles of the river rose into the air. It was not much more spectacular than one mile; they could only see part of it. But the aftermath was incredible. Lance was already turning away but Jacques took his arm.

'Wait. Watch.'

Ewart was frantically undoing his safety line and running up the slight slope towards them, a slightly comic figure in his voluminous yellow plastic clothing. Fifty yards from them he looked upriver and hastily threw the safety rope around the nearest sturdy tree and secured it to the clip on his harness. Lance followed his gaze. A wall of water forty feet high and more than a mile across was rushing down the river, smashing grown trees to matchsticks along the banks, pushing waves sideways up the incline. It rumbled angrily as it came. Where it swept over Ewart it was still taller than he, and the last waves licked at the feet of Lance and Jacques fifty yards away and ten feet higher.

In front of them an eight-foot eel hung in the fork of a tree, writhing about to free itself. Sambo jumped past them with a thick log in his hand and started hitting it about the head. The huge mouth opened as it tried to strike at Sambo, the fangs gleaming. The eel jerked itself free and fell to the ground. Immediately it slithered towards the river, outdistancing even the fleet Sambo. The huge black man threw his log away in disgust.

'How come that horror is still alive?' Lance asked.

'It was beyond the explosion. A few thousand tons of water was pushed upstream, then came rushing downstream again, bringing the eel with it,' Jacques said. 'No matter Sambo, you'll be able to pick up a dead one beside the river for your dinner.'

'Not that big, Mr Roux,' Sambo said. 'That was a grandfather of all eels.' Sambo left them to fetch the skiffs and put them back in the water to gather the crocodiles lying dead on the river banks. It was already mid- afternoon and searching twenty miles of river bank two hundred yards wide was going to take well into the evening.

Ewart made up four parties, led by himself, Jacques, Lance and Sambo. Lance was surprised at the variety and quantity of river life: not only crocodiles but small and large eels, several kinds of water snake, a large variety of fish, large and small crabs, hippopotami, fresh-water prawns or shrimps, and many varieties of snails lay dead on the sodden banks of the river.

'It's sad that one only finds out about the life of the river when you kill everything in it,' Lance said to Jimmy as they heaved at the tail of a dead crocodile.

'It's ironic that the crocodiles will be the first to repopulate the river,' Jimmy said. 'But crocodiles take a very long time to grow to full size, so the other animals will stand a chance.' He laughed. 'For a while, the crocodiles are going to have to feed on each other.'

'Where will they come from?'

Jimmy scuffed a sandy patch with his boot. 'Eggs in the sand, hatched by the sun.'

Lance peered close. The eggs were quite small and the colour of the sand. Jimmy squashed them underfoot. 'When they hatch, the first thing the little crocodiles do is to start eating each other. Only a few actually make it to the water.'

'What's an egg's chance of getting to be this big?' They were dragging a fourteen-footer to the edge of the water with the help of four other men.

'I don't know,' Jimmy admitted. 'One in a thousand, maybe.'

'Naw,' Lance said thoughtfully. 'If they lay that many eggs every year, if they grow as old as my brother says, and if there are only a couple of hundred grown ones to every mile of river, I reckon the chances of an egg becoming a fully grown croc is one in ten thousand or less.' He changed his handhold on the croc's tail. His hands, never soft, had been hardened by the work on the way here but the scales were rubbing them raw. 'These things smell.'

'All carrion-eaters smell,' Jimmy said. 'Even people who eat meat smell bad to vegetarians, I've heard.' The idea amused him and he laughed. 'When we get back to the camp you'll really smell something.'

Lance thought Jimmy meant the carcasses of the crocodiles rotting in the heat but that wasn't it. When Jimmy led Lance to the slaughter ground the smell was coming from the buzzards sitting in a circle around the bloody bare crocodile carcasses or tearing pieces of flesh from them or making a loud squawking noise. Further out sat a circle of hyenas, slavering at the jaws, watching and waiting for the men to leave. Every now and again one would be overcome with hunger or greed and dart forward, scattering the buzzards and other birds, grab a piece of meat and run back, trying to swallow it before the rest of the pack could descend on him to fight him for it. They too had a distinct morbid smell. Lance held his nose.

At dawn the next morning Lance moved the camp ten miles upriver while Ewart and Jacques stayed to oversee the gathering in and skinning of the dead crocodiles. By the time the rest of the personnel arrived at noon, Lance had set up camp and had the jelly prepared for exploding the next ten miles of river after lunch. Ewart expressed himself satisfied with the choice of campsite. They had taken more than 2300 crocodile skins in the eleven miles of river and Lance was surprised that so many skins made only a single truckload. The crocodile skins were laid flat on the bed of a truck in two rows, the heads outwards, the tails fitting together in the centre like sardines in a can. There were many layers of skins on the truck and Lance thought the nine-foot-high wall of open crocodile jaws staring at him a nightmare prospect.

'About an hour and a half before I'll have lunch ready,' Briony said.

'The skinners won't eat the meat of the animals from the water because of their religion or something.' Ewart said to Lance. 'You take Jimmy and go shoot them a good-sized buck.'

'Now?'

'Yes. It shouldn't take long. These woods are teeming with buck. Jimmy'll track for you.'

'I'll go with them if you don't need me for anything else,' Jacques said.

'All right.'

They walked in single file through the jungle, Jimmy in front, Lance in the middle, their rifles over their shoulders. After less than ten minutes Jimmy stopped them. Lance had been looking around and had seen nothing but a grey flash of monkey, the disappearing tail of a ground squirrel, and a large red and white parrot that sat on a branch within arm's reach and watched their passage with disapproving disdain from hooded eyes. They stopped when Jimmy raised his arm. Lance moved as silently as he could to stand beside Jimmy. He peered along Jimmy's pointed arm and saw nothing, just greens and browns and mottled yellow where a few specks of sunlight fell through the dense foliage.

'Speak softly, don't whisper,' Jimmy said softly, not whispering. 'Whispers carry further. See the big forked tree to the left of the path?'

'Yes.'

'Three paces to the left and just behind it.'

Lance stared for a full minute and saw nothing. Then, suddenly, miraculously, as if it had just this moment appeared there, his eyes found the outline of the buck and separated it from the curves of light and shadow. It stood about three feet high and was no more than thirty feet away, standing poised, ears twitching in alarm, the large light-brown liquid eyes watchful. Lance knew he could not kill it. He stood to one side.

Jacques stepped up beside him and sighted along his rifle for a moment, then lowered the barrel.

'That's a doe,' Jimmy said.

'I noticed,' Jacques said drily.

'Let's find a buck then,' Lance said in his normal voice. There was a crashing in the undergrowth and the doe was gone as instantly as she had appeared to Lance. They stood for a moment in silence, looking in wonder at the blank greenery into which she had disappeared. There was silence.

They walked on. Jacques said, 'I don't actually like shooting animals. The thrill is stalking them and getting them in your sights with power of life or death at the squeeze of your finger. Heads on a wall, trophies, don't add anything to the thrill.'

Lance nodded. 'I can understand that. But we have to feed the skinners.' They walked silently away.

Jimmy held up his hand. This time it took Lance less time to distinguish the buck from the surrounding camouflage. It was a different species, bigger, with two thick stubby horns. It looked mean as hell to Lance as it butted the horns against a tree. Lance turned around to look at Jacques. Jacques shook his head; he didn't want to do the shooting.

Jimmy put his finger inside his shirt collar at the junction between his neck and shoulder and then tapped his heart. Lance understood: he should aim into the animal at an angle. He raised the rifle and aimed, waiting for the buck to move around until it was lined up for the shot. He breathed evenly for the minute he waited, then squeezed the trigger gently. The buck gave a small cry, reared up, and crashed to the ground. It had not shown the slightest sign of being aware of their presence. Lance wondered which way the wind was blowing. He felt no exultation, rather a sense of depressing let-down.

Jimmy examined the horns. 'An old one. Look at the scars on him. He's fought in many a mating season.'

Close-up the horns looked bigger and more dangerous, thick as Lance's wrist at their base. Lance felt their scaly texture. The points were not sharp but pointed enough to gore a man with the buck's three hundred pounds of mass behind them. It needed all the strength of the three of them to hoist the buck into the fork of a tree.

'How will we find it again?' Lance asked.

'We'll send the skinners for it, Mr Lance,' Jimmy said. 'I'll tell them where to find it.'

Lance looked around. Forest was forest, but he remembered how Ewart had apparently found two recognizable trees among the many beside hundreds of miles of road; he said nothing.

They waited for Jacques to relieve himself. Jacques zipped himself up and said, 'We're surrounded.'

'Who by?' Lance looked around, raising his rifle so that the barrel rested in the crook of his left arm as he had seen Ewart and the black men do.

'Pigmies.'

'What now?'

'You're leading the party. You decide.'

'Will they take the meat?'

Jimmy answered Lance. 'No, Mr Lance. The camp's not more than two hundred paces that way. The skinners will be here almost instantly.'

'Then we'll just carry on as before. Do you see them, Jimmy?'

'Yes.'

Lance stood beside Jimmy and followed his directions and found one of the watchers, a pot-bellied man about four feet tall with an evil wrinkled face. The black pinpoints of the eyes were staring straight at him. With one hand the pigmy held on to the tree he was in; in the other hand he carried a short length of tube.

'What's that he's holding?'

'Reed-section through which he blows poisoned darts. Some of the others have bows and arrows, also poisoned.'

Lance shivered. 'Let's go.' He willed himself to keep an even pace and not to look back. They had almost reached the camp, around which, Lance now understood, Jimmy had led them in a large curve, before his resolve broke and he looked back. There was nothing to see except trees. He wiped the sweat from his eyes but there was still nothing to see. Jacques did not seem disturbed but Jimmy was nervous, his smile gone. 'What is it, Jimmy?'

'Nothing, Mr Lance. I just don't like the little half-men. Poison darts and arrows . . .' Jimmy rippled all over in revulsion. 'They shoot for the back or, from the front, for the eyes. That poison comes from the black tree snake and there's no known antidote. It kills you excruciatingly and quite slowly.'

'Relatively slowly,' Jacques said as they reached the camp. 'Ten minutes or so. But there are lots of snake poisons that kill slower and only a very few that kill faster.'

'Like the green or black mamba, which takes only three minutes,' Lance said. Safe in the camp, he felt a sense of relief. 'Really Jimmy, you shouldn't exaggerate.' Jimmy gave him a disgusted look and shouted at one of his brothers to send the skinners for the buck.

Jacques laughed. 'It's not often you see one of Sambo's brothers off-balance. But I wouldn't rib him about it too much if I were you; you might start finding black tree snakes in your bed of an evening.'

Was Jacques making a threat? 'Those pigmies give me the shivers too.'

'They give everybody the shivers. Come on, let's have lunch.'

'Will they attack us?'

Jacques shrugged. 'They're unpredictable. You just have to be watchful.'

They sat down at the table. Ewart had overheard the last part of their conversation. 'They won't attack the camp. They might try their luck on small parties out in the open. Usually they'll take out the blacks first because the blacks are their age-old enemies. If you see a poison dart coming or a black man fall down for no reason, start spraying the trees on automatic.'

'Why don't we grab a few and make an example of them?' Briony asked. 'A sort of a preventive measure.'

Lance drew a sharp breath. Jesus, she was a nutter. True, the pigmies made him feel uncomfortable and might be dangerous but, what the hell, they'd done nothing so far but watch.

'That's sure to provoke an attack,' Ewart said. 'They have a very strong family and tribal structure. They'll just send for all the kinsmen of the dead ones and attack us in force.'

'Then kill all the ones here and the others won't know where to come.'

'It's not such a bad idea,' Jacques said, 'and Sambo and his men would love it. But there are perhaps fifteen or twenty pigmies out there and nobody could guarantee we'd get them all.'

'They're being watched,' Ewart said. 'I've also told the skinners that, if they want to keep working for us, they'll just have to ignore the pigmies. There's nothing more we can do now.'

Lance was aware that his mouth was hanging open in astonishment and closed it with conscious effort. To change the subject, he said, 'I've been thinking, Ewart. I could take over on the river this afternoon and you or Jacques can take a break.'

Ewart looked at him for what seemed an hour before he spoke. 'Can you handle it?'

'Sure. I wouldn't offer if I didn't think I could.'

'You're not getting contemptuously familiar with the jelly, are you?'

'No, I'm shitscared,' Lance said honestly.

'That's good. All right, you can take Jacques' shift this afternoon and mine the day after tomorrow.'

Lance broke out in a cold sweat. What had he committed himself to?

'He can take your shift this afternoon if you like,' Jacques said to Ewart. He held his hand above the table to show it was quite steady.

Ewart shook his head. 'No thanks.'

133

'What about me?' Briony asked. 'Can I go out on the river too?'

Ewart rose without answering. Jacques said, 'No.'

'*Kinder, Kirche, Kuche,*' Briony said sharply. Children, church and kitchen. 'You male chauvinist pig! My hands are at least as steady as yours.' She held them over the table to prove it.

Jacques rose and walked away. Briony stared after him with venom in her eyes.

'Are you nuts?' Lance asked her.

'I hear you're a gambler. You should understand. It's the highest game in town.'

'Huh?'

'You'll work it out.' She rose and walked away.

Lance went to the latrine trenches he'd had dug a little way from the camp and brought up his lunch. When he rose from the trench, Jimmy was standing a few yards away, talking to one of his brothers in their own language. He was carrying Lance's rifle.

'Your brother has ordered everyone to go armed,' Jimmy said.

Lance looked at the trees. He'd been in too much of a hurry to lose his lunch to think about the silent, unseen watchers. 'What's he doing here?'

'Watching the little pigs, Mr Lance,' Jimmy's brother said.

'Can you see them? How many are there?'

'This side I've counted nine.'

Lance took his rifle from Jimmy and looked through the scope.

'Look for a hard shape with a regular outline,' Jimmy said. 'Imagine the forest as a black and white picture so that the colours don't interfere.'

After several minutes Lance found first one pigmy and then several more until he could find five. They sat staring impassively into the barrel of his rifle, revolting little men with thick bellies and stick-arms and -legs. The other four

134

were pointed out to him and at length he found them among the foliage.

'They know we know they're there. Why don't they just bugger off?'

Jimmy's brother shrugged expressively and Jimmy said, 'Mr Lance, I can't even tell you what's in the mind of the skinners and they at least look a bit like me.'

'Yes, and those wee things don't.'

'It's the halfbreed bringing us bad luck,' Jimmy's brother said.

'Halfbreed?'

'Mr Roux's servant.'

'Pietie? He's harmless.'

'Halfbreeds are always bad luck,' Jimmy's brother persisted.

Lance didn't know what to say. 'Are you coming on the river with me?' he asked Jimmy.

Jimmy's smile broadened. 'Yes.'

'You seem pretty happy about it.' Lance looked towards the trench where he had left his lunch.

'It has to be safer than supervising that blockhead Ben and his happy crew while they're making the nitro,' Jimmy said with a chuckle. 'Anyway, if we kill ourselves on the river, we have only ourselves to blame. But what shall I tell the ancestors if I die through the stupidity of the lowborn likes of Ben?'

Jimmy and his brother laughed at this. Lance smiled with them. As they walked back to the camp he asked Jimmy, 'Do your ancestors require you to control the manner of your death?'

'No, Mr Lance, no such thing!' Jimmy was genuinely shocked. 'The ancestors control both life and death. I mean, I should know better, being mission-educated and all that, but it's in the black man's heritage, this dependency on his tribe and his ancestors. It absolves him of personal responsibility.'

Lance laughed hearily, the afternoon's work

momentarily forgotten. 'If Mr Roux hadn't said something similar, I would've thought you were having me on again, Jimmy, you sounded so pompous.'

They took the skiff out on the water and Lance practised with the throttles until he could make the boat move with minimal disturbance to the water. It was a lot more difficult than it seemed when Ewart or Jacques were doing it. They fetched an empty bottle and filled it with water and practised lowering it slowly into the river. When they were certain they would not blow themselves up, Lance went to fetch Ewart, who was resting in his tent. Lance was still carrying the bottle filled with water. He winked at Jimmy and rolled it through the flap of Ewart's tent. They watched as Ewart gingerly picked up the bottle and brought it outside with him. Ewart unscrewed the top, dipped his finger in the contents and tasted it. He was not amused.

'I expect you to set a better example than playing dangerous practical jokes,' he said to Lance.

'Yes, but . . .'

'That's all. Let's go, we have work to do.'

On the skiff, chugging upriver, Lance said, 'Humourless bastard.'

Jimmy was more contrite. 'He's probably worried the Bens of this world will emulate you, only with the real stuff inside the bottle.'

Lance was hurt but forgot about it when his glance fell on the half pound bottles of nitroglycerine standing in near rows in the boxes at their feet. 'Watch our for logs,' he told Jimmy. 'If this stuff goes off your ancestors will get you as vapour floating on the air.'

Jimmy's smile was noticeably subdued. 'I heard you volunteered for the job, Mr Lance.'

'I couldn't very well not offer,' Lance said ruefully. 'My brother's helping me get out of trouble so I can't let him do all the dangerous work.'

'The noble die young.'

'You'll go with me.'

'Our men say you're lucky, just like your brother.'

'Sambo says my brother is a good planner. Nothing to do with luck.'

'Lots to do with survival. This is far enough, Mr Lance.'

Lance brought the skiff to a complete halt, the propeller just turning over to prevent the current sweeping it along. Jimmy took the controls. Lance knelt on the deck and moved his knees apart for a firm stance. Who would ever have thought *knees* could get sweaty? He wiped his wet palms on his shirt and carefully took one bottle out of the foam-lined compartment, handling it by the lid rather than the string to prevent it banging against the other bottles. Once he had the bottle clear of the box, he studied the surface of the water but could find no obvious current though there was a small lacy point of bubbles at the bow of the skiff. He took the string right up near the bottle in his one hand and paid it out hand over hand. When the bottle was near the water he leant forward to put more distance between it and the boat. The bottle started swinging alarmingly and he heard Jimmy draw a deep breath. The very sounds of the jungle and the river seemed suspended. Lance wanted to throw the string from him but held his hand steady: whether the bottle struck the boat or the water they'd be equally dead.

The bottle swung within an inch of the boat, then away again, the bottom no more than an inch from the water. If Lance had jerked his hand the momentum added would have swung the bottle into the side of the skiff.

Minutes, perhaps hours, a purgatory later the bottle hung straight and still from the string. Lance couldn't actually see it because of the sweat burning in his eyes.

'How far is it from the water?'

Jimmy expelled his breath with a sigh. 'It's still an inch or so from the water. You can't see it?'

'I got sweat in my eyes.'

'Haul it back in, Mr Lance.'

Lance considered. 'No, chances are I'll bash it against the side. Can you reach to wipe my eyes?'

'No. I'll tell you when the bottle touches the water.'

'All right, hold her steady.' Slowly, excruciatingly, Lance let the now wet and rough string pass through his sweaty hands. He felt a lightening of the load a moment before Jimmy spoke.

'Now!'

Lance paid out more string, a fingerbreadth at a time until, a misspent lifetime later, the line went slack. He wiggled the line gently to make sure the bottle was settled on the bottom, then leant over to place the line gently on the water.

His eyes burning fiercely, he nearly fell back into the boat as fast as he could. He remembered the box of bottled nitro behind him and forced himself to move slowly. When he was sitting up and had felt all round him to make sure he would bump nothing, he wiped his eyes with the sodden sleeves of his shirt. It wasn't much of an improvement but at least it eased the pain while he got his handkerchief from his pocket. When he had wiped the worst of the sweat from his eyes, he leant forward to scoop up some water to rinse his eyes; they were still burning furiously.

Lance's hand was cupped, poised to swoop into the water, his mind already accepting the cool balm to his eyes.

'No, Mr Lance, No!' Jimmy said in an urgent low voice.

Lance was startled and nearly lost his balance. He toppled forward, remembered what happened when the water was disturbed after it was mined with the nitro, imagined the effect the wash of water from his body's fall into the river would have on the fragile skiff and the volatile nitro inside. He grasped the side of the skiff with one hand and fought the panic as he hovered over the water, slowly and surely bringing his other hand to the rim as well. He saw his whitened knuckles against the fibreglass. He wanted to vomit but even the vomit falling in the water could bring disaster. He could hold it no longer and opened his mouth. The spasms shook him and he retched emptily, nothing coming out.

After a while he levered himself upright. He sat for a while to regain his composure, then took his handkerchief from his pocket and spat on it. He wiped his eyes as best he could.

'All right, Jimmy, take us to the next spot,' he said, his voice ringing hollowly in his own ears. What did it sound like to Jimmy?

'Are you all right?' Ewart asked as Lance brought the skiff cautiously to the bank of the river. For the last two hours Ewart, having finished mining his section of the river, had been standing on the side, watching Lance and Jimmy finish the last part of their section.

Lance stepped ashore from the nose of the skiff and helped Jimmy draw it gently from the water. Two blacks carried it away. Only then did Lance answer his brother. 'Yes. I'll throw the log.' He owed it to himself, to his pride, to see this through to the end.

'The oilskins are over there.'

Lance looked down at his clothes. There was not a single inch that wasn't black with sweat. Even his chukka boots, mustard-yellow when he had put them on this morning, were dark brown and he could feel the sweat squelching between his toes inside his socks. 'Don't worry about oilskins. Let's just have the safety harness.'

The harness was brought. Lance's hands were shaking so much that he had to ask Jimmy's help in buckling it up. Jimmy fumbled for a long time; his hands, too, were shaking, though not as uncontrollably as Lance's. Everybody else politely seemed not to notice. Lance stood behind the tree he had selected and looked back to see that everybody else was clear. He tugged at the harness to make certain it was secure. He swung the log Ewart had given him and let go. Immediately there was a hollow roaring in his ears and an oppressive weight rolled over him. He choked and spat out water. He was supposed to do something now. What the devil was it? Dreamily he looked up-river. The backwash!

He tried to run further from the river. The harness held him. He fumbled with it, relaxed, took a deep breath and stepped closer to the trunk to give it more slack. It snapped free. Over the roaring of the river he could hear them shouting at him from behind. Bugger them, he was moving as fast as he could.

He was sprinting up the slight incline, not remembering how he had started, no memory of acceleration, he was just running faster than he had ever run. 'A blinding sprinter, flashing into instant action, barging his mass through the slightest chink in the defence,' one rugger commentator had said of him.

They were still shouting. Yes, the backwash. He looked to his left. Jesus! The wall of water was much taller than he remembered, several times his own height. He stumbled over a root and fell against a tree. He flung his arms around the tree and held on for dear life. The water smashed his face into the tree and branches crashed into his body. When he could not hold any longer, he let go and was swept round the tree. Even as he stumbled along he felt the water rushing down his legs as if he were standing in a bathtub with the plug out. He turned to look.

Rushing towards him in the knee-high water was a crocodile, its jaws gaping to take him. He shuddered and tried to move but his feet were stuck in the mud and his knees were weak. The crocodile was diving for his ankles though, Lance thought with surprising clarity, the jaws opened wide enough to snap him in two at the waistline. The crocodile advanced inexorably forward and down. Lance was totally detached, wondering if it would help to scream. But he was too tired for the effort of screaming.

The crocodile's lower jaw struck the top of his shoe

where it stuck out of the mud. The water had passed. The crocodile stared up at him with bulging eyes and a foul smell came from somewhere inside it. Lance pulled one foot out of the mud and fell over backwards. He lay there, looking at the sky through branches the water had stripped the leaves from until Jimmy came to help him up.

He was savouring the feeling of ten miles of the huge river reaching for the sky when he chucked a small log. He had done it, made the jelly, mined the river, blown it up, killed among others the evil crocodile at his feet.

Briony was right. It was the biggest game in town.

Ten miles upriver the next day Lance saw his first live crocodile. He had chosen and cleared a site opposite a short spit sticking out into the river. When they had sweated the jelly, they carried it on to the spit and placed the bottles round the trunk of a tree standing right in its centre. It was just after midday, nearly lunchtime, and the others had just arrived from the previous camp down-river and were walking down to the river from the new camp-site. Lance saw them out of the corner of his eye as he rose from putting down a jar of nitro. But his attention was taken by the flash of sunlight on something black and slimy hanging from a branch of the tree about three feet in front of him and directly over Ben's bulging backside as the black man bent over to settle another jar of nitro firmly in the mossy grass. For a moment he was nonplussed, then he saw the small beady eyes, the fangs in the open mouth, the flickering forked tongue. Snake!

It was like yesterday on the river, all over again. Lance willed himself not to move.

'Stand very still, Ben. Don't move. Jimmy, tell him not to move.'

The head wavered between Ben's backside and Lance's face. Snakes don't see too well, Lance thought, but now I've attracted this one by the sound of my voice.

Jimmy snapped something in his own language and Ben

141

froze, only his hands moving, inching away from the jar of explosive he had just put down.

'Is it dangerous, Jimmy?'

'Fatal, Mr Lance. It's a black tree snake.'

'Well, shoot it!' Lance was looking straight at the snake. It had turned its slim tapered head towards him and was staring at him, shooting its tongue rapidly towards him.

'Don't speak, Mr Lance,' Jimmy said softly, 'and stand perfectly still. If I move it might strike you.'

Lance stood as still as he could. Hours seemed to pass though he knew it was only seconds. Out of the periphery of his vision he saw Ewart and Jacques and Sambo and some other black men stop twenty feet away and keep perfectly still. He let his breath out very slowly and breathed in as slowly as he could, resisting the urgent need to gasp air. Fatal. No antidote. The poison the pigmies put on their arrows. An excruciating death. The snake had the most elegant muscular control, curving the three feet of its body hanging from the branch ever so slowly towards him, nearer and nearer. Its head weaved from side to side as if it were trying to get a better look at him. There was a pain in his back from the unnatural half-erect position he was holding.

Ben's nerve broke. He dived sideways and, fast as he moved through the air, the snake was faster, striking at his shoulder in a long swooping curve of its free-hanging forepart.

Lance threw himself backwards and rolled up against Jimmy's legs. He heard the clatter of Jimmy's machine pistol on automatic and saw the snake cut in two, the tail still wrapped around the tree, the head falling straight for the jars of nitro. Necrorevenge, Lance thought. The head-part fell in a curve around a jar. Lance prayed no spent bullet would fall on a jar of jelly only ten feet from him. He saw Ben staggering backwards to the edge of the spit. He saw with horror the crack appearing at Ben's feet and the ground breaking away, taking Ben with it into the river. He crawled quickly to where Ben had fallen in, the echo of the shots still in his ears. People were shouting at him, they were always shouting at him.

Ben was floundering in the water, obviously unable to swim. He was still alive! The snake had missed.

'Grab that log!' Lance shouted at him but no sound came from his dry mouth, his tongue sticking to his palate.

He remembered the 'log' he had seen on his first day on the Obangui, the one Jimmy had said was a crocodile. The log near Ben was a crocodile!

Without thinking, Lance jumped into the water and started swimming towards Ben. As he reached Ben, he clearly heard Jacques say, 'Bloody idiot, the man's as good as dead.'

One of Ben's flailing arms struck him stunningly across the ear and for a moment he went under. He came up spluttering, spitting water. Ben was trying to grab him. The 'log' was nosing towards them, a small wake streaming from it. He trod water, drew breath, went under in Ben's arms, then propelled himself upwards and flung his arms up inside Ben's to break the drowning man's hold. His right forearm struck Ben under the chin, more by luck than design, and knocked him out.

The crocodile was only ten feet away, coming smooth and fast and straight towards them. Lance could see the individual scales stretching back from the nose-holes, the bulging eyes gliding along in the water behind with no visible connection. He flung Ben's arm over his shoulder and struck out for the water's edge. With only one free hand and his two feet it was slow going. Why the hell didn't they shoot the fucking crocodile from where they stood on the bank? How near was the thing? He couldn't look back without stopping and then he and Ben would both sink.

He turned his head out of the water to gasp a breath and saw Jacques running to his left along the bank, working the bolt of the rifle in his hands. Head under, forward motion, his heart was going to burst, head up on the other side to rasp air into his lungs: Ewart running to his right along the bank, hands busy on the rifle in his hands, looking over his shoulder at the water. Of course, they couldn't shoot over his head because the angle was too acute, they might hit him or Ben. So they were trying for a sideways shot.

That also told him how near the crocodile was. Lance instinctively drew his knees up under him in a foetal position before he realized the futility of it and kicked out again. Was there a thrashing in the water behind him?

He kicked out with both legs together and touched the mud underneath the water. A few kicks and his feet sank exhaustedly, of their own accord, to the mud. He could barely stay up under Ben's weight. He looked over his shoulder, not really caring if the crocodile took him now. He saw the open jaws, monstrous, the razor teeth, the rough texture even inside the mouth of the animal, whiffed the smell of carrion, saw the spurts in the upper palate as the two bullets hit separately but simultaneously, tearing a huge thick chunk right through the crocodile's skull. The crocodile thrashed once and Lance watched with detached interest, something happening not to himself but to some anonymous person, as the tail curved round to strike his legs from under him.

He drew a deep breath just as he went under and came up swimming, Ben still hanging like a wet weight around his neck. Willing hands helped drag him and Ben on to the bank just as Ben's arms tightened around his neck.

'Aagh . . . choking me . . . you stupid . . .'

They pulled Ben from him. The black man hadn't regained consciousness. He was convulsing.

Lance lay on the ground and watched over his own heaving chest as Ewart knelt beside Ben and, instructing Sambo and his brothers to hold a thrashing leg and arm each, ripped open Ben's shirt. The fang marks were two tiny pinpricks but around them a purple swelling had already developed on Ben's smooth black skin.

Ewart stood up, shaking his head. There was no point in even bringing the snake-bite kit. The poison had already reached every part of Ben's body. He was as good as dead.

'You did him a kindness, knocking him out,' Jacques said to Lance. 'But next time save your heroics for those who stand a chance of living.'

Lance looked away from the heaving body of Ben – lifting Sambo, sitting on his chest, high with each convulsion – to the river and saw two scaly tails flash as a live crocodile took the dead one to rot under a concave bank until it would be decayed enough to be edible. This afternoon you too will be dead, he thought with satisfaction, hating all crocodiles.

The tortured nerve ends had broken through Ben's unconsciousness. He screamed, an awful drawn-out sound, arching his back so violently that the hefty Sambo fell from his chest. One of Sambo's men drew a knife from the sheath at his side and gave it, handle first, to Sambo. Sambo thoughtfully ran his thumb along the blade. Everybody looked the other way, except Lance, who only realized what was happening as it was being done. Sambo looked at the men holding the arms and legs of their dying comrade. They nodded. Sambo plunged the knife into Ben's heart just as he reared up again and withdrew the knife immediately to slice through his throat. There were a few weak spurts of blood and then Ben lay still, a huge bulk of nothing.

Lance reflected on the days Ben had spent at the dangerous task of sweating nitroglycerine from dynamite, surviving to die of snakebite. Sambo had not killed him. Sambo had done Ben the kindness of releasing him from unbearable pain.

Ben had played in the biggest game in town, won a fortune, and been run over as he crossed the street to bank his winnings.

BRUUN

Bruun came on the seventh day, their day of rest after six days of killing crocodiles.

In the morning Ewart took Lance hunting with him. Jimmy and Kombi, another of Sambo's brothers, went with them. Lance noticed that they moved very quietly for such large men. Under his own feet twigs were always popping like gunshots. Only a hundred paces from the camp, Ewart stopped the party to show Lance a dikdik doe and her calf. The doe stood no more than twelve inches off the ground and the calf, already two months old, was no larger than Lance's hand. The doe had seen them and was frantically nudging the playful calf into the protective bushes.

'The dikdik is synonymous with cowardice for many Africans,' Ewart said as the doe finally succeeded in nudging her calf into the safety of invisibility. 'Yet even a dikdik will not desert its young.'

Soon afterwards they found a large buck which Ewart shot without breaking stride; even after it had fallen Lance took some time to find it in the undergrowth. A monkey swinging down on to a low branch to satisfy its curiosity helped him. They left the buck lying and walked on.

'Are the pigmies still here?' Lance asked.

'Four, maybe five, following us,' Ewart said. 'There are fewer at the camp than when they started watching us. They've lost interest and started wandering away.'

'Or to fetch more for an attack,' Lance said, shivering. He could not forget Ben's horrible death from the same snake poison on the pigmy's darts.

'Possibly,' Ewart shrugged. 'I'll worry about that when

149

it happens. Meanwhile we'll keep a watch on those who remain.'

A quarter of an hour later Kombi touched Ewart on the shoulder and pointed. Ewart nodded and they advanced slowly. 'Do you want it?' Ewart asked Lance.

'I can't even see it. I don't much like shooting animals, even for the pot,' Lance admitted.

Ewart nodded. 'Okay, Jimmy, you get it.'

Lance watched as Jimmy went forward, seemingly casually and quickly, but soundlessly. In less than twenty feet Jimmy had disappeared among the trees in a second when Lance's attention wandered momentarily. There was a shot and Lance found Jimmy by the direction of the sound. They walked forward. Jimmy had shot a wild goat that must have stood four feet at the shoulders.

Jimmy was looking at a tree not too far away. 'Would you like a belt of black tree snake skin, Mr Lance?'

'You shot that snake up too badly to make even a small purse out of the skin,' Lance said.

'There's another one, about fifteen feet away,' Jimmy said. 'On that branch just under the rot-mark on the tree.'

Lance found the snake and reflexively brought his rifle up.

'Just shoot its head off, sir,' Kombi said.

The snake was raising its head from the trunk to wave it around in a slow circle, trying to find the direction of the disturbance its vibration sensors had detected. The head was the thinnest part of the body. Lance aimed carefully, controlling the shiver of revulsion. The bullet separated the head from the body. The body uncoiled from the trunk like a released spring and fell to the ground. Jimmy picked up the writhing body and knotted it around his waist. With his boot he squashed the head into pulp. The black body was still twitching spasmodically when they reached the camp. Jimmy immediately slit it down its length and separated the skin. He scraped the skin clean and hung it up to dry while Lance watched, fascinated.

150

Lance wondered whether he could ever bring himself to wear the belt.

After lunch Sambo came to their table and stood a few feet away until Ewart nodded at him. 'The men are wondering if you would sing for them, sir.'

Ewart nodded, thanked Briony for lunch and rose. He walked away with Sambo.

'Entertaining kaffirs!' Briony sneered.

'I didn't know Ewart could sing,' Lance said.

'Sambo meant tell them a story,' Jacques enlightened him. 'Come on, we'll listen. Ewart's quite a military historian, an expert on decisive engagements. Also on the history of the Zulu warrior chiefs. Are you coming, Briony?'

She shook her head.

'Suit yourself. He's not going to give you a command performance later, you know. And he's worth listening to.'

Lance sat on the mossy grass with Jacques, Jimmy as always behind his right shoulder. In front of them, with his back to them, Ewart sat on his haunches, smoking a cigarillo. In front of him Sambo and his brothers sat on their haunches and behind them in a half-circle those of the men not watching the pigmies. They were chattering softly and even Sambo had a smile on his face. A respectful distance behind them the skinners stood in a silent semicircle, their eyes cast down.

Ewart finished his cigarillo and looked at Sambo.

'Dien Bien Phu,' one of Sambo's brothers suggested deferentially.

'The slaughter of the Matabele by Chaka Zulu,' another said. The men behind him murmured approval.

'Rorke's Drift,' Jimmy, in his turn, called softly.

'Rorke's Drift is good,' Sambo said judicially. 'If that is what is in your mind, sir. All your songs stir the blood.'

'Today Rorke's Drift is in my mind,' Ewart said.

Lance had a feeling of an intricate formal ballet; every

151

move in its time and its place. Ewart waited a while, gathering his thoughts while the men became silent and attentive. 'Ceteswayo, King of the Zulus, called his impis before him,' he said at last.

Without looking backwards, Sambo called a translation over his shoulder to the skinners and their headman translated. There was at least a minute of chatter, then silence. 'He was disturbed at the inroads the British had made into his land.' Another pause for translation and discussion. Another sentence. Another pause. It was a slow process.

'This will go on all afternoon,' Lance said. He had seen the film with Michael Caine and Stanley Baker.

'It is the way my people tell a story,' Jimmy said with dignity.

Lance waited for Ewart to progress another sentence, then said, 'I know all about Rorke's Drift. Next time we should get him to tell of the slaughter of the Matabele. I've heard of it but not the details.'

'Part of the pleasure for my people is the anticipation of what is yet to come in a well-known tale,' Jimmy said. 'But the slaughter of the Matabele, now there's a thing.' He waited for Ewart's next sentence. 'I have never understood why white people make such a fuss about a mere six million Jews. Tens of millions of Matabele were slaughtered. By comparison to Chaka Zulu, Hitler was a kindergarten bully.'

Jacques held his hands apart, then brought them closer together. 'Perspective of time. Hitler is nearer to us than Chaka. Also, the Jews were white and lived amongst us.'

'History is history,' Jimmy said. 'What the ancestors did the ancestors did.'

Jacques shook his head. 'That's just clever-nigger talk, Jimmy. Fancy tautologies won't obscure the fact that the black man has a total sense of history which the so-called sophisticated white man has lost.'

They listened to Ewart for several sentences while

Lance wondered what 'tautologies' were. He was too drowsy to ask.

'All right, Mr Roux, I'm sorry,' Jimmy said at last. 'But what has it benefited us?'

'Contentment for the simpler ones.' Jacques waved his hand to indicate the men beyond Ewart. They were expressing surprise and delight at the defence Hook was putting up in the hospital room of the post, as told by Ewart. 'But that's not really the question. The point is, what has the fragmented view of history held by the white man cost him?'

'Aha!' Jimmy said appreciatively. 'Cause means responsibility and responsibility means guilt.'

'You mean the history they teach in school is what fucks up the minds of white people?' Lance said.

'Inelegantly put but absolutely correct,' Jacques said.

'But you said – '

' – that the blacks do not know personal causation and therefore personal responsibility. I stated it as a fact, neither approving or disapproving,' Jacques said. He waited for Ewart to finish another sentence. 'It is simply a different way.'

'But Jimmy, and Sambo, and the other brothers are responsible men.' Lance was embarrassed at the turn the conversation had taken in Jimmy's presence but he could not stop himself.

'They've had our culture impressed on them. They're only a few. Look at those skinners.'

Lance lay back and closed his eyes. 'The hell with your metaphysics.' His roommate was fond of the word. 'I'm going to sleep.'

'The question,' said Jimmy, 'you seem to be implying, is not whether the westernized black is a better man but whether he is a happier man. Sir.'

Lance half-listened to Jacques and Jimmy laying into do-gooders, missionaries and misdirected liberals, and half to Ewart's tale of the defence by the British against

153

the Zulu attack on the post at Rorke's Drift. He had to admire the way Ewart used short, simple sentences to weave a spell that conjured up the beleaguered soldiers and the fanatical attacks by the Zulu impis throwing themselves on the rifles again and again. Eleven Victoria Crosses were won that day and night, more than in any other single engagement before or since, Ewart concluded. The men sat silently for a long time. There was no applause. Finally Ewart rose and there was a murmur of gratitude as the men rose with him. They were still standing there in the glow of a tale well told – Lance wondering how it was that his brother had ever learnt to tell a tale so well – when the whistle split the air. It trilled and rose and fell, a code.

Lance opened his eyes to see the men stiffening. The skinners, sensing the tension, were melting away to their lean-to shelters of leafy branches.

Sambo cradled his machine pistol across his chest, his ear cocked to the air as his eyes flickered across his men to make sure they were all armed. The forest had suddenly gone silent. Lance involuntarily looked up to see if there were thunder clouds. The sky was a clear blue, the rain yet an hour away. He rolled over and rose.

'Armed men crossing the river,' Sambo said.

A parrot called. Lance jumped. It broke the spell.

'Sambo, make sure the men watching the pigmies remain at their posts,' Ewart said. 'The rest of you spread out a bit and carry on as before but keep your arms to hand.'

Lance nervously took his rifle from Jimmy. Ewart saw this and said, 'Chances are it's a friendly visit. Everybody goes armed around here. And they're not approaching by stealth.'

'Better safe than sorry.'

'Of course,' Ewart said easily. 'Just don't shoot first, eh?'

'Sure,' Lance said evenly, but Ewart was already walk-

154

ing across the camp to the first trees. Lance followed him and so did Jacques. They stopped behind Ewart and Jacques moved off to one side. Jimmy tugged Lance to the other side. 'A bit over here, Mr Lance. If we stand too close together we make a target.'

They heard the visitors before they saw them, chatting casually in a tongue strange to Lance. Then they came through the trees, twelve black men in khaki fatigues that were torn and none too clean. Their rifles were slung over their shoulders and they carried no packs. Behind them came Bruun, swaggering in a lightweight white cotton uniform that was stained at the collar, underarms, cuffs, fly and turn-ups.

Lance, remembering the beating Bruun had administered to him in Lubumbashi, suddenly did want to shoot first. The barrel of his rifle rested in his left elbow as he tracked Bruun with it but Bruun paid him no attention. Jimmy murmured something behind him; he didn't catch it but it sounded savage.

'Yes,' Lance said softly, 'but wouldn't it be a pleasure.' Behind him Jimmy chuckled. Lance uncurled his finger from the trigger. The safety was still on. He looked over his shoulder at Jimmy; the black man was not smiling and his eyes were red. Lance decided he would not like to be hated by Jimmy: Jimmy was far too intelligent and wily and determined to have as an enemy.

'Who but Teddy Bruun leads his forces from behind?' Ewart said in greeting, making a show of lowering the machine pistol in his hands.

'Colonel Bruun, Commander-in-Chief of the Armed Forces of His Royal Highness Lobengula the Fourth.'

'Jesus!' Jacques said mockingly between his teeth.

'You do keep turning up like a bad penny,' Ewart said.

Bruun went red in the face and his chest swelled. He made an obvious effort to control himself.

'Temper, Teddy, temper,' Ewart said, watching with interest and obviously enjoying himself.

155

'You, Weber, are one of the few men in the world who unfailingly makes me vindictive,' Bruun said between clenched teeth.

'Me and everybody else.'

Bruun walked past Ewart into the camp and stopped at the head of his men. He inspected the armed men surrounding them and smiled carefully. 'I'm here on official business with only a token force. I have more men across the river.'

Ewart nodded to show he had taken the point.

'I should have known it could only be you who would blow up ten miles of the river all at once,' Bruun said. 'But I never thought you'd even get this far, not with all that lovely dynamite you were carrying.'

'You didn't give your friends enough advance warning to mount a proper attack on us,' Jacques said. 'They sent the second team and held us up for about an hour until Lance here disintegrated the head of their only decent shot.'

'The boy, eh? Cast in the mould of his big brother. Bygones.' Bruun waved away the past with a flick of his hand, the finger Lance had broken standing stiff in its splint.

Lance's hand clenched around the trigger guard of his rifle, the barrel pointing straight at Bruun, the man who had been directly responsible for the killing of that man and his bad dreams. Behind him Jimmy cleared his throat nervously. 'It's on safety,' Lance assured him.

'Since I come on official business and in a spirit of friendship,' Bruun said, 'how about offering me a drink?'

As one man Ewart and Jacques turned their backs on Bruun and took seats at the table. Bruun sighed loudly, theatrically and waddled over to sit down between them.

Bruun's men had formed up in a hollow square and were looking apprehensively at the armed men around them. A few had unslung their rifles and others were fiddling nervously with their shoulder straps.

156

Bruun coughed apologetically. 'Your men are making mine nervous. You know kaffirs, they get twitchy and then they start shooting for no reason at all.'

Ewart waved a hand and immediately his men melted away. Bruun's men broke into relieved chatter and those who had unslung their rifles shouldered them again.

'You mean you didn't train them too well,' Ewart said.

Bruun shrugged, his uniform rippling with the fat on his belly. 'I've only had the job six months or so. There comes a point at which further training is wasted on kaffir gun-fodder.'

Pietie brought a bottle and some glasses to the table on a tray. There was silence while Jacques poured without asking Bruun if the liquor was to his taste. When they all had glasses, they drank and then looked at Bruun.

Bruun raised his eyes to the trees.

'Get to the point, Bruun,' Jacques said.

'My spies tell me you have taken many truckloads of crocodile skins from the river. Is that true?'

'Yes. It is also no business of yours.'

'But I'm afraid it is my business. You will be taking more skins?'

'Yes. Get to the point.'

From the way Ewart was letting Jacques handle the conversation, Lance had already formed the opinion that this was a matter of bribery rather than one of their safety. Bruun's next words proved him correct.

'You are trespassing on the Imperial Hunting Preserves of His Royal Highness Lobengula the Fourth without permission. For this permission you must pay tribute to him and tithe me for my protection against the manifold dangers that lurk in these forests – ' Bruun paused to wave a hand at the forest ' – part of the great and irreplaceable wealth you are gathering.'

Jacques laughed. 'Colonel Theodore Bruun, Comman-der-in-Chief of the Armed Forces of His Royal Highness Lobengula the Fourth and Protector of the Imperial

Hunting Preserves. You are nothing but a grandly styled petty brigand.' His voice hardened. 'Perhaps you'd like to give me one good reason why I shouldn't sick the central government, from whom I have a licence to hunt these crocodiles, on to you for attempted extortion.'

Bruun stretched, an unedifying spectacle as it drew the dark patches in his armpits to the attention. 'You have no licence from the Central African Republic. All you have is an understanding with certain politicians. If I were to tell these politicians of the great wealth you're taking from the river . . . My merit is that I'm cheaper than they.'

There was silence for a while. Jacques poured more liquor in his own glass and Ewart's. When he put the bottle on the table, Bruun helped himself without asking. He was now in perfect control of himself, his face pink rather than red, malevolence rather than rage emanating from him.

'What,' Ewart asked conversationally, 'is to prevent us from killing you where you sit and your men where they stand?'

'I don't think you could,' Bruun said smugly.

Ewart smiled tightly. 'Bruun, you aren't worth shit as a soldier yourself. But a Sandhurst man cannot fail to see the difference between a good soldier and a massacre waiting to happen. Look at my men and then look at yours.'

Bruun giggled delightedly. 'That insult will cost you an extra truckload of skins.' He looked over his shoulder. 'I think your faithful Sergeant Sambo is coming to tell you something.'

Sambo came up to the table and gave Ewart a smart military salute. Ewart nodded. There was silence. Even the buzzing insects of the forest were quiet for a moment.

'We're surrounded,' Ewart said to Bruun.

'Quite so,' Bruun said, satisfaction mingling with disappointment that Ewart had not heard it from one of his own.

158

'Dismiss, Sergeant,' Ewart said calmly. Sambo walked away.

Lance felt a pricking on the back of his neck. He slowly turned a full circle, scanning the trees and the undergrowth. As he had expected, he saw nothing.

'Is he bluffing, Jimmy?'

'Unfortunately, I don't think so, Mr Lance. You won't see his men because they'll be quite far away, beyond the pigmies, but near enough to close in and cut us down in this clearing if they are summoned by a shot or a whistle or something.'

'All right, Bruun, state your price,' Ewart said.

'Three truckloads to recompense His Royal Highness for the devastation you have wrought in the Imperial Hunting Preserve. One truckload to tithe me for my protection. And,' Bruun added with a fat chuckle, 'one truckload for the insult you paid me earlier. Five truckloads in all. With the trucks of course.'

Lance gasped. It was almost everything they had risked their lives to take from the river and this revolting man was laughing while he demanded it all be handed over to him, complete with transport.

Ewart and Jacques looked impassively at their unwelcome visitor, nothing showing on their faces, both sitting at ease.

'Be grateful,' Bruun said portentously to Jacques, 'that I do not demand another truckload for your insult to me. But I think I've proved that there's nothing petty about me.'

'All that remains is for him to prove that he's human,' Lance said bitterly to Jimmy.

'"Petty" is inaccurate anyway,' Briony said clearly from where she stood watching on the other side of the table. '"Gross" would be more like it.'

Bruun stood. 'I shall take my skins and go before the insults of women and children cost you more than you can afford.'

Lance had thought he was pitching his voice too low for Bruun to hear.

'Lance,' Ewart said, 'make sure there's ten gallons of fuel in each of the trucks Teddy will be taking. We don't want him to get stuck on the road and rob somebody who can afford it less than we can. Or, worse still, to return here.'

Bruun stretched again. 'If I had an extra driver, I'd take one of your tankers as well.' He turned to Lance. 'You heard. Get going, boy.'

Lance was shaking with rage. He was about to storm Bruun and butt him in the stomach with his head when Jimmy took his elbow in a firm grip.

'Try it, boy,' Bruun said, licking his lips, 'You, Nigger, let him go.'

'Go on, Lance,' Ewart said. 'See to the trucks. Don't let this scum get to you.'

Lance stubbed his toe on a log as Jimmy led him away. For the first time in his life he knew what it meant to be blind with rage. Behind him he heard Bruun laugh mirthlessly.

'Why did you hold me?' he raged at Jimmy.

Jimmy let his elbow go. 'Wrong time, wrong place, Mr Lance. But your time and place will come, I know it.'

'Black man's magic, shit!'

Jimmy shrugged. 'You had it all worked out?'

'Yeah. Funny thing.' Lance's anger had gone as quickly as it had come. 'I could think quite clearly. I was going to butt him in that fat stomach of his and wind him and then I was going to stomp him only but good.'

'You wait for that pleasure until you're wearing hard, studded boots, Mr Lance.' Sambo said. He had been following them. 'In those yellow desert boots you'll break your toes and if you're really angry you'll never even know it. I've seen it happen. I'll take Ben's place until you can find a man to replace him.'

Lance would never have believed, had he been told

160

before today, that rage could affect him like that. He kept the thought to himself; he didn't want to appear any more naive to Sambo and Jimmy than he had already. 'Thanks, Sambo.' He noticed that the other tanker men were following them.

All the trucks loaded with crocodile skins had ample fuel in their tanks. Lance saw the men looking expectantly at him. He had an idea 'You men fuel the rest of the trucks and the Landrover,' he said to them. As they walked away, he touched Sambo's shoulder to restrain him. He turned around so that he could face Jimmy as well. 'We can't immobilize the trucks here because then we'll be attacked. But what's to stop us rigging things so they don't get too far down the road?'

Jimmy's smile broadened. 'Water in the tanks, or sugar, or just a few strands of these ferns.' He plucked a handful from a bush beside him.

Sambo shook his head sombrely. 'They will know what happened and be alert against attack then.'

Lance had not thought that far. 'I have no intention of attacking somebody's official soldiers. But if they rob me, surely I can cause them some inconvenience until I can seek redress in the courts.'

Sambo and Jimmy looked at Lance strangely and then looked at the ground. For a moment he thought it was because of his pompous phrasing, then he realized the truth: 'You mean my brother is already planning to attack the soldiers and take the skins back? You must be mad!'

'He has said nothing yet of an attack,' Sambo said reasonably.

'But this thing will be settled one way or the other long before it gets to any court. By force?'

Sambo looked at the ground again. Jimmy said, 'In this part of Africa there aren't any courts you can take this kind of thing to.' He dropped the handful of fern leaves to the ground, his smile gone.

Lance felt the rage rising in him again. Bruun would

161

take their skins and go. There were no courts in which they could get compensation. It was unthinkable to attack the armed forces of any properly constituted authority, however despicable. His legs felt weak. He sat down on the running-board of the cab and looked up at Sambo and Jimmy. They were acutely uncomfortable, the normally self-possessed Jimmy shuffling his feet in embarrassment.

'All right,' Lance said savagely, 'I'm naive. This is Africa, deepest Africa, and I'm out of my depth. But I assure you neither my brother nor Mr Roux will even consider attacking the soldiers of another nation, no matter that they be thieves.'

Jimmy shuffled some more. Was there a gleam of pity in his eyes? Sambo opened his mouth to say something, thought better of it, and closed his mouth again.

Lance decided to say no more. He felt drained. He rose. 'Come on, let's lend a hand over there.'

Colonel Theodore Bruun, Commander-in-Chief, sat in the lead truck, his body shaking against the passenger door as he chuckled at his triumph. Just as well those imcompetent Angolan rebels had failed, even after he tipped them off in good time, to take the trucks and dynamite. What a lesson in craftsmanship he had taught the superior Major Weber, not to mention the supercilious Jacques Roux with his plummy accent! It just went to show, an ounce of information was worth a pound of a big soldiering reputation. He knew who their buyer was, waiting in Bangui with the money. Forty dollars per skin! More than ten thousand skins. The man would buy from anybody. And later he would demand another tribute from Weber and Roux. It had been so easy.

Bruun stopped chuckling. Should he have demanded another truckload and driven it himself? No, that would have been less than dignified, driving a truck like a nigger. He did wish he had more drivers but he would

162

train more on these excellent trucks, in readiness for the next time. Still, this time . . .

Roux and Weber had borne their humiliation well. Perhaps he should teach them another lesson. He told his driver to stop. Immediately he was thrown forward as the man stomped on the brakes.

'Easy, you fucking stupid black bastard!' He struck the man on the flat front of his face with the back of his hand.

The truck swayed alarmingly and stopped diagonally across the road. In an hour it would rain and then these drivers would be lethal. He would have to be quick.

He walked back half a mile, covering the ground nimbly for a man of his bulk, his quickening breath betraying his seedy condition. But it was quicker than having those morons trying to turn a truck on the narrow forest track. And no doubt ruining any number of skins by tearing them on the branches of trees.

When he judged he had walked the right distance, he stopped in the middle of the road and waited. 'Come on, you black baboon, it's me,' he said out loud.

Not more than ten feet in front of him the sergeant he had left in charge stepped from the foliage. His task was simple: he was to stay for an hour and make sure nobody left the camp. Then he would lead his men to the boats they had come on and which were now hidden up-river and they would make their own way home, lighter by ten men than when they had come. Bruun had put a driver and a guard in each truck-load of crocodile skins, himself guarding the lead truck.

The sergeant gave Bruun a sloppy salute and stared at him through reddened eyes. Bruun ignored the salute. 'How many pigmies near here?'

The sergeant held up two fingers.

'Any of our men near them?'

The sergeant shook his head.

'Just you?'

The sergeant nodded.

'Point them out to me.'

The sergeant pointed twice. Bruun had no difficulty finding them.

'Give me your rifle. Then walk down the road a bit. When I've finished here I'll give you your rifle back and you take up position on the other side of the road. Stay out of the way of the little men and don't interfere. They'll be attacking the white men in the camp, not you. Understand? Verstehen? Capish? Answer me, you fuck-head!' Bruun poked the sergeant in the chest with each word.

'Yes, Colonel, sir,' the man said.

Bruun took the rifle and watched the sergeant walk away down the road. When there was enough distance between them so that even the dumbest pigmy couldn't possibly think the black man had anything to do with what was about to happen, Bruun turned around and waited for both pigmies to look straight at him. He raised the rifle, wished he could close his nose against the sergeant's smell which clung to the wooden stock, aimed at the stomach of one of the pigmies, and fired. He stood for a moment, watching with satisfaction as the pigmy clutched at his stomach and fell from the tree.

Good. The gut-shot pigmy would be in fair condition to make a dramatic deathbed statement calling on all his kinsmen and tribesmen to revenge his painful demise by killing whites.

Bruun turned and ran shambling down the track to-wards his sergeant, throwing the rifle to him as he passed. It wouldn't help to hang around until the other pigmy, the one he had spared, got the idea of blowing a few poison darts his way.

The dumb little bastards never could distinguish be-tween one white man and another, just as he thought all niggers looked alike.

Bruun was laughing aloud as he heaved his bulk into the

164

truck. Were Weber and Roux ever going to be surprised when the pigmies attacked them!

Lance stood like a sandstone statue, watching as Bruun gleefully waved him goodbye from the window of the first of five truckloads of hard-won crocodile skins, then turned sharply on his heel and walked to the table from which Ewart and Jacques had not risen even to see Bruun disappear into the forest with their wealth. He stood glowering beside the table. 'You two seem remarkably unconcerned.'

Ewart waved him to a chair. 'Sit down. Relax your testicles.'

Lance sat down heavily and poured whisky into the clean glass Pietie, hovering fearfully near Jacques, immediately placed in front of him. He looked for the glass Bruun had drunk from, intending to smash it, but Pietie had cleared it away.

'What do you know about this Lobengula?' Ewart asked Jacques.

Jacques thought for a moment. 'He's the hereditary ruler of a large area of the Bangala province. His main kraal is past Businga, that way.' He pointed, adding, 'Almost directly east of here. He makes his living selling the votes of his people to the politicians in Kinshasa.'

'Corrupt.'

'Corrupt. Despotic. Greedy. Cruel. His name is a byword in Kinshasa.'

Ewart whistled. Lance asked, 'What the hell are you two on about?'

'Perhaps I should have said "even in Kinshasa",' Jacques answered him politely. 'Kinshasa is a cesspool of greed and corruption.'

Briony came from where she had been standing near the mess tent. She stopped near the table and stared aggressively at them. 'When you have finished discussing geopolitics in cultured drawing-room tones, what the fuck are you going to do about getting our skins back? Or are you going to do anything at all?'

Ewart entirely ignored her, lighting a cigarillo. Jacques said, 'Sit down, Briony. We can't do anything until we've dealt with Bruun's rearguard.'

'Which you're not going to do while you sit on your butt here sipping scotch. Or the man you hired to defend your goods and your life.' She pointed at Ewart.

'Ewart is an equal partner in this venture,' Jacques said stiffly. 'He is entirely in charge of this kind of thing and we are bloody lucky to have him. Now keep quiet or go to the tent.'

Briony's mouth quirked at the corners, opened for a sharp retort, shut at the sound of a single shot. 'What was that?'

'A signal from Bruun to his rearguard, I should think,' Ewart said. 'The period they should watch us before leaving starts from that shot.' Ewart looked around to where Sambo was inspecting the firearms of the men and checking their ammunition. 'Sambo, when you finish there I have an errand for you.'

Sambo nodded to show he had heard and continued his leisurely round of the men seated in a rough circle on the ground, laughing and chatting among themselves.

The very lack of tension in the camp – apart from himself and Briony – was winding Lance up like a nervous spring. There was something in the air, something dangerous, and he couldn't quite put his finger on it. 'You're not going to attack Bruun's soldiers, are you, Ewart?' he asked anxiously.

Ewart turned his head to look at him, taking the cigarillo from his mouth. 'Of course we are. They took our property under threat of arms. Now we're going to take it back.'

'Well, get on with it!' Briony snapped.

'But you can't! Those are soldiers. Even if there aren't courts, like Sambo and Jimmy tell me, surely there are channels through which you can get either the skins or the money back.'

Ewart puffed at his cigarillo, opened his mouth to say something, thought better of it and looked up at the sky.

'The channels are Lobengula himself,' Jacques said gently. 'He is Bruun's boss and gets a share of the proceeds. The only other channel is force.'

'You won't be coming with us anyway,' Ewart said. 'You're staying to make sure our trucks and dynamite are still here when we return.'

Lance held on to the edge of the table. 'I'm not objecting because I'm frightened. But there is such a thing as law and order.'

Ewart shook his head.

'Even you can't be that stupid, Lance,' Briony said, almost with compassion. 'You just saw the law and order of these parts. They stole our skins while we stood at the hollow end of a gun-barrel.'

Lance clenched his teeth and said nothing, his knuckles whitening on the edge of the table.

Ewart picked up his machine pistol from the ground and placed it on the table next to his glass and his ashtray. 'This is the law. The higher the stakes, the more likely people are to revert to this kind of law.'

Jimmy leant over to speak close to Lance's ear. 'You'd better tell your brother what you told me about the drivers.'

'What?' Lance said loudly, startled.

'About the drivers.'

'What's that got to do with anything?'

'Just tell it, Lance,' Ewart said tightly.

'It's nothing. I just said Bruun's drivers looked pretty incompetent to me, crashing the gears, stalling the trucks, steering erratically.'

'How long till the rain, Jimmy?' Ewart asked.

'Half an hour, forty-five minutes at the most, Mr Weber,' Jimmy said without hesitation.

'Sambo, let one of your brothers finish the inspection. You come here and bring Kombi with you.' Kombi was one of Sambo's brothers, a huge, silent, smiling man who could move with incredible speed in total silence, a man always in the background, melting into his surroundings wherever he found himself. Briony hated him because she had several times come unexpectedly upon him where he was just standing still and been startled out of her wits when he spoke to greet her respectfully.

Sambo and Kombi came up at a run. Lance wasn't all that comfortable with Kombi either: he had a habit of appearing eerily with no advance sound, one moment nowhere, the next right on you and usually behind you.

'We have to move chop-chop now,' Ewart said to them. 'Take one of the men watching us. Take him only as far as you need to be safe. Make him tell you where their leader is. Kill him silently. Take the leader and bring him here. Soften him up on the way. Questions? No. Then move!'

'Why the sudden hurry?' Briony asked innocently.

'Our trucks take some skill to drive lightly loaded on dry roads,' Ewart said. 'Heavily loaded, on wet roads, incompetent drivers will wreck the trucks. We need those trucks. Besides, once they stop, they have a better defensive position than when they're on the move.'

'See,' Briony said sweetly to Lance, pressing her thigh against his, 'you do do something right once in a while.'

Lance jerked his leg away so violently that he shook the table.

'Lance, make sure the Landrover and one other truck have full tanks,' Ewart ordered.

'I already have,' Lance said through clenched teeth. 'All the trucks.'

'Good.'

'I don't want any part of this killing.'

'We won't kill any more of them than we have to,' Ewart said, ignoring Lance's tone. 'And you're not being asked to kill anybody who isn't already trying to kill you.'

168

'We'll send you back to civilization the same lilywhite innocent,' Briony said.

'Shut up, you vicious cow,' Ewart said without raising his voice. 'People who enjoy killing are a danger to themselves and to everybody else.'

'Now your line is,' Lance said, getting some of his own back, '"Jacques, you're not going to let him speak to me like that, are you?"' Behind him Jimmy chuckled.

Briony turned to look at him. 'God knows I try not to be a snob but you are quite as common as your brother. You don't even have his redeeming feature of ice-cold efficiency at his sordid trade of killing.'

'Briony – ' Jacques started warningly.

'Let her run on, Jacques,' Lance interrupted. 'It's just nervousness talking. I used to be like that before rugger games when I was younger, much younger.' He had been cut to the quick but was proud of the way he now had himself under control.

Briony's face coloured. She turned to Lance and he thought she would strike him.

'If you ever again insult me in front of the kaffirs, I shall kill you,' she said softly, intensely and pushed her chair over as she rose. She walked away with a stiff back.

Jimmy picked her chair up and righted it. Jacques looked at him and spread his hands in silent apology. Ewart laughed aloud.

'You're not altogether the big stupid jock you try to make out,' Jacques said to Lance.

Lance looked modestly at the table.

'My brother, the rugger player and wit,' Ewart said, still chuckling. He looked proudly at Lance. Lance blushed.

The golden moment was spoiled by the return of Sambo and Kombi dragging one of Bruun's men between them. The man's nose was bleeding and staining his rumpled shirtfront. He was dragging his feet.

Sambo and Kombi let him go but before he could sink down, Sambo's massive forearm swung a short arc through the air to catch him stunningly on the chin and send him crashing to the ground.

'Easy, Sambo,' Ewart said. 'If you break his jaw or knock him out he won't be able to talk.'

Lance was watching the tent, certain Briony would not want to miss this. Sure enough, here she came. God, for a beautiful girl she filled him with morbid repulsion.

Sambo and Kombi dragged Bruun's man forward by his arms until he lay face down at Ewart's feet. Ewart lifted his chin with the tip of his boot. 'You can talk now or you can talk later but you will talk.'

The red eyes glared sullenly at him.

'Bruun will have you shot anyway because you allowed yourself to be captured. We only want information, not your life. Talk, spare yourself the pain.' He waited a moment and, when there was only silence, pulled his boot away to let the man's face drop to the ground.

Sambo's number thirteen boot crashed into the man's side, causing a wet plopping sound and the clearly audible cracking of several ribs. The man screamed and raised his hands over his head, a futile motion. Sambo's boot swung back again.

'Wait, Sambo. Bring a towel and a bucket of water.' While they were waiting for the water and towel, the prostrate man was turned over on his back.

'All right. Get going.'

The towel was put on the man's face and some water poured over it. At first he lay quietly, then he started struggling. Sambo casually placed a foot on each of his wrists while two of the men held his feet. More water was poured between Sambo's legs. When the struggles started subsiding, Ewart lifted a corner of the towel to look at the man's face.

'That's what a drowning man looks like,' he said to Jacques and dropped the towel on the man's face again. More water was poured. The struggling resumed, at first violently, then decreasing as the man burnt up the oxygen he had gulped when Ewart raised the towel. Finally the man subsided altogether.

Ewart whipped the towel away and Sambo knelt on the man to push his chest with his powerful hands. The man had lost consciousness. Gradually his chest started to move with Sambo's hands and his breath grew in rasping strength in his throat. He turned over and vomited while Sambo stood clear.

'It's actually just the sensation of drowning,' Ewart said to Jacques. 'He's not swallowing all that much water. But see how his eyes pop when he's straining for oxygen.'

The man, his stomach empty, was turned on his back again. Ewart waved the now soaking towel over his face. He pulled his head violently from the drops of water splashing from the towel and stopped gasping for air long enough to croak something desperate-sounding.

'From the smell of him, I'd say he was never too keen on soap and water,' Jacques observed dispassionately. 'Now he's gone off it for the rest of his life.'

Ewart snapped something at the man in French and he answered, a short spluttered sentence. Sambo and Kombi dragged him upright while Ewart questioned him. After the last question Sambo fished in the man's shirt pocket and brought out a tin whistle on a filthy piece of string.

'Twenty men around the camp, out of sight,' Jimmy said softly behind Lance. 'To wait until the sergeant blows two long blasts on his whistle and then to return to their boats up-river. The sergeant had instruction to wait two hours after the trucks had gone before he blew the whistle.'

Lance was feeling sick from watching Bruun's man being drowned – no matter what Ewart said about his water-intake, the effect was the same. He watched as Sambo and Kombi dropped the man to the ground and let him lie.

Ewart was disposing their men around the camp under such cover as was available. The skinners were brought into the camp and told to sit under the trucks. They were rolling their eyes and chattering softly to themselves.

171

'Why attack them?' Lance asked. 'Why not just blow two blasts on the whistle and wait for them to leave?'

'That's what we're going to do,' Ewart said patiently. 'But what if he lied, if two blasts is the signal to attack the camp?'

'Oh.'

'You could drown him some more to make sure he's telling the truth,' Briony said, pushing Bruun's man with the toe of her boot.

'That'll take longer than what I'm doing,' Ewart said, his patience obviously wearing thin.

'Ewart is an expert,' Jacques said. 'Leave him alone so he can get on with it, both of you.'

Ewart looked doubtfully at the whistle. He poured some whisky into a glass, dipped the whistle into it, set the whisky on the whistle aflame with his lighter, waited for the spirit to burn out, dipped it in the whisky again to cool it. 'That should sterilize it. All right, everybody in position. Jacques, you and Briony over there behind the dynamite boxes. Lance, you with your tanker men. Don't shoot until I give the order.'

Ewart waited a moment, looking to assure himself everybody was in position, then gave two blasts on the whistle. He stood in the middle of the camp, turning round slowly, his eyes on the ground at his feet to concentrate better on his hearing, listening for any disturbance in the forest.

Lance listened too and heard nothing except the usual forest sounds. Though he knew the dynamite could not be exploded by a bullet and a diesel tanker could, he was still glad he was not hiding behind a wall of dynamite boxes. He looked up at the fat belly of the tanker over him and actually smiled: it was a damm sight more solidly reassuring than some flimsy pine boxes filled with dynamite. So what if it was only a psychological edge? Any advantage was worth something.

172

'Five minutes,' Ewart called. He had the stopwatch on his Rolex running. 'We'll give it another five.'

Bruun's man raised himself painfully from the ground, clutching his arms around his broken ribs. He stood swaying not far from Ewart, who ignored him.

Lance listened to the sounds of the forest again. The usual sounds. You would need black magic to hear any different. It was ominous. Perhaps all Bruun's men could move like Sambo and Jimmy's brother Kombi. He looked over his shoulder at Ewart standing in the middle of the camp, his eyes still on the ground.

'If I were Bruun, perish the thought, I would have ordered my men to attack anyway, soon as I was clear,' Lance said softly to Jimmy.

Jimmy shook his head. 'No way. He intends coming back later and claiming more skins.'

'They're definitely moving away, Mr Weber,' Sambo called from his position behind a tree.

Ewart looked at his watch. 'Eight minutes. They're in one hell of a hurry to get away. Okay Kombi, take another man and take this one to near his boat. If he doesn't turn up they may come to look for him though I doubt it. Mr Roux will come with me in the Landrover and Sambo will drive behind us.' He called six men by name. 'You go in the truck and stay close behind us. The rest of you stay in the camp with Mr Lance. Lance, keep the usual complement of guards posted and stay alert. We'll be back in three hours, just after dark.' As he talked, Ewart walked towards the Landrover, checking his machine pistol once more, patting his pockets to make sure he carried enough ammunition.

The pigmies had retreated through the line of black men, carrying their dying kinsman with them. They stopped in a small clearing two hundred yards behind the line of blacks and five hundred yards from the camp. Their wounded brother was laid down in the middle of the clearing and they sat on fallen trees and on the lower branches of the living trees looking down at him. The one who had been with him told them twice how the white man had come up with his firearm and deliberately shot their brother in the stomach, grinning hugely all the time to show his delight in so taunting them.

'He could see you as well?'

'Yes.'

'Clearly?'

'Yes.'

'Why did he not shoot you as well then?'

'Who knows what is in the head of a white devil.'

'Perhaps,' another suggested, 'it is intended as a warning to us.'

'Then the white man would have shot both of them. No, it is a challenge.'

They digested this in silence. 'We should send for our kinsmen and ask their counsel,' it was suggested at last.

One of the lookouts came running into the clearing. 'Two of the white devils and their black familiars are leaving in their roaring machines.'

'Then,' said an elder after it was clear no one else wanted to speak, 'there is no time to send for the kinsmen and hold a council. We attack at once.'

'Sambo and the black man's magic. How did he do it, Jimmy?' They were watching the Landrover and the truck disappear into the trees.

'It's quite simple, Mr Lance. He listens for the birds and other animals disturbed by the passage of men, anything out of the ordinary. Then by the volume and intensity of the sound, he judges in which direction they're going.'

'Jesus!'

'There was a man in my tribe who could lie with his ear on the ground and tell how many men walked a thousand feet away and in what direction. It was his only skill but much admired.'

174

'Yeah, I know about that from lying under the loose scrum and hearing the heavy men of two teams thundering up to throw themselves on me. That's how snakes hear, through ground vibration.' Suddenly, having a handle of his own on the phenomenon, Lance believed Jimmy's explanation explicitly. Anyway, Ewart, who knew about these things, had taken Sambo's word for it immediately and without question. 'Come on, we'd better post guards.'

'And get these skinners back where they belong,' Briony said. 'Our own kaffirs smell bad enough, but this lot are something else. Please,' she added with a subdued smile.

Lance sniffed. The skinners did smell bad. 'Yeah, that's a good idea. Jimmy, find somebody who can talk their lingo and tell them it's safe to go back to their own camp now.'

'Yes, sir,' Jimmy said crisply and called something to one of his brothers.

Lance looked around, his earlier discontent forgotten in his pleasure at being left in command. Not that he bluffed himself he was the best man for the job, he hastened to assure himself, because Jimmy or any of the brothers here would be more competent, but because the simple task was well within his capabilities. 'Now guards, Jimmy, and then we'll rig the lights so they shine into the forest.'

'Yes si – Look, Mr Lance!'

Kombi came running through the forest, long strides crashing through the undergrowth, his hands strangely at his throat.

'Pigmies!' Jimmy said explosively.

Lance was cursing his premature euphoria. There was a small man running behind Kombi, losing ground, his blowpipe to his mouth. Lance was sinking to his knees, shouting, 'Everybody take cover,' without realizing it. Just a few steps more, Kombi, and I'll have the angle on the little man. Run Kombi, you're in my line of fire. Through his telescopic sight Lance could see the pigmy's cheeks bulging with air to expel the dart. The little man stopped and raised his head a little in aim. In the left half of the sight Lance could still see Kombi's body heaving as he ran. Kombi would just have to take his chances. He squeezed the trigger and watched through the scope as the bullet tore the little man's right temple away. He heard the shot from his right and saw another bullet strike the pigmy in the throat.

Kombi stumbled into the camp, his hands at his neck. What the devil was he doing with his boots around his neck? Then Lance understood: Kombi was carrying a man on his back, holding him by his ankles, letting him swing head down on his back. Kombi dropped his cargo. It was Bruun's man whom he was supposed to escort back to his transport.

Lance saw Kombi go down with exhaustion and sprinted forward to fetch him. He heard shouts behind him but paid them no heed. He grabbed Kombi by the collar of his shirt and dragged him towards the safety of the truck ten yards away. His eye caught Bruun's man; the man had several shorts darts sticking out of his chest and was convulsing horribly, just like Ben had. Black tree snake poison. The man was as good as dead. Without thinking about it, Lance pointed the rifle he was still holding in his hand and shot the man through the head.

'Spray the trees on full automatic,' he heard himself shouting at Jimmy but Jimmy was right beside him, Kombi's shirt collar completely covered by the one huge black hand and the one huge white hand. Somebody was shooting and Lance saw leaves and twigs whirl in the sun. Then the sun was suddenly gone and the rain started. They pulled Kombi behind a truck and Jimmy examined him carefully to see if he had taken any darts in the flesh, tearing his clothes from him to speed up the examination.

'No darts. Other man on . . . my back . . . protect me,' Kombi gasped.

'Where's our own man who went with you?' Lance demanded. He had been in command only minutes and already he had lost a man.

'Dead . . . the pigmies got him first.'

He would have to worry about Ewart's reaction to his incompetence later. Right now he should concern himself with the pigmy attack and a possible attack by Bruun's men coming to look for their missing leader. 'You okay now, Kombi?'

'Yes sir. Thank you for pulling me in, Young Master.'

Lance was embarrassed 'Don't mention it. Come on Jimmy. I must take a tour of inspection and you'd better advise me.'

Lance's fear was that the pigmies would use the rain to sneak up on them. He didn't notice the water squelching in his boots but visibility through the rain was down to ten feet. And the pigmies knew where they were while they didn't know where the pigmies were or how many of them there were. He wished someone else had been left in charge.

His tour dispelled some of his despair. He now understood what Ewart had meant when he had told Bruun that the difference was plain between good soldiers and a massacre looking for a place to happen. All his men had taken cover and started firing without waiting for orders. Three of the skinners had not been quick enough and were writhing on the ground.

'Have them put out of their misery, Jimmy,' Lance said, fighting to keep his voice steady, gulping at the fear constricting his throat. Sometime sooner rather than later he would have to come to terms with his own casual and thoughtless killing of Bruun's man. No matter that he was dying horribly anyway: it was another killing on his slate. And he was not like Kombi, who could carry another man on his back to protect him, to die horribly, while he lived. Or was he? It was becoming automatic – he had not thought before giving the order to Jimmy.

'Their own people will see to it, Mr Lance,' Jimmy said. 'Better for us not to interfere.'

'Goddammit Jimmy, it's unnatural to let them do it with knives while we have firearms. Just do as I say!' Lance heard his own voice becoming thin and hysterical. He looked appealingly at Jimmy. He didn't want to offend Jimmy; he needed him now more than ever before.

Jimmy was shaking his head gravely, his perpetual smile completely gone. He took Lance by the arm and led him a little way from the circle of skinners standing silently around their dying tribesmen. 'Sure, Mr Lance, its's faster. But they might turn against us if we shoot their people. After all, we promised to protect them against the pigmies. And we really don't know anything about their ways. What for us might be a mercy-killing for them might be an affront to the ancestors.'

'So we just stand here?' One of the convulsing men screamed. 'Do it my way, Jimmy, or I'll do it myself.'

When they turned around it was too late. An elder of the skinners had his machete out. He mumbled something while he ran his thumb down the blade, his distress clear, drawing blood. A middle-aged skinner said something without looking at him. He hesitated, then leant forward and with one smooth movement slid the blade across the throat of a convulsing man. Blood spurted in small weak arcs as the man jerked several times more before he died. The man with the machete didn't stay to watch the result of his handiwork. He quickly slit the throats of the other two and then turned his back, keening softly, to walk away and sit under a truck. The other skinners took up the lament as they carried their fallen comrades with them under the trucks. As they disappeared into the curtain of rain, Lance thought on what Jimmy had said, red spirals of blood – a mental image but more real than daylight – interfering with thought processes he desperately wanted and needed to be orderly.

'Well, at least they're not leaving and they haven't

turned and attacked us yet,' Lance said to Jimmy as they turned away to complete their tour of inspection.

'They'll hold a council before they do anything.'

'Small comfort you are.'

They found nine dead pigmies around the camp. From the condition of the bodies it was clear they had been caught in sprays of automatic fire: all the bodies were riddled with bullets. The implication was clear and frightening to Lance: his men hadn't actually seen the pigmies they were aiming at but had fired blindly into the trees. The pigmies had come right up to the perimeter of the camp, where the bodies lay, without being seen. When the rain stopped, the pigmies could do it again.

He told Jimmy what he thought.

Jimmy nodded agreement but he was smiling again. 'We killed nine. That means at least that many wounded, some perhaps seriously. And next time we'll be watching for them. Remember, they've got to get in real close to use their darts and arrows. Our weapons have probably ten times the effective range of arrows.'

Lance was not convinced. A pigmy hidden in a tree could kill you silently, horribly. You had to be able to see him before superior weapons could be any use to you. 'Get the floodlights turned on the forest and get them switched on.' After the rain there would be a dull period while the clouds that had brought the rain passed on and soon after that dusk would come quite suddenly.

They came upon Briony, sitting in the cab of Lance's tanker with windows rolled right up. Lance opened the door and climbed up on the running board.

'Where you born in a church?' Briony demanded.

'Huh?'

'Close that bloody door.'

'What do you think you're doing here? I told everybody to stay down and here you're sitting high and mighty and exposed.'

179

'Have you ever heard of poison darts that can penetrate laminated glass?'

'Your sarcasm is wasted,' Lance said calmly. 'The bullets of Bruun's men, when they come back to look for their sergeant, are going to come right through that glass like a sheet of paper. And if a bullet strikes this tanker, you'll go up in a ball of flame. Now, for Christsake, do as you're told and don't try to second-guess me!'

Briony climbed silently from the truck. Lance saw her safely behind a wall of dynamite boxes, watching her clothing cling wetly to her, before he went around the camp once more, making sure each section of the perimeter of the camp was covered and each man had sufficient cover.

Then they waited for the rain to stop. Lance stood with Jimmy in the middle of the camp, not because he wanted to – he had never before known such real fear, not even when the toughs had taken him up Table Mountain. But Ewart had stood thus and Lance now realized it was to provide a focal point for his men. The moment the attack came he would dive for the protection he had chosen, the double rear wheels of one of the trucks.

The rain stopped. The floodlights turned on the forest showed nothing, simply made the shadows more distinct, deeper and more threatening. 'Turn those lights out!' But Jimmy had already given the order. The lights were doused. Lance turned around slowly, anxiously, the forest all round staring back blankly at him. Wherever he turned, there were hiding places behind him from which a poisoned arrow or dart could be shot into his back. He shivered. There was nothing to see except forest but he knew the pigmies were out there.

Waiting.

'They used the cover of the rain to creep up,' Jimmy echoed his thoughts.

'At least they didn't use the same cover to rush us. That proves there can't be too many of them.'

180

Jimmy shook his head. 'No, Mr Lance. Rushing somebody isn't pigmy-style. Stealth is. There could be hundreds out there.'

'Then what are they waiting for?' Lance wanted it to be over as quickly as possible. After dark it might be . . . better not to think too far ahead.

'A signal.'

Lance listened to the sounds of the forest. After the rain the birds always chattered louder than before and the other animals made slithering sounds that often made them appear aurally larger than life.

'Tell your people to listen for anything unusual.'

'They know, Mr Lance.'

Lance wondered if the pigmies were sophisticated or sly enough to play a psychologically debilitating waiting-game. He didn't want to interrupt Jimmy's close concentration with a question.

A parrot called somewhere quite close. The forest went silent for a moment. The parrot called again.

'That's it,' Jimmy said as his brother Kombi stepped out from behind a truck and fired a short burst into the forest. Jimmy shoved Lance forward and dived after him.

Lance fell lightly and rolled, thinking, There was no need for Jimmy to push me; I was right on the ball. He came up on one side of the tyre and peered cautiously around it, Jimmy to his left looking around the other side of the wet black rubber circle.

There was a cry in the forest and the crashing of a body through the branches. Lance was still trying to locate it when Jimmy fired a single shot.

Immediately an arrow glanced off the bodywork of the truck and fell flat on the ground. Lance fired four shots in a shifting pattern in the direction it had come from but did not know whether he had hit anything because nothing could be heard over the cacophony of automatic weapons. There were more arrows and Lance ducked behind the huge wheel, rolling on his back. Jimmy had also rolled

181

over and they lay side by side, watching the men on the far side of the camp perimeter firing into the forest or ducking behind their defences. Behind them the arrows clicked against the metal.

'I didn't know you could shoot left-handed,' Lance said casually, amazed at how calm he was now it had started.

'I'm ambidextrous,' Jimmy said.

'Remind me to try it sometime. I see one.' Lance raised his rifle and zoomed in on the hard shape he had seen in a tree right on the far perimeter of their camp. He aimed for the chest but the pigmy moved just as he squeezed the trigger and he got him through the neck instead. Jimmy caused the falling body to jerk in midair with two further single shots. 'We'd better check behind us. Now!'

They rolled over. Lance saw nothing but emptied his magazine in a square grid pattern and was rewarded with the sound of a falling body. He rolled back to reload. Jimmy had only fired two single shots.

'You got one, I got two,' Jimmy said. 'This can go on for a long time, Mr Lance.'

There was a cry from where the skinners were huddled. Another one of them had been hit. 'Stay down, stay down!' Lance shouted as he saw another one peering with fearful curiosity at the forest from under a truck and taking a poison dart in one eye. 'Call a tally, Jimmy. Find out how many we got, how many more there are, if we lost any of our men yet.'

After a shouted conversation, Jimmy reported, 'We got maybe nine, ten. There aren't all that many more. Our men are okay but the skinners have lost several more.'

'All right. This can't go on. We can't see them and they're close enough to nail us if we take a leisurely look. But bullets don't have to see.'

'What do you have in mind, Mr Lance?'

'Do your people know how one searches a square-grid pattern?'

'Of course. They're soldiers.'

'We've lots of ammo, haven't we?'

Jimmy laughed. 'Enough to start a small war.'

'Tell the men to divide the forest up in sections between them and, when I tell them, start spraying the trees in square-grid patterns on automatic.'

Jimmy's smile broadened. 'That's worthy of your brother, Mr Lance.'

'And tell them not to expose themselves unnecessarily.'

It took quite a while for the ammunition to be passed along and for the men to settle the demarcation of their respective grids. Lance's eyes kept flickering to the opposite perimeter and every now and again he would roll over to peer cautiously past the tyre. What if Jimmy was wrong about the pigmies and they did launch a full frontal attack on the camp? They'd get most of the pigmies but the pigmies would certainly get some of them. And, more frightening, once the pigmies broke through the outer defence and were among them, men fearful of the painful death of the black tree snake poison would spray the campsite on automatic and cause awesome carnage among their own.

'Tell them to get a bloody move on, Jimmy. This isn't a *kaffe-klatsch*. It'll be dark soon and then those pigmies are going to be able to sneak up and *stick* their darts in us, never mind blowing them through a little reed tube.'

Jimmy shouted some more and then the men were ready. Lance, feeling slightly foolish, like a film actor, shouted, 'Fire at will!' He lay on his back, looking at the sky, the sound overpowering in his ears. Without a fully automatic weapon of his own there was no further contribution he could make.

From the forest came the sound of shattered branches and now and again the sound of human cries. A wave of guilt washed over Lance's consciousness. He had not even tried to talk to the pigmies. But how do you parley with men who don't reach much past your middle, have a totally different culture with strange and incomprehensible

183

values, speak no language you or any of your comrades know, and attack you without provocation?

Provocation? Suddenly he knew, and no further proof was needed. The shot they had heard after Bruun had left had been no signal. Bruun had deliberately killed a pigmy to provoke an attack on them.

'Cease fire!' Lance shouted. A surge of hate for Bruun welled through him.

'They stopped firing a minute ago, Mr Lance,' Jimmy said gently.

There was indeed silence. Lance saw Briony rising behind the barrier of dynamite boxes, an FN glowing orange in her hands. The rest of the men were rising too. Lance stood up.

'Whew!' Lance said.

'Down! Down!' Jimmy shouted.

Out of the corner of his eye as he turned, Lance saw Jimmy lunging for him. In front of him he saw the pigmy drop from the tree, blowpipe already to his mouth. He fired from the hip, squeezing the trigger three times before Jimmy's shoulder struck him between the shoulder blades. Yes, the area to his right. Nobody had thought of covering that, assuming he would cover it. But he hadn't.

Lance turned in the air, his finger clear of the trigger – Ewart would be proud of his presence of mind and his reflexes – and landed painfully on his shoulder, the rifle well clear of his body and cushioned against a shock which could set off the next shot. In the air he had seen the dart the pigmy had blown in his death throes, stopped in its travel through the air as time stood still. And a black man holding his hand up to his face, an FN without a clip in one hand, the empty clip falling from the hand rising to protect the face. In the next instant the dart had stuck in the little finger of the man's hand. The man was one of Lance's, one of the tanker men.

Lance rolled and, leaving his rifle on the ground, ran to

184

the man. He grabbed his wrist and jerked the dart out, dropping it on the ground. He dragged the man behind him by the wrist, heading for the row of stacked dynamite boxes. The man was resisting.

'Move, you dumb black bastard! Do you wanna die?'

In passing Lance grabbed a panga from the belt of a surprised skinner.

He slammed the hand of the tanker man down on the dynamite boxes and glanced at the crocodile-blood stains on the blade. No time to clean and sterilize it. The man, frantic with fear at the horrific death staring him in the face, tried to jerk his hand away. Lance held on with all his strength to the slippery wrist – both he and the man were sweating profusely. He spread the little finger from the rest with the point of the panga and chopped at it. His first blow severed the first joint. He didn't know how fast the poison travelled. He chopped again and hit the second joint squarely. Another piece of finger went flying.

'Better chop it off right at the hand,' he heard Jimmy's voice. Jimmy was holding the man's wrist near the hand and keeping the other hand clear by main force. Kombi had the man around the chest.

Lance placed the point of the blade on the little finger where it joined the palm. He didn't want to chop for fear of cutting off more than he intended. With the other hand he pressed hard on the upper edge of the blade. The last joint of the little finger came off and Lance swept it away with the tip of the blade. The man screamed for the first time. Or perhaps he just hadn't heard him before. 'Keep holding him.'

Lance grabbed an FN from a man standing next to him, searing his hand on the hot barrel. He fired five clips into the ground. The barrel was red hot. Jimmy held the mutilated hand up and Lance pressed the barrel against the bleeding wound. There was a sizzling sound and the smell of burnt pork. The man, understanding that somebody was trying to save him, actually grinned broadly at Lance. Jimmy and Kombi let him go. He sat down on the ground, his legs slowly folding under him.

'Bring whisky,' Lance said to nobody, then shouted, 'Pietie! Bring whisky.' He saw the coloured servant peering fearfully from under the groundflap of the mess-tent. 'Whisky, Pietie. Hurry!'

Pietie stared at him, too petrified to move. Jimmy ran into the mess-tent and came back with a bottle of brandy. He handed it to Lance, who dropped the panga and started struggling with the foil around the top. Jimmy grabbed the bottle and smashed the top off against the dynamite boxes. He poured the contents over the hand of the man sitting on the ground.

They stood around the man. Lance picked up the panga and gave it to the nearest black soldier. 'Find its owner and return it.' The skinners were dealing with their own wounded, slicing the throats of those still convulsing, moaning over those already dead.

The man on the ground stared blankly in front of him, cradling his mutilated hand in his lap, the smile still vacuously fixed on his face.

'Will he live?' Lance asked.

'He hasn't gone into convulsions,' Kombi said.

'In a few minutes we'll know for sure,' Jimmy added.

The man gave a shudder and fell over. He lay quite still. Jimmy bent down and listened to his heart with his ear on the man's chest. He rose, smiling. 'He just fainted from the pain and shock. He'll live.'

Briony came through the assembled crowd. Pietie was walking behind her, carrying their large first aid box. There were angry red marks on both his cheeks.

'I had to slap this one a little before he could unfreeze himself,' Briony said. 'He was quite catatonic. That was fast thinking, Lance, even though your surgery is a bit rough and ready. Another second and he would have been dying and as good as dead.'

186

'Some of the poison might still be in him,' Lance said. 'Depends on how fast it travels in the blood.'

'No.' Briony opened the box to find salves and bandages. 'It travels very fast. The slightest amount is sufficient to kill. There's nothing left in him or he'd be dead by now. You'd better get going after the rest of the pigmies.'

'What for? If any are still alive they got away.'

'*Are* getting away because you're letting them.'

'Then let them get away.'

'They attacked us. You should punish them.'

'Bruun provoked them by shooting one of them.'

'How do you know?'

'I worked it out.'

'It doesn't matter. If you let them get away with it, word will get around that we're soft.'

'Excuse me, sir, madam,' Jimmy said carefully, looking at the ground. 'There is another reason for making sure not a single pigmy gets away.'

Lance sighed. 'Okay, Jimmy, what is it?'

'If even one gets away, Mr Lance, he'll bring all his tribesmen and kinsmen against us.'

'That's another day's worry.'

'Then we'll have to kill all of them instead of just one or two now.'

'I'm sick of all this killing!'

'It's still a few now or many later.'

'All right! I'll follow them till darkness but not a second beyond that.'

Briony looked up from bandaging the man's hand. 'That's a wise decision. Only a suicidal maniac would hunt pigmies in these forests after dark.'

Or at any other time, Lance thought, remembering how hard it was to find pigmies once they had hidden themselves. But, strangely, Briony's agreement was reassuring.

'We're not going to catch them before the rain,' Ewart said.

'Can't you go any faster, Sambo?' Jacques was sitting in the rear of the Landrover, his knees braced against the seat in front of him occupied by Ewart, checking the slide of his FN for the second time. He didn't try to hide his nervousness; on Ewart and Sambo the effort would be wasted.

Sambo shook his head grimly and took his hand from the wheel for a moment to jerk his safety harness tighter against the lurching of an uneven road taken at a speed which was threatening to dislodge even his mass from the tight grip of the bucket seat. A moment after he replaced his hand on the wheel the rain fell. There were no warning drops. It came down all at once. Sambo didn't make the mistake of braking or taking his hand from the wheel to engage four-wheel drive. They were sliding sideways down the road and he kept his attention on the road and on the mirror, watching for the truck to come out of the rain behind them and ram the light aluminium coachwork of the Landrover.

'Now,' said Ewart conversationally. He had his hand on the lever to engage four-wheel drive. Without looking, Sambo depressed the clutch briefly, not raising his foot from the accelerator. The engine raced, Ewart slammed the lever home, Sambo let the clutch in quickly but smoothly, the now-driven front wheels took with a bite that set the whole vehicle shuddering. They were still sliding diagonally across the road. Sambo was feeding in power and actually accelerating their forward speed.

Jacques was looking back. The high bumper of the truck was creeping up inexorably on the rear window of the Landrover. The face of the man behind the wheel of the truck was distorted by the rain but his arms could be seen whirling as he tried to apply opposite lock and correct the slide. The bumper nudged the rear of the Landrover.

Sambo cursed in his own language, swung the wheel, changed into a lower gear without engaging the clutch.

The Landrover had turned and was sliding down the road diagonally again but this time at right-angles to its previous position. Slowly, the bumper and hood of the truck appeared out of the rain behind them again.

'They're gaining on us,' Jacques said.

Sambo grunted and fed in more power. All three men in the Landrover listened anxiously to the sound of the drivetrain. If Sambo had damaged the gearbox in that change they would be dead meat before the monster truck running out of control behind them.

They were straightening up very slowly. The truck bumper came closer, then fell away just before the Landrover was completely straight. But now a delicate manoeuvre had to be performed. At the exact moment the wheels came straight Sambo would have to let off the power or they would surge ahead and lose control again. Then he would have to feed in power and accelerate on the treacherous surface *before* the truck slammed into them. Otherwise all would be lost.

They listened tensely as the engine raced and the nose straightened inch by inch. Just before the nose was straight Sambo kicked the clutch, changed gear and lifted his foot right off the loud pedal to let the revolutions fall halfway down the scale. In that moment the truck hit them again and catapulted the whole Landrover forward. Jacques gasped and Sambo cursed. He glanced at the mirror and saw the truck bumper filling the rear window. He fed power, the tyres bit and, almost reluctantly, the Landrover drew away from the monster behind it.

Jacques sighed.

'Are they all right behind us, Mr Roux?' Sambo asked.

'I can't see them. The last time I saw them the driver was still fighting.'

'Keep going as fast as you can, Sambo,' Ewart ordered. 'There's nothing we can do to help them and if we stop we'd just make an additional obstruction in their way and get all of us killed.'

The rain stopped ten minutes later. Without being told, Sambo slowed down. Ewart and Jacques were looking anxiously out of the splattered rear window. Five minutes later the truck caught up with them. One of its fenders had a new dent where it had been apparently swung glancingly against a tree. Sambo speeded up.

Ewart laughed, not from relief but from genuine amusement. 'Imagine Bruun trying to make it in this lot with inexperienced drivers and overloaded trucks.'

Jacques was not amused. 'It won't be so funny if they wreck our trucks and our skins.'

'We'll know within minutes,' Ewart reassured Jacques.

They rounded a curve in the road and found the convoy ahead of them. Sambo slowed down fractionally and looked questioningly at Ewart.

'Drive up right behind them,' Ewart said without hesitation. He wound his window down and waved his arm out of the window, up and down, to tell the driver of the truck forty feet behind them to slow down.

Sambo brought the Landrover to within ten feet of the slewing tailboard of the rearmost truck of Bruun's convoy. A crocodile skin had come partially loose and the head was flapping its open jaws at them.

'That idiot hasn't even engaged four-wheel drive,' Sambo said.

'Let's hope he isn't using his mirror either,' Ewart said. He explained to Sambo what he was going to do and gave his orders.

Sambo shook his head. 'Very dangerous.'

'Do you have a better plan?'

'No sir.'

'Then do as I say.' Ewart swung his door open. He unbuckled his safety harness and reached upwards for the roofrack's side rail. He crooked his arms and straightened his legs as he curved his body out of the Landrover and swung his legs over the door in a smooth movement before the force of the wind could slam it. He stood on the

190

bonnet and watched Jacques climb over the back of the front seat. First Jacques handed out the FNs, then he pushed the door open and, while Ewart held the door, Jacques stepped first on the armrest and then on the window still and, with surprising nimbleness for a man with one crippled leg, climbed over the door on to the bonnet. They let the door go and it slammed shut.

Still holding on to the roofrack, they swung the FNs over their shoulders. They crawled across the engine compartment by holding on to the spare wheel bolted to the bonnet. When Ewart had his hands on the top pipe of the bull-bar and his feet against the spare wheel, Jacques signalled to Sambo through the clean segment of the windscreen. Sambo accelerated slowly, intent on getting the Landrover as near as possible to the truck without the slewing tail of the truck bashing into the Landrover. Even the most incompetent of drivers and soldiers would notice that. And all he would have to do would be to blow his hooter and the attacking party would have lost their main advantage, surprise. Without surprise there would be a pitched battle and men would die.

The truck slid across the front of the Landrover, the loose crocodile head swinging grotesquely. Jacques gestured to Sambo: forward. Another few inches. The truck slewed twice more. Jacques saw Ewart nod and held up his palm to Sambo: hold it there. The truck slewed once more.

Ewart studied the ropes holding the crocodile skins as the tail of the truck slewed past him, no more than eighteen inches from his nose, ducking as the loose crocodile head swung malevolently at him. He would have only one chance because Sambo had orders to let the Landrover fall back the minute he jumped to avoid any chance of crushing his swinging legs between the two vehicles. And if he fell, if he missed, the Landrover would simply slide over him and grind him into the mud.

In his mind there was an image of himself as a boy,

spitting on his hands before a fight. He smiled slightly as the truck's tail reached the apogee of its swing. He relaxed his muscles and, waiting a second for the truck to start swinging back, tensed them suddenly and launched himself into the air in front of him, still empty but soon to be filled with the back of the truck, his hand clawing for the ropes that had better be there. Perhaps he should have spat on his hands, he thought as he heard the Landrover's engine sound fall away from him. He caught the ropes only inches from the side and swung himself on top of the pile of skins before the swinging crocodile head could hit him. He gasped at the foul smell and abrasive surfaces of the skins under his nose and raised his head. He dug his feet into the skins behind one of the ropes and signalled for Sambo to bring the Landrover up again and watched Jacques crouch on the bonnet. When the Landrover was close enough he signalled to Sambo to hold it there. He gave Jacques three swings of the truck to judge it and, as the fourth swing started, stretched out his hands.

'Jump!'

Jacques hesitated the barest fraction of a second – or perhaps his reflexes were simply slow. He jumped and, instead of catching both Ewart's hands, caught only Ewart's right hand with his own right, both their left hands swinging free.

The swinging crocodile head caught Jacques stunningly in the side, winding him. There was no strength left in him. His hand, lubricated with sweat, was starting to slip from Ewart's grasp. Sambo, seeing what was happening, had braked. He had misjudged, lost control and now the Landrover was sliding forward, gaining on the truck, exactly the opposite of what Sambo had intended: If Jacques fell he would be squashed under the weight of the Landrover.

Ewart swung his free left hand over to grab Jacques' right wrist just as their fingers parted. Jacques hung slackly, his feet swinging free, making no effort to help

Ewart by finding a purchase for his boots on the truck and so taking some of the weight from Ewart's arms. Ewart grabbed Jacques' other arm as it swung slowly past him, propelled by the change in direction in the truck's slewing.

Ewart lay still, just holding on to Jacques and breathing deeply, watching the Landrover slide ever nearer to Jacques' legs. Two more breaths. Now. He put all his strength into one sharp heave and catapulted Jacques on to the top layer of skins just as the Landrover's bull-bars ran into the back of the truck, apparently gently though Ewart knew there would be enough force to squash both Jacques' legs. He looked over his shoulder towards the cab but they seemed to have noticed nothing – there had been no sound (or, more accurately, the sound had been swept away by the wind) and no perceptible jarring of the truck. Sambo had regained control over the Landrover and was holding position some distance back.

Jacques was heaving like a fish out of water. Ewart crawled over the rough and stinking skins to his side. He felt his side, where the crocodile head had struck him, but could find nothing broken although that was no proof some internal organ hadn't been damaged.

'Nothing wrong with me except I can't breathe in this stink,' Jacques said testily. It took all his breath and he started gasping again.

'Just winded?' Ewart shouted against the wind, holding his mouth near Jacques' ear.

Jacques probed himself gingerly with his fingers and nodded.

'Let me know when you're ready to proceed. Take your time.' Jacques would know how much time they could afford and the risks if he hurried into something he wasn't fit enough to handle. Ewart lay on his back on the skins and took a cigarillo from his stainless steel case. He lit it at the fifth try and sighed. He was sure that the literature that had come with his lighter had promised it would work in a forty-mile-an-hour wind and they were going nowhere near as fast. You couldn't trust anybody any more. Or perhaps it had been forty kilometres. But they weren't going that fast either. Jacques nudged him in the side to show that he was ready.

They crawled forward over the skins, Ewart to the driver's side, Jacques to the passenger's side of the cab. When they got there, each took hold of the bars that kept the load from the cab. They looked at each other across the skins. Jacques nodded and they swung down on to the running-boards.

Ewart looked at the startled black face that glanced yellow-eyed at him for a moment, then looked at the road again. 'That's right. Just keep your hands on the wheel and slow down easily. If you do anything stupid you're dead.' He pushed the barrel of his FN forward an inch to emphasize his point.

The passenger was either foolhardily brave or simply stupid. He looked for several seconds at the barrel of Jacques' FN swaying in rhythm with the movement of the truck not more than an inch from his nose, then scrabbled for his rifle between his legs.

'Don't,' Jacques said, not wishing to fire the shot that would alarm the rest of the convoy just in front of them. 'It would be fatally stupid.'

The man was pulling the rifle up by its barrel. Jacques swung the FN around by its trigger guard, turning his hand sideways so the barrel wouldn't strike the window frame, and struck the black in the face with the butt. The rifle slipped from the man's fingers. The truck stopped. Jacques wiped the blood that had splashed from the man's face out of his eyes with a shirtsleeve, then opened the door and pulled the groaning man out. 'You're a bloody fool,' he told the man. 'Only idiots fight the odds. Wise men wait their turn.' The man's nose was not only broken but squashed and both his lips were nastily split. No dentist was ever going to restore his teeth to their former glory. There was also a dent a quarter-inch deep in his forehead, running vertically into his low hairline. 'What a pity a handsome specimen like you has to spoil his looks by stupidity.'

Ewart came round the front of the truck, pushing the driver in front of him. 'All right, let's get this truck off the road and repeat the procedure on the next one.'

Bruun knew he had been lucky with the rain. His driver had missed a gearchange and stalled the truck. The other trucks had come very near to crashing into them and into each other but a miss was as good as a mile. Cuffing the man about the ears had taken time, getting the truck started more time. And in that time the rain had come. Bruun had put the truck in four-wheel drive for the man and told him to go very slowly in the rain. He didn't want either the trucks or skins damaged. There was no need to worry about Weber: first the little tin soldier would have to wait for two hours to get out of his camp, then he would have to face the same road conditions. No, Weber wouldn't catch up with him before Bangui. He had thought of putting Weber's other vehicles out of order but rejected the idea – how would Weber continue to lay the golden eggs for him without transport?

Soon it would be dark. Then, even if Weber got lucky, the lights of pursuing vehicles would be seen reflected upwards by the trees like a searchlight, and he could just pull his vehicles off the road in some clearing and either ambush Weber or let him run on a wild goose chase. The prospect was satisfying enough to make Bruun chuckle. He almost wished Weber would get lucky and catch up with them after dark. A rope stretched across the road between two sturdy trees could bend a speeding aluminium Landrover quite appreciably and administer a lesson in shock and small injuries to the occupants without damaging them so much that they would be unable to continue their admirable work of making him rich. Bruun laughed aloud. He looked up at the sky through the windscreen and the branches over them.

'Not so fast, blockhead. Killing yourself will be no loss, but I'm in here with you.'

Darkness, down here at least, in only minutes; above the trees an hour later. 'Switch on your lights.' The man fumbled with the switches. Bruun leant over and turned the one clearly marked LIGHTS.

Bruun looked in the mirror beside him to see if the other drivers in the trucks behind his were switching on their lights as well. The mirror was caked with still-wet mud. He hung out of the window.

'Stop, goddammit, stop!' he screamed. Behind his leading truck only one truck remained and behind that the Landrover was dropping back. On top of the second truck's load of crocodile skins two figures were moving. It was clear that what had happened to the other three trucks was now happening to a fourth.

Bruun cursed as his fingers scrabbled with his holster flap. With his other hand he smacked the driver across the chops again. 'Stop, I said, you black bastard and I meant immediately!'

The driver slammed on the brakes just as Bruun got his revolver free.

'Bruun, in the lead truck, is likely to be more awake than his men,' Ewart had said. 'This one has to go especially smoothly if we don't want to alert him. And quickly, so we can take Bruun himself before dark.'

Jacques had nodded. He didn't relish the thought of jumping into empty space in the dark and hoping to land on some crocodile skins.

Now they were crouching on the skins just behind the cab, one hand on the bars, one hand holding the FN.

It was dusk already under the trees though above them glimpses of a clear blue sky could still be caught from a slow-moving vehicle by the quick and sharp-eyed.

Jacques nodded at Ewart in the gathering gloom and they swung down as they had three times before. Just then there was a shot and the driver slammed on the brakes. At first the truck seemed to dig its nose into the mud, then it turned the nose towards the trees. But its momentum carried it down the road, decreasing the distance between it and the lead truck rapidly. The lead truck was also sliding sideways. Ewart, not wishing to be crushed between the two trucks, jumped, rolled in the mud, and came up with his FN pointing the right way. He shot the driver through the throat as the door swung open and the man tried to jump. The body was crushed between the two trucks.

Jacques wasn't so lucky. The black man in the passenger seat had already been panicked by the sound of the shot and the sudden braking and was swinging the door open just as Jacques swung down from behind him. The door caught Jacques full in the chest and threw him clear. The black man landed on him, flat out.

Jacques struck out for the man's throat with his forearm but missed. The man had jumped from the truck without his weapon and was trying to throttle Jacques. He was pressing Jacques down by superior weight and Jacques, winded by the fall and the man landing on him, hadn't the strength to break the hold the man's hands had on his windpipe. Already the red was starting to flame behind his eyes. He gave up trying to break the man's hold and scrabbled with his hands, for his weapon. He couldn't remember in which hand he had been holding it when he fell. His left hand found the barrel of the weapon and inched along it until he found the clip and trigger guard. He stuck the barrel in the man's side. He was losing consciousness. If there was much mud in the barrel, or even a little, the pressure of gas behind the bullet, having nowhere to escape to, would blow the barrel apart, and him and his assailant with it. No matter. He squeezed the trigger and passed out, his finger falling away from the trigger, his body relaxing, accepting death.

Ewart knew nobody was going to be able to get out of the far truck on this side as it was locked against the truck that had crashed into it. Without looking over his shoulder, he called, 'Stay this side, Sambo.' Sambo would have stopped the Landrover and found cover the minute the trouble started.

'Yes sir,' Sambo called softly. About fifteen yards away, Ewart judged. There was no point in looking; he wouldn't see Sambo.

Ewart crawled under the two trucks near the rear wheels. Both engines were dead and nobody was trying to move the trucks. He held the FN in front of him in both hands, clear of the mud, his elbows wriggling him forward, his knees marking time in the mud behind. Years of demonstrating this to soldiers with live bullets flying over his head, and a few occasions of practising it with real enemies who could shoot lower, had given him considerable speed in this unconventional mode of progress.

In front of him he could see the big black man lying on top of Jacques and overflowing beyond the smaller man. He paused under the edge of the second truck and looked upwards and forward, just in time to see Bruun leaping from the truck. Before he could raise the FN Bruun had disappeared into the forest. The driver slithered out after him and Ewart shot him through the side of his head, rolling aft for the protection of the wheels and axles immediately after in case Bruun had turned and was providing covering fire for his man. There was no return fire. Ewart switched to automatic and sprayed the forest with two clips, taking care not to expose himself more than absolutely necessary. He waited a minute for cries or groans or return fire. There was nothing. The animals of the forest, startled into silence by the shots, took up their song again. Ewart crawled out from under the truck and stood up. He bent over the man on Jacques and saw the very large exit wound in the man's side. It had been torn, not by the bullet, but by the exploding gases entering the

198

man's body through the bullet hole, expanding inside him, still finding no escape and then tearing the bullet hole wide open as they escaped. The bullet had also run around the ribs before tearing them open. Entrails were spilling out.

Ewart rolled the black man off to look at Jacques' body.

Jacques opened his eyes and looked up at him. 'You sure as hell took your own sweet time.'

'You could have rolled him off yourself.'

'I didn't have the strength. The bastard throttled me. I thought I'd had it. I'm still woozy but not so non compos that I was going to push him off and sit up begging to be shot by Bruun when I didn't know what kind of shit had collected in the barrel of my firearm.'

Ewart gave him a hand up and picked up the FN. 'Shit is right. And lung and pieces of bone.' Jacques and firearm alike were covered in mud and blood and smelt of human excrement.

Jacques leant against the truck. 'Bruun got away?'

Ewart helped Jacques sit down by steadying his elbow. 'Yes. There's no point in trying to catch him, even with the spoor he'll leave in the wet. In five minutes it'll be too dark to see the spoor.'

Jacques nodded tiredly and rested his chin on his chest. His system was still trying to recover the oxygen it had been starved of while he had been throttled.

Ewart walked away to set out guards against the eventuality that Bruun would return to snipe at them from the dark and to organize the separation of the trucks.

'Dig a grave for the pigmies and for your own,' was Lance's last instruction to the skinners as he left the camp in search of the surviving pigmy or pigmies. He had sent Kombi on a scouting trip around the camp and the black man had reported that either one or two pigmies were heading straight north, parallel to the river bank.

The party consisted of Kombi to track, Lance and

Jimmy, and another black man whom Jimmy had said was the brother of the man killed earlier by the pigmies when he had gone with Kombi to escort Bruun's sergeant. So much had happened since that Lance had quite forgotten about that. But Jimmy said the man had asked as a right to be allowed to come.

Lance glanced at the man in the halflight under the trees, uncomfortable with the concept of violent revenge. The man seemed alert, his smile only slightly dimmed – not a death's-head grin as Lance would have expected. Lance hung back a little to let Kombi and the man get another few paces ahead.

'Are you sure they were brothers?' he asked Jimmy.

'Certainly, sir.'

'Cut out the sir."Mr Lance" is bad enough. He doesn't seem to be grieving too much.'

'It would be most unseemly for him to show grief publicly.' Jimmy was shocked at the suggestion. 'Anyway, he's not here for grief but from a sense of duty.'

'You mean revenge?' Lance couldn't help sounding disapproving.'

'It's a duty he owes the ancestors. The death of his brother has nothing to do with it,' Jimmy said stiffly. 'We all owe the duty to see that our cousin does not go to the ancestors empty-handed but he feels it more strongly. That's why I asked you to let him come.'

Lance shrugged, not prepared to argue a point of dogma. This, what Jimmy was saying, was just revenge dressed up another way. It occurred to him that Jimmy was getting his back up because he was being forced to defend something he didn't really believe in. Quite probably Jimmy's standing with his own people would be adversely affected if he rejected the time-honoured beliefs too strongly. He said as much to Jimmy.

'That's true,' Jimmy said less aggressively than before. 'But there's something else, something personal that you wouldn't understand. I, me, I wouldn't like to die unrevenged.'

Lance nodded. 'I sure as hell would like whoever murdered me to hang by his neck until he was dead.' It wasn't quite the same thing as Jimmy was talking about, but then the place and circumstances were different.

Jimmy was smiling again as they lengthened their pace to catch up with the other two.

Lance couldn't see the trail Kombi was following. Kombi's eyes would flicker here and there, sideways, up and down, but he kept walking relentlessly forward with hardly a change in direction, never once pausing. They were going a hell of a lot faster, four big men walking with long fast strides, than a four-foot pigmy could trot.

Lance didn't want to turn around at first dark and find they had passed the pigmies, that the pigmies were lying in ambush for him.

'How were they moving, Kombi?'

Kombi looked over his shoulder. 'Running but not too fast, N'kosi.'

'I should run like all the devils in hell were after me,' Lance said to Jimmy.

Without a break in his stride, Jimmy plucked a sprig from a long fern hanging downwards. 'One's wounded and the other one is staying with him.' He gave the sprig to Lance. There was a small spot of blood on it.

'More than wounded,' Kombi said. 'Dying. He's slowing down and the other one with him.'

Lance dropped the piece of greenery. Such a small spot of blood and the man was dying. He didn't doubt that Kombi was reading the sign right. Even a city boy knew brand-new runny red blood from blood that had lost the glint of freshness; something that would happen in minutes. For the first time Lance thrilled to this chase, his satisfaction enhanced by the knowledge that soon, at darkness, he could call it off.

It was a very small clearing. The pigmy stretched out in

201

it had one arm thrown out in his final convulsion and the hand of the other clutched constrictively around the shaft of the arrow he had driven through his stomach, under the short ribs and into the heart. His death must have been very quick. Lance gagged at the sight of a row of bullet holes stitched with obscene regularity across the man's stomach. It was a miracle that he had managed to come this far.

'He killed himself to give the other one a chance to get away.' Kombi rose from the body.

Lance was suddenly aware that it was a very small clearing filled with four very large men and one shrivelled body. He was not sure whether the sweat of the living or the gastric juices of the dead, burbling away audibly as they leaked out of the riddled body, smelled worse. There was a burp from the dead man, gasses escaping. Lance started.

'We'll never catch him now,' Kombi said. 'He left at top speed.' He pointed at a twig as thick as a man's little finger that had been broken and was oozing a sap that was faintly phosphorous in the gathering gloom.

Lance looked at the twig, fascinated. Then he shuddered suddenly and took a step backwards before he could help himself. The broken twig was nearly six feet off the ground, much higher than any pigmy. But he couldn't run into hiding without warning his men. He drew a deep breath and stood still.

'It's a trap,' he said softly, shakily. 'When I start shooting, take cover.' Without waiting for confirmation he raised the FN he had brought in preference to his rifle and squeezed the trigger with his forefinger while his thumb clicked the safety off. The weapon was already on automatic fire. Lance walked backwards as he fired, trying not to panic, to cover the tree systematically. He stumbled over some unseen obstacle and felt rather than saw the hand Jimmy reached out to steady him. He heard rather than saw the arrow and, still falling, twisted his body

202

away. He heard Jimmy gasp behind him. Then he was on the ground and rolling for shelter behind a tree trunk. To his left he could see Jimmy standing exposed and firing at the tree with the FN held in his left hand, his right arm held out oddly at a high angle. Kombi and the other man were also blasting away at the tree with the broken twig. There was a sigh from the tree and the sound of a crashing body.

Lance didn't wait to see it fall. The automatic weapons were still stuttering, following it down. He stumbled forward to Jimmy. Oh, Jesus, please, not Jimmy! Jimmy's face was grim, turned to one side and down to his left, inspecting the shaft sticking out of his side. A fraction of an inch wider and it would have missed him altogether. At least Jimmy was still standing up and not convulsing but you cannot very well amputate the trunk of a man like you can cut off a little finger.

Lance reached out to tear Jimmy's shirt from him to see if there was anything to be done.

'Wait, Mr Lance!' Jimmy said urgently. 'It hasn't touched me yet. It's just pinned the fold of my shirt between the arm and the body to the tree. But if I move I could cut myself on it.'

'And then kaput Jimmy,' Lance said and laughed nervously.

'There's a Swiss Red Cross knife in my trouser pocket,' Jimmy said.

Lance fetched it out very carefully indeed. It had a multitude of blades, an awl, a can opener, a file and, wonder to behold, a pair of small scissors.

'Hold your arm higher, Jimmy.'

'I can't. There's no more play in the shirt.'

Kombi took Jimmy's outstretched arm to steady it. Lance started cutting at the cuff of the shirt. The little scissors coped remarkably well but, attached to the heavy knife, they were cumbersome. Lance stopped cutting and studied the swivel where the scissors were attached to the knife. With two quick twists he broke the scissors free from the knife.

'Hey,' Jimmy said, 'that knife cost fifty American dollars.'

Kombi grunted his irritation at the levity. Lance ignored it.

The sleeve came away and Lance folded it back with the utmost care, keeping his hands well clear of the arrow. The shaft was only a quarter-inch from Jimmy's arm. Free of the constraint of the shirt Jimmy raised his arm and stepped free. Suddenly it was pitch dark. Kombi lit matches to inspect Jimmy's arm for scratches. He couldn't find any.

'If there were even the smallest scratch, I'd be dead by now,' Jimmy said, his voice first bantering, then awed, then shaky, all in one short sentence.

Lance found himself shaking uncontrollably. That arrow had been meant for him. If he had not stumbled it would have struck him in the chest. Jimmy picked up their weapons and took his arm while Kombi and the other man looked away. 'We'd better get back, Mr Lance.'

On the way back, Lance recovered his composure enough to say fairly steadily, 'Thank you, Jimmy.'

After an hour of hard work they had separated the rear ends of the trucks. But the front wheel rims had locked together and neither truck could be moved until this problem was solved.

'Shall I drive back to the camp and bring lights and more trucks and men?' Jacques asked.

Ewart rose from where he had been kneeling in the mud, inspecting the locked wheels. 'No thanks. The torches provide enough light and more force won't help much either. The rims seem to be melted together in places from the friction.'

They walked away to inspect the interlocking latticework of several layers of branches Jacques had had the blacks spread on the ground for the Landrover and the other trucks to get some grip on. Jacques had also had the lines put on. Ewart nodded his approval. They walked back and stood in front of the two trucks they were trying to separate.

'Sambo, I want a hole dug right there, beside the tyre.' Ewart knelt with the black man to look under the truck and pointed.

The big black men were making hard going of the digging in the soft and runny mud in the confined space underneath the truck; it was obviously going to take a long time.

'I'm going to lock the gearbox of one truck,' Ewart explained. 'Then I'm going to run the engine of this one and the wheel will just run freely over the whole and break the weld it has on the other wheel which will be held by the gearbox. Meanwhile, the trucks and the Landrover will be pulling away at both trucks to provide lateral force. The truck with the locked gearbox will be pulled free, sliding sideways. The truck with the rotating front wheel will fall in the hole and go nowhere. We'll worry about pulling it out later.'

'Yes, ingenious,' Jacques sounded exhausted.

Ewart shone his flashlight in Jacques' face and clicked it off before his friend could complain. 'You look tired. This is going to take a while. Why don't you take one of the trucks and go back to the camp.'

Lance sat in the cab of one of the tankers, watching the forest. He had had the floodlights turned on the trees and felt reasonably safe in the circle of darkness which was the camp. He would be able to see Bruun's men or any pigmies – or the skinners who had melted away in the night – or anybody else of a mind to attack the camp. He'd have an advantage. Jimmy had told him it was common knowledge among soldiers that the human eye took at least thirty minutes to get accustomed to darkness after

205

light. Lance was still shaky and hadn't been able to hold down any food. He was sure his rage was making him paranoid, but knowing it and changing it were two different things.

When he returned to the camp he found the skinners singing as they dug a hole for the dead pigmies. Their own dead they would apparently take away to be buried with proper tribal rites and in secrecy, away from the eyes of all others.

The pigmies were laid out in a line next to the large hole. Their heads had been cut off and placed in two rows some distance from the mutilated trunks. Lance had started screaming obscenities at the skinners and had struck several, throwing two bodily into the grave, before Jimmy and Kombi and two others had been able to restrain him. The skinners had melted away, taking the heads with them, while Lance struggled with the men holding him, dealing battered lips and black eyes and bruised shins indiscriminately until they pinned his arms and legs in the mud, and even then he butted with his head at anything within reach.

He had walked around the camp, giving his orders in a low tight voice – guards, lights, burial details, food, care of weapons, distribution of ammunition. The men refused to meet his eyes, leant forward to listen intently, jumped to obey. When he turned his head in some direction the chatter of released tension after dangerous action would stop instantly and the men would slide away to their tasks. Then he had sat down at the table but the first mouthful of food had brought the memory of the dead men and the mutilated bodies back to him and he had been sick beside his chair. He had left the table and staggered to the tanker, climbed up into it and been left alone.

Ewart was overdue. Lance wished he would bloody-well come back and take back the unwanted command of this bunch of fucking savages.

The door on the far side of the truck opened and Lance growled a warning. Briony climbed up into the truck and gave him a glass. He was tempted to throw it out of the window but his mouth tasted foul. He took a mouthful and swirled it around his mouth. It burnt. He spat it out of the window and sipped from the glass. It was straight whisky or bourbon, he didn't know which.

'Thanks,' he said without grace. 'Now go away.'

'Lance, you need all the friends you can get.'

'Oh, fuck off.'

She sat silently.

'With you for a friend I'll never again need enemies.'

'Have you considered what you're going to say to Ewart when he gets back?'

'Yes,' Lance replied, caught off guard by the unexpected question. 'I'm going to tell him to take back his bunch of savages and may he have much joy of them.'

'That's not what I mean.'

'Then what do you mean?'

'What happened here today. You did well, considering you were new to the job – '

'You're damn right I did!'

' – but that's not how Ewart's going to see it.'

'Huh?' Lance couldn't believe his ears.

'He's going to return with all his men, our trucks and our skins intact. He's frighteningly efficient, you know. And he's going to see his little brother, whom he left in charge of a peaceful camp. And his little brother has lost one of Big Brother's beloved Butchers – '

'The pigmies killed him, not me!' Lance was outraged.

'Sure, but you were left in charge of him and he's dead. Big Brother is going to see another of his favourite Butchers with a mutilated hand from your rough and ready surgery. And then you left the camp to follow the pigmies, leaving the camp undefended. Bruun's men could just have walked in and raped me.'

'You should have told me then.'

'I didn't think of it then. But Ewart's going to say you should have. Then you nearly got yourself killed by a pigmy, which Ewart will consider a personal insult. And then, for good measure, you alienated our skinners to the extent that they'll probably be the next ones to make war on us.

'The way Ewart is going to see it,' Briony summed up, 'is not that, by any reasonable standards, you performed excellently, but that, by his own very exacting standards which are the only ones he recognizes, you fucked up. And the fact that you're his brother is only going to make it worse. You'd better be ready with your story.'

Lance thought about it. At last he said, 'You're not just trying to stir trouble?'

'Why should I?'

'Because it's your nature.' Bluntly.

Briony laughed, swung her legs up and turned to lie on the seat, her head in Lance's lap. 'You smell raunchy.'

He sniffed. He couldn't smell himself because he had become accustomed to the odour. But she had had a bath and smelt fresh and desirable. Lance felt an erection rising and willed it to go away. It kept rising.

'Killing makes you randy,' he said nastily.

'Of course.' Her fingers were busy on his zip and in his underpants. She turned over to lie face down on him. He tried to push her away but in the confined space of the cab couldn't find the leverage. Out of the corner of his eye he saw she had her feet wedged against the door.

'Sit still,' she mumbled indistinctly, 'or I'll bite.'

Lance shuddered at the thought. 'Somebody will see!' he said desperately.

She didn't answer. The sucking sounds were unnaturally loud in Lance's ears. He was sure Jimmy, always nearby, would hear. Then it was too late. He arched his back and exploded. He heard her swallow, felt a few tantalizing licks and it was over as she sat up.

Lights were coming down the track.

'Jesus! Get the hell out of here! Ouch!' Lance, fumbling with the zip in the dark, had caught himself painfully.

Her hands nimbly rearranged his underpants and slid the zip.

'Get out!'

'You really should have a bath. You taste of death.' She giggled as she opened the door and slid away just as the lights entered the darkened camp on Lance's side of the tanker.

Bruun watched the activity around the trucks from a safe distance. Better Weber stuck with this mess than he. He could pick them off easily but he had only a revolver and, even if he had an automatic weapon or a rifle, they never bunched up so closely that he wouldn't get his before he had killed more than a few of them. One thing you had to say for Weber, his strenuous methods made soldiers who jumped to commands and took no unnecessary risks. But the result was, of course, totally disproportionate to the effort. You could save a lot of training if you were willing to sacrifice a few niggers until greater numbers started to count.

But right now he had no greater numbers and, even if he could take the trucks back from Weber, no drivers for them.

Bruun struck out through the forest until he could no longer see the lights, then turned towards the road. He walked along the road. His boots hurt, his breathing was painful. Walking, he had often said, was for other ranks. He cursed, a continuous loud stream.

A black man on a bicycle came past him, greeting him courteously and staring curiously in the dark. Bruun turned around to look after the slithering bicycle.

'Hey, you!'

The man stopped politely. Bruun waddled over to him. What a piece of luck. A bicycle might pass here once in six

209

days, a truck less frequently, a car almost never. Tonight the gods were·smiling on Theodore Bruun.

Bruun took the man by the lapels of his tattered coat with one hand, steadying the bicycle in the other. He lifted the man clear of the bicycle and threw him into the undergrowth beside the road. He mounted the bicycle and, putting out a foot on each side every revolution of the pedals to stop him falling down on the slippery mud, rode off, ignoring the outraged cries behind him. The nigger would have more sense than to run after him and try to repossess the bicycle. Of that he was sure, otherwise he would have killed him before taking the machine.

It was tiring work, riding on that road and it was well after midnight when he reached Bangui. He walked the bicycle across the narrow bridge and past the deserted customs post. He knew where to find a man with a car who could be bribed to drive him upriver to his camp.

At two o'clock in the morning he was kicking his men awake. He patiently slapped faces until he had some account of what had happened at Weber's camp. The sergeant, stupid sod, had been captured, had blown the whistle, and then been escorted back to the boats. Within sight of the boats he and the men escorting him had been attacked by pigmies. One escort had died. The other had taken the sergeant on his back for protection and run for it. The men had scrambled aboard the boats and left with all speed, the sound of automatic fire receding behind them. So. The pigmy attack had worked. He also knew how Weber had caught up with him so quickly. He kicked the men almost absently.

Weber shouldn't be allowed to get away with it.

Ewart inspected the camp and listened to what everybody had to say. He approved of the positions Lance had sent guards to. By then Briony had tended to Jacques, strapping up his chest just in case there were bruised ribs, and prepared a meal. Ewart washed his face and hands and

210

ate. Lance also managed to eat something. Jacques demonstrated that there was nothing wrong with him by wolfing his food. It was midnight when they finished. Ewart lit a cigarillo and poured brandy.

Here it comes, Lance thought.

'Tell me about it,' Ewart said.

'You've heard the story from everybody else.'

'I left you in charge. Give me the official report.'

Lance told the story. He was interrupted only twice, one when he told of his suspicion that Bruun had provoked the pigmy attack by deliberately killing one of the pigmies – Ewart said, 'Very probable; we'll look for the body tomorrow' – and once when he explained how they defeated the pigmies by firing grid patterns into the trees – Jacques said, 'Excellent thinking!' He ended by saying, 'We turned back to the camp,' not mentioning the events on their return. Ewart would no doubt get to them soon enough. Lance braced himself for a dressing down.

'My brother, the rugger player, wit, and hero,' Ewart said, raising his glass.

Lance sighed his relief.

'Tomorrow,' Ewart continued 'you and I will discuss a few details of what you did today in the light of the more considered opinion of hindsight. You've done us all proud. For the moment, I just want to say this: the next time you're tempted to heroics, take the time to ask yourself if they're really necessary. Most of the big medals go to dead men.'

Lance nodded, too relieved to speak.

'Now,' Ewart said in the same friendly tone, 'you'd better tell me what happened to the skinners and how come four of my men have their faces battered.'

There was no escape. Lance told him. When he finished his monotone tale he said, with some spirit, 'Those skinners are fucking savages, cutting off the heads of corpses.'

'That's no mitigation for breaking our contract with them so abruptly.' Ewart didn't seem much concerned.

'What the hell are you talking about?'

'We agreed, admittedly at a time when it seemed only a sick joke and an obligation we'd be unlikely to have to honour, that they could have the heads of any pigmies we killed.'

Lance remembered. American dollars, salt, food, and the heads of pigmies. 'That's sick, Ewart.'

'You may think so. They don't. You broke our contract with them. If they attack us, any damage they do will come out of your share of the profits. If we can buy them off, any additional cost will also be borne by you.'

Lance had his mouth open to speak, to say something obstreperous and hurtful, but Jacques raised his voice to cut him off. 'That's fair, Lance. Don't argue.'

Ewart nodded. 'Let's get the unpleasantness over. There remain the four men with bruised faces that says more for the intensity of your anger than for your intelligence. The only creditable aspect of that little episode is their restraint in not tearing you limb from limb.'

Lance put his hands flat on the table. Ewart could be hateful but he was right. 'I'll apologize.'

'Don't. Apologies are not their style. But remember, your undoubted skill with the rifle Jacques gave you, or even your excellent qualities of leadership, those won't keep you alive out here for twenty-four hours without these men. So just pay them common courtesy and consideration when they're acting in your best interests. That's all. We'll save the more pleasant bits for tomorrow.'

'A toast to Bruun walking to Bangui in the mud,' Jacques said.

Jimmy picked Lance's glass from the table and put it in his hand.

'More likely shivering cold and wet in a tree, trying to keep awake so the leopards don't get him,' Ewart laughed.

They drank the toast and Lance went to bed, feeling drained. 'Good night, Jimmy,' he called and was reassured when the answer came: 'Sleep well, Mr Lance.'

* * *

They spent the next day getting their camp in order and rigging repairs to the two damaged trucks. Before breakfast Ewart sent a man to see if he could find the pigmy Lance thought Bruun had killed. The man returned to say he had found the pigmy, ceremoniously laid out but ravaged by the nightstalkers of the forest and surrounded by the daytime scavengers. He had buried what was left of him on the spot.

'You're really getting the feel for this kind of work very quickly,' Jacques said to Lance when they heard this.

Sambo went with two men and renegotiated their contract with the skinners. He had to double their wages and salt rations and allow them to keep the pigmy heads. He had promised Lance to ask for the heads back for a decent burial but judiciously forgot about it when he actually spoke to the skinners. The families of the men killed by the pigmies were also each to be given a hundred American dollars.

'I don't have that kind of money,' Lance said when he heard this.

'Your share of that,' Ewart said, pointing to the truckloads of crocodile skins, 'will be many times more than a thousand dollars or so.'

Towards the end of the day Lance became aware that the men jumped when he ordered something. Before yesterday they had done what he had said but with no great alacrity. He mentioned this to Jacques, who laughed broadly. 'Yesterday morning your authority was derived from being white and, in a secondhand sort of way, from being Ewart's brother. But then you proved yourself a leader of men in your own right. Running out to save Kombi made a big impression on them. He might not be the brightest of Sambo's brothers but he is one of the highest of their high chiefs, a prince, and well regarded by them for his courage.'

Lance was embarrassed. He didn't want to pursue the discussion but Jacques had more to say.

213

'It takes real courage to go into the forest after pigmies. The way they see it, you could have sent somebody else and stayed here on the pretext of defending the camp. But you went yourself.'

'I hadn't actually thought of staying in camp,' Lance admitted.

'Yes, but they don't know that, do they?'

Late in the afternoon Lance told Jimmy, 'Find another man to help us on the tankers. To replace the one killed yesterday.'

Jimmy called for volunteers. All the men volunteered. Lance was touched. They selected the man whose brother had been killed by the pigmies the day before.

The man whose life Lance had saved by chopping off his little finger took, whenever he had nothing specific to do, to following Lance around, walking three paces behind Jimmy. At first it was disconcerting but Lance soon became used to it and was even a little amused though he kept a straight face. The man had polished all his shoes and had to be restrained by Jimmy from polishing his rough-textured desert boots as well.

In the late afternoon, as dusk fell, he sat at the table with Ewart and listened carefully, without resentment, as Ewart dissected every decision he had made the previous day, approving of some, getting Lance's agreement that others were hastily made under pressure and could be improved upon. Ewart concluded by saying, 'In time you will instinctively make the right decisions, no matter what the pressures. For now, give it another second of thought and you'll improve your average.'

Lance came down to the river at midmorning the next day with the jars of nitro, a line of black men walking behind him as if on hot stones, each carrying a single jar of the vicious explosive.

Twenty yards from the river he found Jacques. 'Have

the nitro carried back,' Jacques said. 'There'll be no use for it today.'

Lance turned away without asking questions. A half-pound of nitro in your hands tends to make you very un-garrulous. When he returned empty-handed, having made sure all the nitro was in a safe place and set guards over it, Jacques handed him the binoculars without a word.

'What am I looking for?'

'Cut branches on the far side of the river.'

Lance found them and also some wide slimy tracks up the bank of the river.

'What is it?'

'Bruun. The bugger must have found transport back to his men and brought them down here in the night.'

'The tracks are where they dragged the boats out and then cut branches to camouflage them?'

'Yes. But, as usual, Bruun worked shoddily. He cut the branches too near the bank and didn't worry about covering the tracks left when they dragged the boats from the river.'

'Where's Ewart?'

'He took Sambo and Kombi and went scouting over there.'

'Christ!' Lance searched through the binoculars but found no sign of people. He tried the greater magnification available from the scope on his rifle. Nothing.

'You aren't likely to see anything,' Jacques said, chuckling.

'Then what are you sitting here for with binoculars?'

'Sentry duty. Just in case Bruun decides to invade us.'

Lance looked at the men, all armed, who had helped him with the nitro and were now standing around curiously, trying to appear not to be listening. 'That would be very stupid of him.'

Jacques shrugged. 'Nobody is as unpredictable as a man whose pride has been wounded.'

Lance had a hot flush as he remembered Briony in the

cab of the tanker. But Jacques had the binoculars to his eyes again and was watching the opposite shore.

'I thought Bruun's parish was this side of the river. What's he doing over there?' Lance said finally.

'Causing trouble. Bruun's kind don't recognize borders as anything but minor inconveniences to their greed.'

After a while the men wandered away and then Lance went back to the camp. There was nothing to be seen, nothing happening. He hoped Ewart wasn't getting into trouble. But Ewart was indestructible. Lance sat watching Jimmy kneading the scraped skin of the black tree snake.

Two hours after dusk Ewart came back in a truck, the skiff on the back. They'd taken it downriver, crossed the river, hidden the skiff and proceeded on foot to spy on Bruun's party. They had returned the same way. Ewart was immaculate as ever but looked a bit tired. They had left just after midnight, in the earliest hour of this day.

'He's got more than forty men,' Ewart said as he sat down to the meal Briony had waiting. He ate in silence and rose. 'Tomorrow we'll kill crocodiles,' he said and went into his tent to sleep.

'The superior jungle fighter is the one who sees but is not seen,' one of the old Borneo hands had instructed Bruun's class at Sandhurst.

Bruun chuckled. Already he had caused Weber to lose three days. A day of rest on which you have to fight is a day lost. A day spent making unnecessary repairs is a day lost. And, best of all, a day on which you had to lie in hiding, idling away the hours because of fear of an enemy you could not even see, was a day lost. Weber had shown extraordinary good sense to stay off the water the previous day, setting out a guard with binoculars to watch for an enemy he couldn't possibly know was already in position. But today Weber would have to venture on the water if he wasn't to lose the confidence of his men. Bruun was counting on this.

216

For Bruun had only two choices open to him, having already discarded the only other alternative of attacking Weber, wiping him and his men out and taking the crocodile skins already gathered: that would mean he would miss out on the skins of the crocodiles Weber would kill between here and Bangui, as many as they had already taken and probably more. The two remaining choices were: to withdraw for the time being and waylay Weber with his convoy of skins just before Bangui, but that would be too near the city and its many blabbering mouths and greedy hands; or to harass Weber just sufficiently to make him see reason, which reason was that he couldn't continue without some kind of a compact with Bruun, naturally at a stiff price – Bruun was thinking in terms of four-fifths of the proceeds. If this failed, Bruun thought, he could still fall back on the alternative of an attack near Bangui.

Bruun watched the darkness in front of him. He was thirty yards from the river and dawn could only be minutes away, yet he could still not distinguish the trees right in front of him. He shifted in the dew. He had been lying here for half an hour and was getting stiff. Suddenly he could see the line of the tops of the trees across the river, broken by the upright black shapes of the trees on his side of the river. Seconds later a red glaze shot through the treetops across the river. It would be a while yet before he would see the sun, but it was dawn.

Only minutes later he saw the first stirrings in the shadows under the trees on the far side of the river. At first he thought some animals were drinking dangerously close to Weber's camp but his binoculars showed him men. Aha! So Weber was trying to get an early start. But Theodore Bruun had been up even earlier.

He closed his eyes to accustom them to darkness and looked left and right to make sure the shadows which were his men were in position. 'Don't fire until I do. Pass the message,' he called softly, aware that sound would travel further over water than land. He listened to the message being passed on.

Full light came to the middle of the river, though the sun could still be seen only as a red rim over the tall trees. The river banks had a cool clear light on them. Under the trees it was still almost dark, only the edge taken off the inky blackness, only detailless shapes recognizable. Bruun knew it was tricky light for shooting in, especially over the water, but the intention was not to do Weber's party irreparable harm (that would be counterproductive) but simply to frighten them into negotiating. After all, they were going to have to sit exposed on the river on God knows how much nitro if they wanted to hunt crocodiles.

The river bank right in front of them lit up and the sun blinded them with all its glory and the added reflection on the water. Bruun waited impatiently for the light to reach under the opposite bank as well. Meanwhile he watched them put a skiff in the water and place some boxes in it. Good. They had decided he wasn't coming after all. They were in for a very rude shock. He hoped his men would remember not to shoot at the skiff if any of the white men were in it or in the water. Killing a few of Weber's little black Coldstreamers would be salutary; killing any of the whites must reduce the crocodile-killing capacity of the expedition.

The skiff chugged out on the water, the airscrew turning lazily, the wake non-existent. There were only two black men aboard. Bruun decided to wait until they had cleared the shadows thrown by the trees on the far bank. He wanted to start shooting before they turned the skiff upriver. It is easier to hit a target moving towards you in a straight line than one moving across your line of sight. The skiff was quite a substantial target but the range was right at the limit of their firearms.

Bruun pictured a trajectory in his mind. The latter part of any bullet's trajectory was the most unpredictable – though novices often fell into the trap of thinking that, because it was inevitably downwards, it was therefore predictable. In fact, the further from the barrel, the greater the effect of even small differences in explosive load, microscopic irregularities in bullet or case castings, the condition of the rifling inside the barrel, and even the state of cleanliness of the rifle. At the end of their trajectory similar bullets would have different sink rates, all other things being as nearly equal as human ingenuity could make them, in different conditions of air humidity.

Bruun aimed carefully and fired. He hit one of the boxes on the skiff. There was no explosion. The bullet must have been spent. He didn't bother to fire again. His men were delivering the message loud and clear with spent bullets plopping in the water near the skiff: Come any closer and we'll blow you up.

The skiff turned at a right angle and steadied, then proceeded upriver at the same slow pace. The two black men aboard were hiding behind the boxes. Bruun laughed aloud. The men kept shooting. The skiff turned another right angle towards them. Of course, with nitro aboard, they would not want to turn towards the bank and perhaps run into a submerged log. They would have to make two more right-angle turns, exposing themselves for a considerable time at their present pace, before they could land at the safe sandy spit they had launched from. Before then they would go sky-high and the river with them. Bruun checked again that there was a stout tree for him to grab hold of.

His men were really putting up a good firing rate. Bruun grinned encouragingly at the one nearest to him and found the man hanging foward over a thick tree root, a small hole in the back of his head oozing watery blood, the front of his face blown away by the bullet's exit. Somebody was shooting at them from behind!

'You really should change your make-up, Jimmy,' Lance said as he stepped from his tent in the last coolness of the

219

night that always came with the false dawn just before the heat of the day. Jimmy's eye, which yesterday had been purple, today had a greenish tinge in the light of the Coleman lamp. 'It's going mouldy and you know the boys don't like slovenly girls.'

'Here, catch.' Jimmy threw something at him and Lance caught it. 'The grandfather of all black snakes.'

But Lance had already dropped the cool, scaly, writhing thing and crashed away, upsetting the breakfast table thirty feet away in front of the mess tent. There he stood shaking. 'Christ Jimmy, I only punched you a few times. That's no reason to kill me.'

Jimmy, smiling broadly, picked the thing from the ground. 'You slide this tongue into this hole and in the back is a money pocket with – with – ' Jimmy could go no further, he was laughing so much. From behind him the shadows split with white teeth and loud laughter as his tribesmen, invited to enjoy the joke, declared themselves.

'Go away, you barking hyenas,' Lance said wearily. It was a supreme insult in their language but it set them off in new peals of laughter.

Jimmy brought the belt over to him and Lance accepted it warily. It still felt repulsive and he had never really wanted it but knew no way of refusing. He inspected it politely. It was beautifully soft and handsomely crafted with stitches almost too small for the eye to see.

'Aah, Kleinbaas, genuine snakegut stitching,' Pietie said with wonder in his voice as he came to reset the fallen table.

Jimmy nodded. 'Twisted from the gut of the black tree snake. It will last your lifetime and beyond. It is knotted at every stitch.' Lance looked at the row of tiny knots. 'What are these flaps on the inside at the back for?'

Jimmy slapped away Pietie's hand where the Coloured servant was fondling the end of the belt. 'Money pouch. You put in gold coins or paper money folded double, fold the flaps – so – and it is totally secure against your body once you've put the belt on.' Lance touched the tongue made from the fang of the black tree snake, and jerked his hand away.

'Quite clean of poison.'

Jimmy pricked his finger with it to demonstrate. 'It will get brittle and break in thirty years or so but there's a spare soaked in the grease from the same snake sewn in – here – and then you have that attached. After another thirty years or so, you catch your own black tree snake for another tongue.' It was a joke. They all laughed while Lance stood holding the gift. 'Put it on, Mr Lance.'

Lance took off his belt and put it on the table. Reluctantly he slid the black tree snake-belt through the loops of his trousers and closed it, careful to keep his fingers well clear of the fang. The black men sighed collectively and chanted something.

'Only the most renowned warriors of my tribe may wear such a belt,' Jimmy said. 'Even Sambo doesn't have one yet.'

Lance was touched and relieved. 'Only for ceremonial occasions then, eh, Jimmy.'

'Oh no, Mr Lance, you must wear it every day. It is true, when I promised to make it it was only intended for a dress belt' – Jimmy paused so Lance could understand it was his tactful way of saying it had been a joke ' – but after the battle of recent memory the men all agreed you should have the proper belt as befits a great warrior.'

The men grunted their agreement.

Lance put his hand on the belt. It felt less repulsive by the minute. He had never had any kind of ceremonial dress before and certainly not a money-belt. And made of black tree snake, possibly the most dangerous snake in the world. Voted him by Ewart's world-famous Baluba Butchers. He would certainly wear it. And make a suitable speech. But when he opened his mouth, he was overcome with pride and gratitide and only managed 'Thank you all very much' before he sat down at the table, one hand still on his belt.

'It is truly said,' the men chorused, understanding, and melted away, telling each other, 'What great warrior ever had many words?'

'Your brother said for you to make another batch of jelly, Mr Lance. Today he wants to blow up the river twice.'

'Where are the others?'

'Already at work,' Briony replied, bringing his breakfast from the mess tent.

An hour later he heard the faint reports of the first shots. 'Stop work.' He looked in the direction of the river.

'That's your brother, taking care of the thieves across the river,' Jimmy said casually. 'We'd better get on with it. We have our orders.'

'All right. Continue work.'

Lance didn't much like melting nitroglycerine from dynamite while there was shooting, no matter that it was across the river, but when Jimmy put it like that it more than likely meant he'd had orders from Ewart directly to keep Lance's nose to the grindstone. Over the days, with practice, the process had been streamlined and another hour of work would see the batch completed, well before it could possibly be required. The hell with it. 'Stop work. Clear up. Make safe.' He waited impatiently for the orders to be executed. Jimmy was looking on silently. 'Come with me. Bring your arms.' Lance added unnecessarily, out of nervousness.

Jacques was sitting on a log right at the water's edge. 'I'm glad you came. I was about to send for you.'

'Aren't you a bit exposed out here?' Lance looked in the direction of the opposite bank where the sound of shots continued.

'No. They haven't the range of me and, anyway, you'd have to be a Bisley shot to hit a sitting man from over there.' Jacques pointed and Lance saw the skiff on the river, making its first right-angle turn.

'What the hell are they doing out there?'

'Decoy. Don't worry, they don't have any nitro, only plenty of boxes full of dynamite to hide behind. And nothing is going to hit them except perhaps a few spent bullets which'll do no more harm than leave a burn mark or a graze.'

'So, they're out there and Bruun's men are shooting at them. Now what?'

'Wait. Ewart's behind Bruun. When he's marked enough of Bruun's men, he starts shooting. You'll hear it.'

Lance stared unbelievingly at Jacques. 'Are you and Ewart and Bruun crazy? That's the Central African Republic over there, a *third* country that's got nothing to do with this, and you're fighting a private war on its land.'

Jacques was amused. 'By the time they find out, it'll be too late to do anything but complain through diplomatic channels. Diplomatic channels flow very slowly indeed. We'll be long gone, enjoying our riches in more salubrious surroundings.'

'Haven't you heard of extradition?'

'Take my word for it, there's nothing to worry about, Lance. If you have to worry about something, worry about somebody proving it was us who blew up part of the Kariba Dam and stole the trucks and dynamite there.'

Lance had forgotten about that. 'Aw shit,' he said, defeated. You just couldn't argue with Jacques or Ewart.

'Now. Use the scope on your rifle and study the forest over there.' After a minute, Jacques asked, 'What do you see?'

'I've found eight men, lying on the ground, firing at the skiff. They're smiling, enjoying themselves.'

'There are more men than that.'

'Shall I shoot at them?' It was an idle question; if they couldn't hit him, presumably he couldn't hit them.

'Not yet. Ewart's behind them.'

'I didn't see him.'

'You will, when he starts shooting.'

Lance looked through the scope again and saw nothing

but Bruun's men. His finger itched on the trigger: they were shooting at his men, defenceless on a skiff moving slowly out in the open river. Then he was ashamed of the urge. It was primitive. He was no better than the skinners who cut the heads from corpses.

The firing intensified. At first nothing happened except that Lance saw several of Bruun's men jerk and lay still. The bullets fired by the rest still reached for the skiff or slapped against the boxes of dynamite. Then he saw Bruun rear up like a bull electrocuted at an abattoir and jump over a log. He laughed. When he sighted again, Bruun was out of sight.

'Now you can start firing but try not to hit our own,' Jacques said, 'Not you, you stupid fools,' he said to the blacks who were eagerly fitting long barrels. 'You've barely got the range and without scopes you're as likely to kill our own people as Bruun's men.' They looked sheepish and put up their firearms.

Lance sighted carefully on the back of a head. The man had jumped about to fire at the attackers. Then Lance searched through the obscuring foliage further in and found two of their own men in their position, brief glimpses as they exposed themselves momentarily to fire a shot or a short burst. He found the back of the man's head again and fired when the scope framed the head in an area the size of a soup plate. The bullet caused a fine spray of red mist to flare out on the side of the head further from Lance.

'Good work,' Jacques said, his binoculars still to his eyes.

Lance felt his heart drop. He hadn't expected to hit anything at all, just to be of some nuisance value with spent bullets flying around from his rifle.

'Come on, boy, what's wrong with you,' Jacques chided. 'They're shooting at your brother and a couple of days ago they set the pigmies on you.'

Lance looked at the rifle in his hands. A beautiful instrument, finely crafted for death.

'Come on Lance! Either use the rifle or let Jimmy or me have it.'

It was his rifle. Jacques had given it to him. Lance obeyed blindly, raising the rifle to his shoulder, his finger around the trigger, the thumb of the other hand on the telescopic zoom. He found a head, squeezed the trigger, looked for another head without waiting to see the result but not escaping the smeared red blur as he swung the rifle away, found a head, squeezed the trigger, swung the barrel and the scope to search again while the auto ejector shot the empty casing past his ear. In the minute it took Bruun's men to catch on that they were in a murderous crossfire, Lance killed six of them. When they broke to the right, he killed two more before they disappeared into the forest.

He heard Jacques gasp beside him. He swung the rifle again, looking for Bruun. Bruun had brought all this about. Bruun was just rising, breaking to the left, about to reach the cover of undergrowth which would shield him from Lance.

Lance shot the rifle from Bruun's hand and saw it flying to one side. Bruun's hands flew to his buttocks but Lance was sure he hadn't hit Bruun. He wanted Bruun alive, captured to stand trial for what he had done. He lowered the rifle and rose.

The men sighed their admiration for such shooting.

'Fuck you all,' Lance said and walked away, sick to the heart. The worst was that he no longer felt sick to the stomach at the killing.

Bruun dived for the other side of the log. Ah, and another log to protect his back. Excellent! 'Cover your rears!' he shouted. Two of his men were killed before they could reverse positions. He looked over his log and ducked again as a piece was chipped off it before he could see anything. Some of his men were firing and others were searching desperately for targets. Quite a few were held in untenable positions such as his own. Stupid black bastards.

Then he saw a man slump forward. It was incredible. Roux was supposed to be a fair shot if given some pretty exotic shooting machinery but this was ridiculous. A fluke shot. Bruun looked over his shoulder. He was covered by a log and the undergrowth, which obscured his view of the far bank, also covered him from them. He could crawl along a few feet and regain his previous sightline but that would be pointless: the danger was this side. He raised a twig above the log and it was broken with a single shot. Shit!

There was a series of close, regularly spaced faint pops from behind him and Bruun incredulously saw one of his men go down with each pop. But it was his chance. As soon as they realized they were in a murderous crossfire, they would break without waiting for orders. He would give them a moment to distract the attention of the attackers on this side of the river, then break in the other direction. There they went. Bloody fools, Bruun thought as he saw them fall. He rose almost leisurely and cut in the other direction, away from the mass exit of black lemmings from the trap. There was a shock in his hand, a blow across his backside and he watched his rifle land ten feet from him while his hands flew to his bottom. No wetness but he knew what it was: the bullet had ricocheted off the rifle and cut across his buttocks without breaking the skin, leaving a blood welt an inch deep. Already the pressure was painful and it would hurt like hell when it had to be burst.

Ewart Weber stepped out of the undergrowth, his FN negligently crooked in the elbow of his right arm, the barrel pointing in the general direction of Bruun. Bruun felt like crying, Within shooting distance of Weber and without a firearm.

'You always escalate things unnecessarily,' Bruun said reproachfully.

'So my little brother got you across your fat backside. He could hardly miss.' Weber burst out laughing.

Bruun took his chance. He rolled away into the undergrowth and was crawling ten feet from where the bullets struck by the time Weber got enough control over himself to start firing.

For this, Bruun resolved, he was going to kill Weber, his freak brother and all with them. Then he would take their skins and their dynamite and blow up the bloody river himself for the rest of the skins.

'For a fat man, Bruun was belly-wriggling through the undergrowth amazingly fast.' Ewart was still laughing, 'By the time I started searching, he'd gone. Fancy shooting that, Lance, welting him right across the arse and knocking his rifle out of his hand at the same time.'

Lance's sharp retort was lost in the general hubbub of laughter, backslapping congratulations and the activity of dragging the skiff Ewart had crossed the river on off the truck that had brought it back from down-river.

'All right,' Ewart said, chuckling. 'Get that skiff to the water and bring up the jelly. Lance, can you have the second batch ready to go up-river right after lunch?'

'Are you mad? You can't go on the river sitting on a box of nitro with Bruun and his crazies over there. It'll take only one spent bullet knocking – '

'We counted twenty-one dead. Use your head, Lance Even if Bruun can find them, round them up, re-arm them, how do you think he's going to persuade them to get within range of your rifle again? A man who lost half his force in three minutes.'

'And had another defeat only a couple of days ago,' Jacques added.

Lance went sullenly about his work. When the jelly was ready, he held the men with him until he heard the first batch explode. Watching the river rise above the trees from afar was a somehow frightening experience. Would

227

nature retaliate against them for tampering so grossly with her? He waited for the water to subside and then had the jelly carried towards the river. The idea was to take it up-river before too many of the smaller animals bloated and started floating down-river but not before all the solid debris had been washed away. The scouring parties were on both sides of the river all day long, taking their lunch with them. On the far bank, Ewart had Kombi scount inland and forward but Kombi found nothing worth reporting.

In the early afternoon, Ewart sent Jacques ahead in one skiff to a point fifteen miles up-river. Ten minutes later he followed with the other skiff, loaded with all the nitro.

They divided the nitro in midstream, an operation that had everybody except Ewart soaking with the sour sweat of fear before the main operation of mining the river had even begun. When it went up, the huge spout of water could be seen at the camp ten miles downstream. Ewart had the two big lights with their generators mounted on the skiffs and they worked into the night bringing croco-diles from the banks into the camp where the skinners worked frantically to stay level, pausing only to look up fearfully each time Lance passed them.

'They think you're the *tokoloshe*,' Jimmy said. 'Only the devil would throw them into an unhallowed grave, one morover dug for pigmies who, as everyone knows, are – '

'Why don't you just shut your face, Jimmy.'

It was nearly ten o'clock when they ate, gulping their food because there was more work to be done. Lance's scowl put tension in the air. Finally Ewart laid down his knife and fork. 'All right, Lance, what's eating you?'

'I don't like killing people like a little game.'

'We're not killing people to score points. We're hunting crocodiles to make money and, incidentally, defending our lives and lawful property against unprovoked and unwarranted attack. That's very different indeed.'

'Do you call waiting for Bruun over there "incidental"?'

'That's due foresight against aggressors already in place, if you have to have fancy words for it.'

'Jesus Christ almighty! You killed twenty-one people today!'

'You did your fair share and more.'

'Yes, and when you had your chance to arrest Bruun and bring him to justice for causing all these killings, what the fuck did you do? You laughed, that's what you did, you laughed and let him get away!'

'Don't swear in the presence of ladies,' Ewart said calmly.

'Oh, don't mind me.' Briony's eyes were shining with anticipation.

'Lance, there was never any question of capturing Bruun and no possibility of bringing him to what you call "justice". Bruun is "justice" around these parts. I was just laughing too hard to kill him. I thought you'd deliberately disarmed him to deliver him up to me.'

'You – ' Lance was rising, shaking the table.

'Sit down and eat your food!'

Lance sat down but didn't pick up the knife and fork he'd dropped.

'"So are we Caesar's friends that have abridged his time of fearing death."' Jacques said. 'To have killed Bruun would have been the friendly act of putting him out of his misery but he is no friend of ours. Let him go in fear and long.'

'Okay, okay,' Lance said softly, taking his hands off the table so the others couldn't see how he was clenching them. 'But I don't like this business of fighting our wars in a neutral country.'

'I told you not to worry about it,' Jacques said. 'All we have to do is keep Bruun at a distance for a few days and we'll be gone before the bureaucrats in Bangui even hear about our little target shoot.'

'You mean he'll be back?' Lance couldn't believe his ears.

'Tomorrow,' Ewart said. 'He won't give up this rich a prize simply because he's lost a few men.'

They sat silently, considering this, giving Lance time to digest the news.

'You've done your share,' Ewart said gently. 'Your share of the skins will come to a substantial amount. You could go back home and I'll arrange for you to stay with a friend in Durban until I can get to Cape Town and straighten out the Chinaman.'

Lance felt shame colouring his cheeks. 'I'm not frightened, if that's what you're implying. I just think you're handling this whole business the wrong way. I'll stay till the first lot of skins are delivered in Bangui, then I'll go home.'

Ewart nodded, not bothering to deny he had thought Lance a coward.

Jacques said, 'We didn't throw the first punch.'

Lance rose. He was feeling drained. He walked towards the floodlit area where the skinners were still working to the rhythm of a song only they heard.

'My way is the only way to stay alive round here,' Ewart called after him. 'I don't like it either but I must accept it or we'll all be dead by nightfall tomorrow.'

Lance stopped and turned around. He was going to say that Ewart had known that he would have to kill men to protect his crocodile skins and could have chosen not to come at all. But Ewart was not the kind of man who would even consider the alternative of avoiding trouble by simply absenting himself.

Anything Lance said would have as much effect as the croaking of the frogs in the river. Lance nodded and walked on, hearing the frogs for the first time: they didn't just croak, they whistled and clicked and clucked and wheezed and whimpered. Lance knew in his heart that, had Ewart insisted he leave, he would not have gone. The wealth of the skins was a prize worth risking much for; he was not cured of his gambling yet.

* * *

By break of day the next morning they had moved the camp twenty miles upstream. By eight o'clock enough nitro had been melted from the dynamite to blow up five miles of the river. The men kept looking up from their work, giving Lance curious glances. Lance snapped at them to pay attention to their work. If before they had jumped to his orders, they were now literally falling over themselves not to irritate him, so much so that one man actually spilled half a jar of nitro on the ground in his hurry not to have Lance catch his eye.

'It's your shooting yesterday,' Jimmy said helpfully. 'One man for every shot at that distance . . . Even Mr Roux and I – and, not to be modest, we are excellent shots – couldn't match that. The men have never seen anything like that. They're looking to see if they can spot your magic.'

'Tell them it's the black tree snake belt and to get on with their work.'

Jimmy said something in their own language. The men went back to work smiling.

'There's no word for sarcasm in their language,' Ewart said behind Lance.

Lance had not heard him coming. He jumped, startled.

'They take whatever you say at face value. Fortunately that was a suitable remark.'

'Sorry.' Lance wasn't sorry at all – he was in fact feeling decidedly aggressive – but this was not the issue to start an argument over. He had been too obviously in the wrong.

'There's no word for sorry or apologize in their language either.'

'Nor please or thank you, just like the Zulus,' Jimmy said, trying to forestall an explosion between the brothers.

Ewart smiled. 'You listen well, Jimmy.' To Lance, he said, 'Take Jimmy and have a word with Jacques at the river. He has a plan. See what you think. I'll supervise here.'

'Was he this shitty in the war?' Lance asked Jimmy when they were nearly at the river.

'He was just pointing out, perfectly reasonably, that one does not offend those you have to work and fight with.'

'Whose side are you on?'

'Survival, Mr Lance. I want to live and it's not going to get easier if you carry grudges.' When Lance didn't answer, Jimmy continued, 'You missed the point, Mr Lance. He wasn't reprimanding you or trying to pick a fight. When your brother picks a fight somebody else ends up in hospital. He was paying you a compliment, asking you for an opinion. The men understood this. How many people do you think your brother asks for their opinion?'

'So a lot of grinning savages are more subtle than me,' Lance said rudely, and hunched his shoulders.

'With friends like Jimmy a man has no hiding place.' Jacques had overheard the last part of the conversation. He was seated on a log, his breakfast being served by his white-coated servant, Pietie. 'Your breakfast is under that cover. Jimmy's will come in a moment.'

Lance ate hungrily. He didn't ask what it was about. Every evil would hatch in its own good time. When he had finished and was sipping his coffee, Jacques handed him the binoculars. 'Have a look. Tell me what you think.'

Lance looked and handed the binoculars to Jimmy as a sort of silent apology for his rudeness. 'One man every so often, a goodly distance apart. Jimmy will tell you how far.'

'About two hundred metres apart, Mr Lance,' Jimmy said.

'Bruun must be pretty stupid to try the same thing again,' Lance said.

'Not quite,' Jacques said. 'He brought his men up after light, checking carefully for ambush. He's got a man every two hundred yards for the next ten miles up-river, about a hundred men in all.'

'I don't understand,' Lance said. 'He can't attack us with his men spread out like that. And each of those men will be unable to defend himself against us should Ewart decide to attack them.'

'That's just the point. How long do you think it will take us to clear that side of the river, hunting each man down separately?'

'I don't know. All day? Jimmy?'

'At least two days, Mr Lance. Possibly three days.'

'At which point they'll be back at the beginning again and we have to start all over.' Suddenly Lance saw it. 'We can't work on the river with nitro unless we make a deal with Bruun.'

'Exactly.' Jacques was smiling. 'But we do have an option. We have two skiffs. We put a marksman on one. He drives Bruun's men back. The skiff with the nitro shelters behind the first skiff.'

'I see. You want me to be the marksman.'

'No. I'll do it.'

Lance shook his head. 'I said I'll pull my weight and that's exactly what I'll do.'

Jacques shrugged. 'That's up to Ewart. He decides who does what. He might decide it's too dangerous.'

'We'll see,' Lance said tightly. 'Anyway, why not have a marksman on the skiff with the nitro? Then we can use both skiffs and get it over with so much quicker.'

Jacques appeared to be thinking it over.

'I don't like the idea of two skiffs too near each other in the water,' Lance added. 'It just needs a little clumsiness on the throttle of the marksman's skiff and both will go up.'

'Yes, you have a point there. Talk it over with Ewart, will you. You can say that I agree.'

Ewart listened to what Lance had to say and agreed to it. 'We'll do it that way then, a mile at a time with the two

233

skiffs working towards each other. Jacques can work the rifle on one and I'll do the other.'

'I'll take my turn as well,'

'No.'

'You still think – '

'What I think doesn't matter. Jacques and I are the major partners. We'll take the bigger risks.'

'All right. Then cut me in for a third of what's left after Sambo's share.'

Ewart looked calculatingly at Lance. 'What's in your mind?'

'If I'm risking my life for a share of the skins, I want an agreed part which I'll know I earned rather than depend on your charity for a piece of your action.'

Ewart was obviously delighted. 'That's my brother talking! Now I can see what made you a gambler. You realize, though, that here you're not going to get a second spin of the wheel, don't you?'

'Yes.'

'You're not just trying to prove something?'

Lance tapped his belt. 'Even you and your Sergeant Sambo don't rate one of these. I've done my proving.'

'All right. I'll talk it over with Jacques. Don't make any more nitro than we can use in ten miles. At a mile a time, I doubt whether we'll even make ten miles today.'

'Why not buy Bruun off then?'

'Because his price is everything – all the skins and all our lives. You shot him in the bum and I laughed at him. Jacques and Briony he just hates because they're superior.'

'Then pretend to make a deal and, later – '

'I don't work like that.'

'Even with snakes like Bruun?'

'With anybody. I only have two assets: my skill as a soldier and my reputation around the world for keeping my word, for doing exactly as I promised I would do. I value both. Anyway, it's easier to fight Bruun when he's in

234

front of you than when he's lounging in your camp planning to kill you sometime while your back is turned.'

It was the longest speech Lance had ever heard his brother make about himself; come to think of it, the only one. He watched Ewart walk away, then turned back to the dynamite melting to count the full jars. Later he asked Jimmy, 'Do you think I made a good deal?'

'Oh yes, Mr Lance. Of course, your brother would have been generous with you out of his own share. But your attitude has made a good impression on him. He admires independence.'

'Yes. What I meant was this: How much risk do you think there is of us being blown up on the river by Mr Bruun's men?'

'The ancestors will decide which of their children joins them today.'

Lance thought this over. 'That means you think there's a good chance of being killed on the river.'

Jimmy shrugged, his smile a pale shadow of its former magnificence. 'They could be lucky. A man near the river that we don't see . . .'

'You don't have to come on the river with me, you know. I'm the one who sold his soul to the devil, not you.'

'It will be my opportunity to demand a bonus from Sambo. And it is customary for the bearer to share in a very modest manner in the good fortune of his master.'

'But of course! I should have thought of it myself.'

Jimmy laughed. 'Or your brother or my brother or Mr Roux would have told you. But that is not the reason. What would you think of me if I didn't finish what I started? And how would I look my brothers and my people in the face?'

The man with the amputated little finger looked up from his frying-pan. 'I go with you, Master. If the induna shakes.'

'See what I mean,' Jimmy said under his breath to Lance and snapped something at the man in their own language.

'Thank you but Jimmy has already offered,' Lance said

gravely. The men all laughed at some private joke and Lance felt better. Perhaps it was like Ewart said: What had to be done had to be done. 'I didn't know you were a counsellor.'

'Honorary post that comes with being a prince and a corporal,' Jimmy said. 'It doesn't mean they actually listen to your advice until your hair is grey.'

Jacques had agreed to Lance's proposal and shook his hand to welcome him as a full partner. They were standing near the edge of the water between the two skiffs. Each skiff had a row of boxes of dynamite down each side. There was a break in each row to work or shoot through; the breaks were staggered to protect the backs of the men who would be working the skiffs. Sambo was testing each knot on the ropes that held the dynamite boxes. A box pushed into the nitroglycerine could cause disaster. Ewart repeated the procedure with the knots and also inspected the packing of the jars of nitro to make sure they were all standing up steadily and firmly.

'Lance and I will do the first turn,' Ewart said from where he kneeled on the ground. Jacques looked relieved. Lance felt his buttocks contract.

'All right,' Ewart said when he was satisfied with all their equipment. 'Let's go.'

Both Jacques and Ewart had rifles with scopes from the Landrover's gun rack. Jacques started firing across the river at a steady rate. Lance was too concerned with putting the skiff ever so gently into the water to look. He didn't think Jacques had hit anything or there would be more excitement among the men. They ran the skiffs upriver parallel to the near bank and only thirty feet out, Ewart in the lead skiff looking intently into the murky water for submerged roots or logs that could kill them. They heard the sound of shots from the far bank and ignored them. Nothing struck them. Though they were perfect targets moving at a snail's pace, the range was too great.

Lance found his hands shaking as he checked his rifle. The sweat running in rivulets across his palms and dribbling into his eyes didn't help much either. He raised his buttocks carefully from the boxload of fruit jars filled with nitroglycerine he was sitting on before feeling in his pocket for his handkerchief. With the dynamite boxes running down each side of the skiff it was very cramped and he didn't want to bump anything. He wiped his face and hands and left the handkerchief lying next to him in case he should want it again. He noticed that they had left the protection of the near bank and were angling out into the middle of the river. From the way the sun ran dead into the water and disappeared, he judged it was high noon; the sun woud be directly overhead and give neither side an advantage.

'Your brother will start shooting in a moment,' Jimmy warned him.

Lance stood on his knees next to the box containing the nitro and looked over the protective row of dynamite.

'Your cartridges are going to be ejected right on the jelly and blow us to the ancestors,' Jimmy said.

Lance crawled around to kneel on the other side of the box containing the nitro. 'Thanks,' he said as Jimmy moved his feet to give him more room.

'There's one about thirty degrees to your right, standing up against a spade-shaped tree,' Jimmy said. 'The other one is sixty degrees to your left, lying behind a log under a Y-fork.'

Lance heard Ewart's shot. He raised himself over the dynamite boxes, rifle to his shoulder, eye to the scope, finger on the trigger, thumb on the scope zoom. Jimmy's directions had been entirely accurate. He was turning to the second of Bruun's men before the first had fallen. He fired and turned the scope back towards the first one. The man was just sinking to the ground, half his head gone, sprayed over the trunk of the tree against which he had been leaning. Lance didn't check on the other one. It was easier if you didn't look. Jimmy slowly ran the skiff upstream to where they would lay the first line of jars across the river.

Each skiff laid two lines of fruit jars across the river and then they drifted downstream, keeping on just enough power to ensure directional control, They were back near the Congo (Kinshasa) side of the river and effectively out of range of the weapons on the far side of the river, incredibly lucky shots and spent bullets excepted. That even spent bullets could impart enough concussion to set off the nitroglycerine – Lance had not forgotten Ewart's demonstration of throwing a spoon lightly against a tree to blow it apart – did not worry Lance quite as much as the thought that somebody need just throw a log into the river where they had just mined it and they would all be very dead indeed. No, just dead. Dead is dead is *only* dead. At least he could still think logically.

'What're you sweating for, Jimmy? I got everything under control.'

'I was just wishing, Mr Lance, that, when I was a westernized little nigger at an expensive English school, I hadn't laughed at the ancestors. Who knows how they receive those who mock them.'

'A lot better than they receive those who die through their own carelessness,' Sambo called loudly from the skiff behind them. 'Keep your mind on watching for the roots under the water.'

They could hear Ewart laughing.

'Very funny,' Jimmy muttered.

Lance had to agree. Ewart's laughter sent a cold shiver up his sweat-wet back. Ewart seemed impervious not only to dirt and cold and heat and discomfort but to danger and – dare he even think it? – death as well. Of course it was only an illusion, created by Ewart's meticulous preparation to eliminate unnecessary risks. Very few men would describe the risks Ewart did take as 'necessary'. But for such rewards . . . Most men worked a lifetime to save only

238

part of what Ewart would make on this river in only weeks. And what he, Lance Weber, would make now that he had become a full partner.

It took his mind off the further killing that was necessary to protect their lives and property but time had passed and the moment would not wait. Jimmy was heading the boat towards the middle of the river again.

'They're forty-five degrees each,' Jimmy said. 'One's lying flat on some moss behind a log but you can get him in the angle of his neck and shoulder where he's exposed. That's the one on your left. The one on the right is behind a thick tree and not peeking out much. You want me to do the shooting?'

'You just keep watching for loose bodies in the water, Jimmy. It wouldn't be right to put this on you.'

Lance peered around the dynamite box. 'I can see only one. Which tree is the other one behind?'

'The light tree in that dark patch.'

He heard Ewart's first shot and then another almost immediately. He turned his torso and zoomed as the rifle swung. He got the man spot on, looking down the barrel of a rifle at him. He pulled the trigger a little too abruptly and heard the thud the man's bullet made in the dynamite next to his ear. For a moment everything was still. Lance remembered walking with his mother in the park at Maitland, the high spot of his life till then. How could he have thought, on visiting the park as an adult, that it was a grubby little place?

'You've only wounded him,' Jimmy said urgently. 'He's aiming again!'

Lance saw the man swaying as he aimed again. He squeezed the trigger and saw the man's head disintegrate. All was still except for the whistle of the bullet over their heads.

A spurt of water shot up ten feet from Lance. He turned his rifle towards the other of his targets but the man had disappeared behind the thick trunk again.

'If you can hear the bullet, it's passed you,' Jimmy said.

Lance hadn't known that. He watched the tree. The man was staying behind it.

'What's the hold-up?' Ewart called across the water to them.

'We have one behind a tree and he's not showing himself to be shot,' Lance replied.

'You can be flippant when we've eliminated him. Go downstream and inshore and I'll go upstream and inshore and we'll put him in a crossfire. Okay? Watch you stay well out of his range.'

Lance hadn't meant to be flippant; it was just the way the words came out. 'Yes sir.'

After a while, Jimmy said, 'We're in position.'

Lance, who had been pushing bullets into the magazine of the rifle Jacques had given him, crawled into position and looked around the dynamite boxes. 'I still can't see him. Can you go closer to the side, Jimmy?'

'No, Mr Lance. We might strike a submerged root. I don't think your brother can see him either or he'd've started shooting.'

'What do we do now?'

'We wait.'

'Yeah. But we have nine more miles to do today. He could hold us up all day.'

'Somebody's going to die if we try to winkle him out, one of us I mean.'

'I still don't fancy sitting on a skiff full of nitro on a river already mined with the stuff, just waiting for somebody with a little sense to come and throw a log in the river. What do you say Jimmy, we beach a little downstream and sneak around behind him?'

'Not without your brother's direct orders, Mr Lance. And I can assure you he isn't going to give any such orders, leastwise not to you and me.'

'Who to then?'

'He'll go back to the camp and fetch Kombi. Maybe

240

he'll go with Kombi himself, maybe just send Kombi alone. That's how he always handles this kind of problem.'

Lance kept watching the tree trunk through his scope. Nothing. 'Maybe he snuck away and we're being held up by a tree with nobody behind it.'

'I was watching all the time. He's there.' Jimmy sounded absolutely certain.

Lance remembered what he had been told when they had been ambushed by the guerillas, that patience was the key to survival. But the waiting was frazzling his nerves. He put the rifle down to wipe the sweat from his hands and face. He heard Ewart's shot and scrabbled up his rifle.

'Easy! Don't kick that box of jelly!'

Lance looked over his shoulder. His feet were resting against the box with the jars of jelly. He pulled his knees up. His scope showed him nothing except the solid tree trunk. 'Did Ewart get him?'

'I don't know, Mr Lance.'

Lance studied the water. The surface was an unbroken onyx. It was impossible to tell what lay below. He looked over his shoulder at Jimmy. 'Ten feet closer in, Jimmy, and I'll be able to see behind that tree.'

Jimmy shook his head. Lance looked upriver. Ewart's skiff was actually further out into the river than his own. He could see neither Ewart nor Sambo, just the glint of sunlight on the telescopic sight of Ewart's rifle where it peered through the wall of dynamite boxes. He swung his rifle back to the tree. Still nothing. He waited. It seemed like hours.

'Relax,' Jimmy said.

Lance consciously relaxed each of his muscles, starting with his toes and working up to his head. He knew from experience this exercise took six and a half minutes.

He saw the flash of sun through the tree. No, that was an illusion. The ray had always been there but something had crossed its path. He waited for another flash. A man's arm in a khaki shirt. He shot at it. There was nothing more to see for a second after the blood spurted and the elbow jerked away. Then he heard two shots from Ewart and Bruun's man toppled over backwards behind the tree.

They laid the nitroglycerine and moved downriver to kill the next batch of Bruun's men, lay the next four rows of jelly . . . It was going to be slow work, a long hard day.

When the first mile of the river was blown up, they had a bonus: one of Bruun's men was caught in the tons of falling water and drowned.

By the third mile, Bruun's men had learnt their lesson and were hiding themselves well into the forest but still within shooting range of the river. They fell back still further at the first sign of danger. Late in the afternoon, when they had blown up six miles of the river, Ewart called a halt. 'I want the skins from both banks brought in before dark.'

Bruun's men offered no resistance on the far bank. But every dead crocodile lying there had its belly-skin, the most valuable part, cut to shreds.

'Bruun's winning,' Lance said dejectedly at dinner.

'Only if he can continue to sustain losses on the same scale as today,' Jacques said. 'All he's done so far is slow us down and ruin about a quarter of the skins. For that, more than twenty men is a very heavy price.'

Ewart shook his head. 'No. We didn't see him all day. My guess is he left his men to delay us while he plots something with the politicians in Bangui.'

'If you're right,' Jacques said, 'we must simply clear this stretch of river to Bangui by no later than the day after tomorrow and be out of here the next day.'

Lance waited until they finished discussing ways and means before he asked his question. 'Why should Bruun plot with Central African Republic politicians? He comes from this side of the border.'

'Their common cause is not nationality but greed,' Jacques said.

'Bruun needs them because they can bring more force against us than he can,' Ewart added.

'Then let's pull up stakes and go down the river and just forget about the few miles to Bangui,' Lance said.

Jacques shook his head. 'Our deal is to kill all the crocodiles up to Bangui before the rest of our licence, for the crocodiles downstream, comes into operation. We promised to do something and we shall do it.'

'Then find Bruun first and kill him,' Briony said, giving Ewart a dirty look. 'If our tame hero here hadn't been so keen on indulging his sense of humour when he had Bruun in the palm of his hand, we wouldn't be in this shit now.'

'Fighting Bruun when he attacks us is one thing,' Jacques said. 'Driving down to Bangui to hunt him is quite another. Our new partner has already pointed out that, across the river, the land belongs to a third party, the Central African Republic.'

'New partner?' Briony asked.

Jacques explained the new arrangement to her.

'Phui! So you made him an equal partner! An over-grown boy.'

'He's earned his share by risking his life, same as Ewart and I.'

'Yes, risking his life . . . He's a gambler and you know it. What's more you know most gamblers want to lose. They want to lose so badly it hurts. Just having him on this trip is inviting disaster. Making him a full partner is to ensure disaster. When – '

'Briony, you – '

'When he gets killed – and he will because he's a gambler – have you thought that he'll probably take some of us with him – '

'Thank you for your opinion, Briony. But our decision has been made and implemented,' Ewart said without raising his voice.

'And besides, I'm a woman. That's it, isn't it?'

Ewart lit a cigarillo. When it was clear that nobody was going to reply, Briony rose and, pushing Pietie aside roughly, started clearing the table. She threw one plate against the mess-tent but it just rolled off the canvas and came to rest, unbroken, on the ground-moss. They could hear her clattering utensils about in the tent.

Lance found Ewart's eyes on him. 'You don't believe that pseudo-psychological crap, do you?'

'What I believe is that I heard you say this morning that you have nothing to prove. Just remember that.' Ewart threw two flattened pieces of lead on the table. 'Both of these came out of the dynamite boxes on one skiff and it wasn't mine.'

'I only collected one of those,' Lance said. Ewart had use one skiff all day long, Jacques and Lance alternating on the other one. He realized he was accusing Jacques and turned to him. 'Sorry, Jacques.'

'It's all right. I was about to own up anyway.' Jacques turned to Ewart. 'It was unavoidable.'

Ewart slid the two pieces of lead across the table, one to each of them. 'These could have killed you and everybody else on the river. Don't let it happen again.'

Lance looked at Jacques, expecting him to tell Ewart where to get off. But Jacques said nothing and Lance took his cue from that. It was shitty of Ewart to sneak around behind their backs, spying on them, but if Jacques seemed to think he had to take it he, Lance, was obviously going to have no joy out of making an issue of it. If Ewart had decided men could control the course of spent bullets, a younger brother was not going to change his mind.

Lance fingered the deformed lead, heard again the thud of it next to his head, relived that eternal second of waiting for the world to end in bright lights and tons of water. He wiped his forehead and hands and saw Jacques was sweating too.

'That's right,' Ewart said as·he rose to inspect the

guards. 'I want you shitscared. That way you'll get out of this alive.'

Behind Lance's shoulder Jimmy sniggered.

'Just remember, when I go up, so do you,' Lance snarled at him. 'And you too,' he said softly at Ewart's retreating back.

'The most irritating thing about Ewart is not that he spies on people but that he's right to do so,' Jacques said when Ewart was out of earshot. 'Let's have another brandy. Sit down Jimmy, join us.'

'And wipe that grin off your face,' Lance added as Jimmy sank his bulk into a chair. 'It won't have escaped my brother that you drove the skiff that went so near it collected a spent bullet.'

Jacques burst out laughing. 'We're all rather in the same boat, aren't we?'

The next day, in a roundabout way, Briony's dire prediction became reality.

Ewart had changed their work-method. On one skiff he placed Kombi to drive and Lance, Jimmy and Jacques with scoped rifles but no nitroglycerine. Ewart and Sambo used the other skiff to carry the nitro; they laid it in lines down the river rather than lines across as before, mining two miles of the river at a time. Lance's skiff kept pace with Ewart's about twenty feet away, sheltering it from Bruun's men who were further deterred from approaching too near by Lance firing up-river, Jimmy covering the forest directly opposite and Jacques firing down-river. It went amazingly quickly and by lunchtime they had blown up ten miles of river. Bruun's men were wary and they had only killed one and wounded two more. There was a handful of bullets in the boxes of dynamite on Lance's skiff but none had penetrated very deeply, proving that Bruun's men had retreated almost out of the range of the weapons they carried.

Sambo showed Lance a rifle brought back from the

other side of the river the previous day; it had belonged to one of Bruun's men who had, Sambo said, 'been sent to join his ancestors and account for his folly'. It was a Lee Metford .303 calibre and the date of manufacture was stamped on the barrel: 1898.

'It's criminal of Bruun to send men with such weapons against us,' Lance said.

Jacques didn't agree. 'You'd be surprised what a .303 Lee Metford in good condition can do. No, where Bruun's criminality lies is in not insisting his men care properly for their weapons and in not training them in their use.' He wiped his finger along a streak of rust on the barrel. 'Clean this rifle properly, replace worn parts, and you or Jimmy or I could be very dangerous with it.'

'But not Bruun's men. I feel sorry for them.'

'They have the wrong attitude to their weapons,' Jacques said. 'They feel the rifle itself is the instrument of power. But it's not, if you'll allow me to say so. The instrument of power is the will and the ability of the man behind the rifle.'

'Give a coward or an incompetent a rifle and he becomes less dangerous because his confidence is falsely increased,' Sambo said dismissively. 'Then his death is his own fault.'

Lance weighed the spent bullets taken from the dynamite boxes in his hand. 'Yes, but we give them an advantage by sitting on top of a huge concussion bomb.'

Nobody had an answer to that. Sambo threw the rifle into the river and they walked away to lunch.

'I suggest we forget about fetching the crocodiles from Bruun's side of the river,' Ewart said. 'With slashed belly skins they're not worth much.'

'About ten, perhaps even fifteen dollars each,' Jacques said. 'It adds up to several thousand dollars.'

'It's up to you. What I had in mind is that we go out on the river again this afternoon and continue blowing it up two miles at a time for as long as the light lasts. Then, tonight, we can use the floodlamps to gather in the skins on our side of the river. That way we'll reach Bangui by tomorrow evening. It worries me that we've caught no sight of Bruun. I'm sure he's up to something in Bangui.'

Jacques thought it over briefly. 'All right. I hate leaving Bruun even part of what we've earned but I think you're right.'

Lance gobbled his food and rose to see to the preparation of jelly for the afternoon's work. 'Can you send Pietie with coffee for me please?'

By five o'clock they had done another eight miles with several hours of daylight remaining. Ewart looked at the sun. 'It's gone faster than I thought. One more shift, another two miles, and we'll call it a day. That'll bring us to within fifteen miles of Bangui.'

'What exactly was the agreement about Bangui?' Lance asked, 'I mean we can hardly blow up the river right in the centre of a town, can we?'

'No,' Jacques said. 'We'll go up-river until we come within sight of Bangui and then stop. Probably about ten miles away.'

The skiffs were loaded and Ewart had done his usual meticulous check. They set off slowly, staying near their side of the river. At the upstream end of the two-mile stretch they were going to mine, they allowed the skiffs to drift in tandem down the river while Ewart laid the explosive. For the moment there was nothing to fear from the opposite bank. They repeated the procedure several more times, protected by the breadth of the river and the caution of Bruun's men. On the next to last run, Lance asked Jimmy, 'Do you think they've gone?' There was no sign of Bruun's men.

'I don't know.'

'Keep watching,' Jacques said.

Ewart called, 'Back upstream for the last time.' The two skiffs ran slowly upstream. When Ewart called again they turned, manoeuvred into position and were held

247

suspended in the flow of the river by the slow turn of the airscrews while Ewart laid explosive. 'Okay, next station,' Ewart called and the skiffs started moving forward with the flow of the river.

Lance heard the shot and the thud of the bullet into the dynamite as one sound. There was no return fire; Jimmy couldn't see the man who had fired the shot. There was a whole fusillade and then a shouted command from the forest and the firing stopped. Lance peered cautiously around the dynamite boxes but could see nothing. Jimmy and Jacques had not fired and it was safe to assume they had seen nothing either.

'Okay, next station,' Ewart called.

The skiffs moved downstream. Lance could see nothing in the forest. They laid another charge. Still nothing in the forest.

'Hey, Ewart,' Jacques called. 'I think Bruun's returned and made them hide and wait their chance.'

'Have you seen him?'

'No. But if we go further downstream they're going to get us in a crossfire, we're that near the river bank. I think we should pull out before they throw something in the water.'

'All right. Just let me settle this bottle on the bottom and we can go.' Ewart sounded as calm as ever.

Lance saw a flash of pale white and fired at it. 'I just saw Bruun's hand, Jacques. You're right, he's here.'

'Did you hit him?'

'No.'

'Pity. What range?'

'About two hundred feet into the forest. Three hundred and fifty feet altogether.'

Jimmy's rifle cracked and out of the corner of his eye Lance saw a man staggering drunkenly in the forest and slump face down.

'Three hundred,' Jimmy said.

'Okay, we can leave,' Ewart called. 'Slowly, very slowly,

Sambo, Kombi. Handle those throttles like a newborn babe.'

'Yeah,' Jacques muttered. 'We don't want to do Bruun's work for him.'

'What's Bruun waiting for?' Lance asked anxiously.

'For us to go further downstream so that Ewart will be caught in a crossfire from both sides and we won't be able to shelter him without actually bumping into him,' Jacques sighed.

Lance shivered. It was impossible. Yet there was still no firing from Bruun's men. Bruun was obviously restraining them – and keeping their heads down – until the target was exactly in position. There was nothing to see except the forest. Lance had never realized before that shades of brown and green together made a sinister, threatening combination.

The moment it was clear the skiffs were turning to run for the far bank there was an enraged shout from the forest and a fusillade of shots. Lance picked off two men by firing into what looked like good hiding places. He could see none of Bruun's men but the bullets kept thudding into the boxes of dynamite. He reloaded his rifle while his eyes searched the forest through the gap between the boxes in front of him. He saw Bruun's hand flash again, this time to push one of his men out into the open. By the time he had the rifle to his shoulder, Bruun had gone. The man was running towards the water, swinging a log over his head. Lance hit him in the chest and head with two closely spaced shots. The man fell over backwards, the log flew forward. Lance watched horrified as it fell right at the river's edge and rolled into the water. I don't want to go out with my last thought being Oh, shit, I fucked up again. Or just watching the water rush and ripple around some piece of tree.

Nothing happened but the incident hadn't passed unnoticed. Jimmy didn't pause in his spaced shots but Lance could hear him clearly. 'Next time shoot the log and ignore the man, Mr Lance.'

Lance saw a movement in the forest and fired. He was rewarded with a shout of pain. He wished they would move faster. They were going so slowly he was not quite sure whether they were actually getting away from the men shooting at them. It didn't seem so.

A bullet struck the corner of the dynamite boxes in front of him and a splinter cut into his forehead. He pulled the splinter out and was immediately sorry he had done so for blood started flowing into his eyes. He fumbled for his handkerchief and wiped the blood away. As his eyes cleared he saw Bruun behind a fern.

Lance scrabbled for his rifle. Bruun fired before he could get it to his shoulder. There was a tremendous blow in his groin, like the time a cricket ball had hit him, and he blacked out for a moment: it wasn't long because he fired two shots before the blood again obscured his vision. He sank down to the deck and breathed slowly to try and drown the pain.

'Did . . . I . . . get . . . him . . .?'

'No,' Jimmy said. Lance held his groin. It was wet. He took his hands away carefully to look at them. They were red with blood. He fainted.

When Lance came to, they were in the middle of the river. He listened to the thud of bullets against the dynamite boxes and looked to see if Ewart's skiff was still with them. Stupid! If Ewart went up, so would they. Ewart was standing on his knees and firing at Bruun's men, his rifle moving slowly, the barrel pausing only momentarily as he squeezed the trigger.

'Keep your head down, Lance,' he said, without taking his eye from the scope. 'We'll soon have you ashore. How do you feel?'

'Okay,' Lance looked down at his bloodstained trousers. Someone had ripped his fly open and stuffed a handkerchief into his trousers. What the Chinaman had threatened . . . The thought gave him the same strangely impatient feeling as an erection. There was no great pain, only a dull ache. And he felt dizzy, as if he had run ten miles uphill.

Branches of trees flashed across his face, blocking the sky.

Time must have passed – they were at the edge of the water.

Kombi was carrying him off, stepping gently into the water, lifting each foot clear with caution, then placing it back in the water with utmost deliberation. The others were now standing up on the skiffs, firing across the river in an attempt to keep Bruun's men from approaching the water. Lance wiped the blood from his eyes. He was seeing things.

A man was running towards the water, swinging a log above his head. Jacques, Jimmy and Ewart had their rifles to their shoulders. Sambo was screwing a long barrel to his FN. Moments passed slowly, perhaps not quite a second but longer than eternity. Lance remembered something of Dante. An eternity in purgatory.

The three rifles cracked simultaneously. The log flew out of the man's hands. The man was trying to halt before he hit the water's edge, windmilling his arms. Lance clearly saw Bruun stand behind the man and shoot him in the back. The man, still milling his arms, fell towards the water. 'Jump!' Lance heard Ewart say, his command sharp, his voiced raised only enough to transcend the hubbub.

Kombi grabbed him by the hair to swing him around in front of the huge body and Lance screamed. The water struck him in his open mouth and then his wind was knocked out as Kombi fell on him. Lance struggled for air against the huge black body as they tumbled over and over, being swept painfully against trees, struck excruciatingly by loose objects. For a moment there was air and Lance gasped. Then the second wave struck them and Lance went limp.

He opened his eyes to the sawing of planks for a coffin. It was the wheezing in his own chest. His scalp hurt. But Kombi had one mammoth arm around him, the other around a tree root from which the water had washed the topsoil. He was grinning hugely, blood from a split lip staining his teeth.

Lance couldn't speak yet. He looked around him. Ewart was sitting on a tree branch at least twenty feet above the ground, his clothes already dripping dry on him. Just what you would expect of Ewart, Lance thought. Jacques was lying on his back about fifty feet away, one of Sambo's arms across his chest. They were both steaming gently. Jimmy was standing on his knees in a pool of vomit, even further from the river's edge than Lance and Kombi, retching painfully. All except Ewart looked ragged and bloody. Lance looked down to see if his own clothing was steaming and saw the blood on his trousers and shirt – all over his belly. He whimpered his fear of an unknown future.

As if it were their cue, the others sprang to life, one moment far away in their own distress or relief, the next crowding around him. Ewart stripped off his shirt and wrung it out. Lance could see a deep cut around Ewart's ribs from the middle of his chest and curving around to his back. It was not bleeding much. What you would expect of Ewart. There was also a long thin sliver of glass sticking through Ewart's cheek; he seemed not to be aware of it. Ewart stuffed the shirt into Lance's trousers.

'Give me a rifle.' The croak was his own voice.

Ewart shrugged. 'The battle is over.'

'I don't want to live without my balls.'

'Don't be silly. Let go of me, you idiot!' Lance had grabbed Ewart by the shoulders and pulled his face down close, spraying spittle in his brother's face as his mouth opened and closed wordlessly. Ewart slapped Lance through the face, palm and backhand. 'You've got all your equipment. A piece of something just cut you under the balls. If you don't lie still you'll bleed to death.'

Lance sank back. He tried to say something, he knew not what, but could not even croak. He saw Ewart motion to Kombi. Kombi picked him up in his arms. Jacques said something to Ewart, who raised his hand to his cheek, felt the sliver of glass, pulled it out, looked at it, grimaced and threw it on the ground. A dribble of blood ran down Ewart's cheek and he wiped it away with the back of his hand. While Lance waited to see if Ewart would, just like other people, wipe the back of his hand on his trousers, darkness fell over his eyes and hearing.

'There's nothing we can do about a cut artery,' Briony said, wiping her arms which were covered in blood to the elbow. 'We can't put a tourniquet on that part of his body. Pressure only staunches the flow of blood – there's no way we can stop it. And he's lost so much already that any more will kill him. He needs professional attention, somebody who can stitch him up. A doctor in Bangui – '

'Bruun has crossed the river and cut off the road to Bangui,' Ewart said. 'There's no way we can get through without first waiting till daylight and then fighting what could be a long action. Can't you do anything more?'

'No. He needs a blood transfusion. Can't you dispose of Bruun tonight?'

'It would be suicide. What if you tried stitching him up?'

'No way. It's skilled work, stitching arteries.'

Jacques said, 'Next to Bangui the mission at Lisala is our best bet.'

'That's nearly four hundred miles over terrible roads,' Ewart objected.

'Yes, but the Landrover could be in Lisala by dawn tomorrow, ten o'clock at the latest. Could you take Bruun by then?'

'Perhaps. But if we had to pry Bruun from some prepared position in a hurry the cost in men lost would be horrifying.'

'The men will fight for Mr Lance,' Sambo said from

where he stood just inside the flap of the tent.

'Thank you, Sambo, but that is not the point. We cannot risk the men unnecessarily.'

'He is *your* brother.'

Ewart ignored the implied rebuke. 'The question is: What will do him more harm – four hundred miles of rough travel or a few hours more while we clear up Bruun's ambush?'

'If you could be sure of finishing Bruun off in a few hours . . .' Briony let the sentence trail away. 'But if it's going to take all day to get Lance to Bangui, then I say the rough travel.'

'All right. Lisala it is.'

From the shadows at the side of the tent, Jimmy said, 'I can ride and shoot.' He was almost invisible in the darkness, defined only vaguely by the turban of bandages covering the cuts on his head, his gleaming teeth and the white cloth sling in which his arm rested. It had been the pain of the arm being wrenched at the shoulder which had made him vomit.

'Yes, you can ride shotgun. Only shooting will be required. I'll drive myself.'

'You're not leaving us with Bruun lurking just down the road!' Briony was in an instant rage.

'Jacques and Sambo will be here and all the men except Jimmy.'

'I don't care if Lance *is* your brother! We pay you to protect us and that's what we expect you to do, stay here and defend us.'

'Sambo, make sure the Landrover is provisioned and have it brought round.' Ewart turned to Briony. 'Your husband took me as a partner to make certain decisions. If you or Jacques or any of the men had been wounded, the decision would be exactly the same, regardless of the relationship to me. I certainly do not work for you and, as for defending you, your mouth gives you better service than I ever could.'

Briony was about to slap Ewart when Jacques burst out laughing. She pursed her mouth, turned on her heel and stalked out of the tent.

Just before midnight the messenger came to the position Bruun had chosen. Bruun, dozing against a tree, wiped his eyes. 'Yes, what have you seen?'

'The small truck left the camp of the crocodile hunters, sir. There were three men inside. One was the leader. There was another man but he was dreaming. Still another, a black man wrapped around the head like an Indian trader.'

So. Weber had left the camp in the Landrover. With him an unconscious man and a wounded man who was still conscious.

'Are you sure they left?' Bruun was certain no one had tried to pass here on the way to the hospital in Bangui.

'Yes, sir.'

Weber wouldn't come out of his camp with only two wounded men. 'Did you see which way they went?'

The man pointed south. Bruun kicked him on the shins. The man pointed south again. It was just not possible. The nearest medical help, beside Bangui, was at Lisala, nearly four hundred miles away. Anybody hurt badly enough to need medical attention beyond first aid would die on that trip.

Bruun flipped the messenger a cigarette. 'Return to the guard at the camp. Tell him to send you with report of anything else that happens. Anything, you understand?'

'Yes sir. If anything happens you want to hear.'

'Yes.' Weber's camp was less than a mile through the forest. The runner would cover the distance in under ten minutes.

Bruun lit a cigarette himself. Weber had wounded all right – there had been enough blood on the river bank to testify to that. But, if Weber couldn't get them to Bangui for treatment, he would kill them. He wasn't called The

255

Butcher for nothing. So, Weber was using his badly wounded to play some game. But what? Weber knew Bruun was lying in wait for him on the Bangui road. The road to Lisala or other parts south or southwest was of no importance to either of them because the buyer for the crocodile skins waited in Bangui.

Bruun chuckled. He threw cigarettes to the men sitting against trees a respectful distance from him. Weber was trying to draw him off, using the wounded as a decoy. Christ, did Weber think him so stupid as to neglect the simple precaution of setting surveillance on the camp? He'd show Weber.

'How would you like a taste of white woman?' he called to his men. 'She has hair the colour of ripe maize.'

They clucked their approval. They too had understood that the feared Ewart Weber had gone from the camp, taking with him one of the white men who shot so fearsomely. And dreaming, wounded seriously. They had done that. Something to be proud of. To be rewarded with a taste of the white woman who had hair the colour of ripe maize. Working for this white pig might yet turn out to be better than starving.

Lance came to, fighting the straps constricting his middle and chest. He was drowning, trapped in a net. His clothing was soaking. A star burst behind his eyes as he struck his head against a submerged log. His lungs were bursting; he could hold his breath no longer – he had no more breath to hold. He opened his mouth in a long scream.

'Slap him again, Jimmy,' he heard Ewart say. Instinctively Lance raised his hands and Jimmy struck his wrist.

'He's all right now, sir. Just sit quietly, Mr Lance. We've passed Libenge.'

'Water,' Lance couldn't hear his own voice and tried again to overcome the ringing in his ears. 'Water,' Jimmy gave him a bottle and Lance drank eagerly, spilling some down his shirt, feeling the soothing coolness of it on his sweat-soaked body. He gave the bottle back to Jimmy. He was still dizzy but it wasn't so bad now. After a while he had more strength and opened his eyes.

On every straight stretch of the road the battery of lights across the front of the Landrover was turning the night into day for half a mile or more. Just outside the sharply defined cut-off of light there was total darkness, the forest seen only as a blur of trunks. Ewart was taking the 'improved road' at tremendous speed, as fast as the Landrover would go and that was impressively fast because the weight of the fuel cans on the roof and in the back gave it good stability. Lance instinctively pulled at his safety harness buckles to find them tight.

'What happened?'

Jimmy told him.

'Where are we going?'

'Lisala.'

'That's an awfully long way. I feel better now. We can turn back.'

If there was an answer, Lance didn't hear it. He had fallen into the state between exhaustion, sleep and unconsciousness.

He woke to a thump at the front of the Landrover and saw the goat fly over the spare wheel mounted on the bonnet. He ducked because it would surely crash through the windscreen and immolate them. He heard it crashing against the fuel cans on the roof and then it was gone. He opened his eyes to see the nose of the Landrover pointing straight at the trees and *Ewart swinging the wheel towards the trees* but the whole vehicle was moving the other way with a tremendous roaring of the engine. Then there was a lurch and Ewart straightened the wheel, corrected with more opposite lock, and they were around the curve beyond the village. Lance had not even seen the village but he knew it would be there: it was where the goat had come from.

257

'Budjala,' Jimmy said behind his right shoulder. It was reassuring to know that even in his dreams Jimmy was there, solid as a rock behind his right shoulder. 'About thirty miles to the ferry across the Mongala at Akula. The surfaced road starts just across the river. Then it's a hundred miles to Lisala.'

Lance asked for more water. When he had had it, and dutifully chewed the glucose tablets Jimmy gave him, he asked, 'What time is it?'

'Two hours before dawn, Mr Lance. Don't talk, save your strength. By dawn we'll be in Lisala.'

'There's nothing wrong with me, I tell you. I feel no pain.'

Ewart leant over to put his hand on the seat between Lance's legs. 'It's still seeping,' he said to Jimmy.

Jimmy hung over Lance's back to check the padding. 'It's strapped up tight, sir.'

'All right. He's just getting lightheaded. It's the final stage. Do you feel you're floating, Lance?' Ewart had to repeat the question before Lance answered him.

'I float like a butterfly and I sting like a bee.'

Akula could not even be dignified as a hamlet. There was little more to it than the ferry-keeper's hut and a corrugated iron general store, though the clacking of fowl testified to human inhabitants.

Ewart drove the Landrover straight through the flimsy wooden barrier and on to the ferry. He climbed down and walked over to the mechanism. There was a big old-fashioned padlock on it. Without waiting for orders Jimmy, who had followed him, rifle in the crook of his arm, cocked his rifle and shot the padlock off. They started winding the big handle.

'I'll give you a hand,' Lance's voice reached them weakly.

'Just stay put and conserve your strength,' Ewart called.

Lance tried to wind the window up again and failed. When they reached the other bank and were under way

258

again Jimmy wound it up for him. Lance could only nod his thanks. That was all he saw of the single-lane road to Lisala from the ferry at Akula.

Bruun chose the last half-hour before dawn for his attack. It was his favourite time, when the metabolism of the defenders would be at lowest ebb, when they would still be rubbing the sleep from their eyes after it was all over. Weber and Roux would know this, of course, but it was one of those facts of human nature no commander could do anything to change. And Weber wasn't there while Roux, though not exactly a desk soldier, was more of a staff officer than a field commander. Perhaps he'd be very lucky and find that the wounded white man in the Landrover had been Roux, the wounded black man Sambo – leaving Weber's inexperienced younger brother in command. Bruun licked his lips and whistled to signal the advance. When the men were in position, his parrot call stopped them. Bruun lay in the darkness, studying the position of the guards, waiting.

The first burst of fire killed several of the skinners, huddled around their fire, and one of Sambo's men who was stoking the fire in front of the mess tent. Sambo was shouting commands before Jacques was fully awake and had organized resistance by the time Jacques came running from his tent in his pyjamas.

Their clearing, at this time of night, was not a good place to defend. The fires threw unexpected curves of light as they flared up, providing light for the attackers to shoot by, and soon the first light of dawn would fall in the clearing while the surrounding forest would remain pitch dark for an hour afterwards. Jacques kicked the fire apart with his bare feet as he came through it.

'Out of the tent, Briony!' he shouted.

Briony came flying through the tent flap, her short nightdress flying diaphanously in the flickering light, an

FN cradled in her arms. Somebody was shooting at her and several of Sambo's men sprayed the forest on automatic for covering fire. There were shouts of pain from the forest. Screams from the skinners.

Jacques found himself lying next to Kombi. 'Is everybody accounted for?'

'Under cover sir. One of ours dead, many skinners.' He pointed at the bundle of flesh lying amid the scattered, still burning logs. 'He was making the fire for breakfast.'

'A flesh wound in my leg. Not serious, sir,' a voice with a chuckle in it called to their left. They couldn't see the man.

'Are you under cover?' Jacques asked.

'Yes, sir.' The man still sounded amused.

'Is it bleeding? Do you want first aid?'

'Bleeding almost stopped. First aid later.'

'Your bloody Ewart has left us with our arse out in the cold,' Briony called.

Jacques ignored her. 'Where's Sambo?'

'Over near the skinners, sir,' a voice said from the darkness.

'Kombi, check that all the men have enough ammunition. We're going to have to hold them for at least an hour after dawn, until we can see better.'

Jacques crawled away in the direction of the skinners. He wanted to confer with Sambo. This kind of engagement was outside his experience.

He had only crawled a few paces when there was a parrot call setting off renewed firing from the forest. A truck tyre burst near him and he rolled with the blow as a piece of rubber struck him on the shoulder. He lost the rifle from his numb hand. He saw a man fall, shot in the back because he was inside the defensive ring facing the quiet south side of the forest. The men were changing sides to face their attackers.

'Get back there! That's where the second rush will come from.'

260

It was too late. Bruun had seen his chance and was storming the undefended side of the camp. His men were already inside the perimeter of trucks and dynamite boxes.

'Get out, retreat!' Jacques shouted as, out of the corner of his eye, he saw Sambo rise. Then Sambo was falling over backwards, shouting something in his own language.

Jacques saw Kombi go down on one knee, his FN carving a swathe of death through the attackers before a single shot started the blood spouting from his throat. Jacques was bending to pick up his rifle with his left hand. He saw Bruun knock the man's rifle upwards and then Bruun had a rifle stuck in Jacques' nose.

'Just one move!'

Jacques swivelled his eyes. Briony was on her knees. She shot one man in the chest at point-blank range before another kicked the FN from her hands and pushed her over with the flat of his boot on her chest.

More of Bruun's men came rushing into the camp from the other side, shouting and firing their rifles into the air, several falling to the pangas of the skinners before they realized the other blacks were a threat and starting firing on them. Against firearms the skinners fell quickly and the rest downed pangas. Five of Sambo's men were dead, including Kombi, and twenty or more skinners. Of Sambo and the rest of his men there was no sign. They had simply melted into the forest.

Bruun had not failed to notice this. 'After them,' he shouted, running around in a circle and kicking his men on the shins. 'You stupid fools, do you want them to regroup and attack us? After them.'

They rolled their eyes and looked fearfully at the dark forest but finally Bruun succeeded in getting a sergeant and twelve men to go after Sambo and his men.

'You! Cock your rifle. And you! Stand here, cover them. If there's just one shot from the forest into this camp, kill them. The man first and then, if the shooting doesn't stop, the woman. Understand? Verstehen? Capish? Verstaan?'

They nodded and turned their rifles on Jacques and Briony, who was sitting up on the ground, her hands between her legs, inspecting the muddy footprint on her chest.

Bruun turned his attention to placing guards around the camp, a line completely encircling the camp, each man within sight of the others. They could hear him shouting. 'The man you black baboons let get away was Sergeant Sambo. Do you understand, the right-hand man of the Baluba Butcher? If you don't look lively he'll come back and cut your balls off though God knows why I don't do it right now.'

'He's so frightened of Ewart's return . . . Perhaps he'll just take the skins and go,' Jacques said to Briony.

The man pointing a rifle at Jacques made a threatening movement. Jacques stared him down.

Bruun returned to the camp. There were still fifteen or so of his men left, standing around staring at Briony's nipples, clearly visible through her thin cotton shift. 'Get those skinners to load the skins,' Bruun snapped. 'Your turn will come.' His men herded the gibbering skinners towards the skins they had taken the day before and forced them to start loading them on a truck. Bruun satisfied himself that the work was proceeding at the fastest possible speed and came to stand in front of Jacques.

'How do you plead now, high and mighty *Colonel* Roux?'

'The fact that you're holding a gun on me doesn't make you any the less scum, slimy scum.'

Bruun giggled. 'We'll see. Bring that log,' he ordered one of his men.

Jacques didn't struggle while they tied his hands and feet behind the log. It would have been pointless. He hoped Briony would have the sense not to waste energy on unproductive struggle. Ewart would return not much after nightfall – he simply had to. When he was tied, one of the men pushed him and, unable to put out his hands to save himself, Jacques fell heavily on his chest and face. Bruun kicked him in the side. Jacques bit his lip and remained silent.

'Pull him up,' Bruun ordered. His men dragged the log upright. Bruun punched Jacques repeatedly in the stomach. Jacques remained silent, working his jaws to gather spit. When he had enough, he spat in Bruun's face.

'I wouldn't do that if you were in the desert, dying of thirst,' Jacques said almost conversationally.

Bruun kicked him in the groin and Jacques doubled over to the full reach of his bindings, the only sound escaping him a low, extended whistle. Bruun stalked over to Briony and jerked her upright. He held her at the full reach of his long arms so that she couldn't reach him with her nails or feet. She drew blood from his arms to the elbow. He looked her up and down appraisingly. Her only garment was the thin cotton shift and it reached only an inch past her hips.

'She dress sexy like this for you every night, Roux? No pants, just bum and pussy?'

Jacques did not reply.

Bruun forced Briony to stand on tiptoe so he could get a good look at her pubic hair. The first rays of the sun struck a golden glint and Bruun's men sighed.

'Such a pretty pussy, looks good enough to taste myself.'

'Have a bath first, Teddy. You smell,' Briony spat.

Bruun threw her backwards on the ground. 'You four grab her. An arm or a leg each. Spread her on the table. I'll show her.'

Briony's nails drew blood on each of the four men before they managed to get her on the table. Bruun unbuckled his belt and dropped his trousers. He waddled comically over to the table and stood between Briony's spread legs, rubbing at her with his erection. 'Bring him round so he can see.' He waited until Jacques had been brought to beside the table.

Jacques refrained from telling Bruun he would die for this. In his position such a threat would be ridiculous. He looked away. Bruun grabbed his hair and twisted his head around.

'Watch, you supercilious bastard!' He rammed into Briony and she gasped. 'Nice and tight. You don't use it too much, do you Roux?'

Jacques didn't answer. Bruun let go of his hair to jerk Briony's hips against him as he pumped faster into her. 'Or . . . maybe . . . Weber . . . does that . . . for you . . . too . . . Just like . . . your . . . fighting . . . Aaah!' Bruun fell forward over Briony and she bit his nose. Bruun screamed and jerked his face away. She spat out blood.

'Bitch!' Bruun pulled back, then leant over her to push her shift up above her breasts. He took a breast in each hand and slowly squeezed until she screamed, then twisted the breasts. Her screaming rose to a crescendo and she fainted. 'I was going to keep her for myself, such a nice tight pussy,' Bruun said sadly, dabbing at his nose with his shirttail. 'But now I'll have to let the men have her.'

'You're the kind of animal that gives hyenas a bad name,' Jacques said calmly.

Bruun grabbed him by the hair again, jerked his head down and kneed him in the face. Jacques fell to the ground when Bruun let him go. 'Pick him up,' Bruun ordered his men. 'Then form a queue. Now you can watch all these kaffirs fuck your wife, Roux. When I finish with you, just before I kill you, that's all you'll be able to do, watch.'

Jacques actually managed a lopsided smile. 'Better stretch it all it's worth, Teddy. It's your life. When Ewart Weber catches up with you – as he will – he's going to kill you very slowly indeed. He caught a man raping a nun. He kept him alive for eleven days. By the second day the man was begging to be killed. For you he'll no doubt make a special effort to – '

Bruun struck him in the mouth with his fist. And again. Repeatedly. When he finished Jacques hung limply from the pole, his face a bloody pulp without features. But he twitched satisfactorily when Briony screamed as the first black entered her. The black man was twisting her breasts to make her jerk.

Bruun watched for a while and then went to check on the loading of the trucks.

The moment he turned his back, the men holding Jacques upright let him fall to the ground and kicked him to one side in their hurry to join the back of the queue.

Jacques rolled against the mess tent.

He breathed deeply and let his breath out slowly, deliberately blanking his mind to Briony's cries. First think, then act. Mess tent. Of course. Pietie slept in it and, true to form, should be cowering inside it. But getting loose was only one problem. He turned his head and found, not five feet away, an FN and two clips of ammunition lying on the ground underneath the late Kombi. The FN would probably be empty or near empty but at least one of the clips should be full.

'Pietie,' he called softly. No reply. 'Pietie, it's me, Jacques Roux.'

'Yes, Grootbaas,' his coloured servant called timorously, almost too softly for Jacques to hear.

'Can you see where I am?' Jacques wriggled to make a bulge in the tent.

'Yes, Master.'

'Pass me a knife under the tent.'

The knife was a long time coming as Pietie screwed up his courage. Jacques talked encouragingly to him all the while. Finally the knife was passed through and he manoeuvred the haft in his hand and sawed through the rope holding his wrists. He looked to check whether anybody was watching. Everybody's attention was on the table.

'Pietie, listen to me closely. Cut through the back of the tent and run away into the forest. Get ready to do it now and do it when you hear shooting. Don't come back until after dark. Do you hear me?'

'Yes, Master.' Pietie sounded very doubtful.

Jacques shrugged. Pietie's nerve would probably fail him. But there was nothing to be done about it. He doubled up, cut the rope holding his feet behind the log and left the knife where it was. He rolled towards the FN, grabbing it as he rolled, the clips in his other hand. On his next roll he ejected the clip on the weapon and fitted a new one. Both the clips he had picked up were full, he could feel.

Jacques rolled again and, on his stomach, began firing. The queue of men dropped like ninepins. Jacques' plan was to clear the area around Briony, grab her and drag her into the forest. He rolled again as earth and leaves rose to meet his face where a bullet had struck. Out of the corner of his eye he saw Bruun and several men running towards him. He cursed. It was too late to drag Briony away now. He'd just get both of them killed. He rolled the other way and fired at Bruun. The clip was empty. Bruun dived for the ground, rolled and came up firing. Jacques was into the first under-brush. He kept rolling frantically, then rose and set off as fast as he could through the branches slashing his face and body, his direction parallel to the edge of the camp, at right-angles to the direction he had rolled, heedless of the noise he made because he was certain the shooting and shouting from Bruun's men would cover it.

Jacques ran into one of Bruun's perimeter guards and, before the man could recover his balance, smashed him across the temple with the barrel of the FN. He dived into the undergrowth before the guards on either side started shooting and crawled forward frantically to escape the wild firing. There was shooting ahead of him, spaced shots. He rolled to one side. He was boxed in.

'Run, sir!'

Jacques looked up. It was Sambo, lying at ease along a thick branch ten feet from the ground, picking off Bruun's men as they came rushing up. Jacques rose and ran, his footsteps thunderous beacons in his own ears. He didn't hear Sambo coming up behind him, becoming aware of him only when Sambo passed him and veered to the left. Sambo grabbed him and pulled him behind a tree. His chest was heaving, pounding in his ears. He didn't hear the pursuers but Sambo must have for the black put his hand over Jacques' mouth to still his laboured breathing. There were only three of them, crashing through the forest without looking left or right. Jacques gestured with his FN but Sambo pushed it down. Thirty seconds later they heard three spaced shots. Sambo pulled Jacques to one side and they ran, easily now. The stitch in Jacques' side was killing him but he knew that stopping now would only aggravate it. Sambo whistled once as he ran and was answered with a birdcall. They came to a clearing where a few of Sambo's men rested alertly. Shortly afterwards the men who had ambushed the pursuers announced themselves with a whistle.

Jacques sank to the ground, his chest heaving. There were nine men, including Sambo, ten with himself.

'The men were talking of taking them from the forest,' Sambo said.

Jacques shook his head and tried to smile his gratitude through his split lips. Sambo must know as well as he did that they were too few to take Bruun's many men while Bruun held the sound defensive position of the camp. They were too few to try the trick Bruun had taken them in with, even if Bruun would fall for it soon.

'Your wife,' Sambo said tentatively.

Jacques shook his head again. 'Water.' He drank.

'We'll do her no good if we're dead. What alternatives to frontal assault are there, Sambo?'

'Ambush when they leave the camp, sir, and a harrying action along their way.'

'We're too few for an effective ambush either. They'll expect it near the camp and we have no transport to take us to where we could surprise them. It'll have to be harrying action with such transport as they leave behind or the Landrover when Mr Weber returns.'

Sambo nodded and sat down against a tree to rest. Jacques closed his eyes on his thoughts. One of the men gently took the water bottle from his hands and put a fresh clip in his FN.

'He's too weak to be moved.'

'Then he's also too weak to defend himself, Sister. I must leave and it would be best if he were in my protection.'

'We don't want our mission or our hospital turned into one of your battlegrounds, Major Weber.'

Ewart Weber smiled coldly. How soon they forgot! 'Of course not, Sister. But if Teddy Bruun comes looking for my brother here . . .' Ewart let the sentence die while she formed her own mental images.

She nodded thoughtfully. 'There's nothing wrong with him now that rest and good food won't cure. The more rest and good food, the faster the cure.' She was embarrassed. 'You understand, we must think of all our patients and the children at the school.'

'Of course,' Ewart peeled a handful of notes out of his wallet without looking at the denominations. 'Here, for the mission.'

'Major Weber!' She looked at the notes in her hands. 'All the religious in the Congo already owe you so much – '

'It's on behalf of my brother. I shall recover it out of his wages.'

'How fortunate he is to have a brother like you. This

will keep us going for two weeks or more. We shall say prayers for you and your whole party.'

'Thank you.' Prayers hadn't saved the nuns before; Ewart had. He looked at the angle of the sun on the polished floor. Ten o'clock. 'We shall leave as soon as my man has refuelled the Landrover.' At the door he turned. 'I shall be in Johannesburg in six or eight weeks. If you have a list of medical supplies ready by the time I leave here, I shall arrange to have them sent to you.'

She flew down the passage to her little office, bobbing her head. She was speechless with gratitude.

Ewart shook his head as he went outside. They did much good but it was only a drop in the bucket of suffering the blacks brought upon themselves. The eternal optimism of the missionaries had no room for the probable truth: the blacks could not be converted to the white man's productively competitive ways and their own ways were totally unproductive, what Jacques called the Rule of the Lowest Common Denominator. Saving their souls was only a missionary distraction born of a half-realized despair at failure to improve their present lot. If the meek ever inherited the earth it would be by pure pressure of numbers and entirely the doing of the religious: by providing a health service they were lowering the mortality rate without at the same time lowering the reproductive rate. Ewart, waiting for Jimmy to bring the Landrover back, made a mental note to discuss this idea with Jacques, who would no doubt have figures in his head to prove or disprove it.

In Bangui the administrator whom it had taken Bruun a full day to find and persuade picked up his phone on the second ring. They had finally found Mobutu.

'Brother,' Mobutu greeted him. 'You seek me. How can I be of assistance to my great and powerful neighbour today?'

The administrator did not smile at the hyperbole. Mobutu was apt to embrace you all the better to stab you in the back. 'Brother, there is indeed a small matter. It seems that some of your South African friends are hunting crocodiles in the river between our two countries. They have your permission but not ours.'

'Perhaps not officially,' Mobutu said smoothly. 'But, my brother, if you were to ask certain, and several, men of influence – '

'Yes, yes. That is not the point though. We are not making objection to the killing of the crocodiles. That is a service all round. But another of your jackals, Bruun, is in contention with – '

'Ah, Bruun. A disreputable man. A jackal, as you say, but not my jackal. Lobengula's. Anyway, so what? Bruun is no match for my great good friends Jacques Roux and Ewart Weber.'

No, Bruun's not; that's why he needs my help. 'Quite. But they're fighting their war on our land, on our side of the river.'

'That would be very serious,' Mobutu said calmly, 'if you could prove it. Until you send proof I am powerless.'

The administrator let the silence hang but Mobutu was not to be abashed. 'Is that all then, Brother?'

'No. We do not need proof to act within our own boundaries. It would be regrettable if we had to eliminate too many of Lobengula's men on our land and – '

'And it would be even more regrettable if Roux and Weber were to wipe out half your second-rate army,' Mobutu snapped. 'Talk sense, man. No, let me set an example by telling you some sense, eh Brother? If you were to cross my borders in force to wipe that thorn in my side, Lobengula, and his impertinent jackal Bruun, off the face of the earth, I would, as soon as your forces retreated across the river again, shower medals and pensions on your military and on you like it was confetti. As for Roux and Weber, even your syphilitic military have more sense than to tamper with them, regardless of whose soil they're on; they need no protection from me.'

'I understand. Thank you for your co-operation.'

'Any time.' Mobutu rang off. He was totally immune to sarcasm.

The administrator had dealt with Mobutu before and expected as much but the gesture had to be made. Now he would call the French big brother at the Quai and sick them on Mobutu's Belgian paymasters. Mobutu wouldn't dare give the Belgians the same shit – he'd have to call off or at least delay Roux and Weber, which was all Bruun required the administrator to do to earn his share of the skins.

But the man in the French Foreign Office decided to bypass the Belgians, who were pussyfooting with Mobutu because he was threatening to nationalize the copper mines, and go directly to the South Africans. His reasoning was simple: Bruun was irrelevant because he was an Englishman and employed by Lobengula and therefore indirectly Mobutu's responsibility; Roux and Weber were South African nationals and notorious mercenaries – exactly the kind of people the South African Government were very sensitive about. The South Africans bought most of their arms from France; they would also very shortly require the French veto in the Security Council of the United Nations in the matter of a resolution put forward by one of the more troublesome third world nations. Ergo, the South Africans could call their own nationals, Weber and Roux, back. He made a call to Pretoria and was told the matter would be looked into; he was satisfied – the South African made no idle promises.

The official who had promised to 'look into the matter' first spoke to his minister (who telephoned a General von Hoesch) and then went to call on a Colonel Rocco Burger at the headquarters of the Bureau of State Security. The official, who was a very senior man and more than a little on his dignity, could have called Burger to attend him at his own office. He had not for the simple reason that Burger was a man who acted outside the usual channels and, for that matter, often outside the law. The activities of such men, made public by some mischance, would ruin the careers of many others and the official didn't want sharp eyes to notice Burger visiting him. When Burger objected to what was expected of him the official told him to phone General von Hoesch. When Burger finished talking to von Hoesch, he asked the official, 'Don't the manipulations of our masters, the politicians, ever sicken you?' The official left without answering; he was a career man.

Jacques was no great loss. Bruun would have liked to have killed him but another day would do. He kicked the row of dead bodies who had been queueing before Briony when Jacques opened fire. 'Like a line of targets in a fair ground shoot,' he said aloud. He sent men to replace the guards who had been killed. They were so on edge that they shot two of their own in the party sent to pursue Sambo when it returned without ever having caught sight of Sambo or any of his men. Bruun kicked and slapped them soundly, then put them to work loading the reeking skins on to the trucks. The skinners had quietly disappeared into the forest during the commotion Jacques' escape caused.

'You lot, you too,' Bruun called to the men around Briony. She was unconscious, her breasts red from all the handling, a trickle of blood running down the thigh that hung limply from the table's edge. 'Load the skins. We'll take her back with us so you can enjoy her at your leisure.' Bruun went out to inspect the guards. He didn't want any of them creeping back into camp. Not that he thought Roux would be stupid enough to mount an attack but because a gap in the defences could let through the single sniper sent to kill him.

When Bruun returned to the camp half an hour later, he found to his rage that the men had discovered the liquor in the mess tent and that several were half-drunk already. A man waved a bottle at Bruun. Bruun took his rifle and shot him through the head. 'Drop the bottles. Smash them.' Bruun turned the rifle around the circle of sullen faces radiating hate through reddened eyes. How the hell could they get drunk so quickly? 'Does anybody want to be dead for a drink?'

One young black cradled the bottle of Ewart's best bourbon to his chest and raised his rifle in his other hand. Bruun shot him through the wrist and, when the rifle had fallen to the ground, through the stomach. 'Anybody else?' They dropped the bottles and smashed them. 'All right, back to work.'

Bruun heard the moaning behind him and turned to look. They had found Roux's halfbreed servant and nailed him to a tree, hands and feet, upside down. His stomach had been cut out, his entrails ripped out, his nose and ears cut off, his cheeks split, and he had been castrated. As everything else, they had botched it. The idea was that the man should bleed to death very slowly. But this one had been so hung that he would drown in his own blood before he lost even another pint. The hell with these halfwits, he wasn't going to tell them.

He raised the rifle and aimed – he would kill the halfbreed before he drowned, a fitting further punishment for his men for starting on the liquor. He heard the growl around him and turned a full circle to stare them down before he aimed again, dragging it out, and fired two shots into the head and heart. There was a collective sigh from his men and they continued sullenly about their work.

'You! Make coffee. Many pots of it. When it is ready, bring to me all the men who think they can drive a truck and mugs to feed them the coffee from. Move!' He turned to watch the men at work. 'Wiggle your arses and move it or I'll kill the woman too.' Maybe they couldn't help being born black but if he was that stupid he'd kill himself. Starting on the booze while Roux and Sambo and several men were still on the loose out there and Weber could return any moment with his brother the freak sharp-shooter and perhaps even how thick-headed could even a kaffir be and still be called human?

Bruun looked at his watch. He'd be lucky to get away by two o'clock. But, no matter what, he'd be in Bangui by nightfall to deliver the skins to the buyer and split the money with the grubbing bureaucrat. Split the money?

He'd promised the greedy little black bureaucrat half the money the skins fetched to hold up Roux and Weber for so long that they would see reason and would deal with Bruun. But Bruun had taken the skins by force and any delay was irrelevant. The man had earned nothing. But he would still demand his share and, once the skins were at Bangui, would cause difficulties if he didn't receive his share. Who knows, he might even now be plotting to take Bruun's share as well.

Bruun tore apart a packet of Senior Service and wrote on the plain cardboard inside. He called the messenger, folded the packet so that the message was inside and protected against sweaty hands. He gave the runner instructions about finding the buyer at the hotel. 'Tell him, if he wants the skins he must come to meet me at Lobengula's palace by the second dawn. If he wishes, you stay to show him the way.'

As he watched the messenger on his way through the forest, Bruun decided he had done the right thing: it would be much easier dealing with the greedy Lobengula than with the rapacious politician in Bangui. Perhaps he could even satisfy Lobengula with Briony, though he'd have to clean her up a little first.

As soon as Lance was strapped into the Landrover, Ewart took off, setting an even more blistering pace through the daylight hours than he had before in the night.

KILL

In the fading light Lance didn't at first realize why Ewart had stopped so close to the camp. He had just woken and was still fuzzy. He sleepily watched Jimmy walk around the pole planted in the ground beside the track.

Oh my God, Lance thought, suddenly shatteringly awake, that's a human head on the pole. He unsnapped his harness and climbed down. Ewart put a restraining arm on his shoulder before he came too near. 'Kombi was Jimmy's brother,' Ewart said softly.

'I never even had a chance to thank him for saving my life yesterday,' Lance said.

Jimmy walked around the pole and its grisly crown once more, than took the head off lovingly and cradled it to his chest. He climbed back into the Landrover and Ewart closed the door. All the way into the camp, another ten minutes, none of them said a word. Even Lance did not need to be told what the red handkerchief tied to the pole below the head meant: Bruun's sign. For this, Lance thought, Bruun will die and I'm not going to be left behind, no matter what Ewart says – he can't very well tie me up and tell Jimmy to stand guard over me while they hunt Bruun down because Jimmy was Kombi's brother. He absently put a handful of the sickly sweet glucose tablets in his mouth and crunched them methodically. Nobody was going to say he looked weak and should rest.

They stopped in the camp and climbed down. Lance automatically opened the door for Jimmy. They stood for a moment, taking in the devastation of what had been their orderly camp. Tents had been pulled down, boxes of food smashed open and scattered, a fire had started in the rubbish but not taken. Men were walking around, picking up the last few bullets from burst boxes. Others were standing by an improvised hoist near where Sambo, stripped to the waist and gleaming with diesel oil, was pouring boiling water on an engine out of one of the two remaining trucks. Ewart walked over towards Sambo and Lance followed. The men went about their business, avoiding looking at them.

'They left five hours ago,' Sambo said without looking up from his work. 'At the road they turned south. They have not returned. They took Mrs Roux with them.' Sambo stopped pouring water and tested the glistening black bulge on the engine casing with his thumb.

'Where is Mr Roux?'

'Sleeping. His hands were getting in the way and I asked him to rest.'

'How long before this truck will be ready to run?'

'Half an hour, sir,' Sambo held a burning branch against the black welt. When he took it away the repair was not scarred. 'The other truck has a shattered distributor. They took our spare parts.'

'One truck will do.' Ewart turned on his heel.

'Aren't you going to ask how it happened?' Lance wanted to know.

'That's irrelevant.' Ewart walked away to the shelter where Jacques was sleeping.

Lance would have followed him but Sambo took his elbow. 'This is not your battle, Mr Lance.'

'And perhaps you would like the belt of the black tree snake back as well,' Lance snapped without pausing for thought.

Sambo's lips compressed and his grip tightened on Lance's arm. 'Most of us won't return. Believe me, I mean you well and cast no slur on your courage. But it is not your affair.'

'But it is, Sambo. You claim to be my friend, so – '

'I am.'

There was no doubting Sambo's sincerity. 'So, when my

brother tries to leave me behind, my friends will explain to him that my skill with the rifle is essential.' Lance looked into Sambo's grim face for a moment. 'I count on you, Sambo.'

'Bring the chains. Put them on the engine,' Sambo said to the men standing by. He let Lance's arm go. He turned to Jimmy, standing silently with Kombi's head cradled in his arms. 'The rest of our brother is under the tarpaulin there. Join his head to it so he may go to the ancestors whole.' Lance would have followed Jimmy but Sambo said, 'This engine was put out of commission with a shot intended to go through the block. Fortunately it went only through the water jacket. I plugged the hole with a piece of wood soaked in tree gum. The wet wood will expand and the tree gum hardens when boiling water is poured on it. It's as good as the white man's welding. Let Jimmy be for the moment; he's young and as soon as there is work for him to do he'll snap out of it.'

'I am sorry about Kombi.'

'He took many with him to the ancestors. For such a one it is unseemly to feel sorry.' Sambo took an end of the chain from the man whose little finger Lance had amputated. 'Fetch the master's rifle. He dug it out of the mud and cleaned it for you,' Sambo added to Lance.

Lance took his rifle, thanked the man, wandered away. He found Jacques around the back of the truck, supervising the loading of supplies. He put his hand silently on Jacques' shoulder and Jacques nodded. 'I checked your rifle after it was cleaned. The water didn't get into the electronics of the scope so no damage was done. How are you?'

'Never better.'

'I heard what you said to Sambo. Nobody'll think the worse of you if you reconsider. Sambo's right, it's not your – '

'If you heard what I said to him, you heard.' If Jacques wanted to take offence at the tightness of his voice, let him.

'Don't let anger cloud your judgement,' Jacques said evenly.

'It's not anger. It's frustration at your thickheadedness and Sambo's. Don't you see, if scum like Bruun attacks any of us, it's an attack on decent people anywhere. It's got nothing to do with anger. It's what I said before, Bruun must be punished. Justice. And if the only justice around here grows from the barrel of a gun, sending me home is like saying a high school class can't go to the magistrate's court to see him pronounce sentence because . . . well, because!'

Jacques nodded but whether it was agreement or an empty gesture to avoid argument, Lance didn't know. He walked away and found Jimmy, his arm back in its sling, checking the rifles on the rack in the Landrover. He helped Jimmy for a few minutes, making sure all the rifles were in good order and that there was ample ammunition for each. Then they found a piece of copper tubing and a fuel can and siphoned all the diesel from the truck which would be left behind. Ewart was removing all the wheels and auxiliary parts of the engine to take with them as spares.

'You're staying here with two men to guard the camp,' he said to Lance.

'No.'

'I haven't time to argue, Lance.'

'There's nothing here to guard. You can't afford two men to guard me. Sambo and Jacques both think my rifle will be useful on your little expedition. Ask them.'

'I make the decisions.'

'But would you want to leave me if I weren't your brother?'

'You're walking wounded, you and Jimmy.'

'I'm not staying,' Jimmy said flatly. 'Sir.'

'And I,' Lance said stubbornly, 'am in better shape than you are. When did you last sleep?'

Ewart laughed. 'Four hours this morning at the hospital.

280

All right, you can come if you promise to do exactly as you're told and no more.'

'I promise.'

'I'll deal with your impertinence, and Jimmy's, when we've finished with Bruun,' Ewart said, the smile gone.

'Fucking martinet,' Jimmy muttered as Ewart walked away.

'At least he's consistent,' Lance said. He spat to clear the taste of diesel from his mouth. 'Here, chew some glucose. I never knew diesel tasted so much like castor oil.'

There was nothing more for them to do. Lance was careful not to show his impatience as Ewart insisted on spending half an hour personally checking their equipment and supplies after everybody else was ready to leave. Ewart might still change his mind and leave him behind if there was any suspicion that he might be tempted to break his promise through impatience. Lance thought of Briony in the hands of Bruun and his men and shivered. He looked surreptitiously at Jacques, but Jacques was outwardly calm as he distributed the scoped rifles among the best shots.

At last Ewart was satisfied. Lance gave one last look at the mound of bodies under the tarpaulin, wedged down at the edges with wooden tent pegs against the carrion-eaters of the forest, and climbed up into the Landrover. To Lance's rage, Ewart took one last walk around the camp, returning with a case of dynamite he had found in a dark corner. This caused another delay while unbroken jam jars were found to make nitroglycerine into as the dynamite would have been useless to them without the fuses and detonators, all of which had been taken by Bruun.

The man whose little finger Lance had amputated had a name in his own language which was formed of two clicking sounds made with the tongue against the palate. None of the whites, except Ewart, could even approximate this sound; Jacques had therefore christened him Clickclack. He sat snoring in the back of the Landrover between Lance and Jimmy; he was riding with them because, after Kombi, he was the best tracker. Jimmy too had gone to sleep within ten minutes of leaving the camp. Lance, wide awake after sleeping all day, looked at Jacques, who was driving; Jacques was deep in his own thoughts, his face relaxed in the glow of the instrument lights. He was not driving very fast because the truck behind them had to keep up and the road was still treacherously muddy from the afternoon rains. Lance found their pace frustrating.

'Can't we go any faster?'

'No.' Ewart didn't look up from the chart he was studying in the gleam of the map light.

'I don't understand why Bruun turned south,' Lance said after a while.

'How's that, Lance?' Jacques asked politely when Ewart just grunted.

'Well, the buyer is waiting in Bangui and that's north. Bruun could have been there long before now. For another thing, he seems to come and go in the Central African Republic as he pleases. So why not go there in the hope that we won't follow?'

'Greed,' Ewart said shortly.

Jacques explained. 'He probably spent some time in Bangui getting a partner to help him in some way – we don't know how – but once he had the skins, Bruun decided not to share. So he's heading for his home ground and you can be sure he's already sent for the buyer to meet him there.'

'But his base is east, not south.'

'He might just be clever.'

'Or laying a false trail.'

'No. Look at the road. All our trucks passed here.'

Lance wouldn't give up that easily. 'It would have been a lot cleverer for Bruun to take the skins to Zongo, on the Congo side of the river just across from Bangui, and deliver them to the buyer there.'

'Perhaps. But his disappointed partner in Bangui would simply tell the police chief and mayor of Zongo of the transaction and then they would demand their share. No Lance, for Bruun to keep everything, he must get the skins on his home ground first of all.'

'What about the man he works for, Lobengula?'

'I don't know. Perhaps Bruun thinks he can deal with him.'

'Go to sleep, Lance,' Ewart said irritably.

Lance was not sleepy but he sat quietly. Jacques punched a tape into the cassette and with it the whole of the Landrover's radio system became alive. The radio cut in immediately:

' – or Weber on the Bangui. Please come in. Calling anyone in the party of Roux or Weber on the Bangui. Please come in. Calling anyone in the party of Roux or Weber on the Bangui. Please come in.'

Ewart looked at Jacques, then picked up the microphone. 'Identify yourself, over.'

'Please hold the channel open for Rocco Burger. Stand by.'

'Only the best for us. I wonder what the good Colonel wants.'

'We'll soon find out.'

'Who's he?' Lance asked.

'Operations chief of the South African Bureau of State Security,' Ewart said.

Lance was burning with questions. What could the feared boss of BOSS want with them? How did he know the frequency on which the automatic signal detector would cut in? He didn't ask his questions because there was suddenly a tangible tension in the Landrover. The two black men beside him had stopped their soft snoring and Lance sensed that they were awake and immediately alert, like disturbed cats. There was a buzzing on the radio and Ewart turned a knob minutely until the signal strength indicator burned a bright red.

'Jacques? Over.'

Jacques took the microphone. 'Rocco? I'm here. Over.'

'You're required to return to South Africa immediately and bring Weber with you. Do you read me? Over.'

Before pushing in the button to transmit, Jacques said, 'Now we know what Bruun was doing. Political mischief.' He pushed the button and brought the microphone to his mouth. 'I hear you. Why? Over.'

'There have been complaints from the CAR that you've been fighting a private war on their soil. They've complained to the French. Over.'

And the French complained to Pretoria, Lance thought.

'We deny that,' Jacques said. 'We're on Congo soil at the express invitation and under the protection of its government. Over.'

'Nevertheless, there are political ramifications. You are required forthwith to return to South Africa where you will be recompensed for any losses you might have suffered. Please signify your willingness to comply. Over.'

'Recompensed at ten cents in the dollar,' Jacques said scathingly. He pressed the button. 'Rocco, I repeat, we are in the Congo, hunting crocodiles at Mobutu's express invitation. We are fighting no wars. This is none of your concern. Over.'

'It has been made my concern. Don't be hard-headed. Over.'

'We'd willingly comply but there is a complication. A local bandit called Bruun has taken my wife. First we shall recover her, then we shall fulfil our contract to the Kinshasa government. Over.'

'I've already said you'll be recompensed for any losses. Generously. As an added inducement, investigations into the Kariba accident will also be dropped. As for your wife, I shall recover her myself. Over.'

'How?'

'This is an open line, Jacques.'

'How?'

'From a French base in the CAR.' Burger paused. 'I'll have her back by tomorrow evening. I guarantee it. Over.'

284

'Wait.'

'I'll stand by.'

Jacques whistled. 'High-level stuff. What do you say, Ewart?'

'Generously will still mean only twenty cents in the dollar. As for Kariba, they can prove nothing. He might get Briony back by tomorrow evening but I've seen too many of the paramil operations he's mounted to put her chances of surviving the rescue higher than one in ten. Burger's first priority is to keep his own people alive, so they go in with all barrels blazing. But he's your friend, she's your wife: you must decide.'

'I don't believe the Central Africans will let him operate from their soil. He's bluffing. And Mobutu will certainly not let him operate from here – he'll lose too much money.' Jacques punched the button. 'Thanks but no thanks.'

'Jacques, I beg you, don't force me to – '

Jacques cut the sound of Burger's voice in mid-sentence by switching the receiver off. 'Now we know what trouble Bruun was stirring in Bangui.' He pushed the tape home in the player and the sound of Bach filled the Landrover.

After another hour of the same frustratingly slow progress they stopped to inspect the marks where several trucks had slid in the mud and been dug out. They stood to one side, the lights of the Landrover and the truck shining on the disturbed mud.

'This is where they first came into the rain. Very suddenly,' Clickclack said. There two trucks locked together, slid off the road. They take long time to get all trucks back on road, maybe three hours.' He walked away in the drying mud to inspect the track beyond the scene of the accident. When he came back, he reported, 'No trucks damaged but driving very slowly. Some drivers, most, not very good.'

Ewart bent to pick up some of the drying mud. He crumbled it between his fingers. 'How far are they ahead of us? Two hours, three?'

Clickclack also crumbled mud between his fingers. 'Maybe.' He inspected the crushed moss and ferns and grasses where the trucks had ploughed into them, pushed his finger into the sap on the bark of the scarred tree, looked at the angle of twigs on the branches that had been packed under the wheels of the trucks for traction. 'Little more.' He held up three fingers, then four and made a slicing movement with the edge of his hand.

'Three and a half hours,' Ewart said. 'We'll pull off the road at the first clearing and eat and rest.'

'If they're driving so badly and wasting time getting the trucks back on the road every time they slide off, surely we could catch them in a couple of hours,' Lance said. Eating and resting was the furthest thing from his mind. He wanted Bruun punished and Briony rescued before Burger arrived.

'Use your head. If we strike at Bruun in the dark we'll almost certainly kill Briony ourselves.' Ewart turned away towards the Landrover.

The French official at the Quai d'Orsay was pleased with himself. The South Afrcans would do the dirty work in return for a vote at the Security Council which the Elysée Palace had already decided they should have. All that remained to be done was to tell the man in Bangui that the South Africans would be accommodated at one of the French air bases in the Central African Republic – a formality and a courtesy.

When he put the phone down, he was baffled. The administrator in Bangui had been quite vocal about having the South African Bureau of State Security on CAR soil, no matter how briefly. Even the thought that Mobutu would be taught a stern lesson had been no consolation. But it had been difficult to determine exactly what caused the man's rage. You never knew with the little black brothers, no matter that they wore clothes just like yours, washed with soap, and – important – had been in your class at the École.

Perhaps the man was worried that the whole episode might leak to the OAU, but what did the OAU matter when you had France for a friend? Anyway, the South Africans were most efficient at this kind of sweeping-up operation and even more tightmouthed about who had helped them than the Israelis.

He relapsed into the glow of wellbeing that the exercise of power always afforded him.

Bruun was neither stupid nor untalented; he would never have got to Sandhurst if he were. That the more subtle manifestations of his bullying had been mistaken for leadership qualities is not a condemnation of the British but of armies everywhere. Here, in a desolate corner of Africa where Bruun was his own court of appeal, the manner of his 'leadership' was forthright and brutal, blows and kicks and sometimes summary executions compensating for his laxness in instilling discipline in his men. Considering the quality and attitude of his men it was a masterwork of intimidation on his part to get the lumbering convoy on the road before the afternoon rains came. The men were half-drunk and sullen because he had taken their liquor and their woman from them; shooting Pietie was an open and calculated insult to the tradition of their ancestors – if it was bad luck to let the victim die before his time, to kill him would bring a certain pestilence upon the crops. There was almost an open rebellion when he had thrown the woman into the cab of the truck he would be travelling in: the men had expected to enjoy her on the crocodile skins on the back of the truck. Bruun had cocked the FN he had found and pointed it at the men who were muttering loudest. Bruun also promised each man a thousand American dollars when they got the skins back to headquarters and sold them. This had some effect though several doubted they would be paid.

In the first hour they covered thirty miles. Then the rain had come and the nightmare started. It had been Bruun's plan to turn off the 'main' road beyond Boyabo and head for Bosobolo rather than Gemena, taking a slightly longer way home but with less chance of running into Weber returning from the south.

Bruun blocked the 'main' road beyond the turnoff with his truck and sat watching the other trucks turn, his fist kneading Briony's thigh nervously. She still sat with her hands between her legs, still wearing the same torn and dirty short nightdress, her legs muddy to the knees from being pulled out of the truck to stand in the mud while it was freed from a deep rut beside the road. She looked straight ahead, locked in her own thoughts.

As the last truck turned, Bruun pulled in behind it. These bloody kaffirs drove like drunken baboons; he would have to resign himself to losing one or more of the trucks complete with valuable cargo before they reached safety. From the corner of his eye he caught the lights approaching at speed along the road from the south. He switched the lights of his own truck off and checked that the lights of the other trucks had already disappeared into the trees. He waited. From the way the lights swung from side to side it was obvious whoever was coming was driving at speed and with considerable skill in this dangerous period of extended dusk that came to the forest at this time of year. The vehicle came past at speed, the driver concentrating on aligning it to slide smoothly through the next muddy curve, not paying attention to the turnoff.

It was Roux's travelling gin-palace of a Landrover, Weber driving, his freak-shot brother fast asleep in the passenger seat, that impertinent educated-nigger little brother of Sambo's snoring in the back seat. Just like Weber to let a nigger sleep while he worked. Bruun sighed his relief and drove on. The woman had not even noticed Weber's passage.

* * *

Jimmy shook Lance awake. Lance found himself still strapped into his seat in the Landrover. He must have drifted off to sleep before they even reached the resting place. 'Did I miss supper?' He was hungry. He stretched luxuriously as he climbed down.

'We saved you some. Your brother requests your presence.'

Ewart, Jacques and Sambo were seated at a folding table. Lance sat down and found a tin plate of cold meat and an onion before him as well as a mug of steaming coffee and a bunch of bananas. Nobody had thought to bring cutlery but Jimmy's clasp knife was lying next to his plate. Marvelling a little at Ewart's thoughtfulness in bringing the necessities for keeping the body going even under circumstances like this, Lance fell to, ignoring the knife and tearing the meat with his hands. His eyes started to water as he bit into the onion. He was glad to be alive though there was, for the first time, a dull pain in his crotch – something like being constipated, nagging but not serious.

'While you were sleeping,' Ewart said, 'we turned towards Gemena at Boyabo.'

Lance looked at the map on the table as Ewart pointed.

'We're now here, at the turnoff to Bosobolo. Bruun has taken this road.'

Lance looked again. 'I don't believe it, Ewart.'

'Don't speak with your mouth full.'

Lance swallowed the food in his mouth. 'We already know his drivers are inexperienced. To take them on this dirt track "suitable for cross-country vehicles", that's what it says right here in the key, that's . . . It's a trick to mislead us.'

'Or very clever. Lobengula's place is here, east of Businga. Bruun would usually take the road through Gemena. The turnoff to Bosobolo is easy to miss. But his tracks clearly lead up there. Tell Mr Lance what you have found,' Ewart added to Clickclack, who was standing nearby.

'They drive for Bosobolo. Every now and again they stick. They take a long time to pull the lorries out, sir. Now the ground is drying out and they go little faster but still not very fast. When the sun rises they'll be going quite fast.'

'Did you see them?'

'No. Little Master, I only go to half an hour behind them.'

Lance had no doubt Clickclack had judged the time since Bruun's passage correctly. 'Are they stopping for the night?'

'Once they stop for half an hour to eat, no longer.'

'All right, eat and rest,' Ewart told the scout. 'Pity we can't take them one by one on the run as we did before.'

'Why not?' Lance asked, looking up from blowing on his coffee.

'There will be men riding on the backs of the trucks,' Ewart said. 'All right, the plan is this: We'll move out in an hour and split up, one party to circle round Bruun and ambush him, another to block the road behind. All this will happen about midmorning. Lance, you and Jacques and Jimmy and one other marksman will circle round in the Landrover for the ambush.'

Lance looked disbelievingly at his brother, then at the trees surrounding them. Once you left the track the Landrover would soon be irretrievably stuck between two trees.

'The trees end not too far from here,' Jacques said. 'Beyond there's a plain with grass and only the occasional tree. We'll easily get around Bruun.'

'You'll find a secure position with adequate cover,' Ewart continued, 'and all four of you will aim to kill Bruun in the lead truck. Before you ask, Lance, our tracker says Bruun rides in the lead truck. With Bruun dead his men will be disorganized and Sambo and I and the rest of the men will take them from behind. Please note that you are to do nothing but kill Bruun. If you are attacked you will retreat. Even after we have attacked the remnant of Bruun's force

290

from behind, you are not to show yourselves. We are depending on surprise, a crossfire and superior range, not any kind of frontal attack. Is that clear, Lance?'

Lance drank some coffee. 'Of course. You don't think I'm going to storm around heroically like some Beau Geste character, do you?'

Jacques clapped his hands twice. 'My brother, the rugger player and wit,' he said, a reminder to cool Ewart's obvious anger.

Ewart stared at Lance a moment longer. 'Just remember your promise. I have no stomach for telling our parents you killed yourself while showing off.'

Lance felt his face reddening. 'You go too far, Ewart,' He was going to say more but Jimmy squeezed his shoulder painfully. 'But I thank you for your concern. I'll try my best not to shame you by getting killed.' Jimmy squeezed again and Lance gently removed the big black hand from his shoulder. 'It's okay, Jimmy, I've had my say.'

Ewart laughed briefly but quite pleasantly. 'All right. Spill all your anger here. You're not too proud to take a tip from an old pro, are you?'

'No. What is it?'

'An angry man is his own worst enemy. When you have Bruun in your sights, think of his face as a bullseye. Forget what he's done because remembering will spoil your aim.'

'I'll remember.'

Just before they moved out Lance felt another surge of anger when Ewart took his rifle and inspected it, fitting new batteries to the telescopic sight without consulting Lance. Lance said nothing, restraining himself only with difficulty, and was glad he had for Ewart next inspected the scoped rifles of the other three men in the party, the Landrover's fuel supply, the water bottles, the water in the radiator of the Landrover and all its tyres including the spares. Then he nodded at them and walked away to the truck. He didn't shake hands or wish them good luck.

Lance looked back as the Landrover drove from the camp. Ewart was standing in the headlights of the truck looking after them. He wished Ewart's meticulous insistence on detail didn't make him so hard to get on with.

'You really should show your brother more respect, Mr Lance,' Jimmy said after a while. 'He was going to leave you guarding the truck until Mr Roux asked to have you with us. Your brother means well and it is an honour to serve under him.'

Lance said, 'Thanks, Jacques,' and let his head rest against the back of the seat, snoring only once but most pointedly. Jimmy had missed the point: it wasn't a lack of respect towards Ewart but Ewart's own almost old-maidish finickyness that caused the irritation. It was humiliating to have a brother who didn't trust you to show the little common sense required not to risk your life unnecessarily. What was even more aggravating was Ewart's habit of choosing moments when there was an audience to tell his maniac little brother to keep a low profile. Of course Ewart meant well. But he could be so goddamn overpowering with it.

Jacques punched music into the cassette player and the uneasy silence in the car was broken by a string quartet. Lance relaxed his muscles one by one, starting with his right little toe.

He woke up just as dawn was breaking. They were on a huge plain, whether tableau or basin he didn't know. This was a wonder. One moment in the dense forests of rain every day, next among the dry yellow grasses and the stunted trees of the sub-tropical savanna. And not much more than a hundred miles away, said the map, desert where a man could die of thirst in the heat of the day or freeze to death in the cold of the night. The dawn too was strange here, not the slow seeping of light in the forest, not the growth of orange in the shadows but a full sudden sunlight after only the briefest of dusks in which the red eye of the sun raised its brim above the horizon in a majestic hurry, a balance between dignity and frenzy Lance was sure Ewart would understand.

Jacques waited for full light before he directed the Landrover off the rutted track and into the swishing grass. Lance cast a rearwards glance at the 'road' where the tracks of the trucks in Bruun's convoy had dried like arrows pointing towards the malefactor. He was not surprised that their progress across the uncharted grass was smoother than over the 'road'.

Colonel Rocco Burger looked down at the mutilated body of Jacques Roux's coloured servant. 'Pietie. He often served me coffee or wine on the farm.'

'You know Colonel Roux then?' the French liaison major asked.

'Through his brother, who is a member of parliament in South Africa,' Burger said.

The French major would have been the first to admit that he stood in awe of Burger. It was nothing to do with Burger's appearance, to the contrary; Burger, in his brown suit, cream silk shirt, olive tie and tan brogues, looked like a somewhat unremarkable dandy. He was a whisker under medium height, his wavy ginger hair was greying at the temples and only the most observant noticed the intensity of his clear blue eyes. But this Colonel Burger of the South African Bureau of State Security (known as BOSS), this man who looked like a successful salesman of orthopaedic shoes, was much admired in that small tight circle of men who are sent by their governments to sweep up and bury embarrassments. To put it with a point, the French major thought, Burger was feared by his peers around the world. The major looked at the men around Burger, tough young men in olive-drab camouflage jump suits tucked into their boots. The experienced eye of the French officer did not miss the living familiarity with which they handled their weapons. A man like Burger would naturally have an élite around him.

'I would not like to be sent to fetch Colonel Roux or Major Weber,' the French major admitted. 'When I was a young man, just commissioned, in Indochina, Weber was a sergeant under me. Even then he was a man to be respected.' It was a courteous way of expressing his opinion that this was dangerous work. The French major was also uneasy about being on the unpredictable Mobutu's side of the river but, in the face of Burger's calm, felt it would be unmanly to say so. In any case, even a maniac like Mobutu would hardly raise his voice against Rocco Burger. Especially when Burger was under the protection of France. The major's chest swelled a little. 'How will you do it?'

Burger seemed surprised at the question. 'I shall ask them to come with me, of course, and they will.'

The major was not so sure. He would, given a similar task, set a trap for Roux and Weber and, only when he had them surrounded by superior force, demand their surrender. This Burger was dangerously overconfident. But then he had been instructed to see that Burger got all the assistance he required, not to teach him his business.

'But first we have to find them,' Burger said. He tried to close Pietie's eyes but rigor mortis had already set in. He pulled the tarpaulin back over the dead. His men replaced the tent pegs holding the canvas down.

One of Burger's men gave him a list of the dead. 'Skinners, for the crocodiles. Some of Weber's Simbas, not many. A large number of Bruun's men. No whites.'

'Thank you,' Burger said as he cast his eye over the list. 'You have a theory, don't you?'

'Yes sir. Bruun took them by surprise. They nevertheless gave a pretty convincing account of themselves but were forced into the bush. When Bruun had left they tidied up here, effected repairs to damaged vehicles and gave pursuit.'

Burger looked at the man for a few moments. 'That's probably all true. The question I need answered is this: why

294

did they stay here so long before going after Bruun? The tidying must have taken hours, yet it was obviously make-work while they waited for something else to happen.'

'I don't know, sir. None of the repairs they could have done here would have taken that long.'

'Perhaps the reason for being taken by surprise and the reason for the delay is the same: their leader was elsewhere and they were awaiting his return.' Burger gave the man time to digest this. 'Get on the radio to the villages, towns and cities which have hospitals or nursing missions and are within a day's journey from here and ask if they have seen Major Weber.'

'He could have been buying food or ammunition, sir.'

'No. There's ammunition to spare here and food they could shoot or catch in the river. He needed medical supplies, or was carrying someone to hospital.' He called after the man, 'Pretend you're a civilian friend. Our writ doesn't run here.' Berger smiled faintly as he said this. One could say his writ didn't run even in South Africa or one could say his writ ran anywhere and everywhere he said it did. He was neither vain nor conceited, simply a realist saddened by twenty years of this work, disillusioned by a world in which it was necessary. 'Major, could you please arrange for one of your navigators to be stupid and lose his way. I should like pictures as far south as Gemena and from here east to Businga.'

The major matched Burger's slightly cynical smile. 'No need for the navigator to lose his way. We routinely violate Congo airspace when pilots fly directly from Bangassou to Bangui simply because they're too lazy to plot a course around the bulge of the river. Nobody's ever complained.'

'We'll wait here while my men bury the dead,' Burger said, to the major's horror. You had to admire the man's coolness, the major admitted, but remaining on foreign soil while backed by some of the most notorious paramilitary troops in the world, simply to pay a last courtesy to the dead, that was one for the books. If this ever got in the papers . . . what the fuck had the politicians gotten the Services into this time?

Bruun slowed down when he heard the hooting and the truck behind him sideswiped them in its hurry to get by. Bruun cursed and pulled off the track onto the grass. The other trucks passed them as if the drivers had been forcefed Vindaloo. Bruun looked back through the dust. Far behind them on the plain another dustcloud hung in the air, growing at its leading edge as it faded at the trailing edge. Bruun engaged gear and sped past the line of lurching trucks. He stopped pressing the horn when he saw it aggravated the frenzy his men were in. Goddamn! He kept going on the grass beside the track until he was half a mile ahead of the leading truck, then pulled his truck across the track and stepped down on the road to wave them down. They stopped reluctantly and one truck overturned. Men who had fallen from the backs of speeding trucks came running towards them. The men babbled around him.

Bruun punched at them with his fists and kicked shins for a full minute before he pointed. They all looked. The pursuing dustcloud was settling, the vehicle or vehicles stopped too far away to make out size or number. What had happened was simple; the black baboons had known Weber had left the camp. They had enjoyed themselves with Roux's woman but Roux had killed all but one of those who had finished with her and a good number of the aspirants in the queue. Now there was pursuit and immediately the curs assumed it was Weber, the Butcher himself, and Roux come to kill them. 'Look, you inside-out arseholes! We stop. So they stop. They're frightened of us! How many men do you think they have? Four, five? They can't take us from behind while you sit on the skins. They can't take us from the front because, the moment we don't see their dust behind us, we know they've cut around to lay ambush. What do you use your heads for, sticking into your women's backsides?'

They mumbled among themselves for a while, discussing the logic of it. They looked at their numbers for reassurance. What were four or five men against them? Hadn't they taken the Butcher's camp and the woman of the limping white man while he watched?

Bruun set them to work righting and reloading the overturned truck. He pulled the fender from the tyre of the truck that had sideswiped his own but decided against changing the tyre. These baboons would take all day about it.

While not as sanguine as his men, Bruun was not unduly worried. Weber had only the Landrover and there was no way he could surprise the convoy; Bruun had seen his men shoot into the engines of the trucks they had left behind. Once underway again, Bruun put his hand on Briony's thigh and slid his hand up. He pushed her hands away and squeezed her mound.

'Old Butcher Weber and your husband are riding behind there in our dust. But there's nothing they can do. Colonel Theodore Bruun is in complete control of the situation. They can just swallow dust and look on enviously while a real soldier rides home in triumph.'

'I shall stay awake all the ten days or so it will take Jacques and Ewart to kill you,' she said softly.

He squeezed until she screamed, then let go. 'Mustn't damage the goods for Lobengula, His Majesty,' Bruun said with a chuckle.

She pressed her hands between her legs and turned to look through the rearview window. Even if there had been no dustcloud she would have seen nothing through the tears blinding her.

Bruun laughed aloud. 'Weber's just playing one of his psychological games. They don't work with me.' He braked gently. 'Idea.' He watched the mirror as he brought the truck to a standstill. Wouldn't do to have the tailless monkey behind crash into him. When the whole convoy had pulled up, he threw his door open and jerked

Briony out with him. The men were climbing down from their trucks. The pursuing dustcloud stopped and settled with theirs.

'Fetch me a good straight stick,' Bruun ordered. Some men ran off to the trees while the rest looked at Briony, licking their lips, wondering what new humiliation Bruun had in store for her. One men told of how, he had heard, Arabs to the north punished an unfaithful woman by sticking a strong thin stick between her legs until it came out of her mouth. Some opined it would be a fine spectacle, others thought it a waste of a fine white woman at whom they had not had a turn. One thought Bruun was just going to beat her to boil the blood of the pursuers and they all looked to see if the pursuers would be able to see.

The stick came. It wasn't quite straight but it was tall and strong. Bruun had a hole dug in the hard ground and the stick packed in it with the earth from the hole. He pushed Briony from him and took hold of her tattered and dirty nightdress to rip it from her. The men sighed as she stood naked, her arms at her sides, looking at the ground. Several unbuttoned their flies.

'You are truly sons of your fathers,' Bruun said. 'But put those things away until later.' He pushed Briony into the cab of his truck and closed the door. He tied the nightdress to the pole. 'She is our protection against attack. We can all enjoy her when we have her safe at home where none dare attack us.'

Many of the men whistled their appreciation. Only the son of the *tokoloshe* would think of using a man's own wife against him like this. Perhaps it would be better not to have any more thoughts about what one would like to do to this fat white pig Lobengula had put in command over them.

When Bruun had changed up through the gears, he said, 'Mustn't let them damage the tight pussy any more, eh, or Lobengula might not be satisfied. Old Lobengula smells a bit but he likes his meat fresh and firm with tits that stand out just like your pair.' Bruun leant over to squeeze one of her breasts.

Ewart slowed down beside the pole. 'The clothes Mrs Roux was wearing when they left yesterday,' Sambo said. 'And the fat pig's red cloth.'

Ewart drove on without stopping.

'Are we continuing, sir?' Sambo asked. 'It seems to me it is a warning that they will kill Mrs Roux at our first step.'

Ewart shook his head. 'It's an empty bluff. Bruun knows that the minute she dies, he is defenceless. While she is alive, he has a bargaining counter. Anyway, we're committed. We don't know where the others are positioned and can therefore not call them off.'

'I shall enjoy killing him.'

Ewart nodded. 'He is the only man I can think of that I would enjoy killing. But I'm afraid Mr Roux has a claim superior to yours and his views on how Bruun is to die, should he survive the ambush, will take priority over any others. Though he will no doubt be willing to listen to advice.'

'I've told the men not to kill him in any engagement. Also to make sure he's not too badly wounded.'

Silence fell again. They understood each other. They had been here before.

Lance wriggled his elbows to make hollows in the loose bits of stone on the low rocky outcrop. He put his eye back to the scope to watch Bruun pulling Briony from the cab. 'I have him in my sights, Jacques.'

'He's right on the edge of your range,' Jacques said. 'We can't take chances.'

Lance swallowed. He knew he could hit anything he could see in his scope but in the two essentials of good marksmanship, judging distance and wind speed and direction, he had no skill whatsoever.

Jacques asked, 'What do you think, Jimmy?'

Jimmy shook his head. He squinted his eyes, opened them, shook his head again. 'Very much maybe, even with Mr Lance's rifle and scope.'

Jacques ordered, 'Lance, Jimmy, pick our spot.' He put his rifle down and looked through his binoculars.

Lance left it to Jimmy. He kept his scope on Bruun's doings. When Bruun ripped her only piece of clothing from Briony, he said, 'That man has no decency.'

'That's the least of what we're going to kill him for.' Jacques sounded detached, as if it were another's wife. Lance remembered what Ewart had said about an angry man being his own worst enemy.

Bruun's convoy started towards them again. Behind it the dust plume of Ewart's truck started moving, slowed briefly at the pole with the sagging pieces of cloth, and continued. Ewart wasn't going to call it off.

Jimmy said, 'That spot of darker green beside the road, about thirty degrees left, that's nine hundred feet.' He and Jacques turned the knurled knobs on their scopes. Lance just waited; his electronic scope would do it for him. The fourth man, who had not yet said a word, looked at the settings on his scope but did not change anything; he had apparently already selected the same spot.

'Excellent, Jimmy. Lance, you shoot Bruun's right wrist, on your left side, Jimmy, you hit his left wrist, on your right side. You, Mtembo, shoot the front tyre of the truck. Understood?'

'Sure.'

'Yes, Mr Roux.'

'Even so, Bwana.'

Jimmy, grinning broadly, said, 'Mr Weber's orders were to shoot to kill.'

Jacques smiled over his rifle at Jimmy and Jimmy's grin stretched nearer his ears.

Lance too had heard Ewart clearly. But if Jacques and Jimmy thought a quick death by bullets in the brain and heart too good for Bruun, who was he to argue. Had his

300

wife been violated, his servant tortured to death, his brother's dead body mutilated? Anyway, Ewart had put Jacques in command and the rest of them were following Jacques' orders. He caressed the zoom switch with his thumb as the trucks came nearer, Bruun's right wrist on the steering wheel of the truck always in the crosshairs right in the middle of an area the size of a soup plate.

'Try not to hit my wife,' Jacques said. 'Right, on a silent count of two and three, fire. One.'

And two . . . And three . . . A casing ejected from Jacques' rifle struck Lance painfully on the back of his left hand and deflected his aim just as he fired. He saw Bruun falling away and feared he'd killed him. Jacques wasn't going to understand it had been an accident. Then Bruun's hand flashed in the sunlight streaming through the cab window and Lance could clearly see the neat hole drilled through the palm below the splinted finger. So little time had elapsed that no blood had flowed from it yet. He resisted the temptation of a second shot; a bullet ricocheting about in the cab would kill Briony.

'Cease fire,' Jacques said. 'Only Lance hit him, through the palm. He moved just as we opened fire.'

The truck was still running forward on its flat front tyre but neither Bruun nor Briony could be seen. The other trucks were bumping each other in a frenzy, jockeying for position. Some were trying to turn around.

'Lance, block their retreat,' Jacques ordered crisply.

Lance shot out a tyre on the rearmost truck just as it turned. 'We're going to be short of tyres. Shoot the drivers,' Jacques said. 'Shoot all the drivers you can see, all of you.'

'For Christsake don't hit the tankers,' Lance said. 'They're needed and, anyway, we don't want them splashing exploding fuel on the skins.'

Ewart brought the truck Sambo had field-repaired to a smooth stop behind Bruun's convoy. There was steam escaping from the radiator but no matter, they would soon liberate new transport from Bruun. Ewart and his men deployed on either side of the track and almost immediately disappeared in the long grass. When they opened fire at the milling disarray of Bruun's convoy almost simultaneously with the four marksmen on the hillock starting to kill the drivers of the trucks careering around out of control, without any leadership, the men on the backs of the trucks were mown down in the confusion. Many were mortally wounded under overturned trucks, others were run over, still others were crushed between trucks slamming together, their screams rising above the sound of tortured metal.

Too late they started firing back. Lance, lying on the warm earth with the sun heating his back, dispassion exalted by distance, saw a man fall forwards towards him. None of Ewart's people were behind him; he had been shot in the back by one of his own. Bruun's men were firing blindly, panicked. They couldn't see their enemy, though they knew they were in a crossfire. One of their sergeants, establishing his authority, lashed out at several men and persuaded five to storm the hillock with him. Lance watched them come to within four hundred feet, then killed the sergeant and the two men closest to him. The remaining three found cover in the grass and their insistent fire forced Lance and the others to keep their heads down.

'Pay attention to what you do, Lance,' Jacques snapped.

'Sorry.' Lance raised his torso off the ground and killed one while the man was still raising his rifle to fire at the tempting target.

Jacques pushed him down violently, smashing Lance's head into the ground. 'Are you crazy!'

His words were drowned by two shots in quick succession. The other two had risen from the grass to Lance's invitation and Jimmy had shot them.

'It worked,' Lance said, picking pieces of flintstone from his forehead. 'The only blood on me is where you bashed me.'

Jacques gave him an exasperated look. Lance looked away at the scene in front of him. 'Bruun's stopped his truck.'

They watched as the door opened and Briony appeared, Bruun's arm around her neck, an open clasp-knife to her throat. Bruun shouted something they couldn't hear.

'Cease fire,' Jacques said. Very faintly in the distance they heard Sambo shouting something indistinguishable. Firing from Ewart's group ceased. Bruun's men were still firing away. Bruun screamed at them but was careful to keep his back to the truck and Briony in front of him..

'Clumsy bastard,' Lance said. Through his scope he could see a trickle of blood down Briony's throat where Bruun had pricked her with the point of the knife. 'Jacques, I have a clear shot at his head.'

'Don't shoot! His dead weight alone would cut my wife's throat.'

After screaming at his men for a full five minutes, Bruun finally brought order. The men realized nobody was shooting at them but those who had found cover were reluctant to come out, those who were still looking for cover reluctant to stay in the open. Unable to kick or beat them into compliance, Bruun's voice rose to hysteria as he shouted threats at them.

'Weber!' Bruun's voice carried in the strange new silence.

'Yes, Teddy, I'm here,' a disembodied voice from the grass replied.

One of Bruun's men, wounded, groaned loudly and the sound carried across the tall grass. Another man kicked him into silence. Bruun's men were standing in awkward postures, as if caught by an unsympathetic camera.

'Drop your weapons and come out with your hands in the air or I'll slice Roux's woman like I were butchering a pig.'

Ewart's laughter sounded eerie on the plain. 'Go ahead, Teddy, be my guest. It'll be just like cutting your own throat.'

Bruun cursed, a stream of obscenities which nobody interrupted. Lance marvelled at its repetitiveness. When Bruun stopped, Ewart called, 'If your own men don't do it first, of course.'

'Briony is smiling,' Lance said.

'She knows it's only a matter of time before we break Bruun's nerve,' Jacques said offhandedly.

'Why doesn't Ewart suggest to Bruun's men that we'll let them go if they kill Bruun?'

After a silence, Jimmy answered Lance. 'Same reason we don't shoot him, Mr Lance. He might kill her as he goes down.'

Mtembo, the silent one, snorted. 'The N'kosi never let men like that live.'

Lance drew a bead on Bruun's open mouth as he shouted orders at his men. His finger itched on the trigger. He lowered his rifle and looked at Jacques, who was studying the activity through his binoculars. The sun was getting very hot. Soon his shirt would stick to his back. Now that the activity and excitement was over, he could again feel the full pain right at the junction of his legs where the stitches had been put in. It was boring, lying here waiting, watching, waiting, watching. He was beginning to understand why soldiers went crazy and started shooting up their comrades. It had nothing to do with cowardice; just plain boredom. Yet it didn't seem to affect the three professionals with him. They seemed to be stolidly unimpressed by the uncomfortable tedium of it all. He wouldn't be surprised to find that, over in the grass, some of Ewart's men were napping

'Wake me up if anything happens,' Lance said to no one in particular. He put his rifle down flat beside him, as Jimmy had taught him, turned on his back and closed his eyes. He wondered drowsily what Jacques and Ewart were going to do about the standoff: They couldn't fire at Bruun or he might harm Briony, perhaps even kill her, but Bruun had to keep her alive and in good health or they would launch another and this time final attack on him.

In five or six minutes the sun would touch the horizon. The eight trucks neatly lined up beside the road threw long shadows. The late afternoon light fell revealingly on their scarred metalwork.

Rocco Burger walked down the track from his helicopter between the row of trucks on one side and the row of dead men, feet neatly to the road, on the other. A medical orderly had his thermometer in the rectum of a corpse. He pulled it out, took the reading, wiped it clean with a piece of cotton wool, returned it to its protective plastic sheath. He looked at his watch as he rose and waited for Burger to come up to him.

'The wounded were all shot in the head sometime around one o'clock, sir. The others died perhaps ten-thirty, eleven o'clock.'

The French major had been trailing Burger. He looked at two photographs in his hands, blown up from the aerial reconnaisance overflights. 'That's near enough.' He pointed to the little clockface in the lower right-hand corner of each photo. 'This is the neatest battlefield I've ever seen.'

'That's what makes Weber so frighteningly efficient as a soldier,' Burger replied, 'the fact that he can never be hurried, that he is always so well prepared that he has time in hand to tidy up behind him, leaving no loose ends.'

The French officer reflected that he should have observed this when Weber had served under him, not be told by Burger who was deducing it from Weber's trail. 'What happened here?'

'I can give you only a mixture of deduction and guesses. Weber and Roux followed Bruun here, at no great distance I should guess. Perhaps one came ahead to lay the ambush. They caught Bruun off guard.'

'The fool should not have stuck to the road. He should have gone across the grass.'

'I think it is highly possible his drivers were inexperienced.' Burger pointed at the row of damaged trucks. 'Weber and Roux probably caught Bruun in a crossfire. You'll have noticed that all the dead are Bruun's.'

The French officer nodded.

'Then Bruun threatened to kill the woman unless they withdrew. He reorganized his remaining force and drove on with such transport as he could move and find drivers for. Weber came behind him, killed the wounded Bruun had left behind in his hurry, tidied up in his usual manner, then set off after Bruun again to – '

' – to stay just out of sight until he could separate Bruun and the woman.'

Burger smiled briefly. 'Forgive me for correcting you but I think Weber will stay just *in* sight of Bruun until he can separate Bruun from the woman. It all ties in; it's Weber's style to let the other man's weaknesses work for him. Bruun's weaknesses must be greed and impatience. And, since I'm told Bruun is an intelligent man, those weaknesses must be quite strong to overcome his intelligence to the extent that he takes something which belongs to Weber or Roux.'

'Yes, I can see. What makes Weber such an outstanding leader of men is his excellent grasp of psychology.' They walked back to the helicopter. The French major sniffed distastefully. The dead were starting to smell. 'This time he didn't delay to cover the bodies.'

'He left the bodies uncovered as a warning to anyone who tries to take his trucks and their valuable cargo. We'll start again tomorrow at dawn, at Lobengula's camp.'

The French major shivered: he had never in his life had Burger's certainty that what he was doing was right – no, more, the only right. Burger was neither arrogant nor insensitive: he just didn't give a damn who saw him doing right. 'Lobengula might be difficult. He has friends in Kinshasa. If he hadn't, Mobutu would have dealt with him long ago.'

'My men are used to dealing with petty bandits,' Burger said casually, his eyes on his map.

Suddenly Burger's freshfaced young men reminded the Frenchman of himself as a boy, standing beside a tree-lined avenue, watching the Germans march triumphantly into Paris. The Germans had had the same youthful innocence and curiosity. They had been equally deadly. But, to his surprise, the major was no longer worried about being so deep into the unpredictable Mobutu's country. Burger's aura of competence was contagious; it was comforting to be near him. Then the major remembered the last man to inspire him with such confidence. It had been Ewart Weber.

Incredibly, after the tidying operation, Ewart had held up the pursuit long enough to make a short speech.

'I am pleased with all of you,' he had said conversationally to the men standing casually around him. 'Not one of you exposed himself to enemy fire. That is only what I would expect of men I trained myself. But I want you to know I noticed. We are few and the loss of even one man could tip the balance against us.'

That was the full extent of his speech but the men walked to the trucks looking thoughtful. Lance didn't need to be told Ewart didn't often make speeches and distributed such praise infrequently. He sighed with relief – Ewart had apparently not seen his stupidity. He swallowed as the memory returned.

'Hey, you can't just shoot the wounded!'

Jacques turned another man over with his boot. Half the side of his face was missing but he was still alive. Jimmy shot him through the head. 'Perhaps you'd like to nurse them back to health,' Jacques said. 'Then they can humiliate your wife, when you have one of course.'

Lance had looked away. This was barbaric but Jacques had a right to be bitter. These men had to be punished but

307

surely not to the same extent as the man who had inspired and led them in their evil, Bruun.

He swallowed to ease the dryness in his throat. He swung up into the cab of the half full tanker Bruun had left behind. Jimmy didn't look particularly evil, yet he had shot the wounded. Some other time he would search for the moral.

The door beside him swung open. 'Move over, I'll ride with you for a spell.' Ewart climbed up. The convoy moved off, the Landrover in the lead, the tanker behind it, followed by two trucks.

After they had driven for a while, Ewart said, 'I miss nothing, Lance. That wasn't very clever.'

'Somebody had to do something.'

'Yes. Wait until they exposed themselves, then kill them without exposing yourself. Don't do it again.'

'I've already decided it was stupid.'

Ewart seemed content to let it rest there. They drove for an hour in the dust of the Landrover without speaking. Lance swallowed several times and sipped water. The dry throat was a delayed reaction. It had been stupid to take such a risk. As always, Ewart was right.

'I don't quite see what we proved back there,' Lance said. 'The position is still the same.'

'That's a common layman's mistake, to think in terms of single decisive engagements.' Ewart was in a good mood.

'How is it a mistake? You have to have a decisive engagement to settle things.'

'Name one.'

'Dien Bien Phu, the one you know all about. Blood River. Rorke's Drift.'

'No, none of them. Before any decisive engagement there is a long history of other engagements and man-oeuvres. The Indochina example was the culmination of eight years of guerilla war. The other two you named were also preceded by much activity.'

'I still don't see what we achieved back there.'

'We recovered some of our property. We extended our transport capability with the choice of more trucks and the addition of a fuel-tanker. They're quite important details. We reduced Bruun's force by almost two-thirds but, most important of all, we gained a psychological advantage. Bruun is now on the run under a demonstrated threat. His hold on his men must be slipping. There is also the desirable side-effect that he is now forced to care for Briony well and ensure her survival because she is all that stands between him and us.'

'But he still has her.'

'Only until we can take her from him at a time of our own choosing when we judge any possible risk to her to be at a minimum. Bruun must sleep sometime. Do you think he can trust any of his men like we can trust all of ours?'

'No. He keeps getting them killed. But he may not sleep until he gets to his base, where he can find reinforcements.'

'They'll be of the same quality, or worse, and we'll cut through them like a reaper through corn.'

'Anybody with a gun is dangerous.'

'And don't forget it. I'm only talking about relative ability. Bruun with, say, forty men could hold a prepared position against us indefinitely. I'm talking of men like he has now. With men like ours and a like number, Bruun could fight us on equal terms. It would be a fatal mistake to judge his ability by his gross exterior. I'll tell you something else about decisive engagements and then I'm going to sleep.'

'What?'

'The victors are always the ones with greater moral certainty of the justness of their cause than the losers. That, our moral certainty, is our only advantage over Bruun.'

The tanker and the two trucks they had liberated from Bruun had fallen back to stay out of the Landrover's dust. The Landrover stayed in visual contact with Bruun's convoy, stopping when it did, always behind it.

At dusk Bruun stopped to eat and refuel and so did they.

'That's the second night Bruun's drivers have been on the road. They're going to do damage to our trucks if they have to drive another night.'

Jacques laughed. 'Even if Bruun ordered them at gunpoint to stop for the night, they would not. They're only eight hours from the safety of Lobengula's kraal.'

'They might ambush us in the dark.'

'That's a chance we'll have to take,' Ewart said. 'If it happens, Bruun will have to stay and command it himself. Jacques and Clickclack will then see what they can do to get Briony away from Bruun in the resulting confusion.'

'It won't happen,' Jacques said without much interest. 'They're running for Lobengula's. What possible purpose could be served by trying to ambush us?'

Lance fell asleep as soon as they moved off again. He had wanted to stay awake and talk to Jimmy but he was absolutely fatigued.

Briony shivered once, then stiffened her limbs to prevent it happening again. She wasn't going to give Bruun the satisfaction of gloating at her discomfort. And asking him for something to cover herself and keep her warm was unthinkable,

'You're not so stupid.' The eerie glow of the instrument lighting gave Bruun's cheeks the appearance of bulging over his jawline.

Briony didn't react. He had wanted to blow up the tanker he was forced to leave behind but Briony had said, 'Do you really want to force Weber to wipe you out right here?'

'I don't need any advice from women.'

'If one drop of burning diesel splashes the skins, Ewart will attack immediately.'

Bruun had decided to let the tanker be. While he had the woman, all Weber could do was follow at a discreet distance. Once at his home base, Bruun could find rein-

310

forcements and a defensible position. Weber simply didn't have enough men to storm even a mudhut.

Burger sat in an easy chair in the officers' mess, the French major and the commanding officer of the base on either side of him. The others gave him a clear berth, not because of his seniority, for this was an informal mess, but because he was held in awe. The younger officers kept looking at him and looking away in embarassment when he caught their eye.

'I'm sorry my appearance does not match the rumours your subalterns have heard about me,' Burger chuckled.

The commanding officer laughed aloud. 'Nietszche has always bored me.'

'When I was a very young policeman in a small town, he impressed me. Later, when I had read some history and had seen more the wider world, I was appalled at my naivety.'

Burger was totally unselfconscious about being largely self-educated.

'It is to your credit that you could change your mind,' the commandant said, refraining from adding, *considering the environment you work in.*

Burger knew what he meant. South Africa's allies were often critical of her policies but Burger had come to expect it. 'I prefer the Calvinist faith of my forefathers. One righteous man . . .' It was not that simple but Burger didn't want to embarrass the commandant with a deep philosophical discussion.

'France's greatest gift to South Africa, beside the Mirages: the Huguenot craftsmen.'

'And the vines.' Burger held his glass to the light. 'Your mess really has an excellent cellar.' He sipped. 'I grow maize on a farm in the Orange Free State. When I retire, I should like to grow grapes in the Western Cape.'

'And I shall breed horses in the Camargue,' the commandant said, surprised at his easy fellowship with this man. He had expected a shallow, objectionable bigot, but Burger was quiet and thoughtful. The commandant's liking for the man didn't prevent him feeling vaguely uncomfortable because of his presence, however relaxed he might be sitting next to him drinking wine.

Burger knew what was bothering him. 'By tomorrow night my business here will be finished and I shall take my men away.'

'Our orders are to co-operate. There is no time limit.'

'That's very kind of you. But after tomorrow the danger of adverse publicity becomes too high.'

The commandant could not help sighing. 'We must arrange leave at the same time. You are invited to visit me in France.'

When Lance woke, Jimmy was snoring beside him and Ewart was at the wheel. 'What time is it?'

'Two hours to dawn. We'll be at Lobengula's by dawn. How do you feel?'

'All right. It's almost impossible to believe, now, that I could've bled to death.'

'You were muttering in your sleep.'

'I had a nightmare about that stupidity back there, making myself a target.'

Ewart nodded but remained silent. Lance was glad his brother didn't make a point of it. One thing about Ewart, you always knew where you were with him; if he had spoken to you once about something, that was it and the slate was wiped clean.

'Briony once told me that this crocodile hunt was the biggest game in town.'

Ewart was amused. 'You can't stake anything higher than your life.'

'After what's happened, I'm not so sure Briony will agree.'

Lights flashed at them from the darkness and Ewart brought the tanker to a halt. 'Jacques wants his breakfast.'

'If we stop now, Bruun will get to Lobengula's before we do.'

'That's what we want him to do. He must be separated from Briony before we can take him. Anyway, I never let my men fight on an empty stomach. Or with full bladders.'

Breakfast consisted of hot black coffee and rusks to be dunked in the coffee. 'Do you have a plan?' Lance asked Ewart.

'I'll make it when I see the lie of the land.' Ewart put his mug on the running board of the tanker. 'Line up for arms inspection.'

Lance fumbled frantically with the clip on his rifle. He had not reloaded after the engagement yesterday. 'I fixed it,' Jimmy said softly behind his right shoulder. Lance sighed. Jimmy was worth his weight in gold; it would have been embarrassing to have Ewart catch him unprepared.

This time Ewart made no speeches. When he had inspected the arms and the vehicles, they went silently to their transport and drove off towards the red glow in the eastern sky. Lance and Jimmy were back in the Landrover with Ewart and Jacques. Clickclack had been replaced by Mtembo the marksman.

This time nobody slept.

The French major was nervously checking his sidearm in the dim green light inside the big Alouette. Burger and his men watched him with interest. There was nothing else to watch.

Burger never carried arms himself – they spoiled the hang of his clothes and his men were armed to the teeth. His function was to deploy his men, not to fire weapons. Occasionally, about once a year, someone would attempt to fire at him; always in the past one of his men had killed the attacker first. After more than twenty years as a high-risk policeman, Burger had only two bullet wounds in his body; it had become part of the legend about him.

Burger looked at his men. They were good men,

handpicked, an élite trained by himself. Despite the risks, men competed to serve in his unit; after a two-year shift they could choose between the better positions in the armed forces and police, often as instructors ten years before they would otherwise become eligible for promotion to such responsible work. There were also a handful of university graduates doing their time in the rough end of field work before settling down behind a desk.

Burger suppressed a smile. Viljoen, his eyes on the French officer's fumbling hands, was moving his lips. He was praying. A good boy from a Free State farm, none too bright but very religious and an excellent marksman with truly exceptional reflexes. Viljoen wasn't praying for his life in any coming engagement but because he thought helicopters were the devil's handiwork. His fear of flying was a running joke which Viljoen took in good humour.

The navigator stood in the cockpit door. When he was sure he had Burger's attention, he opened his right hand three times, fingers and thumbs stiff. Fifteen minutes. Burger nodded to show he understood. Talking was out of the question in the racket the engines and rotors made and the helicopter's intercom system didn't reach this far back. Burger always rode with his men, rather than on the flight deck.

He looked out of the small window above Viljoen's head. The edge of the sky was red and he could distinguish a horizon now. Arriving a few minutes after dawn would be good timing; he must remember to congratulate the navigator. Just before dawn and at dawn was a particularly dangerous time for fighting men struggling to accustom their eyes to the changing light. In the conditions pertaining to those few minutes, ever-moving shadows assumed gigantic threatening proportions. The human metabolism is at its lowest ebb just then and men fire nervously. Burger had once, as an observer in an Israeli war, seen a battlescarred sergeant wipe out half his own platoon because some green officer had chosen the exact moment of dawn to advance. To lose men in an engagement was an unpalatable necessity Burger did everything in his power to avoid; to have his men shoot each other because he chose his moment badly, a humiliation too devastating to contemplate.

'Well, old goosepimple, soon you'll see the dawn break over your new home,' Bruun said jovially as he brought the truck to a halt in the inner circle of huts. 'I'll get Lobengula's wives to clean you up a little for presentation to your new lord and master, Lobengula's majestic person in all his flabby glory.'

Briony shivered. 'That shows how much you know about Africa, Bruun. The wives will kill me rather than let their man at me. And you know why you can't give me to the men to clean up, don't you?' It was all true but she didn't want to be too far from Bruun. Her chance might come to revenge herself. But not if she were elsewhere.

'I'll do it myself then,' Bruun said with relish. 'Remember, you asked for it.' He craned his head out of the window. There had been no sign of Weber's vehicles for a couple of hours but that didn't mean Weber wasn't there: he might simply have had the lights on the vehicles doused.

Disembodied whites of eyes were crawling out of huts to stare at the trucks and tanker that had arrived. Bruun took his shirt off and threw it across her lap. 'Cover your shame, woman.'

Briony sniffed at the shirt. 'It stinks.'

Bruun struck her lightly across the face. 'Be grateful I don't want to mark you. Put it on.' He didn't want to have to fight off the inhabitants of Lobengula's main kraal when a naked white woman arrived in their midst.

Briony put the shirt on.

Bruun pulled her out of the truck by her wrist. 'Come on. Before your bath I have to arrange a little reception party for that supercilious snot Weber. He had his chance

315

and he boobed. Now I'm going to make sure he doesn't get another go.'

They were within sight of the glowing embers of last night's fires in Lobengula's kraal. Their own fire, over which the dynamite was being sweated, was screened by the truck and the Landrover.

'Ten minutes to dawn, Lance,' Ewart said from where he sat on the running-board of the tanker, tying double knots in the laces of his boots.

'We're nearly finished. Just the last bottle.'

Ewart rose. 'We attack at dawn.'

'Why?' Jacques sounded amazed.

'Because that's our moment of advantage that'll never come again. The more of Bruun's men kill each other in the confusion, the fewer are left to resist us.'

'Finished,' Lance said as he screwed the cap on the last fruit canning jar and wiped the excess nitro from the outside of the glass. Ewart distributed the six jars of jelly to himself, Jacques, Sambo, two of Sambo's brothers and Mtembo.

'What about me?' Jimmy said.

'I want you and Lance to have your hands free on your rifles.'

'But –'

'That's all!' Ewart addressed them all: 'Kill anything that moves except Mrs Roux. I don't need to tell you to watch out you don't shoot at one of us.' He paused a moment but there was no comment. 'We'll go in, spread out, all of us except my brother and Jimmy. When we have Mrs Roux, we'll retreat with her. Lance, you and Jimmy hang back behind us, keep your eyes and ears open and shoot at any flanking movement.'

The men moved silently into the forest which, almost unnoticed, had replaced the savanna during the long night.

'I don't call that much of a plan,' Lance said softly to

Jimmy. 'We'll get Mrs Roux killed just like the man Burger is supposed to be likely to do.'

'We don't have enough men for fancy plans, Mr. Lance. Better not talk. There might be guards.'

'Shut up!' Sambo's voice came out of the halflight in front and to the left of them.

They were approaching Lobengula's kraal. To their left a cock crowed, in front of them there was the excited sound of villagers waking up to an unusual event. Lance thought the kraal was taking a long time to wake up. Bruun must have been at least thirty minutes ahead of them. Perhaps he had used the time to subdue the more exuberant spirits and arrange a defence. Lance shivered and sweat broke out on the back of his neck.

They crossed the cleared fields and reached the first huts. Lance could see the backs of the men in front against the red glow coming through the trees. The hubbub was straight ahead. He instinctively halted as he reached the first hut. It would not do to have people crawling out of the huts and shooting Ewart's party, or Jimmy and him, in the back. Jimmy had done the same. Lance saw one of the shadowy figures look back. That would be Ewart, checking. He saw Jimmy go down on one knee against the curve of a hut and followed suit. A smell of old food and unwashed bodies emanated from the hut.

'Now,' Ewart called and fired a brief burst into the air as he fell to the ground, one hand holding the fruit jar of nitro clear. Lance saw the shadows fall to the ground. He watched the area beyond them and to his left for return fire. There was none, but the noise of many voices ahead of them stopped briefly before resuming at a higher pitch.

The shadows, now better defined as the light grew, rose and ran forward. Lance waited for a moment in case there was a delayed reaction from the huts, then loped after them.

'Not so fast, Mr Lance,' Jimmy shouted at him. Lance fell back to keep pace with Jimmy.

317

Lance saw a movement to his left and fired from the hip. It had been his own shadow. He ran on. They could now see the open circle in the middle of the kraal. On the far side was a long mud building with small windows. Lance was sure this would be Bruun's barracks. There was a silhouette on the roof but, while he was still aiming, a shot came from Jimmy's side and the man tumbled down with a shout.

It was day now, though not fully light as the sun was still low behind the trees. The crowd in the open circle looked at the armed men in consternation, then turned and ran away, towards the low mud building. Lance saw Sambo, smiling hugely, firing into the air to speed them.

'Use them for cover,' Ewart shouted and his party fell in behind the running mob.

Lance sank to his knee and searched the roof through his scope. Where there had been one rifleman there could be more. He saw a glint of light on metal and fired at it. A headless man rose and tumbled backwards. The bullet, flattened on the rifle, had taken his head away, Lance thought quite calmly. Later I shall have nightmares. But I shan't be sick any more. Now there is work to do. I'm becoming just like Ewart. He fired at another glint of light on the roof and missed. He searched the ground on his side for a flanking movement around the crowd to get at Ewart's party. There wasn't any.

The blacks in the crowd were falling. At first Lance was nonplussed: Ewart and his men were running in an easy crouch behind the crowd, not firing. He realized Bruun's men were firing into the crowd. There was a stutter of what he thought was a heavy machine gun. A bullet smashed into a pot behind him, shattering the pot. He rolled and faced backwards but there was nothing and another bullet struck the ground near his shoulder. He rolled behind a hut. The machine gun wasn't firing at him. Nor was the danger behind him. It was one of the men on the roof of the barracks.

318

He peered around the hut as several shots sounded from Jimmy's side. He heard Jimmy laughing. 'You can come out now, Mr Lance. I got him.'

'Thanks.' The man Jimmy had shot was tumbling forward down the roof. More shots from the roof. Out of the corner of his eye he saw Jimmy's rifle drop and Jimmy raising his hand to his head. Lance shot the sniper on the roof twice, once in the wrist of his trigger hand, once in his head as he jerked up at the sting. 'Are you okay, Jimmy?' The machine gun was scything through the blacks now.

Nothing from Jimmy. Lance felt a tear running down his cheek. He rose to storm the men who had killed Jimmy.

'Mud in my eye,' he heard Jimmy croak.

Lance sank to his knee again. He had been one step from the deadly open area between the huts.

'Huh! Why the fuck don't you speak up? D'you want to get me killed?'

'He hit the hut and sprayed mud into my eyes,' Jimmy called. 'It burns but I'm okay now.'

The crowd was turning, trying to overrun Ewart's party. Lance watched in fascination as Ewart and his men stood fast and let the sweating, panicked mass of flailing limbs flow around them. They had all turned to protect the jelly from the crowd. They disappeared in the sea of black.

'Watch your left!'

Lance swivelled his eyes to Jimmy's command. The flanking movement Ewart had predicted had finally come. Bruun was probably not as stupid as he appeared, and he was certainly ruthless beyond anyone's imagination. Having driven the maddened crowd back on Ewart's party with a machine gun, he had now sent men to flank Ewart on both sides to cut him down in the open when the crowd had passed. In the clearing, once the crowd had passed, Ewart would be without cover and under fire from three sides.

Lance watched the six men run out from behind the

barracks and join the fringes of the crowd. Picking the first two off without hitting any innocent in the crowd was easy. The other four took cover behind the crowd. Lance got one more. He heard Jimmy's FN on automatic.

'Not the crowd, Jimmy! Jesus Christ!' He was too late. Jimmy had cut down all the men on his side and several of the crowd as well. The crowd had turned and was now surging towards Lance.

He searched for the three armed and uniformed men on his side and caught sight of a tattered cap. He shot its owner in the forehead. The remaining two turned back to the barracks and Lance thought: Idiots! The crowd is their only protection. He got one in the back. The sound of running feet shook the ground. The crowd was nearly on him! He rose, reversing his rifle to strike out at them with the butt to force them to run around rather than over him. In that moment one of the men on the roof shot him. Lance felt the blow in his thigh, the stunning shock of it, and went over backwards as his knees collapsed. He turned desperately on his stomach and held his hands over his face as the feet pounded over him.

The sergeant nearest the door slid it open on its runners. Viljoen closed his eyes. The others looked out at the rich green of the forest speeding ten feet under them, the sun glinting on the night's moisture. There was a slight haze as the drops evaporated from the leaves. Later in the day the nature of the haze would change. It was one of those rare moments of beauty few ever experience.

The magic moment was over. They would be at Lobengula's kraal in about five or six minutes.

His proximity to the hut saved Lance but he was bruised and sore when the crowd passed. He picked his rifle from the dust and rolled tight against the hut. He took the clip

320

out to look through the barrel. He didn't want to blow himself up. He fitted a fresh clip. Through the ringing in his ears he heard Jimmy call. Jimmy sounded desperate.

'Okay,' Lance shouted, his voice very loud in his own ears.

'Then be of some bloody help,' Jacques' voice came from far away.

Lance could see what had happened. Bruun had overdone the persuasion of the crowd. When the remnants of the crowd had passed, Ewart and his party had mounds of dead bodies to hide behind. Now Bruun's machine gun was searching the piles of dead bodies, jerking them momentarily to life, in the hope of finding the attackers. There was no way forwards or backwards for Ewart's party. But Bruun could slip away through the back door of the barracks. Lance looked over his own shoulder but there was nothing behind him. The crowd had disappeared into the forest as if it had never existed. Lance studied the situation. He tried firing through the window from which the machine gun stuttered but the angle was wrong.

'That's a waste of time,' Jimmy called. 'Your angle is wrong.'

'I know.'

'And they got a steel plate to protect them.'

Lance hadn't known that. There was nothing else he could think of. He searched the piles of dead bodies and found Ewart – easily distinguishable from Jacques because the back of his shirt was free of sweat whereas Jacques', was blackly wet. The machine gun stuttered to a standstill. Ewart rose easily and, as he straightened his knees, flung the jar of jelly at the corner of the building. Lance wondered why Ewart hadn't thrown it at the door. Ewart fell flat, his hands over his head. Jimmy picked off a man on the roof trying to shoot at Ewart. Lance was far enough away from the blast for it to be no more than a swift breeze when it struck his face.

'Ewart,' Lance called, 'I've an idea.' He had understood what his brother was about to do.

Jimmy stopped him from making a mistake. 'Don't call louder, Mr Lance. Wait a bit. He's been deafened by the blast.'

The machine gun again probed the bodies with its bullets. Lance searched the roof and the ground on his side but could find nothing to fire at. Jimmy fired once but Lance didn't know at what.

'Ewart,' he tried again.

'I hear you. Keep your voice down or you'll give them a direction to shoot at.'

'I have a plan,' Lance had lowered his voice to the same level as Ewart's. 'Once you have the two ends off the building and get them in a crossfire from the sides, they're going to escape out the back where you can't see.' From the gaping hole the nitro had blown in the corner of the barracks, it was obvious Ewart would have to attack diagonally from the front and the back of the barracks would be blind. 'Jimmy and I can't do anything here but we can cut off the back exit.'

Ewart thought about this for a while. 'All right. But don't expose yourselves and don't try anything stupid. Jimmy, I'll hold you responsible.'

'Yes, sir.'

Lance and Jimmy retreated until they were behind the huts, out of the line of fire of the barracks, then ran around the outside of the circle and through the trees until they were behind the barracks.

'We could sneak right up there and be standing on either side of the door as they come through,' Lance opined before they split up.

'Your brother just threatened to kill me if anything happened to you.'

'He did?'

'You heard him. What's that on your leg?'

Lance looked at his trousers. One leg was soaked in

blood. He felt nauseous. In another part of his mind he knew it was ludicrous to be sickened by a little of his own blood when he had been killing others almost with equanimity. 'I ran all that way with a broken leg.'

Jimmy raised his trouser leg. 'A flesh wound. Just a large scratch. You stay here and I'll go over there.'

They took up positions in the trees, three hundred feet away, about fifty feet separating Lance and Jimmy on either side of the door. Besides the door, the wall was blank.

Once in position, Lance thought of killing the two men still on the roof of the barracks but decided it might give their position away. He would bide his time. Jimmy apparently thought the same for he didn't shoot at the exposed men either.

Ewart waited patiently for the machine gun to run out of ammunition again. Meanwhile he signalled to Mtembo on his left. Mtembo inched further left. When the machine gun stopped again, he rose to hurl his fruit jar of nitroglycerine at the building. The jelly was already flying through the air when the rifleman on the roof of the building shot at Mtembo, hitting him dead centre in the chest. One of Sambo's brothers got the rifleman with a brief burst.

It was sufficient breathing space for Ewart's men to split off left and right to cover the gaping holes blown into the corners of the building. There were casualties lying in the rubble and a few of Bruun's men behind the rubble.

Ewart waited until both parties were in position, then opened fire on automatic through the hole. His men followed suit and he heard Jacques, on the other side, take the cue. Sergeant Sambo rose to his majestic height and threw his fruit jar of nitro through the hole, then fell flat before anybody could shoot at him. There was a tremendous explosion and great chunks of masonry hit them. Almost immediately there was a similar explosion from the other side.

Ewart pumped his ears with the flat of his hands to restore his hearing, or at least remove the ringing from his ears. When he peered cautiously over the pile of bodies he was lying behind, he found all the side wall and a good deal of the front wall of the barracks in ruins. The machine gun was still firing into the piles of bodies in front of the barracks but its traverse was not great enough to reach him and his men, or Jacques' party, at a similar angle to the other side of the barracks. Not many could be left alive inside the barracks but Ewart had too few men to storm them; they'd be picked off as they silhouetted themselves where they crossed the rubble. He didn't want to throw any more explosive into the building for fear of killing Briony.

It was a stalemate. Everything would depend on how quickly Bruun's nerve broke.

The wound on his thigh was more than a scratch, Lance thought, but at least the bleeding had stopped. There was a sort of loose flap of skin which the coagulating blood had stuck to his wound, blocking the flow of further blood. It couldn't be too serious if he had not opened it again by running.

He heard the explosions and grabbed at his rifle to pick off the men on the roof under cover of the noise but he was too late. One of the riflemen had been shot from the front and Jimmy got the other one in the middle of the back.

It was pretty frustrating, waiting here with nothing to do. It had been a stupid idea coming around here where he couldn't even see what was going on. No wonder Ewart had grabbed it; it would keep the little brother out of harm's way. He should have suggested instead that he and Jimmy take up position on each side of the barracks and a good distance away. Then, when the walls at the sides had been taken out, they could fire in, picking off the people inside at their leisure. He rose to tell Jimmy of his idea. The rear door of the barracks was opened quickly and a man thrust out. He turned to the door as it slammed behind him and hammered on it with the butt of his rifle.

Lance fell flat again. He was taking aim when Jimmy said, right behind him, 'Don't shoot. We'll wait for all of them first.'

Lance was so startled he almost pulled the trigger. 'How'd you get here?'

'I walked, Mr Lance.'

The door opened again and four men filed through, all of them Bruun's askaris. Behind them came Bruun, one hand twisting Briony's arm up behind her back, the other holding a short, broad-bladed knife to her throat. Bruun stood just outside the door, looking nervously left and right. Behind him, in the barracks, the machine gun still clattered.

'At least he's covered her,' Jimmy said.

'And covered himself with her. I'll take the three on the left. You take the two on the right.'

'Mr Lance, your brother said – ' Jimmy started warningly.

' – said for us to cut off the escape,' Lance said firmly. 'Do as I say.' He aimed and fired immediately. He killed two of his targets but the third brushed past Bruun and slammed the door before he could get him in his sights. Jimmy got his two.

Briony chose that moment to stamp on Bruun's instep and start struggling. By the time Bruun had her under control again the door behind him was bolted. With his back still to the door, he shouted orders that were ignored. The knife was still at Briony's throat and a thin trickle of blood ran down her neck where it had cut her in the struggle.

Lance thought for a moment, then gave voice to the obvious. 'We're in trouble.'

325

Jimmy nodded soberly. They couldn't go forward over the open ground to Bruun because of the risk of being picked off by Bruun's men if they decided to open the door, and Bruun would of course not come to them. Lance had played his hand too soon.

Bruun edged along the wall of the barracks, his back to it, Briony protecting his front. Lance and Jimmy followed on a parallel course, just inside the forest. Near the corner Bruun stopped. Lance and Jimmy stopped too. This was more satisfactory, Lance felt. They now had Bruun bottled up between him and Jimmy on the one side and Ewart and his men on the other.

'All we have to do now is drive him around the corner and into Ewart's loving care,' Lance said. 'We'll just fire near him.'

Jimmy put his hand on Lance's rifle. 'A cornered rat goes mad and sinks his teeth into whatever is nearest. Look through your scope how red he is, how unevenly he breathes. He'll kill Mrs Roux if we fire near him.'

Lance looked. Bruun's eyes did gleam strangely and run around crazily in their sockets.

The decision was taken from Lance's grasp. There was a violent explosion from the front of the barracks as Ewart, knowing from the shooting at the back that Briony had gone, had the last two jars of nitroglycerine thrown against what was left of the front wall, demolishing most of it and the machine gun crew behind it. Only enough of the wall remained standing to keep the roof up. Ewart and Jacques immediately led their men into the rubble from both sides, killing the survivors as they went. When they had passed into the wreck of the building, Bruun looked cautiously round the corner, then went round it, still dragging Briony with him as protection.

Lance had Bruun's unprotected back in his sights for a moment; what if the bullet went right through Bruun and killed Briony? He and Jimmy ran as fast as they could across the open area and into the mess of mutilated bodies on the ground. Lance felt a hot flow down his leg and knew the wound had opened but there was no pain and he ran on. Bruun was making for the trucks. Lance dared not look to his left to find out what Ewart and Jacques were doing inside the barracks because he feared falling headlong into the bloody bodies smelling of their spilled gastric juices.

Once Bruun threw out a hand with a bloodsoaked handkerchief around it – the hand through which Lance had shot him the previous day – to save himself, and Briony's weight hanging on his arm in an effort to obstruct him, from falling and perhaps parting company. Jimmy got off a snap shot but apparently missed. Bruun had regained his balance before Lance could aim.

Bruun had nearly reached the trucks before Briony succeeded in tripping him. They both fell heavily but Bruun kept his hold on her and they came up with Bruun still holding her arm behind her back and the knife to her throat. Bruun now had his back to the tanker.

Lance and Jimmy stopped twenty feet away. 'You want this bitch killed, Junior?' Bruun gasped. Lance wished Ewart or Jacques were here. He ignored Bruun. 'Shoot out a front tyre on each of the vehicles,' he said softly to Jimmy.

The moment Jimmy raised his rifle, Bruun pushed the point of the knife through the flesh under Briony's chin.

Jimmy ignored her scream and shot out a front tyre on each of the trucks and the tanker in quick succession.

'Now we can talk, eh?' Lance said when the echoes of the explosions had died away. 'You let her go and I'll give you the keys to our Landrover and tell you where it is.' He didn't have the keys but it didn't matter. All he had to do was keep Bruun talking until Ewart or Jacques arrived. From the direction of the barracks there was only the sound of the occasional single shot; it wouldn't be long now.

'You little freak!' Bruun sank behind Briony's shorter

327

body until only the top of his head was visible and his arms and legs bowed out beside her. 'Just for you, I'm gonna slice her real slow.' He twisted the point of the knife under Briony's chin and she screamed again. He pulled the knife out and jabbed the point into her throat lower down, just beside her bobbing adam's apple. 'Slow, real slow,' She screamed again as he increased the pressure on the knife. Her struggles were no avail against his strength.

'His elbows and knees, Jimmy,' Lance shouted, aiming and firing as he did so. Through his scope he saw Bruun's elbow disintegrate, out of his other eye he saw the knife curve through the air and behind it, under the tanker just ballooning into flame, Ewart's face as he came rolling under the tanker. Lance fired the second shot, to shatter Bruun's knee, before he realized what he had done.

Lance heard Ewart screaming in the burning fuel under the tanker. *I did that, I'm burning my own brother.* He tried to rush forward into the flames to pull Ewart out but Jimmy had him firmly by the collar. Out of the corner of his eye he saw Briony struggle out from under Bruun, who had fallen on top of her, and drag the burning Bruun away to roll him until the flames were doused with his own weight. Bruun's arms and legs flapped comically.

Jacques came running up, took one look at the situation, and slapped Lance, still pawing the ground against Jimmy's restraining weight, heavily through the face. 'Do you want to do it or shall I? Quick man, he's suffering.'

Lance was in shock. He looked at Ewart's frame dancing in the flames, bone already gleaming white and orange where flesh should be. He had done this! He started forward again and Jimmy grabbed his collar again. He struck out at Jimmy but Jimmy held fast. Sambo came running up and opened fire on automatic at Ewart without waiting. There were tears streaming down his face. He held his finger on the trigger long after the dervish of the flames had sunk to an unidentifiable heap.

328

'He could not wait,' Sambo said to Jacques.

'You did what was right.'

Briony was taking each of Bruun's arms and legs in turn and twisting them, squelching the marrow in the shattered bones of the elbows and knees between the fragmented shards of their pipes. She laughed gleefully as Bruun screamed in agony each time the nerves in the marrow grated.

Jacques put his arm around her and pulled her away.

'Give me a knife.'

'No. A quick death is too good for him.'

'Oh no, I've decided to let him live.'

'Give her a knife,' Jacques said.

Jimmy led Lance away from the edge of the flames. Lance was docile now and Jimmy let his collar go to offer his Swiss pocket knife. Jacques opened the blade for her and handed her the knife. The others gathered around curiously.

Briony cut away Bruun's trousers with great care and then his underpants. 'He shat himself,' she stated the obvious.

She lifted the shrivelled penis with the fingers of one hand, then took his testicles and squeezed. Bruun screamed.

'That's the last you'll ever feel there.' She pulled his flaccid member up, sliced with the knife, and rose with penis and testicles, still in their sac, in her hand. She walked away through the bodies.

When Bruun stopped screaming, he started begging. 'Please kill me. For God's sake, kill me now.'

'May you enjoy crawling and begging all the days of your life and may the days of your life be many,' Jacques said.

'Amen,' Sambo said. 'He'll bleed to death through the hole where his balls were.'

'Then get a dressing to press on it,' Jacques snapped.

He waited for Clickclack to tear a tattered shirt from a black corpse and press and bind it into Bruun's crotch. Bruun screamed again and begged some more. Everybody ignored him.

Lance had turned around and was looking at Ewart's funeral pyre. Jacques took his arm. 'It's not good enough just to kick a dog. We must teach his master the same lesson. Come.' Lance went docilely with him. Jimmy took his rifle from his unresisting fingers and reloaded and cocked it. Lance clicked the safety on and then off again. 'He's okay,' Jacques said to the anxious Jimmy.

They walked away to the circle of bigger huts set off to one side which was obviously the 'palace' of Bruun's master, His Royal Highness Lobengula IV.

'Is Mrs Roux beautiful?' the French major asked as they stepped from the helicopter behind a screen of Burger's alert young men.

'Yes. Why?'

The French major waved his hand vaguely at the carnage. 'The story of Helen of Troy . . . I thought you said Weber had only a few men.'

'Highly trained men.'

'And he's still Weber.'

'Yes.'

The French major fingered his sidearm nervously as he looked in the direction of the short vulgar burst of automatic fire coming from a separate circle of larger huts. But Burger did not seem concerned, his eyes on the dead bodies around their feet. Burger was picking his way daintily to avoid getting gore on his trousers.

The French major was sick when he came to what was left of Bruun. He didn't even have enough control to bend over before the vomit ran down the front of his uniform.

'Please! You're white men. Please kill me now!' Bruun moaned.

'You're Bruun. Who did this to you?'

'That Roux bitch. Kill her. Then kill me. Please!'

'Shall I attend to him, sir?'

Burger waved the medical orderly on. 'Sure. Do anything to ensure he lives as long as possible. But no mercy killing, understand? This man deserves everything he's got coming to him.'

'Yes sir,' the orderly said.

'There could hardly be much coming to him that hasn't happened already,' Burger's aide said.

'Wait and you'll learn how Africa treats deposed despots.'

A sergeant came to report that the area around them was secure and they could advance towards the sound of the firing. Burger waited courteously for the French officer to finish wiping the front of his uniform with his handkerchief. 'My God. Even in Indochina or Algeria I never saw anything like this,' he said in apology.

'Warn the men not to open fire indiscriminately,' Burger told the sergeant as they moved off in line abreast towards the sound of automatic firing. Even behind the line of solid men the French major would have preferred to run in a crouch but Burger walked at no more than a brisk pace, and upright.

'We're a bit exposed,' the French major ventured to suggest.

Burger shrugged. 'Weber has disposed of Bruun's force. To Weber's men we're not a threat. There's nobody to fire on us.'

'Those regular shots remind me of executions at dawn.'

'As you said yourself, Weber's compulsively neat.'

The Frenchman decided to keep his mouth shut. He'd already made enough of a fool of himself.

The erstwhile palace guards were easily identifiable by the long ostrich feathers they wore in their headdresses. There had been eight of them and they were all dead, lying in a little group. The Frenchman thought that whoever had trained them had been criminally negligent:

331

he had not even told them to spread out. Not that even excellent training would have saved their lives against Weber's men, but at least they would have taken one or two of Weber's men with them before they succumbed.

The largest hut was Lobengula's Council. Except for an ornately carved throne, the floor was bare. Briony would fire a short burst from the FN at the feet of whichever of his fat wives Lobengula was trying to hide behind until the wife fearfully broke free from him, then he would run screaming and blubbering to grab another to hide behind while Briony fired more short bursts at his heels. Then the whole process would be repeated.

Sambo and his men were laughing aloud. Jacques was smiling broadly and Lance had a detached look on his face. He's a bit young for so much killing, Burger thought. It's probably come as a bit of a shock to him that so many men can die so quickly.

Jacques saw Burger and turned towards him, his rifle swinging with the movement of his body. 'Just let my wife have her fun and then – '

Viljoen must have thought the rifle a threat to his commander.

'No, Viljoen, no!' Burger called urgently.

Viljoen was already firing. While Jacques was still crumpling to the floor, Lance shot Viljoen in the chest and in the face without raising his rifle from his side. How easily I kill, he thought. Later I shall regret. I shall have a whole eternity to regret – the barrels of Burger's men were swinging towards him, I'm coming Ewart, to join you in the flames.

'Ooph!' said Burger as Jimmy's rifle barrel forced the air from him. For a moment the air felt cold.

'You stupid kaffir,' Briony screamed as Sambo jerked the FN from her hand, 'you've broken my finger nail!'

Lance's mind cleared. 'Tell your men to lower their rifles,' he said to Burger. 'Jimmy, take your rifle out of his stomach and stop frightening his breakfast.' Lance swung his own rifle slightly so that there could be no doubt he was aiming at Burger.

'Lower your arms,' Burger said calmly.

'My bearer, the prince and quick thinker,' Lance said. He tried to smile at Jimmy but his face was stiff. The hollow echo of something Ewart had once said would be his peroration for his brother until he could think of something else. He turned to Burger. 'You're the man who's come to save us.'

Briony had been kneeling beside Jacques' body. She flew up and at Lance, scratching his face and kicking out at him. It took two of Burger's men to restrain her. The orderly gave her an injection which quickly stilled her struggling and screaming. Her husband's death had finally unhinged her.

'I'm Rocco Burger, yes.' Order was finally restored.

'I'm Lance Weber. My brother is dead. I'm sorry about your man but he shouldn't go around shooting my friends.'

Burger shivered despite himself. Out of the corner of his eye he saw the French major, who had known the elder Weber personally rather than from files and newspapers, take an involuntary step back. This young man might be in shock but he also emanated purpose as chilling as the air in a morgue.

'We'll call that an accident. I've come to fetch you and Mrs Roux back to South Africa.'

'To stand trial for the Kariba allegations?'

'Because your presence here is a political embarrassment. The file about the Kariba incident will be lost.'

Lance looked at him for a long time. 'How do I know you will keep your promises?'

'I believe you understood that Jacques Roux was not threatening me but offering me a friendly greeting.'

Lance nodded.

'And a trial will get in the papers and we'll have the political embarrassment all the same.'

'I shall return with you after I have sold some crocodile skins that now belong to Mrs Roux and me.'

'No. We will leave immediately.'

Lance shook his head stubbornly. 'I cannot pay my brother's – my men before those skins are sold.' He looked meaningfully around the hut.

Burger followed his glance. In the confined space, none would escape the bullets of the many automatic weapons. 'All right. You have one hour.'

'I'm talking of days. First I have to find the buyer.'

'No. The buyer is here. There is a light plane tethered in a field near here. It would have been logical for Bruun to have a buyer waiting here for him. I'll have my men find him and bring him to you.' He gave orders to his men. Half a dozen of them left the hut. 'The rest of you, at ease.' Reluctantly his men lowered their weapons still further.

'Lower your weapons,' Lance said to Sambo. Lance sank into the throne. Lobengula and his wives had slunk out unnoticed. The buyer was brought. He was a short, plump man with a few strands of hair glued across his bald head. He wore a white silk suit in which he had obviously tried to burrow into the ground. He was apprehensive of all the armed men. Since the skins had the heads still on them, he readily agreed to pay forty-five American dollars per skin but insisted on seeing all the skins first. Burger reluctantly let him use the helicopter to inspect the skins and trucks on the plain. When he returned, the buyer took off his shoe and sock and ripped off the plastic envelope taped to the instep of his foot. From it he withdrew some slips of paper and handed them to Lance.

'Sight drafts on the Union Bank of Switzerland,' he said. 'Good as cash.'

Lance looked at Jimmy. Jimmy inspected the pieces of paper and shook his head.

'How do we know that?'

The little man broke out in perspiration. Burger intervened. 'Because little men like him know that, if they attempt to cheat men like your brother, they're as good as dead.'

Lance took the flimsy slips of paper for which so many men had died. 'With this much "cash" on me, I'll need a bodyguard.'

'Not while you're under the protection of the South African Bureau of State Security.' Burger actually chuckled. 'Don't worry, I'll see you safely to a bank once we're back in South Africa.'

Lance gave Sambo several of the slips of paper. 'That's your fifth plus fifty thousand dollars for services over and beyond the call of duty.' He gave Jimmy a sight draft for fifty thousand dollars. 'My bearer shares in my fortunes.' With Ewart and Jacques dead he couldn't bring himself to say 'good fortune'. Both Jimmy and Sambo stuck these fortunes in their pockets without checking the amounts. 'What will you do now?'

'This gentleman will need protection on the way to Bangui,' Sambo said.

'I'll pay you the same fifth,' the buyer said eagerly. Sambo shook his head. 'Three-tenths.' Sambo nodded.

'And then?' Lance asked. He didn't want to leave these men.

Sambo shrugged. 'Jimmy has a head for business. He'll invest and we'll grow old and fat with doing nothing. We're too few now to rebuild our tribe.' He embraced Lance and Lance walked away in his infinite sadness, wiping tears from his cheeks.

Jimmy walked behind Lance's right shoulder, as always. They came to where Bruun lay on the ground, his bleeding stemmed by the medical orderly. A few of Lobengula's people, mostly women, had returned and were seated in a circle around Bruun. 'Take me with you,' Bruun croaked. 'Please man!'

Burger stopped. 'Only my nationals, Bruun, and even if you were one I'd leave you.'

335

'Then kill me, for Christ's sake. What's a bullet to you? These women will skin me alive!'

One of Burger's men, a look of pity mixed with revulsion on his young face, raised his weapon but Burger shook his head. 'This is not our business.' He walked on, saying to his aide, 'That's what I meant about the way Africa treats fallen despots. African revenge. They'll keep him alive and in pain for many days.' Beside him the French major shivered and wished there was something left in his stomach to vomit. Just being near these South Africans – the dead Weber, his still-living younger image, and Burger with his men – was enough to chill a man to the bone.

Lance stood for a moment over Bruun, listening to the man's pleading, then walked by, feeling nothing.

At the helicopter Jimmy, shaking Lance's hand, said, 'Get your leg sterilized and bound up.'

Lance nodded. He couldn't speak. He feared a future in which Jimmy would not be there to guide him. Stellenbosch was suddenly a long way away and a lot of time had flowed down the river.

'We'll meet again,' Jimmy said with conviction but his smile lacked its usual lustre.

Lance swallowed and embraced Jimmy. Were there words to persuade Jimmy to come with him?

Then Jimmy was walking away and Lance shakily pulled himself up into the helicopter. Inside Briony was turning against the restraining straps and moaning. On the other side of the door lay the bodies of Ewart and Jacques and Viljoen in clear plastic wrappings – Sambo would bury his dead where they had fallen. Lance, wiping tears from his face, turned away towards the door, straining to think of something to call after Jimmy.

Lance put his hand out to help Burger into the helicopter but Burger refused the proffered hand. He looked past Lance at the bodies as he pulled himself up by the rail beside the door.

'You've proved your manhood, but at what price?'